CARRIER

WITHDRAWN

TIMOTHY JOHNSON

A PERMUTED PRESS BOOK

ISBN: 978-1-61868-647-3

PERMUTED
PRESS

Permuted Press, LLC
permutedpress.com

Published in the United States of America

For Heather, always.

CHAPTER 1
THE CARRIER

One

The carrier *Atlas* tore across the cosmos, leaving a black wake of stardust.

It lurched forward with its rigid, hulking hull, like a giant, tumorous tentacle, and the thrusters beamed like a cluster of sapphires, gleaming with the stars in the endless expanse.

Beneath the skin of the carrier mining ship, the engineering decks housed the key to the stars, the *Atlas'* light drive, which had begun to rumble and play its disquieting song, spinning up to bend space like a rubber band. At full thrust, it had taken the *Atlas* weeks to reach the edge of New Earth's solar system, taxiing to minimum safe distance before it could engage the drive and take the long stride faster than light toward its destination, the outer reaches of the known galaxy, deep space.

The *Atlas'* crew called it "the black," as if it were an amorphous being that could get inside and drive them mad, and the pulse of the light drive didn't help. It rose and fell in a mechanical hum like a wave of sound that bored through their ears and into their minds. Its song resonated throughout every deck, crawling up the maglev tram system, which ran the length of the *Atlas* like a spine. The hum bellowed in the *Atlas'* cargo bays, huge warehouse compartments in the carrier's ribcage-like belly.

The mechanical whine of the light drive reached even as far as the residence decks at the fore where the *Atlas'* chief security officer, Stellan Lund, woke from a terrible dream as he did every sleep cycle, knowing he had died.

With indiscernible cries still ringing in his ears, he sat up in bed, feeling his heart pound. It clicked behind his ears, and his head swelled so much it might burst. But there was no pain, only the deep, outward pull of his arteries opening wide, like his whole body breathed.

The air processing system whispered through the vents that everything was all right, that it didn't matter where his mind had taken him. He was back aboard the *Atlas*. He had returned home.

The dream was recurring, and that was all he knew about it because, even as he turned and pressed his bare feet against the cold metal deck and the sensation shot up his legs like electricity, the dream faded. But there was always a sense of familiarity, that it had happened before, that he'd previously visited those darkened corners of his mind. He could almost see it, like his own reflection beyond the fog of a mirror. He couldn't hold onto it, though; it faded until there was nothing.

From Stellan's personal data link that clung to his wrist, a cascade of blue holographic panels leaped into the air, and he found he had some time before his wake cycle began, enough to get more sleep if he could coax his mind into returning there.

He rubbed his eyes, doubtful that they would stay closed for long, and when they opened, they fixed onto his sidearm, a rail-fired HC30 heavy pistol, which hung in its holster from the handle of his closet, always within easy reaching distance. He traced the cool steel of the barrel with his fingertips. As familiar to him as his own hand, Stellan's pistol had been at his side for as long as he cared to remember. When he touched the grooves on the grip where his fingers would fall, it felt like reassurance from an old friend, and the final pit of fear left his stomach.

He removed the weapon from its holster and felt the significant weight, not too heavy or too light, but just right. His hands had memorized the rubber grip and the steel cylinder, the resistance it gave when he moved with it.

Stellan's sidearm had always been there for him when he needed it most, when he had let his guard down, and when he felt shame for exercising the most basic human instincts: the will to survive.

That was another time, and he was another person then. He no longer talked or even thought about his old self. Nowadays, he and his sidearm spoke rarely, only in the firing range to keep each other sharp, and they never mentioned their history. Instead, they looked forward.

And then flames danced before his eyes. Stellan tried to resist the heat out of disbelief. He raised his hand to shield his face and turned away.

A city blazed. The skyline comprised crumbling towers, and the first hints of dawn rolled over the horizon.

A bullet whizzed past his ear, and he sprinted to cover behind a burned-out husk of a car. The back seat still smoldered, and noxious fumes from the vinyl and cushioning assaulted the back of his throat. He stifled a cough as he darted behind rubble from a crumbling building. Glass crunched underfoot.

As he was trained, Stellan watched the high ground, optimal locations for snipers, tracing the rooftops with his deadly eye, the barrel of his MK7 Kruger assault rifle. He looked at the places he would be if he wanted to pick off a few Unity Corps soldiers, the New Earth Council's law enforcement unit. The shadows of open and broken windows drew his attention. He skipped the ones with flames behind them.

A hand pressed his shoulder.

Stellan realized his eyes were closed, and when he opened them, the city vanished. The moan of the light drive and the whisper of the air processors returned. Gentle fingers wrapped over his shoulder, and he reached for them instinctively.

Daelen's hand was cold, even though her touch was warm. The dream and the city melted away like burning cobwebs in a dark cave.

"You all right, love?" Even with his wife's voice a whisper, its soft inflections and drawn out vowel sounds reminded Stellan she'd grown up near London. Of all the things he loved about her, he loved the way she sounded the most, like her lips were gentle with her words.

"Fine."

"Another dream?" she asked, her voice rising with worry.

"Yes."

She fell back, the sheets splashing around her. A concerned sigh escaped her mouth, almost as if she'd been holding it back. As the medical officer aboard the *Atlas*, her mind drummed up the worst biological reasons for his dreams. She had no experience in psychology and didn't have much faith in willing someone to get better. She believed in treatment, and she worried her husband suffered from a tumor or perhaps a virus that attacked the brain.

3

She sat up and rolled behind him, wrapping her arms over his shoulders, her hands finding his. She pulled them close to his chest and squeezed.

"Go back to sleep," Stellan said. "Our wake cycles don't begin for another few hours."

"Not without you." Whatever was bothering him, she wanted to hold onto him and become his anchor. She couldn't heal his body this way, but perhaps she could comfort his soul.

"I don't know if I can," he said.

"Just lay with me then."

Stellan longed to go back to her, to bury his nose in her hair and breathe deep, and he had the similar thought that if he just held onto the sound of her voice and the smell of her hair, the way it spilled over her shoulders like ink, maybe it would keep those dark thoughts at bay. After all, he was exhausted. Sleep would be worth the risk.

So he turned and kissed her softly. They rolled together, and he was gentle as he raised the sheets, wiggled his arm under her neck, and crossed his other arm over her abdomen. He kissed her shoulder and heard her lips part into a smile in the dark.

Soon, they both returned to sleep, and Stellan's dreams were worse than they'd been in years.

Two

Stellan woke with screams once again rattling his head. The voices morphed into the *Atlas'* emergency alert and then to the wake alarm on his link, like a child tugging at the fabric of his pants. Even as he woke and his mind grasped at reality, the voices lingered.

He sought Daelen with his hand and found only the warmth where she had been, her scent lingering in the sheets. He lay for a moment, his nightmares fading, wondering where she could have gone. He checked his link again to see if he had overslept, and found he had not. She must have left early.

He stood and carried a yawn to the bathroom, feeling happy to be awake even though exhaustion tried to anchor him to the bed. A persistent droning in his mind yearned for sleep, but he had enough of the restlessness for a while. His dreams would have to wait for him to return, and he knew they would.

A blue light swelled around the doorframe and mirror in the bathroom. In the reflection, his own eyes appeared so ghostly blue that he thought for a moment they looked lifeless. He'd seen that vacant stare before, when all the color seemed to drain from the irises. And even though his eyes twitched with his gaze, he thought it was an accurate depiction of how he felt. Windows to the soul and all that.

Stellan slid the shower door aside and entered. He opened its valves, and a steady stream of warmth spread across his chest. He leaned forward on the wall and let the water run over his head and down his back, across several long, jagged scars, some wounds that just would not heal and had become so deeply part of his being that they manifested themselves on his body.

As he washed, he touched the long, sweeping edge just under his rib cage where burning shrapnel had once threatened his life. He recalled the pain, how remarkably little there had been. Simply, a piece of metal had nearly cut him in two, and he remembered the warmth of the blood flowing down his belly and into his lap as he propped himself against a tree, still firing, still fighting.

His fingers found another, a thick bloom of scar tissue like a flower on his shoulder, where a bullet fired from one of the most unexpected places had passed through and left him awestruck at more than he could possibly bear.

Again, that was another time, but he asked himself, if that were true, why did he continue to recall it? Why did his mind relentlessly pound him with memories he no longer cared to revisit? If he'd moved on, why did those thoughts remain so close to him, lying in wait just under the surface of the shallows until the waves came?

He returned to the bedroom, the blue glow reflecting off the sheen of water still on his naked skin. After Stellan finished drying himself, he slid open his closet door, revealing several black officer uniforms hanging in line. He put on a pair of pants and then dropped to the floor for his morning pushups, his chest heaving and his arms pumping like pistons.

When he finished, he grabbed a white t-shirt from the closet and pulled it over his head. With a chirp, the *Atlas* announced someone's desire to enter.

"Come in," Stellan called.

The door opened, and the bright light from the outer hall hurt his eyes. A large figure stood rigid with his head almost reaching the top of the doorframe. Stellan finished rolling his shirt over his chest and tucked it into his pants.

Stellan's pupils adjusted to the glare, and he saw a black uniform like his. It was one of his men. Judging by the silhouette's sheer size, it was Doug Fowler.

Stellan believed in symbols, and while Doug had no formal training in anything that would be applicable to security, he'd hired the big man for his inherent ability to intimidate others with his physical size. Since coming aboard, Doug hadn't had to use force, which was a testament to Stellan's theory. Whether people didn't want any trouble or Doug frightened them into shape, it worked.

"You're early," Stellan said.

"I was hoping we could talk."

"On the way," Stellan said. "Give me a sec."

"You ever think of maybe turning some lights on in here?"

Stellan reached into the closet, chose the officer coat his hand first touched, and threw it over his shoulders. A trail of bulbous silver buttons on his coat slashed up to his heart and then diagonally to his throat. The stiff collar stood straight up at the nape of his neck, bristling the tips of his short blond hair. A blue stripe lined the sides of his pants down to his black leather boots.

He stopped for a moment to look in the mirror. *Symbols*, he thought. He hated the uniforms, but he couldn't deny the authority they represented. Though, something was missing, and it wasn't the Council patch he'd torn from the coat's shoulder.

"Yeah, yeah. I'd fuck you," Doug said. "You're beautiful. Let's go."

Stellan looked sternly at Doug and reached for the last piece of his uniform: his sidearm. He wrapped the holster around his waist and instantly recognized its weight, by which he could even count the thirteen rounds in the magazine. It sparkled in the bathroom light, which sensed no occupancy and faded.

Stellan left his cabin. The light from the hall cleaved the room in two as he offered himself to the ship and its crew, and they gladly swallowed him whole.

Three

The hallway outside Stellan's cabin resonated with vibrant life. The clamor of the marching crew and the bright lights replaced the drone of the silence and darkness of his cabin. He found it disorienting.

He glanced down the main thoroughfare of the residence deck, which was arterial in design with perpendicular branches like veins. The walls bowed outward to make the space feel wider, but the volume of people threatened to push them further. Advertisements for products sold in the ship's stores and films that showed on the lounge and recreation deck lined the walls, along with safety messages and reminders: *Remember, safety isn't just a goal. It's a state of mind.*

The time for the *Atlas'* shift change had come. The heads of Stellan's fellow shipmates bobbed and swayed, some going to work, others returning to their cabins. It was hard to tell who was coming and who was going because everyone looked exhausted, and in twelve hours, it would happen again. The *Atlas* had two shifts, maintaining New Earth's twenty-four hour clock.

Stellan finished buttoning up his coat and checked his pockets one last time to be sure he had everything. From bow to stern, the *Atlas* was several kilometers long, and shift change was very much a commute. If he forgot something in his cabin, it wouldn't be easy to return.

His hand landed on the butt of his weapon, and it pulsed with warmth. The grooves meant to help him maintain a steady grip pricked his fingers lovingly, begging him to remember how it felt.

"So, I know you said in the meeting yesterday that if anyone asks we should just tell them we haven't gotten our destination yet," Doug said.

The two officers began walking toward the back of the ship, blending in with the crowd.

The *Atlas'* people bottlenecked in entryways and narrow passageways. Some stopped to chat with acquaintances and friends, and Stellan and Doug politely asked them to break it up and move along. The corridors met their capacity, and the crowds slowed to compensate. Stellan thought, if the *Atlas* had the ability to stretch to better handle the heightened flow of the volume of its crew, it would have. But the *Atlas* was not alive. It was a machine, and machines offered no such flexibility.

"People are asking, and it's just eating you up that you don't know," Stellan said. "And you were hoping, since the Captain and I go back, maybe he let me in on the secret and I could be a bit more forthcoming with details away from the others."

Doug nodded, looking uncertain. "Something like that."

"To be honest, Doug, I wish I could tell you. I really don't know where we're going. The Captain's kept me in the dark about it, too."

"Don't it bother you?"

"No," Stellan said. "He does what he does for reasons he doesn't have to explain to us. His crew is his priority, and he wouldn't do anything that would endanger us. Everyone should know that. If they ask, tell them that."

"That your military training talking?"

"Chain of command is one thing, but this isn't the military," Stellan said. "It's trust. Trust your Captain."

They continued in silence, passing through the residential deck security checkpoint, nodding at another officer stationed behind a desk, following the animated holographic signs that hung from the ceiling, displaying the destinations ahead, their temperature, gravity, and pressure. All Stellan and Doug needed to know was that the font color was green. They knew the layout of the ship by heart, and green meant the environment integrity hadn't been compromised. Yellow, orange, or red would have gotten their attention.

Stellan knew Doug wasn't finished. It was in the way Doug didn't speak and in the way he avoided eye contact. Introspection was abnormal for him. He normally thought with his mouth.

"What about that Council woman?" Doug said. "You trust her?"

Stellan didn't answer because anything he said in response would be a lie. No, he didn't trust her, and he couldn't help but sigh. He hoped Doug wouldn't interpret it as a response, but it was evident from Doug's hardening face that he understood it as irritation.

"Go ahead and start your rounds, Doug," Stellan said, trying not to sound dismissive.

Doug stopped, and the crowd flowed around him like water. Some of the crew bumped into his arms, not even budging the big man. Doug appeared to feel a cocktail of surprise, amazement, and vexation, which Stellan knew he'd process as resentment.

"We'll talk later," Stellan said.

"Sure thing, Chief," Doug said with contempt. As Doug lumbered away, Stellan remembered how much he hated the isolation of authority. He couldn't tell Doug that the abnormality of not knowing their destination set him off, too. He couldn't tell Doug that the presence of a Council agent aboard the *Atlas* was both irregular and, for reasons not many would understand, alarming.

Turning to face the march to the tram and onward to the bridge, he felt a sense of absorbing into the crowd, but he knew better. He knew the things he carried—his uniform, his weapon, his duty—separated him from them. Because he was their protector, they would never accept him. They would never be comfortable with him in the way they were comfortable with each other. His responsibilities to protect them formed barriers, and even as he passed and met eyes with neighbors, even as he smiled and nodded, he knew they returned those sentiments out of a sense of obligation. Few relationships he had on the ship were legitimate, and most existed because of his badge, not in spite of it.

He hated it, but it was the price he paid for their safety. He often felt it was his penance to feel outcast. He could only hope they trusted him. For some, trust was earned, and he wondered if he'd had such an opportunity on their quiet ship. He hoped one day for that chance. He also hoped he would not let them down.

So he continued on, counting the bobbing heads, watching for signs of danger and harm, because they were his flock, and he was the shepherd, trying desperately to fit in.

Four

The platform at the maglev tram station seethed. The crowd swelled dangerously close to the edge, threatening to spill into the magnetic bed. It was the kind of crowd where someone would bump into you, and it wouldn't even faze you. You'd understand. There was no room for the luxury of personal space, and if you wanted a seat on the tram, you'd give up every bit you had.

The holographic displays on the platform's pillars informed them a twelve-car tram would arrive in three minutes. The station manager, Robert Powell, dozed in a leaned-back chair in his booth as his holoterminal blinked and covered his face in blue light. Stellan knocked on the booth's glass, startling Robert, who looked around in a panic and then smiled at Stellan in embarrassment. Stellan shook his head with a smile of his own and walked away with a friendly wave.

He carefully slithered between each warm body toward the platform edge, trying to be as considerate as possible. Some of the crew turned, angry that someone was squeezing in front of them. Once they saw it was Stellan, their demeanor changed in the way anyone hides scorn in the face of authority.

Standing on the yellow line at the edge of the platform, he turned to face the crowd. Looking at either end, he watched their knees to ensure everyone maintained safe clearance. He watched their shoulders to ensure they kept their balance.

Behind the crowd, a holographic monitor projected New Earth's news from the wall, and Stellan read the headlines scrolling in a ticker at the bottom. Anchorman Shelly Sheltonson's relentless smile and perfect teeth reported that sixteen people resisted arrest and opened fire on a Unity Corps unit in the District of Australia. None survived. In the Canadian Province, a family refused to surrender religious texts, violating the Freedom From Religion Act. The parents were being processed; the children would be sent to reform school and already were lined up to be adopted by a noble family that was loyal to the New Earth Council. Terrorists staged attacks in the Mediterranean and greater Europe. The Unity Corps was hot on the trail of the leader of the organization that claimed responsibility.

Stellan knew the rebels never actually claimed responsibility because the message was more important to them than ownership. The Council had declared the war over years ago. Somebody had forgotten to inform the rebels. That message was clear to him, even though most of New Earth's citizens ignored it.

A dull pain on his upper arm brought his attention back to the platform.

"Yow!" he yelled, his hand reaching for the hot spot near his shoulder. He looked down and found his friend, Wendy Lin, one of the *Atlas'* engineers.

A clean canvas now, her blue jumpsuit would later be covered in grease from servicing gravity cranes in the cargo bays, and even now, old stains streaked her chest, shoulders, and legs. They were especially dark at her knees and elbows. Though, with her black hair tied into a ponytail at the base of her skull, her clean face shined with the precious innocence of a younger sibling, even with the shrewd twist across her brow and the swelling of her jaw muscles as she grit her teeth. In her normally narrow eyes, which were now merely slits, he found more fire.

"Where were you last night?" she asked. And then she socked him in the shoulder again. Her fist impacted with all the force of a tennis ball, a quick jolt with little weight behind it.

"Would you stop it?" Stellan said, grabbing both of her arms and moving her away from the platform edge. "Daelen didn't feel well, so I stayed with her. I'm sorry I didn't message you."

"Yeah, I bet you are," Wendy scoffed.

Stellan's attention returned to the crowd. His duty was too important. Still, he was curious. On the outruns, the crew played basketball in the empty cargo bays. Stellan and Wendy were on the same team, but he had missed their game the previous night.

"What did I miss?" Stellan asked.

"What do you care?" Wendy asked. "We might as well consider you an alternate if you're going to keep missing games."

Stellan put his hands in the air. "Hey, don't bench me, coach!"

She shook her head in dismissal.

"Rick Fairchild played," she said with a grumble.

"Rick? Really?"

"Apparently he played a lot in his day. Can't run worth a damn, but he's a pretty good shot. He won it for us at the last second."

"What was the score?"

"Forty-nine to forty-eight."

"Close game."

She glared at him. "Yeah, but we would have destroyed them if our team captain had been there."

"You still won," Stellan said. "Close games are more fun anyway."

"That's not the point."

"Oh?" Stellan said. "I thought having fun was the point."

"No, I mean, that's not why I'm mad at you."

Stellan understood, but he didn't feel much like getting into it then. His curiosity had been satisfied, and had appeased Wendy. He returned his attention to the crowd.

"What are you doing anyway?" she asked.

"Watching."

"Watching what?"

"Everyone."

"That's silly," she laughed, her body loosening. "You can't watch everyone." It was good that they could move past his absence at the game. That was what he liked most about her. While she had attitude and her temper could flare quickly, she didn't dwell on things.

"It's not as hard as you'd think. Most people just have too narrow of a focus. They watch hands or faces, and it's impossible to watch everyone's hands. I look at their shoulders, their hips and knees. Those parts of the body move first. They give away what a person's going to do. It's the same idea we use in self-defense."

Wendy lifted one foot from the floor and shook it, examining her bent knee leading the direction in which her foot moved.

"Speaking of which, you have to show me some moves some time," she said, bouncing.

"Why?"

"In case I ever need to know."

"Do yourself a favor," he said. "If there's ever trouble, run. Fighting will get you hurt, no matter how good you are."

"Don't you think that's a little hypocritical coming from someone who fights for a living?"

"My job is to prevent and resolve conflict," Stellan said. "Fighting only makes things worse."

"I've seen you fight."

"You've seen me defend myself from people who are out of line."

"There's a difference?"

"The difference is I'm supposed to be in that situation, not you."

"What if there's nowhere to run? What if I'm trapped?"

Stellan couldn't imagine a scenario on the *Atlas* where Wendy would be trapped or would ever need to know how to defend herself. He knew learning self-defense bred overconfidence; he also knew that meeting rising conflict led to terrible places. He wanted to protect her from that. It was more than just his job. As a friend, it was his duty to protect her.

"Don't worry," Stellan said, forgetting the crowd and looking her in the eyes. He put his hand on her shoulder. "You're safe here. No one's going to hurt you."

They shared a moment of silence where Stellan couldn't be sure if Wendy doubted her safety because she doubted him or if something had happened. She looked disappointed, not reassured.

Violence had never brought him anything worth fighting over. Except for the times he was using his skills to defend another, he felt like he could have resolved every conflict he'd ever been involved in if he'd just walked away. At some point, which he felt was late in his life, he'd learned that lesson. When he'd turned his back, it felt to him like his life had turned around with him.

The floor beneath them rumbled and then became stable again as the magnetic bed activated. The whole room tightened. The walls constricted.

The maglev tram hovered into the station silently, emerging from the tunnel like a giant worm. Only the linear motor at the front whispered as it winded down. Stellan held out his hands sideways, flicking his fingers inward to tell the crowd on the platform to back away from the edge.

When the tram stopped, the floor shuddered, and the paddles in the magnetic bed slapped the belly of each car, clamping them securely into place.

Then the doors parted, and people funneled in. Stellan shrugged. There wasn't much more he could do, so he ushered Wendy gently into the tram.

"I hate the tram," she said.

"It's all we've got," Stellan said. "Could you imagine the alternative?"

"Point taken," she said as the doors closed. "I hate walking."

Five

It was early when Daelen walked into the infirmary, a long room lined on one side with examination tables arranged like cemetery plots. On the other side, workstations and laboratories led back to her office. Beyond, another door led to private exam, recovery, and operating rooms. The last room on the medical deck was the morgue.

Daelen's shift wouldn't begin for a while, and she hoped to have some time alone. Instead, Daelen found Margo Tailan, the medical intern, asleep on one of the exam tables, her white lab coat draped over her body, her elbows and hips jutting like sharp peaks in a snowy landscape. Daelen felt slightly disappointed that she wouldn't have the deck to herself, but a warm smile curled her mouth anyway. She pinched her lips to contain her laughter.

Seeing Margo asleep on the exam table reminded Daelen of the time she spent as an intern. Margo looked peaceful, but Daelen knew how her back would ache when she woke. Those exam tables weren't meant for sleeping.

Back then, Daelen focused on her career, granting herself no time to pursue personal pleasures, such as the warmth of a man who might love her, and the time she spent as an intern had rocketed by as if it had its own light drive.

She didn't let time pass her by so quickly anymore. She could feel it with her mind, wanting to slip, and she feared waking one morning and realizing all she had were the lives she'd saved. That wouldn't be terrible; practicing medicine and helping people fulfilled her sense of purpose, but she yearned for something more. At some point in her life, she realized what she wanted was not just to give people back their lives but to also give her own life back to herself. The key to slowing down time, she learned, was creating memories.

Daelen walked through the exam area toward her office and the private rooms beyond. She grabbed her lab coat from behind her office door and swung it over her head, placing her arms in the holes. Wind from her flapping coattail blew several short strands of her black hair out from her neat ponytail, and she absently brushed them behind her ears. Out of her pocket, she drew her reading glasses, small oval lenses attached to thin black rims, and she sat at her desk, staring at her blank holoterminal.

Life is about creating memories, she thought. *It's about creating, not just holding onto life and keeping it in this world for as long as you could, but actually creating it.*

She lifted her left arm, and her link fanned open several 3D holographic windows. She flipped them sideways and found her personal folder. Every crewmember had a personal folder on the *Atlas'* servers, retrievable solely on their own links, but Daelen thought that, in this case, she might as well have marked her folder "secret."

The smile fell from her mouth, and her eyebrows pushed together in a sharp furrow, the wrinkles like fine cracks in porcelain.

She pressed on the folder with her palm, and it fanned open several files. She flipped them and found the file marked "results" and threw it to her holoterminal. The terminal lit up and projected a flat screen with text. Reviewing the results, she realized she loved the document. She reached out absently, attempting to touch it. If she could, it might become more real, more memorable. For the first time, she wished it were paper, something she never understood the value of until now.

Her fingertips pierced the holographic image. It was as tangible as the idea it represented. That was to say, the thought of motherhood burned in her mind, not yet in her palms.

But for that, she was almost thankful. It was safer this way, easier to control. She released a deep sigh of relief when she realized she still had time. She wouldn't begin to show for another few weeks, perhaps a month, which was when they were scheduled to return to New Earth and when she'd return to the surface of her home planet for good. Expectant mothers weren't allowed to travel in space, nor were children.

She'd come to love her life on the *Atlas*. Like everyone aboard, the freedom had drawn her to the ancient halls of that forgotten carrier ship, yet she couldn't wait to see her belly begin to bulge. The yearning to see her child's face flooded her chest with warmth, like a deep yawn that stubbornly would not be released.

While it was quiet in the lab and she had some time to herself, she wanted to revel in the thought of motherhood. She wanted to coddle something, so she held onto the idea that, by focusing on her child, she was creating the memory of its conception, a joyous time in her life she would remember fondly.

She wrapped her arms around herself and closed her eyes. She imagined looking down and seeing her abdomen expand, and she began to hum. Her voice matched the note of the *Atlas'* light drive, and it soothed her instead of irritating her. The hum, to her, had always rubbed her temples like sandpaper, but she began to hear it as a song, her mind filling in the gaps of the melody.

The swelling of the hum rose and fell; her chest heaved. The sound of the light drive resembled a mechanical heartbeat, and she thought about her child's heartbeat. She yearned to feel it, and she placed her hand on her stomach and continued to hum with her eyes closed, rogue strands of her hair leaving her ears and falling across her cheek. She didn't brush them back this time.

Over and over, the hum rolled, swaying her body as if it laid hands upon her hips, and her voice matched that note. Her voice hung onto the hum like swinging from the limb of a tree. She heard the song she would sing to her child. It was a pleasant melody. She thought about maybe writing some words to it, but no, that might spoil it.

"What song is that?" Margo asked wearily from Daelen's office doorway, her eyes little more than a squint. The melody left Daelen, and her eyes opened to find her hand still on her belly, which was flat again.

"I don't know," she said. "Just something I made up, I guess." She grabbed the results document from her terminal and dragged it back to her link, the fan of documents closing back into her wrist. Her eyes darted toward the doorway, a desperate attempt to see Margo without turning, but the intern rubbed her face and yawned, shuffling forward into the room and into her chair at a small desk in the corner.

Daelen doubted Margo had seen her pregnancy results, but she undoubtedly saw her close them and hurriedly pull them from the terminal, the sure sign of someone attempting to hide something. If she asked, Daelen had not prepared a lie.

"Those tables really aren't as comfortable as they look," Margo said, wincing from a pain that shot through her back. "What are you doing anyway?"

A lie. Daelen frantically searched for a lie. She couldn't find one, so she decided to stall.

"What do you mean?" Daelen asked and immediately realized she was asking for trouble because Margo wasn't only observant; she was analytical. Daelen thought Margo would make a great doctor someday, which is why she had chosen Margo for the position from hundreds of applicants.

Margo rolled her head back with her eyes closed, stretching her neck. Her collarbone jutted like a bridge between her shoulders.

"You're in early, poring over a document, which you stash away like you're hiding something."

No. Daelen had to stop her.

"You're humming, and you're holding your hand on your abdomen, and you—oh my God, you're pregnant!" Margo's eyes shot open, wide-awake and instantly alert.

Daelen hushed her, attempting to place her finger over her lips, but she was so frustrated her fingers simply balled into a fist.

"What if the Captain finds out!?" Margo asked.

"I don't know. Why don't you go tell him?" An awkward silence wiggled between them, and Margo flushed with embarrassment, suspecting she'd overstepped the bounds of their relationship. Margo revered her mentor. They had worked together a lot since she started the internship weeks ago, the day the *Atlas* last left New Earth. But she didn't think they were friends yet.

"I'm sorry, Dr. Lund."

"It's all right." Daelen offered a reassuring smile. Margo felt a little better, but then her own self-interest set in. Like Daelen in her early years, Margo obsessed over practicing medicine, and she began to worry about what would happen to her internship if Daelen were grounded.

"You can't keep a file like that on the server," Margo blurted. "I mean, *should* you keep a file like that on the server?" Her voice rose in a forced innocent tone.

"Why not?"

"Someone might find it."

"Like who?"

"The Captain." Captain Gordon Pierce always had a way of leaving a first impression of intimidation, but he was a good man. A principled man.

"Please," Daelen said. "Gordon would never snoop on his crew. It would violate his code."

"Stellan know?"

"No."

"When are you going to tell him?"

"I haven't decided."

"What does that mean?"

"It means I haven't decided."

"Haven't decided what?"

"Anything, really."

"Are you going to keep it?"

"I haven't decided," Daelen said with a sigh that bordered on boredom. "That's enough about me. What's wrong with you?"

Margo didn't want to talk about herself because her future was through Daelen; however, she felt the floodgate of information close on her teacher. Margo didn't want to push any harder because she didn't want to insult Daelen. She thought she should have been thankful Daelen had let her stick her nose so far into such private matters.

"Nothing," she said. "Why?"

"You're sleeping on an exam table," Daelen said, motioning with her arm.

"Oh yeah, that," Margo said, stretching her back. "It was really supposed to be a short nap."

"That's usually how it starts," Daelen said, crossing her legs and adopting the posture of an attentive doctor.

"I've just been feeling run down," Margo said. "Don't know why."

"Maybe you're working too much."

"I have been working a lot," Margo said with a self-promoting smile. Daelen shook her head dismissively and laughed.

"Even though I was exhausted, I just couldn't sleep last night. Most nights, it seems, anymore," Margo said with a sigh. "So I came down to do a little more work on those blood samples we took from the crew as we were leaving orbit."

"Find anything?"

"Everyone is clean."

"Good. Look at them again, and when you're ready, we'll examine them together." Margo turned eagerly toward the microscope on her desk, which pinned down a slide with a blood sample, as if holding it at gunpoint. She wiped her eyes again and looked into the lenses.

It pleased Daelen to see the zeal with which Margo went back to work, especially when the lesson she was teaching her had nothing to do with the blood but the folly of repeating a process too many times, of the inefficiency of too many redundancies and safeguards. It was a lesson she'd better learn now rather than later if she was going to practice on New Earth.

Anything looked wrong if you stared at it long enough, and she hoped to force Margo into making a mistake or at least thinking she'd made a mistake. There was time for her to learn how to determine when the job was done and to walk away with certainty and confidence.

Before she moved onto that lesson, however, Daelen wanted to teach Margo something else about space living and the human anatomy.

"No you don't. You," Daelen said and kicked the back of Margo's chair. "Talk."

"I don't know. I've just been really tired and haven't been able to sleep for the last couple of weeks. I get headaches sometimes. And that hum," Margo said, pointing to the ceiling, "makes it all worse."

Yes, Daelen thought, the pulse of the light drive, the beautiful song of her unborn child. She cocked her head sideways to listen, and she lost any affection she had for it. It seemed different to her now. It seemed unnatural, like the rolling sound of the siege weapons of Hell, and she felt dirty for ever thinking otherwise.

"Sometimes, I wonder if it's something serious," Margo said.

"You ever notice the *Atlas* has no windows?" Daelen said passively, as if she hadn't even heard the last thing Margo said. In fact, she didn't really pay attention because she already knew what was wrong with Margo. "They'd be structural weaknesses on the hull. There really isn't much to look at out there anyway. Just black."

Margo looked around the lab and blinked with confusion.

"There's no night and day out here, and our bodies need that," Daelen said.

"Didn't they do something to the environment systems that would help us maintain our circadian rhythms? Something with the lighting?"

Daelen raised an eyebrow. "It helps, but to varying degrees. I'm sure you're aware we all don't have the same physiology."

"So why would they tell us they took care of the problem when they really only mitigated it? That's very deceiving."

"Yes," Daelen said. "It is."

Margo was quiet. She reflected on how Daelen spoke ill of anything regarding New Earth and the Council that ran it. She wanted to know what had gotten her mentor, a rising star in the medical field, to forsake her career for a post that normally was occupied by second-rate physicians and those who'd done something to deserve punishment.

"Why do you stay here?" Margo asked. "I mean, you could practice anywhere, yet you choose the *Atlas*. Why?"

"Is love an adequate answer?" Daelen asked and supposed not, since she didn't think Margo would understand it. "You haven't practiced medicine on Earth, so I'm going to level with you," Daelen said, leaning forward and placing her elbows on her thighs. "It's boring. You're a mechanic following directions. The first thing they give you at any practice or hospital is a book, and then they tell you all the answers are in that book. You're expected to follow it to the letter."

She bent to open a cabinet beside her desk and ducked her head in. Some medical supplies fell out with the sounds of plastic packaging crinkling. Her voice reverberated like she was in a cave.

"The other part, perhaps the worst part, is nothing is ever easy. Everything's complicated. No one uses intuition anymore because that means liability, and because of that, things tend to take much longer than they should. People get sicker. People stay sick longer. Sometimes, it just makes sense to jump to the obvious conclusions. And here, it's fairly obvious you're not getting enough sun. You're probably also not getting enough exercise, since you're here all the time. And, I know your diet isn't exactly healthy."

She emerged from the cabinet and closed its doors, two bottles of pills rattling in her hand.

"On Earth, we'd be running a gamut of tests, and it might take weeks just to come to the conclusion I've already come to because we always have to be one hundred percent certain of a diagnosis. All the while, you're suffering from your symptoms. Here, I can tell you to take these vitamin and melatonin supplements, get some exercise, and let's see how you feel in a couple of weeks. Your body is probably just having difficulty adapting to this unnatural environment." A smile stretched her face, but when Margo took her pills with wonder of the simplicity of it all, Daelen's smile faded.

"That's it?" Margo asked.

"It's actually quite common out here. You find ways to deal with it."

Daelen realized she loved these moments, using her own mind to solve problems for patients. She loved pulling out an answer and showing her patients everything would be all right, even if it meant forgoing proper procedure. With a child, she would be grounded and perhaps lose the privilege to practice medicine altogether, everything she'd worked for her entire life.

As much as her colleagues scoffed at where she chose to practice, Daelen found value in its simplicity. Unfortunately, it had become complicated.

Ultimately, she didn't know what she was going to do. For the time being, she thought she would just have to keep smiling. No one could know. Not yet.

Six

The gravity cranes in cargo bay seventeen boomed like hand grenades. They pumped their mechanical arms and bobbed like oil rigs, stripping the very air. When the *Atlas* reached its destination, the cranes would fire bolts of energy designed to manipulate gravity and pull large bodies of earth into the bays. Until then, the engineering crew serviced and cleaned them, hoping to keep them pulling for another half century or more. It was how they lived between worlds.

Wendy struggled against the bulkhead hatch door, pushing with her shoulder and grunting. Even on well-oiled hinges, the doors were almost too heavy for her to open. Finally, the door swung wide, and the pounding of the gravity cranes struck her like a blow to the head. She had forgotten to put on her hearing protection, so her hands quickly covered her ears. She had to abandon one to search through the small sack she carried on her back for her earplugs. With her head tilted to her shoulder in an effort to keep some of that eardrum-rattling noise out, she nimbly wiggled her hearing protection into one ear and then the other in between crane pounds.

The gravity cranes continued their rolling onslaught, but they sounded far away, faded. The earplugs made it bearable. More importantly, they protected her hearing. At a distance, even within the bays, the cranes weren't so bad, though their pounding was still eerie. Working so close to them and even underneath them, the noise could blow eardrums.

"Stupid!" she cried, smacking herself on the forehead.

When she reached to close the door, a hand touched her arm. She turned, and the face she saw was as familiar to her as her father's. Rough and unshaven, Rick Fairchild smiled. The pallid skin of his long face and thin neck stretched up to his dark, short hair, resembling a spent match.

"Allow me," he said.

"No!" Wendy shouted. "I got it!" She took a deep breath, and the smell of the cargo bay, a mixture of grease and coolant fumes, calmed her like coming home. It reminded her of the repair shop her father had owned on New Earth, where she learned she loved to build and fix machinery, an affinity that had alienated her from the other girls and left her in the company of middle-aged men who spit, cursed, and smoked but who brought her presents on her birthday and listened when she started to fawn over boys.

After remembering their faces, smiling even through exhaustion and filth, pulling the door closed didn't seem so hard. The door closed, the hinges turning easier that way, like it wanted to close.

Rick playfully stretched her headphones apart and placed them over her ears, pulled down the microphone arm, and placed it near her mouth.

"Better?" he asked, grasping her small shoulders. His voice sounded smoky in the radio with a touch of static in the channel.

"Much," she said, and they exchanged a warm smile.

"So what's it going to be, boss?" Wendy asked, tightening her ponytail, the spotlighting in the bay reflecting off her dark, sleek hair like water. "Where do you want me?"

"How many times do I have to tell you all I'm not your boss?" Rick said almost indifferently, placing a cigarette rolling paper on the palm of his hand and tapping some tobacco onto it.

"You're the senior."

"That's just the Captain's way of reminding me I'm old," Rick said, rolling and sealing the cigarette with the tip of his tongue. "One seventy-seven won't start; a cable in the back is loose. No one is able to reach it."

Wendy pointed at him and hopped with excitement. The fact of the matter was Rick knew what needed to be done, and the rest of them knew he had the answers. So they followed his lead. Whether he issued orders or not, he ran the engineering crew, and everyone knew it but him.

"What?" Rick said. "Okay, I get it. Come on."

"Yessir!" she said with an animated salute.

They walked the line of gravity cranes as if they were cannons on a castle rampart. The cargo bays each had ten cranes, and they were numbered by the bay in which they were located. Crane one seventy-seven was the eighth crane in bay seventeen, if you counted crane zero, which had fallen beyond repair and was awaiting replacement, scheduled for the next return service at New Earth.

"I've been wondering for a while now," Wendy said. "Why do you do that?" She pointed to the self-made cigarette hanging in his mouth.

"What? Smoke?"

"No, roll your own."

"Because I never let anyone do for me what I can do myself," Rick said. "And it's cheaper and tastes better. The ones you can buy taste like dirty air."

Wendy grabbed the cigarette from between his fingers and puffed it. She wasn't a smoker. Very few people smoked anymore. The health risks had all been mitigated or become curable, but it was an inconvenient habit because smoking wasn't allowed on public property on New Earth. Smoking also wasn't allowed on the *Atlas*, but a lot of what went on in the cargo bays was overlooked.

She didn't like the cigarette taste in her mouth, though she liked being around a smoker. It was another thing that reminded her of her father's repair shop, along with the men who disgusted most people. To her, the smoke and fumes in the air weren't contaminants. They were elements of character and depth only someone like her could appreciate and understand.

When Wendy and Rick passed crane one seventy-four, it hissed, spewing a cloud of white smoke from underneath. Then the manifold under the frame fell off, slamming the deck with a solid, unyielding sound of heavy metal on metal. A small shockwave set Wendy and Rick off balance; Wendy almost fell, but Rick caught her arm.

"You idiot!" Thomas Foster yelled from the back of the crane. Another man, Edward Stone, his jumpsuit bulging at his midsection, his shoulders and bald head slumping, stumbled away from the side of the crane. His eyes drooped, and he nervously rubbed his arm.

"I'm sorry!" Edward shouted.

Beneath the crane, a dark liquid poured onto the fallen manifold in spurts, like one of the machine's arteries had been severed.

"You're so damned worried about 'where we're going this time'," Tom said mockingly with a lazy, almost drunken, sway of his head and hips, "that you forget to watch what the hell you're doing."

23

"It's not that," Edward said timidly. "I don't know."

"You don't know what?" Tom said. "We're going to Hell, and there's nothing you can do about it. So, you might as well hold on tight and do your job."

"Hang on a minute, Tom," Rick said. "Accidents happen, and it's just lubricant. We have plenty of time to fix this."

"Accidents? Plenty of time?" Tom said. "There's enough work around here that I don't need someone to create more for me. We'll be lucky to get this bay online at all, and we've certainly had our share of accidents."

"Take a break," Rick said. "I'll help Edward with this after Wendy and I tend to one seventy-seven."

For a moment, Rick thought Tom might actually stay, but the man was eager to get to his second job of holding down a barstool.

"Fine," Tom said. He dropped his tools on the deck and walked off toward the end of the bay and the bulkhead door with his familiar limp, an injury that reminded them all to be ever mindful.

"Hey, boss," Edward said. Rick turned to Edward patiently, containing his annoyance. "I don't mean to be a nag or nothin', but where we going?"

"It doesn't matter, Eddie," Rick said. "Every planet's the same. The universe's trash is our treasure." Rick forced a smile, a pleasantry he reserved for someone whose mind was slow, someone who wouldn't be able to tell the difference between genuine friendliness and sympathetic compassion or even pity. Though Edward didn't seem to notice the disingenuousness of Rick's expression, he also didn't seem satisfied with the answer. He stood still, timidly rubbing his forearm, a look of concern wrinkling his round and aged face.

"Plug up that leak, Eddie," Rick said.

"Oh, right," Edward said. He jumped into action, sliding on his back under the crane, his stomach pressing against the edge of the frame. "I'll be back in a few minutes."

Wendy and Rick continued down the line to crane one seventy-seven. The last embers of Rick's cigarette dimmed, and he flicked it out into the bay.

On cursory inspection, crane one seventy-seven looked to be in good working condition. The frame and panels shined, which was a rarity among cranes; even brand new cranes didn't remain clean for long. Yet, it stood unmoving, a long, dead arm hanging out into the wide-open bay, like a dead man's finger breaking topsoil.

"Here we are," Rick said. "I think one of those docking station all-stars at Earth tripped over something during inspection." Rick and Wendy shared a quick laugh at Rick's sarcasm. The dockhands at New Earth weren't as inept as the engineering staff on the *Atlas* claimed, but it had become an inside joke that unified them. If she were honest, Wendy might have admitted that she tired of the joke, but it reinforced the crew's unity, as if humans banding against other humans was a natural behavior they couldn't deny.

They slid under the crouching four-legged giant and pushed all the way to the back, where the crane was nearly flush with the wall. They pulled themselves by the far lip of the machine's frame, as if peering over a ledge, frightened by what they might find.

"See it?" Rick asked.

"Oh," Wendy said in surprise, as if to question that this minor problem was what these experts couldn't fix. "Yeah."

She spun sideways and pushed her shoulder against the wall. Her slender arm squeezed up behind the machine's frame, and her fingers wrapped around the loose cable. She pushed it in until it snapped into place.

"You get it?" Rick asked.

"Yeah."

They listened. Nothing happened.

"Let me see," Rick said, nudging Wendy out of the way.

"Maybe it just needs a rest," Wendy giggled. "Maybe it should sit this one out, too."

"That might put this whole cargo bay offline," Rick said, grunting with frustration. "It wouldn't be the first time, though."

"What do you mean?"

"I've seen pristine ships go adrift. I've seen cranes fifty years past their prime outlast brand new ones. And through all of it, for my money, the *Atlas* is the best carrier in the fleet because it has one thing the others don't."

"What's that?" Wendy asked.

"Love."

Wendy laughed.

"I'm serious," Rick said. "This ship is home for this crew, and the people here would die to protect it. I think the *Atlas* knows that, so when those all-stars in Earth orbit forget to order a part we need and promise to get it to us the next run, things just seem to keep up anyway, to persevere like this old bitch can fight through the pain."

"You talk like it's alive."

"It is."

Rick grunted and pulled down on the cable until it would budge no more, wiggling the connector in its socket. When that didn't work, he pulled a wrench from his belt and violently banged the side of the frame. On his face, Wendy thought she saw frustration and anger, but the crane knocked and slowly rose into a roll of booms, joining the other cranes in the chorus of chaos.

"Love, eh?" Wendy said.

"Sometimes it's tough love," Rick admitted.

A pair of feet shuffled beside the crane, and Edward Stone dropped to his hands and knees and peered at Wendy and Rick.

"Hey, boss," Edward called. "The leak's plugged, but I'm not feeling so hot. I think that's why I dropped that manifold. Do you think I could bail for the day, too?"

"All right," Rick said. "But go see Dr. Lund. Let her look you over. We're going to need you if we're going to get these cranes in shape by the time we get there."

Edward shuffled away toward the end of the cargo bay. When his headset was out of range, Wendy and Rick looked at each other.

"Tom was right about one thing," Rick said. "We certainly don't need any more accidents around here."

Seven

The lift doors parted onto the command deck, and Stellan stepped forward. From the lift lobby, which housed multiple elevators to the command deck and other decks, a hallway stretched. On both sides of the hallway, department managers sat at workstations with holographic terminals, relaying information and issuing commands to their subordinates throughout the ship. For a moment, Stellan heard only the cacophonous knocks of their fingertips against the glass keyboards as they typed messages and entered commands, and he heard chirps, audial responses the workstations announced as the department managers dragged and dropped files between applications. It all amounted to a stereo orchestra of chaos, but it meant order throughout the ship.

For Stellan, reporting for duty had become more routine than eating breakfast, which he realized, since his mind had been elsewhere, he had unintentionally skipped. First in the Unity Corps and now as chief of security on the *Atlas*, he began his days by checking in with his superior officer.

As he walked down the hallway toward the bridge, the department managers were so absorbed in their work that he didn't know if they noticed the sounds of his boot heels when he passed. Their hands were capable, though. From the command center, this group of men and women held the *Atlas* together. Both literally and figuratively, the command center was the core of the ship, and upon it, everything else spun.

"Give me a status update," said Council Agent Adelynn Skinner from the bridge. She had boarded the *Atlas* in New Earth orbit. The irregularity of her presence had been a controversial topic of conversation among the crew. Most Council agent activity was confined to New Earth, but agents had the freedom to do essentially anything they wanted, answering only to the Council itself. They were the Council's dark hand, operating in shadows and secrecy, the necessary evils of a unified world.

Stellan knew more than most about the world beneath that world. He saw beyond the agents' masks, and that knowledge put him at great unease. Skinner wasn't to be trusted.

Ahead of Stellan, the bridge loomed, a brilliant white sphere, the command crew appearing to levitate. Around them, the *Atlas'* interface system's 3D application windows hovered in real space, enabling them to interact with the ship's controls.

The agent faced the helm away from Stellan, arms crossed and weight shifted onto one leg, her slender body's posture crooked and unnatural. Her champagne hair poured down her back.

Instinctively, Stellan's eyes were drawn to the belt that hung around her waist, slanting and holding onto only one hip. On the side that hung low, a handgun dangled precariously in a holster, daring someone to try to disarm her. Even for Stellan, though, it would have been a dangerous proposition.

She was allowed to carry a weapon. She also was not required to wear a link, a fact that might have been to the disadvantage of anyone else, but for her, it meant she couldn't be tracked. If she could figure out ways to open doors on the ship without a link, and Stellan was sure there were ways, she could be like a ghost, moving anywhere and doing anything she pleased. That thought disturbed him the most.

"Thrusters at seventy percent," said Arlo Stone, the *Atlas'* pilot. His voice hung flat in the air, monotonous, as if bored and reciting a script. "We have hull integrity, and our EM field is holding. Light drive spinning up. Like I said, the board is green."

The agent sighed. "Just tell me where we are, Mr. Stone."

"We just passed the outer reaches of our system," Navigator Cooper Evans interjected. "We'll be ready to jump whenever the Captain is ready."

"Once we engage the light drive, how long until we reach our destination?"

"I adjusted the course your 'navigational specialists' charted while we were docked at Earth. Talk about poster children for continuing education. I'm amazed they can navigate their way out of their own shoes, and someone put them in charge of charting a course for the deepest run any carrier has ever made," Arlo said, shaking his head.

"Arlo," Skinner warned.

"I'm sorry, but the most direct route was right in front of them. Sure, we have to shoot a gap between a star and a singularity, but it's not rocket science."

"Actually," Evans said, "it is."

"You know what I mean."

Skinner rubbed her forehead. "Arlo."

"We should arrive a day early."

"Ahead of schedule," she said, blinking with surprise. Her fingertips fell to her mouth and pinched her bottom lip. "Good." Something in the tone of her voice suggested she wasn't so pleased.

Skinner turned and walked out of the bridge, an application window buzzing near her head. She swatted it away.

The department managers looked disturbed by her presence, like a wave of uneasiness as she passed. Some flinched. One raised her shoulders like a breeze made her shiver. Skinner's high-heeled boots ticked the metal deck like tap shoes.

The iris in her left eye glowed with a brilliant green, as if bejeweled with an emerald. It was beautiful and captivating to the point that Stellan almost missed the deep scar that trailed from the outer corner of her other eye. It streaked back toward her ear like lightning, branching into a Y. The iris in that eye was a pale blue, almost white, and Stellan knew that meant it had been replaced.

He wondered how she could have survived a wound like that, and then he thought she smiled at him. He could have sworn there was a hint of a curl at the corner of her mouth and a slight crease in her cheek.

He nearly stopped her to ask for her weapon, but the crest of the New Earth Council emblazoned above her heart reminded him of his place. Her uniform bore no other identification, no name, service number, or rank, but the crest signified military.

She passed Stellan like he was invisible, walking straight and steady without diverting her course, while Stellan yielded his shoulder. She entered the lift, and as the doors closed, there was no mistaking her smile this time. It was more than a greeting. Stellan saw something behind it, recognition, perhaps a mischievous intent.

When the lift doors closed, he gazed at them for a moment. He knew her from somewhere, had seen her before, though he couldn't place her. An image taunted him from the back of his mind. She was softer, with the unmistakable fear of inexperience in her eyes, darting quickly from being on high alert, but both of them green as copper fire, the kind of blaze that consumes a city, and in the smoke that blanketed the streets, someone screaming his name.

"Stellan?" Arlo said, calling down the hallway. "*Atlas* to Stellan."

Stellan blinked at the closed lift door and turned toward the bridge. Arlo was craning his head and looking at him with a wrinkled brow.

"You all right, Chief?"

Stellan nodded and waved a hand in dismissal. He continued past the department heads, who relaxed with the familiar sounds of his rubber boot heels and his confident stride. The atmosphere was returning to normal.

The circular mouth of the bridge door closed behind him, and he stepped onto the opaque white glass walkway. The bridge was a spherical room, the walls and platform ahead that same thick glass. Behind it all, a white light emanated, and it was hard to judge exactly how big the room was.

Stellan supposed the optical illusion was intentional because the bridge was a complete holographic environment. A small application window swooped over his shoulder, greeting him with a chirp, inviting him to make a command. He pressed upon the face of the window with his palm, and it shrank into nothingness.

The walkway culminated in a round platform, which was where Captain Pierce usually stood to command. Beside the platform, ramps led down and around to the front of the room where Arlo and Evans sat at their workstations.

Arlo removed his brimless cap, scratched his shaved head, and replaced the cap above his brow. It wasn't cold on the bridge. Arlo just always wore that hat. Stellan assumed it was a comfort thing.

Beside Arlo, the blue glow of the navigator's holographic interface reflected off Cooper Evans' smooth, boyish cheeks and danced in his eyes like wildfire.

"The Captain was looking for you," Arlo said.

"He isn't here?"

"He's already gone up to his cabin. And I'm sure you saw the spooky Agent Skinner." He snorted and wiggled his fingers in the air for melodramatic effect.

"Can't you ever take anything seriously?" Evans said. "She *is* kinda spooky."

Arlo picked up a cushy ball from his workstation and threw it at Evans. "Everything spooks you. You watch too many movies."

"What did the Captain want?" Stellan said.

Arlo shrugged. "I don't know. I just work here."

Evans looked to Stellan with appealing eyes. "Is there something wrong, Chief? With this run, I mean."

Arlo laughed. "Stel, tell Coop there's nothing to worry about. He won't listen to me."

As with Doug earlier, Stellan wanted to tell them that he didn't feel good about it. He wanted to share the anxiety so that maybe they could reassure each other that everything would be all right. That wasn't his place. It wasn't his duty. His duty was to ensure their safety.

"Of course nothing's wrong," he said. "She's just here because it's such a deep run, to be sure everything goes smoothly."

"Yeah, but an agent on a carrier?" Evans said. "Everyone is saying that's highly irregular."

"It isn't that irregular," Arlo said. "Is it, Chief?"

Stellan paused longer than he would have liked. "The Council does what it wants. Always has. Regularity is irrelevant. You two should learn to just accept it," Stellan said and winced at the lapse in his discretion. "But there would be no point in endangering us, Cooper. Trust me. There's nothing to worry about."

"Yeah, go change your diapers," Arlo said. "The Captain wouldn't let someone on the ship if he thought there was any danger. And if she does try to pull anything, the Chief here will drop the hammer. No doubt about it." He playfully punched Stellan's arm. It had more force than Wendy's blows earlier, but without the discontent behind it, it somehow hurt less.

"What if the Captain didn't have a say?" Evans said.

A small window expanded from Arlo's workstation, framing an unshaven face lined with time. The man's bespectacled eyes stared unflinchingly beneath eyelids that had begun to overlap. Despite his apparent age, he exuded a kind of power, which promptly stopped Arlo's assault on Stellan, and the pilot righted himself at his workstation.

"Arlo," Captain Gordon Pierce barked, "has the Chief checked in yet?"

"I'm here," Stellan said.

"Come to my cabin," Pierce said.

"Sir," Stellan said with a nod.

"Arlo, Ms. Skinner informs me we will arrive at our destination a day early?"

"Yes, sir," Arlo said uncertainly. "Evans and I found a shorter route those nincompoops at Earth missed."

"She says it could be dangerous. You think it's the best course?" Pierce asked.

Arlo scoffed. "It isn't dangerous. The radiation from the star won't be a problem, and while we may not be rated to operate near event horizons, it's just a teensy-weensy, little baby black hole. I know this ship better than anyone, and—"

"Arlo."

The pilot sighed. "Yes. It's the best course."

"Good work. Pierce out." The window shrank into Arlo's workstation, winking out of existence.

"Well, I guess he didn't mind," Arlo said.

"I can't believe you dragged me into that," Evans whined. "Now, if we die, he'll think I had something to do with it."

"If we die, we'll be dead, and no one will care."

"My mom would care," Evans pouted.

Stellan walked back down the narrow passageway that led away from the bridge, to the lifts, and off the command deck. One lift in the center reached as high as the captain's private deck, and as Stellan moved toward it, he let the bickering of the *Atlas'* two most influential technical operators fade behind his ears and out of his mind.

Eight

In Captain Gordon Pierce's quarters, conflict hung in the air like a fog.

Pierce sat in an old-fashioned wooden chair behind an oak desk, the scratches and gashes on the surface and along the edges showing its age. Gaps between panels and around drawers exposed the shrinkage of the wood over time. On the lip of the desktop, Pierce's thumb rubbed nervously back and forth over one particular spot, which had become a smooth indentation from years of wear.

"You shouldn't have allowed one of your men to change your ship's course without consulting you first," the Council's agent said, meandering before the Captain's desk and running her fingers over the spines of Pierce's book collection on the shelves. She narrowly avoided a pile on the floor and stepped over it respectfully, as if it were a corpse she didn't want to disturb.

"It's what Arlo does," Pierce said.

"By allowing it to continue, you become responsible for his insubordination," she said passively.

"My men need to know I have faith in their abilities to do their duties," Pierce growled. His thumb stopped rubbing, and he stood. Skinner faced him, still calm, pressing her hands together into a triangle. "They don't get that with me breathing down their necks. Command is about trust. I trust my men to use their best judgment. And it's a two-way street." His high and tight silver hair glinted like sparks.

"I used to believe something like that, but no," the woman said, her green eye a bright flash of fire. "Command is much simpler than that. It's about making your men follow orders." She sauntered around his desk and leaned on its worn edge, arching her back. Her breasts swelled beneath her tight black top.

"It's almost a fight in itself. You find their weaknesses, and then you exploit them," she said and leaned closer. "The best leaders get their men to follow orders without them knowing it," she whispered. "Some are better equipped for that than others."

Pierce grabbed her shoulders, his forearms bulging.

"I think the results speak for themselves," Pierce said through gritted teeth and pushed her away. "I gave my men a destination and ordered them to get us there, and they're getting us there a day ahead of schedule. That's called exceeding expectations, and I didn't have to put a gun in their face."

The woman doubled over with laughter, and her golden hair fell across her face like a shroud.

"Are these great leadership qualities of yours why you're here commanding a carrier?" She brushed her hair straight back over her head, allowing it to fall where it may.

"What is this really about, Adelynn?" Pierce said, his voice trembling with sincerity. The color in her cheeks faded. Her smile diminished.

Pierce and Agent Skinner hung onto each other's gaze, like exhausted boxers embracing, ready to end their toil but neither willing to let the other come out on top. They knew someone always had to win, and even though it didn't matter who the victor was, through sheer stubbornness, neither would cave. Neither could give in any more than either of them could travel through time and change the past. Yet, there was a softness to their faces, a sense that they both wanted to let their differences go. The longer their eyes refused to look elsewhere, the harder they felt the pull, like gravity, toward forgiveness.

A knock on the hatch door broke that fragile moment.

"Come in," Pierce called out. They silently agreed to settle their differences later.

The metal scuffed as the door swung open, casting a slice of light on the dim room. Stellan stepped forward into the foyer of Pierce's cabin, a small living room with a couch, a meeting table, and more books.

Pierce shot one final warning look toward Adelynn and walked into his foyer to greet Stellan. Adelynn followed.

"Stellan," Pierce said, "Ms. Skinner has finally found it appropriate to share with us why she's here, where we're going, and why the Council decided to send us there."

"Why now?" Stellan asked. Skinner offered no response but an inquisitive look, with her bright green eye and her other sickly, blue eye. Stellan wondered which had the ability to peer into his soul. Pierce shook his head in frustration.

"Because we're out of comms range and can't tell anyone," Stellan said.

"Correct," Skinner said. "You're as sharp as I thought you'd be. Don't act surprised or feign insult. You both know how secrets work."

"It doesn't mean we have to like it," Pierce said.

"No, I suppose not," Skinner said. "Then again, who cares what you like? Make no mistake, gentlemen. What I tell you now is not out of some sense of obligation. You need to know now so you can make proper preparations to do your job and complete the mission."

Skinner had absolute power here, and the *Atlas* was at her disposal. Still, Stellan and Pierce had an edge. The *Atlas* required a crew to run it, and they were confident this crew, *their* crew, would go nowhere under her direct command.

"Let's hear it then," Pierce said.

"Please, sit." She motioned toward the conference table with a graceful hand. Pierce and Stellan took seats opposite each other. Skinner sat adjacent to them. She waved her hand over the table, and it lit up, projecting streaks of blue light that appeared out of thin air and poured onto the tabletop like falling steam.

The light settled, and a holographic planet appeared. It rotated lazily, a soup of browns and reds looking like nothing more than a mixture of mud and clay.

"This is the two hundred and fifty-ninth identified celestial body in the Apophis system," Skinner said. "This is where we're going. As you may know, Apophis is one of the farthest systems we've been able to reach, and two five nine is out farther than any planet we've ever mined. That alone makes this mission special. The *Atlas* will set a record on this run." Stellan and Pierce caught her mocking tone.

"We can handle it," Pierce said.

"Indeed," she said. "As you don't know, two five nine has something we've never seen before, and the Council wants it."

She reached forward and grabbed the projection with both hands, a gesture Stellan thought looked much like the Council's crest on her upper left breast, two hands wrapping around New Earth. Then she pulled the projection apart, and it separated into two halves, revealing an inner layer, which was gray in the projection.

"Under the crust is a thick layer of an unidentified material. There's an entire layer of the stuff wrapped around the whole planet. Solid. The excavator *Shiva of the Trinity* is on-site now and will break ground in the next few hours."

"Why now? What's the rush?"

Skinner shoved two five nine aside, and a big red ball crept into the view.

"Apophis, the star of this system, is a red giant. Soon it will engulf its own system, and our precious cargo will be gone forever. It's already dangerously close for our ships."

"So you don't know what it is, but you plan to rush to it, put it on our ship and have us take it to Earth, banking on the hope that it's something good?" Stellan said.

"Yes."

"I'm sorry, but I can't allow that."

"Why not?"

Stellan had to be careful. "This is a civilian ship," he pressed his index finger down on the table, "and its crew depends on us to keep it safe and secure, to ensure they return home in the same condition as they left. What you expect us to do is just reckless. You already have us running out deeper than we've ever been and dangerously close to a red giant, and now you want to put some alien material on our ship? No."

"This is a Council ship, Mr. Lund," Skinner said, "and to the Council, Apophis two five nine is the only planet in the galaxy that matters right now. Think about the possibilities. It could cure disease. It could be the secret to eternal youth. It could be a new fuel that would extend the range of our fleet tenfold. It could end instability and conflict on New Earth."

"The war?" Stellan said, descending into reflection. He closed his eyes and remembered. He didn't want to. Flames danced before his eyes. The smell of smoke filled his nostrils. Inexplicable anger rose from deep within him. "Or it could make us all dead! Have you thought about that!?" He slammed the table, and the image of Apophis fractured and distorted. It disappeared and was replaced with a message informing them the holotable had encountered a problem and needed to shut down. The table chirped for their attention, requesting it be manually restarted.

"We have," she said, "but if your crew follows proper procedure, there should be no problems, should there?"

She was right, and Stellan knew it. The *Atlas* had protocols in place to prevent harm to its crew, and as long as there were no accidents, there shouldn't be any danger. As long as there were no accidents.

"Well," Skinner said, slapping her thighs. "I suppose you two have some work to do." She stood and walked toward the door.

"May I ask where you are going?" Pierce said.

"Keeping tabs?"

"I just want to know where to find you if we need you, since you declined to wear a link." Pierce tapped his wrist.

"There's a stool with my name on it down at the bar if you must know," she said. "Ingenious, by the way, turning half of the mess into a full-service bar. If I were you, I'd hope the Council doesn't find out about that." She pulled the hatch, and the metal rubbed again, sending a shiver through their eardrums.

Stellan stared across the table at Pierce, and Pierce watched the door almost longingly as it closed behind her.

"I really ought to have someone up here to fix that door," Pierce said, gazing into another realm.

"We're working with unknowns here, Gordon."

"It isn't the first time," Pierce said and stood. He walked to a small table in the corner where a half-full, unlabeled bottle of golden whiskey waited.

"Yeah, but we used to be able to get our own recon if the brass shorted us on intel. Take every precaution we could. This is just reckless," Stellan said.

"What do you want me to do?" Pierce asked, picking up the bottle and removing its glass stopper. He smelled the fumes, and a pleasant look crossed his face. "Good for meditation," he said to no one in particular. He leaned the bottle over on its side as a man might dip a woman in a dance. The head spilled into the rocks glass.

"You know, we're out here running back and forth, and I think all we need, all anyone needs, is a fine bottle of whiskey to keep them warm at night," Pierce said. "You ever think about the old days?"

"The Unity Corps?" Stellan asked.

"Yeah."

"I try not to."

"I remember some of those long, cold nights in the field. We couldn't risk even starting a fire to warm our hands. The wind would blow, and it was like Mother Nature was taking bites right out of you, blowing the heat right off your face like it was dust. The rain turned to needles, and you couldn't shake the chill from your bones. We'd pass around that whiskey that, who was it? Torrington? The whiskey that Torrington's father made? And even though I'd tell you boys to shut your mouths, you'd drink and tell jokes and stories and laugh. And all that heartache would melt away. I didn't realize I loved that. Out here, there's no wind. There's no rain. No adversary for our spirit, and I wonder if we need that to feel alive sometimes."

When Stellan tried to recall those times, he didn't think of the cold. He recalled heat and smoke. He remembered the whole world burning.

"I want you to do your job," Pierce said. "The best you can. I want you to keep an eye on her. We're playing nice now, but we still have some leverage. She may not admit it even to herself, but the crew won't take orders from her. She can't fly this boat herself. She needs us, and I'm not about to risk the *Atlas* or this crew. The first sign of trouble, and we're out of there, regardless of what she says. I'll tie her up myself if I have to." Pierce carried the glasses and the bottle to the table and slid one to Stellan. The table continued to chirp, asking one of them to reset it.

"I'm not about to see lives end out here," Pierce added and sipped his whiskey. He exhaled the heat through clenched teeth. "If it comes to that, this time, I'll take the responsibility when we get back."

"Why risk it at all?"

Pierce held another sip in his mouth and thought for a moment, gazing into nothing.

"Maybe some risks are worth taking. Maybe because I need to know I still can," he said. "And anyway, we don't have much of a choice."

The two of them swirled their whiskey, staring down into their glasses. Pierce laughed, and Stellan understood the fear of losing his edge, of becoming as worn down and soft as Pierce's ancient desk, as the old books he kept around him. He supposed Pierce kept them because it reminded him what happened when you let time and complacency rub against you for so long. When Stellan put on his weapon at the beginning of every wake cycle, it reminded him that he needed to be like it, ready to fire when called upon. And the truth he had come to realize was he wasn't sure whether he still could, whether the decay of age had reached his spine and made it brittle.

"What if she's lying?" Stellan asked. "You know she's lying about something. They never shoot straight with people."

"She's here in a supervisory role only. Mining crews have never been out this far. She's just here to help make sure everything goes smoothly."

"You don't really believe that."

"I haven't the luxury of believing anything, but I have to accept what she tells me."

"And what if she brings hell down on us?"

"That's not going to happen. I won't let it."

"Still," Stellan said, "what if?"

"We'll figure something out," Pierce said. "Like always. We'll do what we have to do and find a way to live with it."

Stellan took comfort in his Captain's optimism, but he hadn't touched his whiskey and felt then that he couldn't stomach it. He pushed the glass away and stood from the table, pulling the hem of his overcoat to straighten the wrinkles.

"I don't think I need to tell you the crew's at a bit of unease," Pierce said. "With that woman aboard and our destination a secret, I'd expect some of them to act a little out of the ordinary. Take extra precautions. We've got enough on our plate having to deal with Ms. Skinner. We don't need unrest among the crew."

"I'm going to make my rounds," Stellan said.

Pierce nodded, still staring into his glass. Stellan opened the hatch door and barely noticed the scuff sound, but it shook Pierce from his trance. Pierce watched his friend leave and felt a sadness he couldn't understand, like seeing only glimpses of a premonition of dark times. It nagged at him, so he finished his whiskey and picked up Stellan's glass. It was a gift, and Pierce didn't take back gifts. If Stellan wasn't going to drink it, no one would. Pierce walked it to his bathroom and poured it down the drain. The

Atlas' water filtration system would detect it as a contaminant and jettison it out to space.

Pierce walked back into his office where he sat in his creaking chair behind his antiquated desk. His hand absently fumbled for the bottom drawer and pulled it open. From it, he retrieved a single bullet. He held it close to his eyes and tumbled it in his fingers like an alien object full of wonder, curious about the way the light gleamed across its metal skin.

"Like always," he said.

Nine

Pierce entered the bridge, his footsteps on the glass walkway announcing his presence to Arlo and Evans, who quickly hid a game they were playing against each other using an application they had illegally installed on their links. They closed the application and turned to their workstations just as Pierce stopped on his command platform and leaned on the railing in front of it, his shoulder blades poking up under his heavy officer's coat.

"Light drive spun up and ready to fire, Captain," Arlo said. "Say the word, and I'll kick off the training wheels." The *Atlas* breathed as the steady fire of the thrusters propelled them forward and the light drive swelled.

"Destination solution achieved," Evans said. "Coordinates locked. Scans indicate no anomalies. Should be smooth sailing, Captain."

Pierce looked down upon the two young men on his bridge, one who'd barely escaped his teens. The danger they accepted to fly in space and break the law of relativity was minimal. In the history of space exploration and mining, there had only been one ship lost. At least, there had only been one ship they knew of. The price they would pay for a mistake would be absolute. One miscalculation, and the whole ship and everyone aboard would perish. More than that, it would be like they just ceased to exist. They wouldn't have time to process the end, and no one on New Earth would know what happened to them. They just wouldn't return home. Perhaps they flew into a star or too close to a singularity. Perhaps they slammed into an unmonitored asteroid. Perhaps the light drive glitched and warped the ship along with space.

The dangers were infinite. Pierce saw a thousand different anomalies and variables, and not all of them were in the deep black. However, the chances were remote that any harm would come to them from out there. Statistically, with all the thorough protocols and redundancies, they were more likely to die in a fire or earthquake on New Earth. They were safe here.

The only dangers that concerned him were within the *Atlas'* hull.

Arlo and Evans looked up to Pierce looming on his platform; he did not see the impatience they clearly bore. He saw dependence.

He thought about the *Atlas* and its civilian crew. He never considered himself a civilian. He wasn't delusional. He was cognizant he had left the military years ago, and he presumed he accepted the command of the *Atlas* as a form of retirement, graceful or not. He presumed Stellan had joined him on this ship for similar reasons, though Stellan's reasons were probably more for seeking escape, as he still had so much life left to live. They all did.

He had faith in Stellan. He had faith in himself. Trust. He knew they could handle any challenge they would encounter, and he knew they'd all come home, one last triumph from the greatest beyond from which any man could ever return.

He took an oath to himself then, and it transcended every oath he'd ever taken. He'd sworn to uphold peace and order once. He'd sworn to serve humanity as captain of the *Atlas*. He'd maintain both of those oaths, but above all else, he'd do what was necessary if the time came. He would accept the consequences and never look back. If that meant defying the Council's agent, so be it; necessity was the only justification he needed.

"Captain?" Arlo said.

"All right, then. That's it," Pierce said. Standing straight, he took a deep breath, his wide chest billowing like a balloon. "Start the countdown."

Arlo's voice boomed throughout the ship as he announced the *Atlas* would jump and counted down from ten. The pulse of the light drive grew. The sound changed in volume and intensity but not pitch. The pitch never changed, and Pierce considered that was the reason it was so maddening. It echoed a perfectly constant frequency, like being tied down while water drops tapped your forehead. It was impossible to escape.

"Seven, six, five..."

A steady stream of something in the air flowed over them. It might have been static electricity, but their hair didn't stand on end. It might have been like the sudden magnetic tightening of the deck when the tram arrived at the platform, but there were no knocks of the stabilizing paddles. All sound became distant. The bridge expanded, as did the distance between each of them.

"Three, two, one..."

They all knew these effects were no trick of perception. The light drive warped space around them. It would draw their destination closer while pushing their point of origin farther behind them. It was how they were able to travel faster than light.

"Zero."

"Mark," Pierce said.

Arlo pressed a window on his workstation. The light drive silenced. They could only hear themselves breathe. Then everything inside the hull of the *Atlas* snapped back into place, returning to normal, even the mechanical rise and fall of the light drive.

The *Atlas* trembled and then streaked across the stars faster than light, disappearing into the great expanse of the deep, dark black.

CHAPTER 2
BLACK MADNESS

One

If anything about spying on Agent Skinner surprised Stellan, it was that it didn't feel good. He'd expected it to feel justified, like he was serving some kind of poetic justice by spying on someone who professionally invaded others' privacy. She deserved deceit and mistrust, but something about playing such cloak-and-dagger games didn't feel right. It felt like cheating. He knew she wielded lies and deceit with grace, like delicate fingers that gently pushed the chins of onlookers to direct their gaze, and those tools felt foreign to him. They felt wrong in his hands, like they'd been made for someone else.

If there was anything that didn't surprise Stellan, it was that she wasn't at the bar where she said she would be, and it concerned him that perhaps he had done precisely what she wanted and was looking in the wrong direction.

"Where are you?" Stellan said with his eyes above the crowd, the din of vagrant voices stealing his words from his own ears.

He weaved between patrons, the body heat pooling in the air like a haze. A stereo played old rock tunes in the corner. Laughter sprouted like gunfire in a war zone. He felt out of place.

Every wandering elbow that stabbed his chest and every stumbling crewmember he caught made him wonder why they congregated here. Having the bar on the ship was a risk. They risked speaking regretful words with fleeting tongues. They risked poor performances on the job. They risked accidents that could cost lives.

Stellan couldn't afford these risks himself, but he supposed it felt nice to let go. He supposed it was the spirit of why they were on the *Atlas* in the first place. They just wanted to get away. And he remembered what Pierce had said; maybe he just wanted to know he still could risk something. Maybe risk was what made them feel alive.

Leaning over the bar and scanning for the agent's face, he recognized everyone with the lighthearted expression of release, an extra curl at the corner of their mouths, wide eyes wired with energy and excitement. They were sensations he thought Skinner would be incapable of feeling.

Behind the bar, a small holoterminal displayed the news feed from New Earth. Shelly Sheltonson's unwavering stare informed them a political representative for a district in Eastern Europe won his re-election, a nail-biter right down to the end, and Stellan knew it simply had gone according to plan. The Council passed a bill that would improve public transportation services. Of course, Shelly failed to mention the tax increase that would pay for it. Global law enforcement brought to justice a man accused of stealing what they appraised to be a fortune in copyrighted digital property. Their tax dollars at work. All was well in the Council's land. There was no more about the ongoing fighting, and everyone could rest easy tonight.

Jude Washington slid a beer down the line, and Nathan Philips, a tram operator, caught it and nodded, waving his link over a tip meter that accepted the transfer of funds.

"Hey, Jude," Nathan said. "Would you turn that off? No one cares about that shit."

Jude nodded, turned off the news, and turned to Stellan. "Looking for someone, Chief?" Jude removed a towel from his square shoulder and set to work drying a pint glass.

Stellan leaned in to ensure Jude could hear him over the noise. "You see a strange woman around lately?"

"I see lots of strange women," he said. "That's why they come here, to let the strange out." Jude tipped the clean glass toward Stellan, offering him a drink. Stellan shook his head.

"This one you would have never seen before this run. She isn't wearing a link, and she's carrying a weapon."

"You're talking about that Council agent," Jude said. "Haven't seen her tonight, but I've been pretty busy. You could ask Suze." Jude pointed toward the other end of the bar to Susanna Barton, the bartender who made her tips with a low-cut tank top and plenty of cleavage. As usual, the concentration of patrons was a little heavier down at her end of the bar.

"What do you know about her?"

"That she's okay with people looking but won't have any touching."

"No," Stellan said. "The agent."

"Just what people say. People seem to think there's something wrong with this run because she's here."

Those people are perceptive, Stellan thought. He found it encouraging that, even without his experiences, she made the crew uncomfortable. Most people didn't know what he knew about how agents really worked. They only knew what they saw in movies, but another face lay beneath that mask. It took Stellan years to see it, but once he had, it was all he could see.

"Is something wrong?" Jude asked.

"No," he said. "Officially, she's just here to ensure everything goes smoothly, since this is such a deep run."

"Hogwash," a drunken man called. Stellan thought he really needed to become a better liar. Down the bar, Thomas Foster slouched over an empty glass, his belly harboring a wet stain that was either spilled beer or drool. His intense eyes wobbled in his skull under the brim of a grease and sweat stained baseball cap.

"This run is fucked," Tom said. "He knows it." Tom's finger wavered at Stellan. He tried to stand, and Nathan Philips grabbed Tom's shoulder and pulled him back down.

"Get off me!" Tom pushed Nathan off his stool with surprising strength. Nathan hit the deck along with some half-full glasses.

The crowd fell silent, and someone stopped the music on the stereo.

Stellan felt all the eyes in the bar, wondering what he was going to do. Tom was a regular at the bar, very regular. He was also a regular in Stellan's holding cell, and the people on the *Atlas* had gotten used to seeing Stellan haul Tom away. This time felt different. Their gaze weighed heavier. Stellan wondered if this was a routine instance of Tom having too much or an exercise in communication, a demonstration.

"I want to hear you say it," Tom slurred. "I want to hear you admit you know something is wrong with this run, and I want to hear what you intend to do about it."

"Everything's under control," Stellan said.

With a belch, Tom smashed his glass on the deck and gazed silently into the shards.

"Except for you," Stellan said, reaching for Tom's shoulder. "Let's go sleep it off."

"Don't touch me!" Tom yelled and lunged at Stellan with a cage of fingers. Stellan deftly twisted Tom's arm, feeling the soft pop of strained tendons.

In a moment of frustration, he followed the submission maneuver with a punch to Tom's nose, splitting the skin at the bridge. To everyone else in the bar, the movement appeared so fluid and natural, all part of a single defensive maneuver, that no one thought twice about the strike. But Stellan knew it was excessive.

"You hit me, you son of a bitch!"

From his belt, Stellan removed a pair of black handcuffs and restrained Tom's hands behind his back. Between groans, Tom continued to curse at Stellan. He slapped Tom on his back like a gentle whip with the reins of a horse.

"All right, everyone!" Jude said from behind the bar. "Show's over. We're closing up for the night."

A moment later, the stereo filled the bar with Paul McCartney's voice, singing "Hey Jude." Some of the bar patrons gleefully sang along to the opening lines, pleading with their bartender to stay open, already forgetting Tom and Stellan as they disappeared into the crowd on their way out the door.

In a far corner, a shadow fell upon a woman who had observed the entire scene with great interest. One of her eyes watched Stellan leave with Tom Foster, and the other followed blindly along.

Two

As Stellan hurled Tom into a holding cell, he couldn't shake the feeling that perhaps Tom provided the best empirical evidence that he'd lost his mind. He couldn't remember how many times he'd brought Tom to this cell to sleep off the terrible mood drinking had put him in, but so far, it hadn't worked. Tom had learned nothing, and Stellan recalled the old saying that doing something the same way over and over again and expecting a different outcome was the definition of insanity. In frustration, Stellan knew he sometimes threw Tom into the cell a bit harder because he hoped, one day, the far wall would knock some sense into him.

The cell door crashed into its frame, and a red holographic panel appeared. Stellan sighed as the locking mechanism latched, and Tom spat blood onto the floor.

"You didn't have to hit me," Tom said, pinching the front of his shirt to examine the new pattern of blood spatter that adorned it. His lip curled into a snarl of disgust. "You owe me a new shirt."

"No," Stellan said. "I think we're pretty even."

"We ain't," Tom said, "not by a long shot."

"Do you know how many times I've brought you here without writing you up?" Stellan said. "I can't remember, and I was sober every time. I don't expect you kept count."

"Write it up," Tom said. "I don't care." Stellan sensed their impasse like an invisible wall, and he thought, perhaps, instead of Tom slamming the steel wall at the back of the cell, it had been him, banging his head all these years.

"I think you do," Stellan said, but what he really meant was he hoped Tom cared. Otherwise, it would all have been for nothing.

Daelen burst through the door to the holding room. She had shed her lab coat, and she moved more freely in her plain and practical pants. Her hair, pulled into a tight ponytail, poured onto her white, long-sleeve shirt. Even as she carried her small black bag filled with medical supplies and instruments with a grip on its handle so tight that blooms of white appeared around the creases of her skin, joints, and knuckles, Stellan thought she looked sweet.

But she didn't look at her husband. Instead, she inspected Tom's injuries from afar, and she feared his nose was broken. That would be harder to gloss over in her report.

"Jesus," Daelen said. "What did you do to him this time?" She spoke plainly, and her demeanor indicated no real concern. But in the way lovers learn to read between the lines in each other's faces, Stellan knew she was angry, and he knew she would deny it if he asked. He also knew silence would be better than the wrong words.

"Twisted my arm real good," Tom said, rubbing his shoulder. "Then he hit me." Tom looked to Stellan with an accusatory scowl. Stellan wanted to roll his eyes because he knew Tom was playing up his wounds, but he also knew Daelen was watching. He wondered if he would be sleeping on the security deck that night. He already knew the cot in the cell next door was the most comfortable.

"You've got to stop this," Daelen told Stellan.

"He attacked me," Stellan said.

"I wasn't going to hurt nobody," Tom said shrugging.

"If I hadn't been there, you would have picked a fight with someone else!"

"Stop it!" Daelen yelled. "Stop all of this." She swept her arm out in a wide arc.

"Why are you looking at me?" Stellan said. "I'm just doing my job."

Daelen brushed Stellan's cheek with her fingertips. Her eyes drooped like she was heartbroken, and she walked toward the cell.

"Just open up," she said with a sigh. Stellan waved his link over the holopanel. It chirped and flashed a green light. The door rumbled on its track.

Daelen walked into the cell slowly, almost timidly, but she wasn't afraid. Under other circumstances, she might have even knocked to request permission to enter. She had developed this approach over the years. Every time she had approached a patient, she saw in their eyes a reluctance to open up and let her in. They all understood they would need to allow her to touch them, and while she found the men often didn't mind, except for the shy ones, she considered it respectful to approach them slowly. Other doctors might have considered it professional to simply break through that barrier of awkwardness, but Daelen was more compassionate than that. She understood there was a doorway, and to find it, she had to establish a relationship with each patient. She was a caregiver, the roots of which were in kindness and friendship. Daelen believed those were her best tools, and she considered it a shame that other doctors would readily cast them aside as irrelevant.

She knelt beside Tom and set her bag on the floor. With her hands spread across his face and her thumbs at the bridge of his nose, she gently tilted his head back, unconsciously making an O shape with her mouth. She waved her hand over his face, and a flash of light emanated from her palm. Her link displayed an X-ray image in a 3D window. She pinched her fingers on the center of the window and then expanded them, which blew up the image, and she squinted as she examined it, short strands of her dark hair falling into her eyes.

"Well, it isn't broken," Daelen said, relieved, and closed the window. "Cover your eyes." She demonstrated with two cupped hands. Tom complied. From her bag, she pulled an aerosol can, shook it, and sprayed it into Tom's wound on the bridge of his nose. He breathed sharply between clenched teeth.

"Baby," she said with a smile, placing a small bandage over his wound. "Open up," she said and opened her own mouth wide. Tom complied again, and Daelen popped a pill onto his tongue.

"For the pain," she said. "And the hangover." Her hand grasped his shoulder warmly, a corner of her mouth rising.

She zipped up her bag, stood, and left the cell. Stellan followed her and closed the cell door, the panel flashing back to red. Together, they walked toward the door that led from the holding room.

"Thank you," Tom said to Daelen.

"Get some sleep," Stellan said, and before he turned, Stellan caught a look on Tom's face that was less the indifference and disregard Stellan had so often seen. In Tom's drunken rages, which Stellan had also often seen, Stellan regarded Tom as more of a cartoon than a real threat. And while this look didn't scare Stellan, there was a seriousness in it, as if Tom had suddenly become a real person. The greasy hat and t-shirt with stains of origins unknown disappeared, and Stellan only saw Tom's stone face, stronger than ever, though Stellan was sure the alcohol still coursed through his veins.

Tom turned to his cot, the oldest and most uncomfortable of all the holding cells, the one Stellan purposefully reserved for Tom on occasions just like this. He didn't want to make the experience as bad as possible out of spite. Instead, Stellan hoped Tom would realize he wanted to stop coming to this place and make a positive change in his life. Unfortunately, Tom projected blame, and he held grudges. He faulted no one but Stellan, so tough love taught him nothing. Although, he routinely swore off drinking as he vomited into a bucket in his cell, pleading with Stellan to let him go because he'd learned his lesson.

The door out of the holding room opened, and Stellan's finger ran down a touchscreen slider that dimmed the lights. Stellan and Daelen stood in the doorway, the light from the main security office falling onto them. They had the room to themselves. Stellan's men were either off shift or on rounds. They stepped out of the holding room, leaving Tom to the quiet dark.

"You won't write this up," Daelen said, "but I have to. You know that."

"Yes."

"That will put another mark on your record, and then I feel like the bad guy," she said. "Why can't you just write this up?"

"He'd lose his job."

"Love, what if you lost yours?" Daelen said, placing her hand upon his chest. "Gordon can only cover for you so much. It's your life. It's everything you love. It's our life. And because of your inability to put responsibility on the shoulders on which they belong, you put all of that at risk."

"He'll come around."

"No," Daelen said. "He won't. There are two kinds of alcoholics: ones that quit and ones that self-destruct. Tom's the latter."

"How do you know?"

She looked back at Tom through the porthole window in the door. He rolled on his cot, attempting to get comfortable.

"Because he feels he has someone else to blame."

She buried her head into his chest, and Stellan wrapped his arms around her. She liked how powerful yet gentle they felt. He held her tight because he knew she liked that, and almost absently, she touched her belly. The life that grew there would change everything for them. It raised the stakes, and if he were to be grounded with her after giving birth, she decided it wouldn't be the worst thing. Though, she knew he would be miserable and didn't want him to resent their child.

"I have something I need to tell you," Daelen said, looking up into his ghostly blue eyes. A few locks of her hair hung liberated from her ponytail, and he brushed them behind her ears. She loved that, too.

"Anything," he whispered.

Before she could speak, Stellan's link chirped. An alert window with a red flashing border leaped to the front.

"I have to go," Stellan said. "There's a fire in the water plant. Tell me on the way?"

"Oh my God. No, it can wait. Go."

Stellan kissed her on her forehead before running for the tram. Daelen walked out of the security deck and down the hall toward the medical deck. She knew there would be plenty of time to tell him later, when it was right. It should be a special moment. It should be a happy time, and she knew in her heart there would be plenty more happy times ahead.

Three

Edward never liked the tram. There was nothing wrong with it, but he didn't like the feeling of being stuffed into a metal tube with a bunch of people. He preferred to walk the long corridors of the *Atlas*. It better put into perspective for him the size of the ship and his place on it. It oriented him, and it gave him the opportunity to see familiar faces one at a time rather than all at once.

This time, however, the problem was his memory kept slipping. He couldn't think of a better word for it. Time occasionally jumped forward, and he would be farther down the hall than he last remembered. He was having trouble recalling names that went with those familiar faces.

He kept walking and hoping his mind would clear. A small part of him knew there was something wrong, but a more dominant part pushed down his pessimistic side, thinking maybe he just needed some rest. Perhaps some time alone would fix him up, make his bad dreams go away, and steady his trembling hands. Maybe a nice walk by the water plant, which had always been relaxing to him like the sea, would cure him.

A thin window lined the wall beside him, offering a view into one of the giant tanks. Some part of him wanted to see a pair of dolphins or a school of fish swimming in that deep blue world. He felt like he could dive in, and he thought briefly about smashing that window and bringing the pool to him. The only thing that really stopped him from pounding on it was the knowledge that it was shatterproof glass. It would even hold up in the event the corridor he was in decompressed.

After a while of staring at the water, he decided to take Rick's advice and go to medical, hoping he would feel better by the time he got there.

A sudden and unexplainable urge to run away surged in his mind, but he thought it possibly was anxiety over what Dr. Lund would tell him. He steadied his feet, prepared to move on, and some men came running past him in a clatter of boots that sounded like popcorn. He thought about one of those men exploding like a popcorn kernel and how funny that would be, his insides on the outside, but then he realized that wouldn't be funny at all. It would be terrible. Where had that thought come from?

When he reached medical, he admitted the walk hadn't helped. In fact, he felt worse, and his memory seemed to be slipping more often, like it resisted turning short-term thoughts into long-term memories.

His bald and drooping head sat upon slouching shoulders, which began to shake along with his hands. He fumbled and pressed his palms together, as if tightening his muscles might still them. It didn't.

The medical deck was quiet. The clean smell was like a fresh coat of paint. He looked between some of the empty exam tables, thinking maybe someone was sorting through the storage drawers under them, and he peered through the window into Dr. Lund's office at the rear.

"Hello?" he called. No one answered.

He liked the fact that no other patients were there because he actually felt a little embarrassed. The Stone family wasn't much on doctors. When they were ill, they let their bodies work it out.

That subservient part of his mind had won out over the dominant part because of doubt, and he reasoned it really wouldn't hurt to at least talk to a doctor. Now that he had gone to the medical deck, the dominant part of his mind argued it had fulfilled its end of the deal. He went, and there was no one there. Period. Case closed. Game over. He thought he probably was fine anyway and that he was silly to even come.

But that wasn't true. The truth was he was scared. He'd heard the stories about men losing their minds in space. He'd heard that, when faced with the endlessness of the black, when men actually saw what infinity looked like, their minds couldn't handle it and began to break down. He'd heard that the light drive could sometimes smear minds like butter. He was afraid of this "black madness" the other crew had mentioned, and he was afraid that they might take him and lock him away somewhere. *They.* Always, you had to look out for *them.* After all, if black madness was real, *they* couldn't afford to let that knowledge out. *They* couldn't let it compromise the mining program. Even more, *they* couldn't let it compromise space travel as a whole.

Call it an occupational hazard. Put up signs that said how many days it had been since someone lost their mind.

Of course, the black laughed at the concept of days. It laughed at the concept of time. The black was endlessness. The black was omnipotence. The black was God.

Edward turned to leave when Margo Tailan burst through the door at the back of the room carrying a tray of test tubes filled with blood. They jingled as she walked.

"Hello," she said. "May I help you?" She shuffled across the room and set the tray down at a workstation between two exam tables.

"I was just here to see Dr. Lund."

"Oh, well, she had to make a house call," Margo said. "Is there something I can help you with?"

Edward felt conflicted. The subservient part of him wanted to talk to this young woman, but the other, the dominant part, argued he had fulfilled his promise to himself. He had come, and the doctor wasn't in. Oh well. Case closed. Moving on. This girl was here, but she wasn't a doctor. She was just an intern and would probably do more harm than good.

"No," Edward said. "It's okay. I'll come back later."

"If you come back later, you'll need an appointment. I really have nothing to do but analyze these blood samples, and I've done it a thousand times already."

The subservient part of him suggested that if he left now, he might be compelled to come back later. If he just talked to this girl, he would have better fulfilled that promise to himself and would be less likely to feel the need to return. The dominant side agreed.

"Okay," Edward said, slipping his hands into his pockets so Margo wouldn't see them shake.

She patted the examination table beside the workstation and sat down in a swiveling chair. "Have a seat."

Edward sat on the examination table and dangled his feet. Even though he knew the girl in front of him was smarter than he'd ever be, she wasn't Daelen and wasn't gaining his confidence, but Edward marveled at how sitting on this table made him feel like a kid again. He wanted to swing his feet, and in some sense, that desire made him feel a bit better.

"So, what's the trouble?"

Edward fumbled with his hands in his lap, and miraculously, they were still, as if whatever sickness inside him had vanished. He surmised it would probably be only for the moment.

"I haven't been feeling well lately."

"Which is why you're here. I gathered that."

"Well, it started with some really bad dreams. Then I started feeling run down like I couldn't sleep enough. There was a bit of nausea, and lately I've been having the shakes."

"The shakes?"

"Yeah," Edward said. "My hands shake, and I can't stop them."

Margo's first thought was to look the symptoms up, but she remembered her conversation with Daelen earlier and decided she needed to learn to trust her intuition. Daelen would be impressed that Margo had learned from her lesson and was already practicing.

"Have you been vomiting?"

"Some," Edward said.

"The bad dreams, I wouldn't worry about them," Margo said. "The fatigue and shakes, that sounds to me like your body isn't getting enough nutrition due to the nausea and vomiting."

"I eat well."

"As we get older, our bodies process food less efficiently, and it's quite possible you have inflammation in your intestinal tract. Nothing to worry about. It's most likely temporary."

"So it's nothing serious?"

"Well, no doctor will tell you anything for certain without running some tests to rule anything out, but I don't think there's cause to worry just yet. No reason to jump to the worst case without knowing for sure."

Relief washed over Edward. For a moment, the halves of his mind rejoined, and he was no longer in conflict with himself.

"Tell you what," Margo said. "As you can see, I'm the blood girl. Let's take some blood, and we'll run some tests. In the meantime, I'll give you some vitamin supplements to take every day and give you something to help you sleep. I'll request you come back in if your tests show anything troubling, and I'll consult with Dr. Lund when she returns. If you don't hear from us in the next couple of weeks and you still aren't feeling well, come back in. But make an appointment then."

"Okay," Edward said.

Margo opened a nearby drawer and removed a syringe and some disinfecting swabs. She wiped the area on Edward's arm clean and placed the tip of the syringe on his skin. It pulled blood from his veins automatically, making a whirring sound as it worked. Edward thought of a drill but felt no pain.

Margo ejected the tube from the syringe, labeled it, and added it to her tray. Then she reached into a cabinet and found some vitamin supplements for him.

As Edward left, Margo smiled. Edward was her first real patient without Dr. Lund's help. She was sure Daelen would be pleased, and it would look great on her record to be practicing unsupervised so quickly.

Edward left the medical deck, feeling the best he'd felt in weeks, staring down at his vitamins in awe, with Margo enthusiastically waving to bid Edward farewell.

Four

Stellan had always found the water plant peaceful. The gentle lapping of the water against its containers reminded him of a more natural environment where his world sang a sweet song like wind blowing through trees, sunbathing, and crashing waves. It almost seemed like firmer ground, as if he might be able to take his shoes off and feel warm sand between his toes. In the water plant, the *Atlas* lived.

He sometimes went there just to think. Most of the crew couldn't even gain access because of the importance of that resource. It was secluded on the back of the *Atlas*, and so it was quiet.

However, even subtle sounds or sensations interrupted the peaceful meditation time. When all else was quiet, the arched ceiling amplified the occasional condensation drip in a far corner. The creak of the wobbly, grated walkway that ran between the tanks reminded him machines processed their water supply, not nature.

If such inconsequential things could ruin the atmosphere, however, the water plant was in a state of ruin and pandemonium.

The fire, which was now extinguished, had filled the air with smoke and the smell of burning metal as it had scorched the walkway between two tanks. It hadn't been a large blaze, but it was enough to permanently darken the path and ensure it would need to be replaced. A couple of low-level maintenance workers for the water plant inspected the damage and were already discussing how they would cut the metal and weld a new section into place.

The *Atlas'* automated systems had performed admirably. The air processing system had redirected its return ventilation from the facility, so the smoke wouldn't be circulated to the rest of the ship. And since it detected a human presence, the ship did not seal it off and depressurize to starve the fire, which would have been the most effective way to deal with it.

Of course, if personnel hadn't been able to get the blaze under control by smothering it with a fire blanket, the *Atlas* would have sucked all the air out of the facility.

Stellan was thankful that the *Atlas* hadn't murdered his crewmates. He had enough on his mind without having to deal with the deaths of some of his crew.

He kneeled on the walkway and drew his sidearm. Using its barrel, he lifted and inspected the smoldering remains of what appeared to be an ENV suit, which created a total, pressurized environment for personnel to wear in depressurized locations, such as the cargo bays when loading the ship.

The fire had filled the air in the room with so much smoke that Stellan felt like he was in a furnace. It was warmer, too. Fresh beads of sweat surfaced on his brow. Hazy smoke obscured the spotlighting above the walkway. In the gloom, the lamp above him resembled a moon, and the light that reflected from the water back onto the ceiling danced like shimmering stars.

While Stellan inspected the charred ENV suit, the smoke thickened, assaulting his lungs. He coughed into the crook of his elbow. His eyes burned, so he closed them.

"Can someone get some ventilation going in here?" he yelled.

He heard the popping sound of dancing flames and the organic applause of wind through trees. He looked up, and the walkway on which he stood had become a fractured road. The hull on either side of him became skeletons of burning and burned-out vehicles, and beyond, skyscrapers rose through billowing smoke. In the distance, the syncopated thrumming of automatic gunfire cracked the sky. Ahead of him, a column that held the statue of a man lay toppled and broken in the center of a city square.

When he looked back down toward the ENV suit on the ground before him, he found the body of a soldier, facedown. A large exit wound from a gunshot formed a crater on the back of his head. The blood still oozed onto the pavement and trickled into the gutter of the street. The soldier's hair stuck up like a dovetail, and a flap of his skull clung to his scalp by a thread of skin.

"Dammit," he heard a voice say, and it was familiar but distant. "We're not welcome anywhere."

A hand pressed his shoulder.

The dream that haunted Stellan even when he was awake receded like he was rising from deep waters. Re-entering the world where the walls were metal and the light drive sang in his ears was like coming up for air.

"I'm sorry," Stellan said. "What did you say?"

Before him, Carter Raines, the water plant manager, gawked at the pile of smoldering ENV suit and stirred it with his boot. In the darkness of the facility, which the lingering smoke obscured even more, Carter's dark skin made him almost invisible.

"It seems like someone's always leaving something burning on my doorstep," Carter said. "You fly the flag of the independents at home and wake up one night to your front porch on fire. It's the same damned thing here."

The crew of the *Atlas* flew to get away from New Earth, to be free between worlds. If that was living on the rim, the water plant crewmen were hermits. They were trying to escape it all, even the other crew on the ship.

Carter had never fought in any rebellions. At least, Stellan didn't think he had. Ten years earlier, Stellan would have blown Carter away if he suspected so. But Carter had sided with the rebels, and like Stellan, he sought the freedom of space. Once enemies, the *Atlas* had made them allies in the pursuit of escape and solitude.

"It's so bizarre," Carter said. "And reckless. Who'd want to endanger our water supply? If we lost that, we wouldn't live more than a week out here. We wouldn't even have enough to get home. How did they even get the damned suit to burn?"

ENV suits were flame-resistant and designed to withstand extreme temperatures, but once you got them to burn, they'd burn for a long time. The plastic made for exceptionally thick and dark smoke.

"An accelerant?" Stellan asked. He lifted one side of the suit and found burn patterns consistent with his suspicion.

"Probably," Carter replied. The two men working on the walkway beside him caught his attention. "Hey! You better cover up these tanks before you get to cutting!"

"Why don't you keep them covered all the time?" Stellan asked.

"So it can breathe," Carter said. Stellan didn't understand, and Carter inferred so. "You gotta let the water breathe. Otherwise, it gets stale."

"Doesn't it evaporate?"

"Exactly."

"Isn't that what we don't want?"

"Most people don't realize that we put water into the air, too," Carter said. "Because space is so dry, we got to. But we capture and reuse what we can. Losses are negligible. Yes sir, waste not, want not is a commandment here."

Stellan smiled at Carter's passion. "Did you see anyone who shouldn't be here?"

"No," Carter said. "Me and the others were treating tanks A-14 through A-18 in the other wing."

Stellan felt eyes watching him and knew it was because every inch of the water plant was covered by surveillance. He thought to check them but realized it probably would be a waste of time. Skinner had done this. He was sure of it. Even if the surveillance proved it, they couldn't do anything to her. She was untouchable.

It didn't make sense to him. Why would she bother drawing his attention to the water plant when she could do nearly anything and get away with it even if he was witness to it? He decided it must have been something important.

"If you ask me," Carter said, "someone was just trying to keep us busy."

"Why do you say that?"

"Think about it," Carter said. "Someone started a fire where there's plenty of water but where they knew everyone would come running. They weren't looking to do any harm. Leastways not here."

A diversion, Stellan thought, and he wondered where Adelynn Skinner was now that she had him right where she wanted him.

Five

Like a ghost, Adelynn Skinner appeared before Thomas Foster's cell, sitting backwards on a metal chair with her arms crossed on top of the chair's back. She whistled a sad tune. Tom woke, feeling the tide of alcohol receding from his mind and the slight pain of hangover and detox, which took its place. When he saw the Council agent, the surprise shot adrenaline through his body, erasing the grogginess and ache, and he shuffled against the back wall. At once, sobriety surged in his brain.

"God, I hate that song," she said. "It comes out of nowhere sometimes. Like, I haven't heard it for years, but all of the sudden, it's there, playing over and over in my head. You know what I'm talking about?"

"No," Tom said. "What song?"

She clapped, and the sound sent a sonic wave between the bars and directly into Tom's brain. He flinched from the pain.

"That's just it, isn't it!?" she said. "That's what's so incredibly irritating! What song, indeed!?"

She looked up into the corner of Tom's cell, as if her sickly blue eye could see through the walls, maybe even through the hull, though she was merely straining to recall.

"It's right there," she said. "On the tip of my tongue. I feel like I could stick it out and peel it off." She stuck her tongue out and pinched the tip. "Ike thith." She wiped the saliva off her fingers with her sleeve. Her warm, almost genuine smile struck Tom as menacing. He didn't trust her.

"So anyway, I'm not here to shoot the shit," Adelynn said. "What's your problem with ol' rent-a-cop? He steal your woman or something?"

Tom wasn't sure if it was a trick. He wasn't a smart man, but he had enough street sense to know these agents, which he'd only really ever read about, were nothing if not manipulative. If they ever were honest, it was transient, so Tom cautiously leaned forward, eyeing the pistol that looked comically large for her thin waist, expecting her to draw and blow him away.

Tom lifted his left pant leg.

"See this?" His knuckles rapped against the metal rod where the lower half of his leg should have been. "It's his fault."

"Did he shoot you? How inconsiderate."

"Nah," Tom said. "I lost it because he wasn't doing his job."

"Do tell," the agent said enthusiastically. She leaned forward like she actually was interested.

"People lose it out here sometimes. I mean really lose it. They call it the 'black madness', like it's some excuse for guys who just can't handle their shit, but that ain't it. It's like the light drive, it spreads your brain thin like butter. Or, you know how humans can't comprehend infinity? It's like they finally get it, as if they looked out there and saw just more black going on and on and couldn't take it."

"Fascinating."

"Well, we had this one guy, Danny, who worked on the loading crews with us, and he started showing the signs, you know? The shakes, nervousness, paranoia. Sometimes we'd find him just standing in places, not knowing how he got there. So we tell Stellan about it, and he says he'll take care of it. One day, he takes Danny away. He's supposed to lock people like that up, like he's got me in here, but Danny's back a few hours later. He seemed all right for a while after that, but the next thing I know, he's aiming a gravity crane at me. He locks on and fires and boom," Tom clapped, "I'm flying across the room. I hit the deck and look back, and my goddamn foot on up to my knee is still standing there."

"Sounds to me like this Danny is to blame."

"Danny's innocent. The guy wouldn't harm a fly. People who get the madness don't act rationally. Sometimes they just stand there like a statue. Sometimes they do violent things even if they don't mean to. The black madness twists their whole world, so you can't blame them."

"I see. I lost a piece of myself once, too," Adelynn said, affectionately running her index finger across her temple over the deep scar that looked like a seam between her ghost eye and ear. "Why didn't you get a new one?"

"Too expensive."

"Oh, come on," Adelynn said. "The Council'd fix you right up if you asked. Might have to twist their arm and make a case about it affecting your productivity, might have to buy into some debt, but every man's an investment, they say."

"I guess."

"No, I think you don't want it replaced. I think you want the reminder," Adelynn said. "When you lost it, how did it make you feel?"

"Well, at first, I didn't even feel any pain. That came after."

"That's not what I meant." She waved a hand. "When I lost my eye, you know what I did? Well, first I spent six weeks in a Council-run hospital."

"Aren't they all Council-run?"

"Indeed," Adelynn said, laughing. "Anyway, once they had me fixed up, I found the motherfucker who left me for dead and blew his dick off. You know why? There was something inside of me that just screamed that I had to do it, to make things right, to put things back into balance in the universe. So when I ask how it made you feel, I mean *inside*, how did you feel?"

Tom thought for a moment. He looked inward with a kind of introspection he hadn't used in what felt like years, and it had been so long because he'd been so focused on everyone else, how everyone else was so full of shit the very smell of them sent him reeling. He realized he didn't like the person he'd become. The anger now defined him, and he realized everyone probably saw him as a child prone to temper tantrums because the reality was he never focused those feelings on anything but booze.

"Angry," Tom said.

"Angry like you feel there's no justice in this world? Angry like the universe needs balancing? Angry like you want to get even?

"Yes."

"I think I can help you, Tom."

Six

After he left the water plant, Stellan couldn't shake the feeling that Agent Skinner had won something. There was this feeling, somewhere deep within his mind, like a voice, telling him the game was already over. Or perhaps he was playing a part in Skinner's story, something she'd already seen in her mind and written. The ending was merely a destination, and they just had to get there. With the way things were going, he didn't think he would like the ending very much.

However, Stellan didn't believe any one person had the ability to see all the angles and predict an outcome with certainty, especially when it came to humans, who were utterly unpredictable. He thought even she had use for luck, and maybe that luck would change.

He likened it to hand-to-hand combat. As he had shown Wendy earlier that wake cycle, people project their actions before they move. Attacks can be broken down into stages, and the first stage is always a preparation. The turn of a shoulder indicates a fist is coming your way. A step forward, a bent knee, and a turning hip might be a kick. Although, that foresight relied on physical observation and had limits of what you could see.

While a person was predictable, people were not. There were too many variables when multiple humans began to interact, and he knew fighting a crowd was much different than fighting one man. At some point, though, it was still prioritizing attackers and watching one movement at a time. Only defensive maneuvers mattered. It was less looking for openings in an opponent's defense and more feigning openings to get attackers to commit and fall into traps.

Fighting was a mind game, a game of chess in dance form.

Yet, he'd already played into Skinner's hands. Perhaps she could see beyond his movements; perhaps she knew what he would do before he did. That scared him, and the water treatment plant hadn't been the first time. No, he couldn't pinpoint it in his mind, but like that voice, deep in his unconscious thoughts, a feeling suggested she'd used him once before. He just couldn't figure out when or where.

The more important question was, to what end? She'd called him away, turned his gaze toward one of the most important parts of the ship. Why? Like a magician, with a sleight of hand, she worked while their attention was directed somewhere else. Only, he was sure she wasn't in it for innocent entertainment.

Stellan couldn't admit defeat, yet he had to admit she'd pulled one over on him. He was angry with himself and knew he would have to get ahead of her if he hoped to keep the *Atlas* safe. That much he knew for sure.

When he got back to the security deck, Stellan found security officer Floyd Coulson dozing with his feet up on his desk, his hands clasped over his round belly, which trembled with each snore. Stellan had hired Floyd simply because of how nice the guy was. With no prior experience in law enforcement or anything relevant, the man was soft. But that didn't matter because the crew on the *Atlas* rarely got out of hand, and Floyd performed mostly administrative duties. Since Stellan believed in symbols, he simply needed bodies to wear the uniform and appear around the ship. Actually, most of his men were little more than autonomous sentries with basic weapons safety training. They knew how to handle a weapon without hurting themselves, but they didn't know how to use it to hurt others.

Regardless, it didn't mean he could allow Floyd to sleep on the job.

Stellan walked into the office and tapped the soles of Floyd's shoes, meaning only to wake the man, but Floyd's feet must have been precariously close to the edge of the desk. The gentle nudge was enough to push his feet off the desk, and before they hit the ground, Floyd's butt slid off the chair and onto the steel deck.

"Whoa!" Floyd yelled, instantly awakened.

His chair rolled backward and slammed into another chair, spinning around each other like long-lost lovers.

Floyd lay still on the deck for a moment. Stellan bent to help him up, and Floyd waved him off.

"I'm fine," he said. "Just my pride." The old man sat up and rubbed his lower back with a grimace. "If I didn't have so much padding back there, I reckon I might have broke something." He attempted to stand and cried out. "I'm not convinced I didn't."

"That's what you get for sleeping on the job," Stellan said, offering Floyd a helping hand. This time, he took it, even though his eyes told Stellan he was too proud.

"I know, I know," Floyd said, looking down at his link for the time. "I'm sorry. I closed my eyes for a minute to rest 'em, and, well, that must have been an hour ago." He smiled innocently.

"That's all right," Stellan said, flopping into a chair with a sigh.

Floyd looked to Stellan with concern. "What's wrong?"

"There was a fire in the water plant."

"Oh my," Floyd said. "Anyone hurt? Was the plant damaged?"

"Everything's fine. Minor damage to one of the walkways. The odd part is it seemed like whoever set the fire wanted only to draw attention, not to do any actual damage."

"Any suspects?"

"One," Stellan said. "By the way, I won't be in the office much the rest of this run. You know that Council agent? The Captain asked me to keep an eye on her, and I'll be asking everyone to keep their eyes peeled as well. You haven't seen her around, have you?"

"Nah," Floyd said. "I *wish* she'd shake her fine tail around here. Hey, maybe we could give her a tour! Then you might be able to introduce me."

"When I see her, I'll find out if she's interested."

"Well, that would be mighty direct."

"In a tour, Floyd."

"Oh, of course."

Stellan remembered he had Tom in lockup, and he checked the time on his link. It had been a few hours since he'd left, and he was sure Tom was still asleep. He decided to check in on him anyway.

He could see the light in the holding room was still off, as he'd left it. From where he sat, nothing had changed, so he could have assumed Tom still lay in his cell. Stellan wasn't much of the type to assume.

"Where you going?" Floyd asked when Stellan stood. "You just sat down. Put your feet up. Take a load off for a while. Trust me. It's highly underrated."

"Lethargy is the tide of the mind," Stellan said. "My father used to say that. To be honest, I could use some sleep, but one thing my dad always taught me was to do things as I think of them. That way, I'll never forget to do anything. As long as my mind never moves faster than my legs, that is. Though, that's never been a problem for me."

Stellan smiled, and Floyd returned the expression. At the thought of sleep, Stellan swore he could hear the screams and the first hints of his dreams rising, but they quickly receded. The fear that he was losing his mind lingered.

"I prefer to make to-do lists. Unfortunately, I always seem to misplace 'em!" Floyd said with a hearty chuckle.

Stellan walked toward the back of the security deck between the rows of desks his men would occupy when they weren't on patrol. It pleased him that they were all empty except for Floyd's. With everyone on edge, they needed to be at their posts.

As he approached, his mind again whispered a prediction, and he didn't like what it had to say. He didn't *believe* what it had to say, and in spite of that feeling, he picked up speed into a faster, more determined walk until he reached the door to the holding rooms, where he peered through the porthole window into Tom's cell.

Tom wasn't there.

Stellan turned, angry again. "Where's Tom?" he growled.

"Who?" Floyd's brow folded in confusion.

"Tom Foster," Stellan said. "I had him in D cell."

"I didn't see a report." Floyd hurriedly flipped through reports on his workstation.

Stellan had cause to be angry with himself again. No matter how hard he tried to help people, even when he did the right thing, events continued to unfold into disappointment. Daelen had been right about that.

"I didn't file one."

Floyd shrugged and closed the windows on his workstation, pleased to again be at rest.

"Maybe one of the other officers let him out. I've been pretty hard at work," Floyd said with a wink. Then he squinted in recollection. "Although, I think I've heard some footfalls come and go. Probably just some of the other guys."

It was just as well. Stellan didn't have time for a guy like Tom Foster while there was a Council agent aboard his ship. Tom had probably sobered up or was passed out by now, and he wouldn't be a danger to anyone else.

"Strange, though," Floyd said, with a look of wonder and strain of recollection. "Maybe Daelen came looking for you because, now that I think about it, I remember the tapping of a woman's heels."

Seven

Thomas Foster had always found the darkness cooler than the light. The absence of illumination suggested an absence of heat. He understood the two were connected in nature, but he also understood the *Atlas* was nothing if not unnatural.

The walls in his residence did not radiate light. When the Council agent released him from the holding cell on the security deck, he had returned here and chose not to turn his lights on, but the accent lighting from his bathroom produced a faint blue glow that reflected off the floor and walls like a thin sheet of ice. He rubbed his cheek with frosty fingertips.

The haze of his hangover was beginning to settle, yet dizziness made him reach for the wall beside his bed. Curled over, he felt he might vomit again. He couldn't remember how many times his stomach had purged its contents because it had become so routine. Each retch was the same as the last, dry and painful.

The wall felt warm and comforting, like the exhaust grill of a gravity crane as it fell into slumber. He envied the thought because he couldn't sleep.

The weight of the handgun in his lap dug into his thighs, and it felt dead, like a severed arm, bent at the elbow, with rigor mortis settling in. His mind blazed with the thought of it in his possession. Exhausted as he was, the racing thoughts were beyond his control.

The edge of his bed was unforgiving, and numbness had set into his buttocks. If he didn't know better, he would have felt the gun was a part of him then. It would fit naturally in his hand, like it belonged there, though he dared not take it. He was aware the power alcohol had over him, and he feared the gun might take hold of him if he picked it up properly, as if the grip would extend long fingers that could wrap around his wrist in a friendly salutation.

He only dared trace the chassis with his clammy, dead-feeling fingers, circling the barrel, pinching the front sight and flicking the safety off and on.

Confusion veiled his mind. Tom felt like a bullet fired from a gun. He knew what he wanted to do. It would feel just. Something had already sent him on the path, pushing him forward, closer toward making a decision.

He flicked the safety off.

Like that first drink of the night, the logical, reasonable part of his mind fought against the compulsion to take this path, digging its fingernails into the floor of a narrow corridor as something dragged it toward certain damnation.

He flicked the safety on.

He was used to being scorned, and Stellan was responsible for that. Stellan singled him out when all he was trying to do was cope with the life they all led, their monotonous journey through the endless black. They all had their way of dealing with that life, and so what if drinking was his? He never hurt anyone.

He flicked the safety off.

Tom sighed. He needed a drink.

He flicked the safety on and slid the gun under his pillow for safekeeping. He patted the pillow as he stood and walked to the door. He turned back toward the bed, looking almost longingly toward his hidden treasure.

It would be so easy, but that compulsion inside told him the time wasn't right.

Tom left his room then, with the handgun hidden, conscious that he had decided nothing. Somewhere deep down, he knew he had.

It pulled harder when he tried to not think about killing Stellan Lund.

Eight

As the *Atlas* barreled toward the line that marked the deepest any carrier had ever run, Pierce wished he could see it. Because of the nature of travelling faster than light, the *Atlas* wouldn't allow the use of the monitors on the bridge to look outside the ship. Even if the *Atlas'* systems would have allowed it, they would have only seen a blur of starlight. It splashed around them, and it would have been impossible to make anything out. So they had to rely on Navigator Evans to tell them when they would cross it, and even that would be an estimate because the ship didn't strictly exist in any one location.

That didn't stop Pierce from yearning for it, though. It was a curiosity he hadn't experienced in a long time, like the excitement of a child in a toy store, unsure of what he will get but knowing something will come to him. He supposed they all felt that way.

"Approaching the line, Captain," Evans said, his chair partially vacated because of how far he leaned forward. A bright red window expanded at the front of the spherical room, hovering in front of Pierce's platform, challenging him. In white letters, it notified them that the *Atlas* was approaching unsecured space.

"So it seems," Pierce said, waving the notification away. "Arlo, how's my ship?"

"Board's green. I think she's eager to get out there."

"*Atlas* was a he," Evans said.

"How many times do we have to go through this?" Arlo said. "Regardless of a ship's name, it's always female."

"Why?"

"Because you treat a woman with respect. You care for her. You love her."

"And you can't care for or respect a man?"

"Both of you," Pierce said, "shut it. It's just a ship."

"Yes, but is it a little boy ship or a little girl ship? When it goes to a public restroom, what's on the door?" Arlo asked.

Evans snickered, and then his eyes lit up. He shushed them. "We're about to cross!"

Pierce thought of a mouse emerging from its hole, sticking its nose out reticently, scanning the room, and then making a break for it. The difference was they weren't taking the time to look around. They were bursting through the wall with such intensity that it would shatter.

"We should be on the other side now," Evans said, and the air became still as they all held their breath, waiting for something to grab them from the depths of space.

Nothing happened.

They exhaled and smiled. Some of the department heads cheered. For a moment, Pierce allowed himself to think everything would be all right. He thought the risk they took on this run, even though they had no other choice, would pay off. The Council agent was not there to sabotage their ship, and they might even get a mention in the history books for bringing the first shipment of this alien material back to New Earth. He might even make commander and be given his own explorer ship and make this sort of experience, this kind of rush, a routine.

However, the attack came from within, and Pierce never again made the mistake of thinking such foolish thoughts.

CHAPTER 3
A LONG WALK

One

The *Atlas* shuddered, and the intensity of the throbbing light drive diminished. Pierce struggled to keep from flipping over the railing of his platform.

The red warning returned to the front screen and indicated there was an emergency. Reports and windows flooded Arlo's workstation in machine gun fashion.

The *Atlas* replaced the red emergency window with a video surveillance feed. A middle-aged, balding man, his shoulders and head drooping, stood in an airlock, nervously shuffling on his heels. He was speaking, though no one stood beside him. The feed did not have audio, so the officers on the bridge could not hear what was saying.

"Dad?" Arlo said.

"Arlo, report!" Pierce barked. Arlo gawked at the surveillance feed.

"Sir, there was an unauthorized airlock activation in cargo bay forty-nine," Evans said.

"Mr. Stone," Pierce said. "How's my ship?" An emergency deactivation of the light drive could cause massive damage to the *Atlas*. It was largely unpredictable and, therefore, unknown because the variables were incalculable.

Pierce asked, not out of concern for the *Atlas*. As he had said, it was just a ship, and they clearly hadn't torn apart. He asked because he hoped to focus Arlo on his duties.

Arlo, clearly in shock, stood from his workstation to leave. Windows continued to accumulate on his terminal unabated. His slow, uncertain gait turned into a hurried walk. His mouth closed and his eyes narrowed. Pierce

68

didn't like that look because he knew it came from an emotional response, which placed blinders over his eyes.

"Arlo," Pierce said. "Arlo!"

"No damage," he said. "We're coasting." Pierce grabbed Arlo's arm as he passed. Arlo tried to shake the Captain off, but his grip was too strong.

"We'll get him out of there," Pierce said, his gaze relentless. Arlo suddenly found that strength and determination sapped from him. Looking at Pierce was like looking into a mirror, and Arlo understood that the emotions he'd felt had been fake. He could look at his Captain no longer, feeling ashamed.

Just the apparent fortitude of Pierce's demeanor broke Arlo down, but like resetting his brain, he regained control and knew he'd been a slave to shock and fear. If he'd left the bridge as he'd intended, he would have broken down before he could reach his father. With his Captain, Arlo felt confident that everything would be all right.

"Evans," Pierce said, "can you override and shut it down?"

"N-no, sir. He must have done something on his end." Pierce released his grasp on Arlo, who couldn't yet move. He didn't have the strength.

"You have the conn, Cooper," Pierce said.

"Sir?"

"It's okay. We're just coasting." Pierce raised his hands to calm Evans. "Just keep an eye on things until we get back."

Pierce ushered Arlo toward the lift.

"Until you get back, sir?"

Pierce and Arlo walked determinedly past the department heads, who all stopped working even though requests for orders and confirmations flooded their workstations. They couldn't resist watching Pierce and Arlo's faces, one unwavering and one wrinkled with worry, both men shadowed by their intent, which would almost certainly put them in danger, as even without the light drive firing, if that airlock opened, they could be sucked into oblivion, and an ENV suit would only ensure a slower death by asphyxiation in the endless black.

"We'll never get there in time," Arlo said in a daze.

"Forty-nine's not far from the central lift," Pierce said. In truth, Pierce also doubted they would get there in time. Edward had only to press a button, and the airlock would open in minutes. Without an ENV suit, he might be gone before then.

They entered the lift, and the doors closed like a mouth into a throat that took them to the belly of the ship, where they ran as fast as they could to cargo bay forty-nine.

Two

When Edward looked inside himself, he found a gaping hole like a wound that he feared would never close. Outside of him was space. Inside of him was more space. Only a shell separated them, and maybe the best thing to do was to crack it and blend those spaces together. Why keep lovers apart?

Even with the feeling of cold nothingness, Edward Stone did not despair. Nothing mattered to him anymore, and that was a good thing. It meant he had no ties to the ship. It meant he had no ties to this life.

Killing himself, though, wasn't his goal. It was a means to an end. He had to bring out what was inside him and rejoin it with the stars. Death was just a byproduct.

Yet, between these moments of insanity, he would find lucidity. He wasn't alone, and he didn't want to die. The realization when he occasionally found his mental footing made him afraid, and it was the fear that drove him to accept his fate, as it was probably for the best that he removed himself. It would be better for the ship and the crew. It would be better than spending the rest of his life in a dark hole. And it would be better for Arlo, his son.

Since Emily, his wife, died, he'd felt like a burden in someone else's hands. He was aware of his grief, and he recognized the impatience of those around him as he continued to carry it years after she passed. He felt afflicted; any normal person would have moved on. He could not. Grief had become his disease.

And then, sometimes he thought, even though he didn't believe in a God, maybe he would see Emily in some form or another. Maybe when he died, he would get to feel her once more, if only for a moment, even if it was only his brain revisiting those sensations and impulses, creating the illusion that she was real. He would know no pain, emotional or physical, in the end. And, he realized, he wanted this. The only reason no one else wanted death was for the uncertainty of what lay beyond. Madness had only made him realize he no longer cared that he would become stardust in the endless black.

And a popsicle. That's what he would be; a frozen, bloody mess of an Edward popsicle. It was too bad pets weren't allowed on the *Atlas*. He imagined he would make a good treat for someone's doggy.

Oh, God. He didn't know what he was thinking. He never knew what he was thinking anymore, and the confusion was as fleeting as his sanity. It was like his mind had a will of its own, and he held its moral compass in his hand. Free from those bindings, his mind could search out anything and make it feel right. Tearing out someone's eyes could feel right if they looked at him the wrong way. Tearing out his own eyes could feel right if he'd looked too long into the darkness.

Edward's hands throbbed in the flashing warning lights within the airlock, and he wondered if he had done this to himself. He rubbed them together as if to wipe away grease, and then he balled them into fists and squeezed so hard his fingernails bit into his palms.

The button lay in wait on the wall. All he needed to do now was push it, and the airlock would open wide and shoot him into space where everything inside him could rejoin the larger gaping hole they all lived in.

It would be so easy. The *Atlas* would just take care of it. One button press, and he would be a burden no more.

That's when he heard his name, faint, foggy, far away, leaving the tongue of a friendly voice on a scream. He stood at the edge of oblivion, his cold hands cradling his head.

He just didn't know anything anymore, but he had somehow made peace with that.

Three

To the engineers on the *Atlas*, spilling oil together was like spilling blood. They wrote the constitution of their brotherhood in grease. They were part of the same class, and that was a bond like no other. They were in some deep shit, but they were in it together. And together, they would trudge through it because, without them, the *Atlas* could not function.

When Rick Fairchild screamed Edward's name, he screamed because it might as well have been him in the airlock. Whatever was going on in Edward's head, whatever the sickness was that infected men's brains, be it the black or something else, it didn't discriminate. It came to them at random while they were working alone in dark corners, and it would take them away from that bond and bring them back in shambles.

At least, the ones who'd been around as long as Rick had seen it. Younger engineers like Wendy dismissed their stories with skepticism. She'd believe him now. As she ran beside him, he could see the understanding in her face.

Rick ran, his aged lungs burning, and he was already beginning to feel his right knee give out. After so many years of working on the ground, his body knew that was his place and tried to keep him there, working the undercarriage of giant machines until he died. His body and time conspired against him, but he defied them. For Edward, he would take the pain.

Rick could not slow before reaching the door, and he used his forearms to cushion the impact when he barreled into the metal frame. He thought for a brief moment he might be able to plow through the door and save his friend, but it would not give. He winced from a sharp pain in his elbow and slammed the door with his fist in frustration. That hurt, too.

"Edward! What are you doing!?" Wendy called. Through the small porthole window, they saw Edward would not respond. He remained, head in hands, internal dialogue weighing the decision to blow himself into space.

"Eddie! Come on, man!" Rick screamed. "Shut it down and open up!" He pounded the door, but Edward remained statuesque.

Footsteps stomped behind them. They turned to find Stellan and Daelen. Margo followed in tow, carrying a small bag of medical supplies. They gasped. They must have run all the way from medical.

"Where are we?" Stellan asked, peering into the airlock and knowing immediately that Edward would be no help.

"We just got here. He's not responding." Rick's greasy hand smeared across his sweaty brow. Wendy covered her mouth, a worried response. She stood back.

"Okay, see what you can do with the controls," Stellan said. Rick pulled a switchblade from his pocket and stabbed behind the door control panel, popping it open, sifting through the wires.

Daelen began setting up the only way she could. She prepared for the worst. However, Margo froze, looking in the airlock at Edward in astonishment, her brain struggling to make sense of it. How could she have been so wrong?

Daelen shook the intern's shoulder. "Margo. Wake up. Give me a hand."

Stellan searched the door for weaknesses. To create the greatest seal, the door was not on hinges. It slid out from a pocket in the wall and into the other side. Pressure created the seal. It was made of the same metal as the hull, which was designed to resist extreme temperatures, so torching it was out of the question.

Knowing all this, Stellan grabbed a nearby piece of scrap metal and attempted to break the seal, hoping the *Atlas* would detect a breach and shut down the airlock.

Behind them, two more pairs of rushing footsteps echoed in the empty cargo bay.

"That's not going to happen, Stellan," Captain Pierce said.

"If you have a better idea, I'm listening." Stellan grunted as he pushed and twisted the scrap metal, cutting his hand. Blood oozed from his grip and between his fingers. It ran down the broad side of his tool.

He looked at Pierce, who nodded toward Arlo.

"Dad!" Arlo yelled, running past Stellan without regard to his efforts and pounded on the door. "Dad, what are you doing!?"

In the airlock, Arlo's voice was like a finger to a switch. Edward's hands pulled away from his face, and he turned to the window in the doorway. His eyelids gaped, and he blinked in wonder.

"I thought I'd go for a walk," Edward said. "They're so beautiful. The lights out there. They shine for me. I want to know what's beyond them." Edward looked at the final barrier between him and oblivion and giggled excitedly.

"Just come back in here, Dad! We'll talk about it and work it out."

Edward turned toward the door and outstretched his hands to show his son there was no danger, that there was nothing to fear. He leaned against the door, his face only inches from his son's. They shared foggy breaths across the glass. Edward's arms wrapped around the door, as if waiting for his son's embrace. They couldn't see that one of Edward's palms rested on the airlock button.

"Don't be afraid. This is for the best." Edward paused, and there was a moment of blankness in his eyes, his mind stalling, and then his consciousness returned. Edward blinked, dazed by a bright light. He looked around the room in confusion.

"What? Hey, Dad, look at me! We're going to get you out of there." Tears formed in the corners of Arlo's eyes.

"Keep him talking. I almost have it," Rick said.

"You're better off without me, son," Edward whispered, his breath fogging the glass.

Edward eased into the airlock release button, and the flashing yellow warning lights changed to a solid red accompanied by an audible buzzing warning. Depressurization began. He moaned at the pain in his ears.

"No!" Arlo frantically beat the door. Stellan dropped the scrap metal. Rick stepped back from the control panel. It was useless now. If they opened the door, the *Atlas* would seal off the entire cargo bay, and they'd all be sucked into space.

"How long?" Stellan asked Pierce.

"It takes a couple minutes to equalize the pressure," Pierce said. "He won't last that long, though."

In the distance, the gravity cranes pounded, their strikes reverberating in Stellan's chest. They crashed relentlessly upon his ears, making it hard to think of anything else, and he decided to not fight it.

"What do you need to do here?" Stellan asked Rick.

"Just cut this wire," Rick said, fingering a white wire.

"Can you operate the grav cranes?"

"Yes."

"Get on that one, and target me."

Rick understood. The cranes required unobstructed view of a target before it could lock onto it. With the inner door sealed, Rick wouldn't be able to lock onto Edward. It had to be Stellan.

"As soon as you cut this wire, both this inner and outer door will open," Rick said. He handed Stellan his knife and ran for the crane.

"This is crazy!" Daelen raved. "That thing will tear you apart."

"Margo, get me an ENV suit," Stellan said. "The rest of you clear out and lock the bulkhead hatch." Margo sprinted toward the entrance of the cargo bay where several ENV suits hung on a rack.

Stellan took Daelen's arm and ran his hand over her elbow and down to her fingertips. He kissed her, the goodbye kiss they hoped to never have. Both of them knew what Stellan was planning was risky, and both of them knew he had to try it. For Stellan, saving one man's life wasn't about compassion. It was about compulsion. He didn't owe Edward or Arlo anything; he owed everyone everything. If there was something he could do, he would do it. It was worth the risk to save his own soul. He owed it to himself. It was his penance.

"You have to go now," Stellan said. He looked deep into her eyes and caressed her cheek. "I love you." Daelen broke into tears of helplessness and pain, a pain Stellan understood and for which he bore the blame. It was a pain he knew she could endure because she was strong.

"You sure about this?" Pierce asked.

"I'll be fine," Stellan said.

Margo returned with the ENV suit and handed it to Stellan. Captain Pierce wrapped his arms around Daelen and forcibly picked her up. Margo and Wendy had less trouble with Arlo. He had accepted he could not help his father and that his father's best chance was Stellan. Even so, Arlo's gaze lingered on Stellan, and he nodded with thanks. They all ran to the bulkhead hatch.

From Pierce's arms, Daelen screamed for Stellan. Through her tears, she watched him quickly step into the suit, and she was unable to resist thoughts of their unborn child living without ever knowing him. In her distress, she knew she was only being more of a burden, but she could not help herself. Her concern was an explosion in her chest that her mouth could not contain. Every sound she made held no meaning because he might die without knowing he would be a father, that he'd created a life. She regretted not having the courage to give him that.

In the airlock, Edward looked bad. He groaned with pain and covered his eyes. Falling to the deck, he curled into the fetal position.

"Edward, listen to me," Stellan said. "When that door opens, you need to exhale. Blow all the air out of your lungs, and keep blowing."

Edward began to levitate as the artificial gravity in the room let him go.

Inside the ENV helmet, the ship around Stellan felt tame. The suit filtered every sight and sound, and it eased his nerves. He felt calm for someone who, in a moment, would willingly blast himself into space for a man who was probably already gone, and then Rick Fairchild would hit him with a gravity bolt, which could very well tear him apart.

Stellan flashed a thumbs up to Rick who responded with his own from the crane's sealed operator booth. Rick prayed his aim was true. He hoped he could bring both of them back from the abyss. He wondered if the last person to service this crane had done a thorough job.

Stellan wrapped the wire over the blade, his hands steady. He closed his eyes, and a prayer of reflection passed over the back of his eyelids.

And then he cut the wire. The blade slipped through the jacket and bit through the copper.

The inner door slid open first, giving Stellan a brief moment before the outer door opened. It was an advantage he had not counted on, and he grasped the frame of the door to catapult himself into the airlock. Then the outer door opened, breaking like a levee, releasing the innards of cargo bay forty-nine into the black.

The silence was breathtaking.

Edward's body became rigid, his skin bloating and turning purple. His eyes remained open, captivated by the stars, and Stellan thought he was already lost.

Stellan reached Edward's heel with his fingertips. He was amazed to find even with the speed at which they were traveling, such slight application of pressure moved their weightless bodies, and for a moment, Stellan was afraid Rick would fire too soon. Stellan reached Edward's ankle and then his calf, but he did not yet have a hold on him. If Rick fired now, Stellan would not be able to bring Edward back.

Though, Edward could already have been dead, and there might not have been anything Daelen could have done for him. Yet, Stellan continued to grasp, and then he had Edward's waist. Still, it wasn't enough. He reached out to Rick in his mind and told him to wait just a moment longer. And then he had Edward's shirt collar and then was hugging him around his chest and wrapping his legs around Edward's waist.

"Now!" Stellan screamed, and as if on cue, Rick fired the crane.

The invisible bolt made the air wave like heat rising from blacktop, and Stellan became aware of a ringing in his ears like a concussive blast had erupted nearby.

In seconds, they shot back through the airlock and into the cargo bay. When they skipped across the deck and slid to a stop, Stellan knew Rick was successful in shutting the outer airlock door, and the last thing Stellan remembered before losing consciousness was Edward's horribly swollen and purple face and the ringing in his ears descending into screams. But those were his own.

Four

As darkness overtook him, Stellan's dream began to finger the back of his neck and the base of his skull once more. Slowly, it took hold, and he fell into another world. He realized, though, that it wasn't just a dream. A familiar feeling grew, and before he lost consciousness, he understood it was a memory.

Stellan's father once told him life was like a series of long walks. You move from place to place, stopping when there's a nice brook running under a small wooden bridge or an unoccupied bench in a city park, a cool breeze flowing through trees like whispering voices. You like to take your time in the nice places, but when you stumble upon bad neighborhoods, you step faster as you hope to make it home.

The longest walk, though, is the one you wish you'd never made. It changes you, and it's impossible to escape without enduring pain like a seed in your belly that grows with time, digging its roots deeper into part of the person you become.

Stellan thought about this as he leaped from a UH-43 Phantom helicopter onto the well-groomed grass of St. James Park in London. His Kruger MK7 assault rifle slapped the clips on his tactical vest, and he joined his Unity Corps squad as they squatted in the field, scanning the tree line and blending their painted faces into the darkness. Dawn crept its slender fingers over the horizon. They hoped to be gone by the time the sun rose, before the world woke and saw what was happening.

"Gentlemen," Pierce said from the front of the squad, "let's take a walk." He said these words when their boots hit the ground on every deployment. He was captain of their squad, and Stellan was his first lieutenant. They understood that Pierce meant to downplay the things they did. Back then, they believed some people simply opposed peace. There was no reason for them to understand. The New Earth Council sought to unify the world, to bring all the people of New Earth together.

Some rebelled, and when they did, the Council sent its Unity Corps units in. Force was the tool of their trade, and they had no illusions about the evils they committed. But they believed, in the name of peace and the advancement of civilization, becoming monsters was necessary for the greater good, to help the Council steer its people into the future where a perfect world waited.

Stellan and the men he served with couldn't understand why these people would fight against the future, why they didn't want to be part of a unified, peaceful world. He had decided that it must have been a form of insanity or sickness, something innate that resisted unification, something instinctual that made them fight each other.

Perhaps it was a need to fight something, and if they didn't fight each other, there would be no one else to fight.

So, they set out upon London, up the Mall between Buckingham Palace and The Strand. Burning cars clogged the historic road between poles that lifted tattered Union Jacks into the air. The oak trees that once made the streets and sidewalks such a beautiful vista had become skeletons. Having been blown off by the shockwave of a vicious explosion, their discarded leaves rolled on the ground, edges glowing with expiring embers.

Behind the squad, Buckingham Palace lay in ruins. The bomb that started the revolution with a flash had torn the roof off like a lid on a hinge. Rubble lay in the gardens like ancient, crumbled monuments. Smoke billowed like dirty cotton.

With the unification of all the countries of the world into New Earth and the birth of the New Earth Council, England's parliamentary government was no longer needed. No longer a country of its own, the state of England needed a single representative, and its people once again turned to the institution of royalty. Leaders were no longer sovereign, but they served in and used those facilities. At some point, the English simply couldn't let their traditions go, so they had continued to treat their Council representative like royalty.

None of that mattered anymore, though. It was the beginning of the war they'd all seen coming for years. Some of them had waited eagerly.

The heat was almost unbearable. Even so early in the morning, the summer temperatures and humidity were palpable, and around them, flames from burning cars licked the air, threatening to ignite the oxygen they breathed. Stellan tried to resist the flames with a raised hand, peering through the cracks between his fingers.

The whole city blazed, warming the dawning sky with an orange glow. Crumbling towers loomed like fingers reaching from the earth. Stellan couldn't believe the ruin. Simmering anger rose to a boil in his stomach. He couldn't wait to squeeze his trigger.

A bullet whizzed by his ear and buried into the dirt at the side of the road. He heard the crack of the gunshot at the same time, so he knew the shooter was close. He sprinted to cover behind a burned out husk of a car. The back seat still smoldered, and noxious fumes from the vinyl and cushioning clawed the back of his throat. Stifling a cough, he darted behind rubble from a crumbled building, glass crunching underfoot.

As he was trained, Stellan watched the high ground, optimal locations for snipers, tracing the rooftops with his deadly eye, the barrel of his rifle. He looked at the places he would be. The shadows of open and broken windows drew his attention. He skipped the ones with flames behind them.

A hand pressed his shoulder.

The gunshot prompted his whole squad to take cover. To keep moving toward their objective, Pierce ordered them to displace one at a time, the last man in their line sprinting toward the front and notifying the next man with a slap on his shoulder. They had greater numbers, and the sniper would have to be bold to fire another shot while they covered each other.

Pierce had either underestimated the shooter's mettle or overestimated his intelligence.

Charles "Chuckles" Torrington, the squad's SAW gunner and homemade whiskey provider, sprinted toward the front of the line. The back of his head exploded. His body shot up quickly and then lazed to the side, descending into the debris that cluttered the streets of the falling city.

With the second shot, the detection systems attached to their combat eyewear revealed the sniper's position. A grid system opened before their eyes and then closed by the side of the road at the edge of a terrace. A rifle barrel peeked over a concrete railing, and Stellan's squad fired upon the location, cracking the sky like thunder.

Pierce held up a fist, and the shooting ceased. The last echoes of their gunshots expired, and a deep silence crept into their ears. Only the pops of the nearby fires dared spoil that calm.

"Clear!" Pierce declared and walked to his fallen man, kneeled, checked his pulse, and removed his dog tags. "Dammit," he whispered. With the eulogy spoken, Pierce dropped Torrington's chain into a pocket in his vest.

"Let's move," Pierce said twirling his finger in the air. "We're not welcome here."

"We're not welcome anywhere," said Jesus Demenez, the squad's demolitions expert, clapping Stellan on the shoulder.

Leaving Torrington's body for retrieval later, they moved up the Mall and into the Strand and then across Trafalgar Square where Nelson's Column lay toppled and in pieces. The buildings surrounding the square were burned or burning, and Stellan thought the square resembled a furnace. The smoke blotted out the moonlight, and while it was hard to breathe, the squad could move easier under the cover of the black fumes.

They struck northwest into Piccadilly Circus. The walls of the buildings, which would normally play loud advertisements in an exciting spectacle, displayed pulses of broken and distorted images. A black hole sucked in the north wall as if some large cannon had shattered the building's facade. Anteros danced on the fountain in the center, having released his arrow, and they crossed the circle as if the god pointed the way.

More gunfire thrummed in the city, only these shots were deep and rapid, the unmistakable tapping of light machine gun fire. Demenez went down, taking rounds to the neck and upper thigh. Scott Whitman took a round in the chest, and Pierce dragged him by his collar into a nearby alley, Whitman's hands pooling with blood.

Stellan darted down the steps of a subway station and thought it perfect. The station would have multiple exits, far too many for the machine gunner to cover. Stellan would be able to flank the nest.

The lights in the station flickered, the cold tiles appearing to blink like thousands of eyes. Water from broken pipes streamed into a pool and then followed a staircase down farther into the station. The turnstiles all displayed red X's. All were locked down, and Stellan was sure no trains were running.

A whimper echoed through the halls, and its alien sound startled him. It was higher pitched than a man, but it did not sound like a woman.

Part of him wanted to ignore it and move on the machine gunner. The other part, perhaps a paternal part, compelled him to search out the source of the cries.

As he rounded a corner into a narrow hallway, he found a boy, perhaps eight or nine years old, crouched into a ball with his head in his hands. A rifle stood between his knees.

Something split in Stellan's mind then. As he stood at the end of the hall, watching the boy sob, all sounds amplified. His breathing became too loud, so he held it. His heartbeat thumped fast and deep so that, at first, he thought it was the faraway barking of the machine gun, so he tried to calm himself.

He detached his rifle from the front of his tactical vest and leaned it against the wall, and before he knew what he was doing, his knees bent. He tried to be gentle and not appear threatening.

Killing people was easy because they had no say in the matter. Calming them was delicate work.

"It's going to be okay," Stellan heard himself say, and part of him, the soldier part that had split in his mind, admonished the other part. Neither part knew what he was doing.

The boy shot up with remarkable speed like he'd trained years to hone his reflexes. He probably had. The rebels turned away no soldier, and Stellan recognized the smoothness in the boy's pull of the rifle to his shoulder, the confidence in his grip, even though the barrel swayed and shook because he was far too young to hold such a weapon steady.

It reminded Stellan of himself at that age. He'd wanted to learn to shoot, but his father told him his body would dictate when he was ready. When he could hold a man's weapon, he could learn how to use it and what it meant to use it. This boy knew more about pain and death than Stellan had known at that age, and it was tragic because Stellan grew up to kill for a living. At that time, he feared for where this boy's life would take him, and at once, the soldier disappeared. Stellan wanted more than anything to make sure this boy got to a better place.

With an outstretched hand, he stood, still hoping to calm the boy, to touch something within him that could see Stellan as someone who was not his enemy.

"I won't hurt you," Stellan said.

"You already have," the boy said.

"Kid, I've never seen you before."

"Why can't you just leave us alone!?" The boy's shake intensified, and Stellan understood it was from anger. He expected the gunshot, so when it came in all its deafening fury, rattling through the ancient tunnels of London's Underground, Stellan was ready; his hand was ready. It moved without permission from his mind, and even as his brain received the message from his shoulder that a bullet had passed through it and blown a hole out the other side, his right hand unholstered his sidearm and sent a round into the boy's chest like an automatic mechanism.

The exchange had been so fast that, before he was aware he had discharged his weapon, Stellan thought the kick of the boy's own rifle had sent him flying backward.

The child lay still in a heap, blood pooling beneath him, forming wings on the concrete floor. Stellan stood there horrified long enough to watch the boy's blood streak down the hallway to some stairs where it cascaded down into the tunnels below.

At the same time that Stellan felt he'd just killed a piece of himself, that he'd given the last drop of innocence to the Council, something burning within grew until, like lifting a veil from his eyes, he could identify it.

It was anger, as if it had passed from the boy to Stellan, and for the first time in his life, he questioned his beliefs. He wondered if the sins he committed to recast the world through fire were worth it. In an instant, he had not only lost his innocence but his humanity, and he understood that, while he had been thinking all the wars and fighting to bring peace to the world were necessary, if they ever achieved a perfect world, he would not be welcome there. And he realized, he might be cast out and eventually die, but humanity would always bear a mark of shame for the deeds he'd done. Like a black mark on some universal score card, his actions would be ever present to remind them they'd achieved perfection through imperfect means.

They could not kill humanity to be humane.

Stellan fell to his knees. He dropped his sidearm like a piece of trash, and the tears in his eyes welled but would not break and slide down his cheek, as if they, too, were so ashamed they would not dare touch his skin.

A hand pressed his shoulder.

"Damn," Pierce said. Stellan heard it faintly, far off, as if his mind were overburdened and could not accept additional stimuli.

A woman Stellan would come to know very well hurried in front of him, the soot on her fair cheeks drawing lines to her dark hair. When she flashed a hand-held device over the boy's chest and evaluated the 3D holographic X-ray, he understood she was the doctor they were sent to evacuate.

"Huh...huh...how?" Stellan was able to muster.

"How did we get her out so quickly?" Pierce asked. "We didn't. She was brought to us. It seems we were the distraction, pounding on the front door while someone else snuck in the back."

Another woman turned the corner, covering their rear with a pistol, and passively looked over her shoulder, her fierce green eyes flashing like emeralds.

"We have to move," she said.

"He's gone," the doctor said. She walked to Stellan and knelt beside him. "He's gone," she repeated. He did not flinch when she touched his hand.

They retreated back to the park. Along the way, they remained alert, but they met with no opposition. The way Stellan understood it, the revolution had paused out of respect for a lost child, and on some level, he appreciated it

As the Phantom descended upon the lawn, the grass trembled with the down-forced air. The rotor blades chopped like a drum roll. Stellan boarded last, unable to shake from his mind the image of the child he destroyed.

"We have men down in the field," Pierce said to the pilot.

"Guess it wasn't just a walk in the park," the young pilot said from the cockpit. His smile faded when he looked at Stellan and saw the oblivion forming in his eyes.

They flew above the rooftops of the high-rise buildings and between the skyscrapers, a blanket of smoke obscuring the ground, and Stellan looked over the cityscape. The sun crowned on the horizon and brought the first hints of gold to the ruined city and the snaking Thames. He wanted to stay a little longer. He wanted to watch as day broke and bore down upon the city with its full, relentless gaze.

He wanted to watch it burn.

Five

Ensign Cooper Evans remembered reading a statistic that estimated most people who witnessed crimes or knew information that could have prevented crimes never stepped forward. The study reached back decades, and the findings never changed. As far as Evans knew, the study had continued along with the Council's pleas for the people of New Earth to say something if they saw something. As far as he knew, that statistic would never change because it was a symptom of the human condition.

Whatever the reason, be it fear, negligence, or the assumption that someone else would step forward, people pretended to not see the bad things in their neighborhoods. They ignored it for their own sake.

He had promised himself years ago when he read the study that he'd never be one of those people. He told himself that if he ever saw anything or had any information that could help prevent something bad from happening, he'd stand up and speak out.

However, when his moment came, fear paralyzed him, and he could only do what he was told. He could only follow orders because he lacked the courage to stand up for what was right.

As Agent Adelynn Skinner watched the rescue from the surveillance feed on the bridge, it took everything Evans had to keep from shaking in front of her. Until he was in a room alone with her, he didn't know just how much she scared him. She didn't have to tell him she could do whatever she wanted without threat of recourse, and even if she wasn't thinking that, he couldn't keep it out of his mind.

There was something about her facial expression. He had trouble looking at her for fear he'd see her ghost eye looking back.

She watched surveillance footage of the events that transpired in cargo bay forty-nine, and she looked like she enjoyed it. Out of the corner of his eye, Evans thought he could see her smile. It didn't occur to him that her face was a blur to him and that the smile could have been his imagination.

"Go back," she said.

Evans commanded the *Atlas* to rewind the recording.

"Stop. Zoom in."

She examined a close-up of Captain Pierce carrying a distraught Daelen Lund. Evans wondered if she saw the heartache as Daelen was torn away from him.

"Follow them," Skinner said, and Evans commanded the *Atlas* to show the feed behind the bulkhead door. Daelen collapsed without her husband, convinced he was gone, cracking to her very foundations.

Evans wondered if Adelynn understood Daelen's pain. He wondered if she even could, if she ever felt love or yearned for the support of another.

A notification displayed on the screen that informed them the event record had reached its end.

"That's all there is," Evans said. "There's nothing left."

"Indeed," she whispered so softly the sound barely reached Evans' ears.

Six

When Stellan's conscious mind regained control, it measured reality by the searing pain throughout his body. His shoulder blade throbbed with warmth, a familiar sensation that he knew meant bruising. His neck and lower back felt like broken glass. His hand burned from the cut he'd sustained from the scrap metal. The bandage squeezed his fingers.

Margo must have dressed it; Daelen would never have wrapped it so tightly.

He opened his eyes, and the light washed over his corneas like bleach. Though everything was a pure, burning white, he could see enough to know he was in a private treatment room on the medical deck.

Distant, foggy voices leached through the walls. He couldn't make out the words, but he could tell it was a man and a woman. Their voices pushed and pulled, spiking in volume and tone. They were angry.

He worked his way off the table and onto his feet, his body fighting every movement with stabbing pains. His eyes regained some of their ability to focus, and he saw the examination table he had just stood from. The walls were white and clean. A diagram of the human anatomy adorned the wall opposite the foot of the examination table. The adjacent wall was a closed door surrounded by frosted glass. On the other side, he could make out two blurry figures. The argument continued until he opened the door and found Captain Pierce and Daelen in the hallway.

"We just can't do that, Gordon!" Daelen raged, and Stellan's hand missed the doorframe for support. He crumpled to the floor, and both Pierce and Daelen reached to catch him and missed, the redness draining from Daelen's face and leaving the pallor of fear.

"Can't a guy get some sleep around here?" Stellan asked, his eyes still blinking to adjust.

"What are you doing up!?" Daelen said. "You're going to injure yourself worse."

Pierce wrapped his arm around Stellan's back and hoisted him up.

"I'm fine," Stellan said.

Pierce helped Stellan back to the table where he sat on the edge, legs dangling, rubbing the back of his neck.

"How's Edward?" Stellan asked.

Daelen and Pierce glanced nervously at each other, and neither answered. Daelen grasped Stellan's arm, and his vitals expanded from the face of her link.

"Lie back," she said, and he did, grunting in pain. "What hurts?"

"It feels like I was torn in two at my waist." Daelen placed her hand over his stomach, and her link displayed an X-ray of his abdomen. She searched the image with a furrowed brow, and then she took her hand away and looked at him with glassy eyes.

"You're extremely lucky you weren't."

"Edward," he said.

"You need to take it easy," Pierce said.

"Will I live?" Stellan asked.

"If I have supervision," Daelen said.

"Then tell me about Edward."

An uneasy silence filled the room like a gas, and with each breath, it became more unbearable.

"You saved his life," Daelen said.

"He's probably going to wish you hadn't, though," Pierce said.

"What do you mean?" Stellan asked, and Pierce turned away, putting his hands on his head and releasing a deep breath through puckered lips.

"Edward suffered massive cardiovascular and tissue damage," Daelen said. "We can fix that when we get him home. Until then, he will be in terrible pain here. I can keep him sedated and comfortable, but that's about all I can do. My surgical equipment isn't adequate for repairing his injuries."

"And not only will he have to come to terms with all that," Pierce said, "but we have no idea what kind of mental state he will be in when he wakes."

Stellan sat up, and Daelen restrained him.

"What were you two arguing about?" Stellan asked.

"Gordon wants you to put Edward in confinement," Daelen said. She looked anxiously at Pierce. "Of course, if you do, I won't be able to keep him comfortable. All my equipment for that is stationary here. When he wakes, if he isn't mad, the pain likely will drive him to it."

"If we leave him here and he wakes, he poses a risk to you, to the rest of the crew, to the entire ship," Pierce said.

"Edward deserves treatment, Gordon!" Daelen yelled. Stellan sensed a resurgence of their conflict, and he would have to keep the peace by deciding. Should he do what was best for the individual, or assuming the worst, should he do what was best for the ship? It was true that Edward could wake and hurt someone else. It wouldn't be the first time someone suffering from the black madness had done such a thing. Still, Edward had only proved to be a threat to himself, and if Stellan locked him up, he wondered what good it would actually do. At least in the medical bay, someone could monitor his health.

"Do what you can for him," Stellan said to Daelen.

Pierce shook his head in disgust. He couldn't believe they were going to leave a madman where he could continue to be a threat. Pierce was finely tuned to pull back and see a situation from a distance. Stellan could not do that. He could not accept one man's fate was less important than the whole, and it was why they made a good team. Together, they saw both sides of a situation.

"Fine," Pierce said. He pointed a determined finger at Stellan. "But if anything happens, that's on you." Pierce stormed out of the room, and it stung Stellan like a smack across his face. He buried his head in Daelen's chest, and she cradled him, brushing his hair with her fingertips.

"Don't worry, love," she said. "Edward will be all right."

"I know," he said. "It's Gordon. Something's wrong. I haven't seen him like this in years."

They sat, breathing each other in for what felt like a lifetime. Neither spoke for fear words would disturb the stillness in the air, the warmth that nearly brought Daelen to tears because she was so thankful he had returned to her unharmed.

In a nearby room, no one grieved over Edward Stone's body, which lay in a chamber that cured his decompression sickness and augmented the healing process. It wouldn't heal his mind, however.

Seven

Arlo was alone, flying in the black. The bridge's wall display projected the outside view of space and stars, as if he drifted in the abyss in a chair that rested on a lonely platform. Arlo sat at his station, gazing into the systems ahead as they drew nearer.

An impossible door cut a hole in the darkness, and light poured in from the command deck. Pierce entered the bridge, carrying his choice whiskey. The glass platform around him lit to help him find his footing in the endless expanse. He passed his command platform and walked down the ramp to Evans' empty workstation, which revealed itself as he neared.

Pierce sat with a pleased groan. His legs and back ached from a long and hard day, and it felt good to finally sit and relieve the strain from them. He offered a glass to his pilot, who silently declined with a raised hand. Pierce set the two glasses on the deck and pulled the stopper from the neck of the whiskey bottle. He kicked it back with a few swallows and set the bottle back in his lap, licking the burning from his lips and breathing the heat from his throat.

"You want to re-engage the light drive?" Arlo asked.

"Not just yet," Pierce said. "We have time."

Arlo would not look at him, but he could tell his pilot had been weeping.

"You okay?" Pierce asked.

"Not really."

"That's understandable," Pierce said, taking another sip. "These days, I seem to be finding more reasons to drink this stuff. As if I need one." He laughed modestly, wiping his mouth with the back of his hand.

A delicate silence fell on the room, like the vacuum of space, while Pierce waited for Arlo to continue, to open up, something he'd waited years for Arlo to do, but Arlo had always kept his emotions hidden behind a facade of arrogance and immaturity, another persona. Pierce saw through it. Everyone else only saw the cocky pilot Arlo wanted them to see.

"Thing is," Arlo said, "what's bothering me most isn't what he did but something he said. He said he wanted to go for a walk. When I was a kid, we'd go for walks out in the woods by our house where there was this clearing, and away from all the city lights, you could see the whole sky. The stars were so bright, and he'd point and say, 'Wonder what's beyond all those lights. The things I've seen just in my short time. I bet someday you'll know. You'll have a chance to just reach up and peel back the sky, and you'll see.' It was times like those that made me want to fly."

"The *Atlas*," Pierce said

"It's no explorer," Arlo said with a shrug, "but maybe someday."

"That's pretty rough, kid."

"That's not it either. I don't know," Arlo shook his head in frustration. Pierce reached out and grasped Arlo's shoulder, encouraging him to go on.

"I wanted to be with him. No, it wasn't like I wanted to go in there and die with him, but I kept asking myself why I wasn't there for him when I knew he needed me. Mom died, and I was out here. I got him this job, fooling myself that it was helping him. Now, I keep wanting things to go back to the way they used to be when we'd take off in the middle of the night. He'd sneak me out of the house when Mom was asleep, and it was like our secret. I wonder if that was what was on his mind in the airlock. I wonder if he missed me and if that drove him there."

"Why don't you go be with him now?"

"No," Arlo said, shaking his head.

"Why not?"

"I guess I'm afraid. I'm afraid he's going to blame me."

"No, you're blaming yourself," Pierce said sternly. "A father's job is to teach, and if something happens to his child, something he could have prevented, he blames himself. And that's justified because a child's mistake is also a father's mistake. A father's mistake is a lesson. Understand it. Learn from it. Use it."

"What is there to learn? An old fool tried to flush himself out an airlock."

"Sounds like you have some forgiving of your own to do," Pierce said. He settled back into Evans' chair and took another sip of his whiskey. "You know why I love this stuff?" Pierce said. "It's simple. Everything's gotten so complicated, but whiskey is and will always be simple. Pure. You taste it, and you know it's genuine. Honest. Only three ingredients go into it, and because of that, they each heavily influence the taste and experience. Something as simple as the region a whiskey is distilled in or the cask it's aged in lends to its character. Its identity. And when it comes out of the bottle, you know it's unapologetic and proud of what it is. It reminds me of simpler times, and when I drink it, I think the only thing stopping life from being as simple as what I'm holding in my hand is me."

"What are you saying?"

"I'm saying don't let your emotions cloud your judgment. He's still your father. He's still alive. And he's going to need you. That's all that matters," Pierce said. "I'm a father. Did I ever tell you that?"

Arlo finally looked at Pierce with wonder through his glassy eyes.

"Hard to imagine," Arlo laughed. With the smile, a large tear streamed down each cheek. He wiped them away.

"It's true," Pierce said, chuckling, but his demeanor quickly became serious. "She's about your age. To be honest, I don't even know how old she is right off." He paused to calculate. "Twenty-eight. She's twenty-eight." He turned the bottle of whiskey in his hand and watched the stars morph through the glass.

"What happened to her?"

"I really don't know," Pierce said, trailing off into his whiskey bottle, rubbing it gently with a square thumb.

"What do you mean?" Arlo asked.

Pierce turned to Arlo, smiling. "I think she learned a little too well," he said. "She became a lot like me."

"If she's anything like you, I'd like to meet her," Arlo said with a grin. Pierce shot him a sharp look.

"I mean that in the best possible way," Arlo said. The two of them laughed.

"I wasn't always as I am," Pierce said. "Two things are constant. The world keeps turning, and you never stop learning."

"What are those? Song lyrics?"

"No," Pierce chuckled.

The laughter didn't last long. It was nice to visit that place of humor, but they both knew it wasn't a time for that. It wasn't a time to hide behind laughter. It wasn't a time to cover their faces with smiles. If being on the *Atlas* and running through deep space had taught them anything, it was how to measure and define their reality. It was what it was, and they accepted that this was the best it was going to get. They learned their situation was only ever as good or bad as they reasoned it to be, and sometimes, facing the hard talk, the real talk, was necessary to find out where things stood because, out there, they had nothing to distract them from the truth.

"So what do I learn from this?" Arlo asked.

"That it's never too late to make amends," Pierce said dreamily, still rubbing the bottle, wiping away a blemish. His rough hands, the hands of a soldier, wrapped around the bottle's neck and slowly twisted, as if to throttle the life out of it. Arlo feared that it might shatter in Pierce's grip.

He reached out to his captain then, and Pierce put the bottle of whiskey in his pilot's hand.

The two of them drank in silence until the whiskey was gone and the Apophis system emerged ahead, brilliant as a rising sun breaking dawn for a wayward pirate ship.

CHAPTER 4
HOUR OF THE WOLF

One

In many ways, the darkness of space simply felt like perpetual night. The stars in the distance reminded the *Atlas'* crew of the times they'd spent gazing into the night sky with wonder and awe. Seeing them through a monitor on the *Atlas* wasn't so different than viewing them from the surface of New Earth. They laughed about how naive they'd been in their formative years when they just didn't understand the scale of the universe. As if they understood as adults. As if they'd ever understand.

According to folklore, the hour of the wolf is just before dawn when wolves lurk outside bedroom windows. The stories are simple, but the danger is real. The wolves are ourselves, and as we descend further into unconsciousness, we find them, ready to pounce, beneath the surface of our minds, beneath what we knew was there. In the hour of the wolf, our demons are at their strongest, and the darkest of our dreams wait no longer. They crash through our doors and windows and find us where we feel safest. They sink their teeth into our heels and drag us to the most horrible places we can imagine because we are them, even if we can't control them.

However, for the *Atlas* and its crew, the hour of the wolf was an instance of time no clock could measure. The space between New Earth and a mine site could be one night, and this run was the longest night of their lives. A cosmic wolf lay in wait. They all felt it.

The *Atlas* itself slept, lazing in the endless expanse, the backdrop of stars impossibly far away, as if the carrier were a galaxy of its own, hopelessly isolated by distance, any semblance of hope for help should they need it far behind them in the *Atlas'* black wake.

In the midst of the hour of the wolf, the time where, if the *Atlas* had arms, it could almost reach out and touch the borders of the Apophis system, they slept one last time. In their deepest sleep, something synced in their minds, like the teeth of a lock latching onto a key. As the key turned, they saw the deepest, darkest corners of their minds.

During this time, the wolves stalked them, mad from the bloodlust, starving from such a long night on the prowl, and their wrath would be supreme. The wolves, now hunting in a pack, wielded sanity like wind across a swaying rope bridge, their minds hanging in the balance.

Stellan sat on the edge of his bed, sweat beading on his brow, his heart pounding. Daelen's touch graced his shoulders, and she pulled him close.

The cranes in the cargo bays rumbled hungrily. When they reached the *Shiva*, the work would last days, and it would be backbreaking, making each of them regret their choice to ferry back and forth between worlds, scavenging for resources and materials. Some would collapse from exhaustion. Equipment would break down. There would most certainly be injuries, perhaps a fight or two over who wasn't pulling their weight.

But when the work was finished, the *Atlas'* appetite sated, they would rest with New Earth in their sights, most of them not all that eager to return but looking forward to the trip nevertheless.

The *Atlas'* crew lived in that time between worlds. They found peace in the black, where the hull was their border and everything in between was home sweet home, the safest place in the universe. It was a pleasure to essentially not exist, for the world to just leave them alone.

In that time between worlds, the New Earth Council could not reach them. They lived on their own and by their own rules, free to govern themselves.

Though, they still had duties to fulfill, the work that granted them the freedom when there was nothing but open space surrounding them, most certainly not the steady and strict hands of the Council.

So the *Atlas* slept. All deckhands and engineers slept. All support crew, including medical and security, slept. The department managers and other non-essential officers slept.

The *Atlas* was cool, dark, and calm, and it was easy to forget that, for a time of peace and happiness, they would pay with a torrent of pain, like a cosmic balance.

Unwittingly, they committed themselves to their fears, and none would sleep well the night before reaching the mine site. None expected the wolves, and even if they had, it would have done them no good.

Stellan, though, was more prepared than others, having faced recurring nightmares for as long as he could remember, and he thought he was beginning to understand them. He thought about Edward Stone, perhaps the wolves' first victim of the run and who lay in a hyperbaric chamber. He would have to wait through the agony while the crew did their jobs. Stellan thought no one understood the balance of sanity better than Edward.

Stellan lay back down next to Daelen, finding relaxation and renewal in the warmth of her skin and the sweet honeysuckle scent in her hair. He wrapped his arms around her, filling the nook behind her knees with his own, and he held her tight.

He closed his eyes, and as the *Atlas'* dawn approached, they descended together into the wolf's embrace.

Two

Stellan didn't really return to his dreams so much as they returned to him, bringing with them that agonizing heat that threatened to char his skin and combust the air in his lungs. They brought the fear and cold sweat, the waves of adrenaline and panic, things he was never supposed to feel as a soldier but did.

He opened his eyes, and the record began to play again. Though, this time felt different, like his mind was dipping further into something it didn't understand. Perhaps it reached for the darkness of his memories, or maybe it reached out to the black of space. Perhaps they were the same thing.

Most of the dream was the same. The immaculate grass of St. James Park. The path through the Strand and Trafalgar Square. The thrumming of choppers and gunfire in the early morning sky. The fires, oh yes, the fires. They burned the same. Through all of it, he knew, although it looked like the same city, it wasn't.

When they worked their way into Piccadilly Circus and found the puncture in the side of the building, which held the machine gun nest,

Stellan again retreated down the steps to the Underground station. Then, the record of the event began to blur. Something encroached upon it. Under the city, descending into the tunnels below, Stellan found perfect silence, like sound stopped entirely, as it did in the vacuum of space.

The sobbing broke that silence.

Stellan leaped over a turnstile and into the back hallway where he found the boy, rifle standing between his knees as he crouched on the floor, head in hands, and Stellan decided to play it a little differently.

"It's me again," he said. "I want to help you."

"You don't have the stomach for it," the boy said.

"This time, I do."

Before the boy could stand and aim his rifle, Stellan drew his sidearm and shot him in the chest. The boy's head snapped forward so hard Stellan was sure the force of the round pushing through his sternum broke his neck as well. He fell to the cold tile floor, his rifle tumbling just out of the reach of his dead fingertips.

From the fading echo of his weapon's blast, a familiar sound rose from below, rolling in waves. It rose in intensity but never in pitch. What Stellan first thought could be the onset of an earthquake became the sound of a light drive.

A moment later, the crash of gravity cranes joined it like a walking giant, and Stellan pushed forward to meet it.

As he descended deeper into the subway station, the dim tunnels brightened. The billboard advertisements for films he'd never see and products he'd never use became red public and safety notices, informing him that, if he went any farther, personal protective equipment would be required. Others displayed general Council propaganda. Privacy was a small price to pay for safety and security. *Cooperation is mandatory. Anyone could be an independent: Report suspicious behavior to a Unity Corps officer immediately.* The Unity Day celebration was coming: *Buy your Unity Bonds today!*

He was on the cargo deck of the *Atlas*, and it had become bitterly cold. It penetrated deep into his bones. Frost streaked like drawings of frozen tree branches on the metal deck beneath his feet. The radiant thermal units should have kept them warm, but the floor burned with cold like the icy black fingers of space had crept in and grasped the *Atlas'* innards.

No voices carried down the desolate hallways and corridors. Other than the hum of the light drive and the crashing of the gravity cranes, the carrier sounded dead. The feeling that all life had left the ship passed over him like a winter breeze, impossible to ignore. He felt abandoned.

Stellan turned and found an open, empty cargo bay replaced the confined tunnels of the London Underground. The gravity cranes churned; otherwise, the bay was empty.

"Hello!?" he called. Only his echoing voice answered.

So he did the only thing he could do. He continued to walk, wary of the openness, as if the top had been torn off the ship and millions of eyes gazed upon him.

He peered around a corner into a long corridor, which led up and around onto the ramp to a tram station. A section of the hallway flickered, the walls themselves winking at Stellan, as if to tell him something in jest.

"Hello!?" he called again, his voice reverberating in the blank, empty corridors.

Stellan walked up the ramp, and that section of the hallway behind him flickered again and then went dark. The rest behind it toward the cargo bay fell into blackness like dominoes, and he didn't notice the spreading darkness.

He found a completely deserted tram station. No news displayed on the monitor, but a clock reported the time was nearing a shift change. The station should have been bustling with personnel, but it was only filled with empty space. Standing in that abandoned place, it felt wrong, like he was seeing behind the curtain of a magic act, like he shouldn't have been there.

Then the magnetic bed rumbled and hummed, and he realized he was holding his breath. The tram hovered into the station, whirring down like nothing was wrong or out of place, and the pads from the magnetic bed slammed onto its underbelly, locking it in place.

A moment passed.

Stellan looked toward the front of the tram for the operator to stick his head out the window so he could watch the platform edge as he opened the doors, but no one opened the window to the operator's cab. The tram simply idled for a moment as if it was waiting for Stellan to do or say something.

Then, the doors parted. Bloodied and broken bodies lay crumpled on the floor of the tram, and above them, a mob loomed, torn flesh hanging from their bloody lips, bloodstains on their clothing. Terror and madness filled their eyes. They stared menacingly, swaying back and forth like they were struggling to stay upright, overcorrecting with every shift in weight.

The gaping holes of their eyes gazed into some abyss beyond him, ahead of him, all around him, not seeing him at all.

"What have you done!?" Stellan cried.

And then Bill McGuire, a portly, balding man who worked in the water processing plant, lazily fixed his gaze on Stellan. Another focused on him, as if Stellan's words had pulled him away from the edge of oblivion like a magnet.

"You know what you have to do, Stellan," a boy's voice said. "Do you have the stomach for it?"

The boy he'd killed in London shuffled into sight and peered at Stellan, the color in his skin completely sapped, the red rose hole in his chest still oozing. With gray lips, he smiled, and then his face cracked into a raging scream that punctured Stellan's ears. The sound filled the room like static, bouncing off every wall in a circus of echoes.

It was a war cry. On the boy's command, the mob flowed from the car, lurching like a symphony of bodies, an unseen conductor ushering them along. They moved together sluggishly, an amassing horde becoming a wave of savagery.

Stellan pulled his rifle to his shoulder, a conditioned, systematic response, a slingshot into readiness. He peered down the scope, feeling himself come to that edge where only one step remained before taking a life.

"Stay back!" he yelled. They continued their lurching and grasping, and he knew what he had to do.

He stood firm and solid, like a mountain rising from the earth. He supported his weapon as if bracing a friend from behind, helping it find its target. Breathing was critical. If he lost his cool, he would hyperventilate. If he hyperventilated, his hands would shake, and his rounds would not land their mark.

Confidently, he squeezed the trigger, prioritizing his targets by distance, taking the closest one down first. His first shot carved a canyon in Bill McGuire's head, splitting it down the center like a banana peel. He hoped one shot would break the trance that enchanted the others, that it might shock them into realizing he would kill every one of them if they forced him to with their continuing advance.

It didn't work. They lurched forward without even noticing their fallen comrade, reaching toward Stellan with a lust that drove them harder as they drew nearer, a psychotic excitement glazing their faces.

Stellan drove his second shot through the chest of Morgan Thurgood, and the round exited and pierced the neck of Abby Schindler, spraying a red mist into the air like a thin veil over the others.

He unloaded every round in his magazine, dropping body after body. When his rifle was empty, he discarded it and drew his sidearm. An impossible number of them continued to spill from the tramcars.

The horror his mind did not have time to register was he knew all of these people, their names and faces. He'd sworn to protect them, yet they continued lurching and grasping.

There were too many of them. He did not have enough ammunition. He turned to run, but the corridor behind him had become as black as space without a star in sight, a universe completely devoid of life.

He stood at the edge of nothingness with nowhere to retreat. He stood at the edge of oblivion.

And then they enveloped him, taking him to the platform floor, tearing and clawing, biting and scratching, until his own blood and tears obscured his vision, and he heard his own screaming fall into a moan and then an uncontrollable exhale and then, finally, silence, nothingness, the perfect vacuum of the black.

Three

For the moment after Stellan woke, something from his dream lingered. It wasn't pain or fear. Unlike past times, the screams immediately silenced. There was no mistaking that it had only been a dream and that he lay in the safety and comfort of his own bed.

He reached for Daelen, as he always did when he woke, and found her still and breathing quietly. Normally a light sleeper, she didn't stir. His link reported that it was hours before their cycle would begin, but he knew without even trying he would not be able to return to sleep. That illusive thought taunted him like a buzzing fly, compelling him to get out of bed. He needed to focus. He needed to shoot something. He needed to know he still could.

Standing with the intention of going to the firing range on the security deck, he hesitated with the guilt of hiding something from Daelen, of sneaking off in the middle of the night, only because, if she woke, she would not let him leave. She would convince him to talk or hold him until he slept. Something told him that was the wrong treatment.

He dressed quietly and, after watching Daelen sleep for another moment, left their cabin. He thought of nothing on the way to the security deck. His mind was clear, as if he were still in combat, in that space that was reserved for instinct. When life hung in the balance, and he knew beyond all doubt that he would die, the clarity was unmistakable. They had called it the understanding and acceptance that they were already dead. He hadn't felt it in years.

The tram platform was as empty as in his dream, but the news streamed across the display in the back. The quiet felt all right. It felt nice, actually.

When the tram whispered into the station, he marveled at the persistence of his dream, how it stood out in his mind like his subconscious had passed a message to his consciousness, something dreams normally didn't do. The stabilizer paddles slammed the tram's belly, and it startled him from his thoughts. Nathan Philips leaned out of the operator's cab window, pressing the button to open the doors.

"Evening, Chief," Nathan said. "Can't sleep?"

Stellan smiled, boarded without answering Nathan, and sat in silence for the entire ride, staring at the empty tramcar and perfectly clean floor.

When he arrived on the security deck, it was as if long hands had stretched around it in a shield of warmth. It wasn't quite excitement as much as it was a sense of anticipation. Something in Stellan's core, whatever part of his being that went beyond the physical world, shimmered beneath his skin. The hair on the back of his neck rose as if a hidden mouth blew across it, but when he turned, nothing was there. Just empty space.

At the rear of the security deck, there was a locked door only he had the authority to open. Behind that door, dead things. Stellan knew, if he opened that door, they would come for him; his monsters would bite him on the neck and tear out his throat, and his dreams would become reality.

He waved his link over the access holopanel that stretched over the door, turning it from red to green. The band of light disappeared, and the door hissed. A breeze of cold air brushed his hair. The door dilated like cat irises. After half a century, its rails were still fresh with grease. He appreciated the design and engineering that made such a device last so long, awaiting the time when it would need to fulfill its purpose. It was inevitability, and Stellan understood something was expected of everything. Purpose was intrinsic. All a man could do was understand his purpose and be ready when the time came. Birth was like an event horizon, the point of no return, and life was the black hole, a contest to see who could hold on the longest.

The black hole always won. Nothing escaped it, not even light. After the horizon, only crushing darkness awaited.

Stellan stood at the opening and wondered, for a moment, if something would lurch from that space, enraged by the years of neglect and looking to lay its wrath upon the sorry soul that released it.

The walls began to warm. Illumination initiated subtly, red hues rose into oranges, reminding him of the way dawn gently rolled over New Earth's horizon, and then clearing into yellows and brilliant white. No gangly monstrosities waited to pounce and slash his throat. It was a storeroom for security supplies. More specifically, it was a weapons cache.

Stellan was already intimate with the handguns and rifles that lined the walls. He traced their barrels and triggers with his fingertips, remembering the sounds they made, like beating war drums. The syncopated rhythms of war were written in his mind like sheet music. If there were monsters here, he would kill them.

These models were old but proven. He favored the rail-fired, bullpup MK7C Kruger assault rifle, the carbine variant designed for close quarters. The Kruger line of rifles shed all non-essential parts for decreased weight and increased maneuverability. It was a no-nonsense weapon, forgoing a flashy appearance for precision and power that would change the mind of anyone who spoke ill of it. Its style was in its performance.

Stellan picked up one of the MK7Cs and immediately recognized its deceivingly light weight, which resulted from a special aerospace-grade titanium alloy construction that only Kruger could do right. He wondered briefly how he had been able to put it down. Holding it felt good, like its grips had been molded just for his hands. It felt right.

He grabbed some spare magazines on his way out of the storeroom and closed the door. Turning down a side corridor, a storm of excitement swirled in his chest. He couldn't remember when he last had the chance to fire a Kruger rifle. He would have to go back to the basics.

The firing range had only two lanes. His men rarely used it anymore. When they got a new officer, he or she would train there. That fire would rekindle some of the spirit of the others, and for a time, the firing range would see some use. It had been a long time, however, since they received a new officer.

Stellan set the rifle down on the bench top in front of him and examined it. He wasn't quite ready for it, so he pulled his sidearm from his holster. He found the right position, cradling the grip in the web of his right hand. His index finger pointed down the barrel, and he lined up the sight at the floor. They were just getting reacquainted.

His left hand completed the circle around the grip. His thumbs lay together, pointing at the target at the far end of the range, a holograph that would count hits digitally.

Stellan started a little high, letting his sights fall as he exhaled. His breath quivered, and he had to remind himself to pull the trigger with the tip of his index finger, not the first joint, else he risked inadvertently jerking the barrel of his weapon.

Seconds marched by, and his window of accuracy was closing. If he didn't fire soon, his arms would sway and his aim would suffer. For a moment, he considered lowering his weapon, but something compelled him to squeeze, and when the trigger broke the threshold and fired a round, the blast and kick surprised him.

The display at the end of the range calculated his accuracy at ninety-three percent, which meant he was only centimeters off from the bull's-eye at twenty meters. Though it wasn't bad, he could do better.

He fired again and again, and his accuracy hung around ninety-three. He couldn't hit the bull's-eye.

When his sidearm clicked empty, he replaced the magazine and returned the weapon to its holster. The rifle called to him.

Looking downrange through its holographic scope, he recalled his dream. Most of his shots hit their marks, and he wondered if the pressure or the dream had made him more lethal. Hitting a stationary target didn't prove anything anyway. Hitting multiple moving targets was another statement altogether.

Stellan's fingers danced on the control panel beside him, activating the crowd program. Five targets appeared downrange, moving slowly forward. He took aim and waited, biding his time. One of them jumped ahead. The rifle kicked, and the target shattered. Another replaced it at the back. The accuracy display calculated ninety-four percent. Another jumped ahead, so he took that one out, too. His accuracy rating edged up to ninety-five.

That was good. It was coming back quickly. He looked at the targets with his rifle lowered and tried to imagine they were people. He saw their heads bob and weave, saw their arms swing. He could almost hear their shuffling feet.

He took aim and fired, slowly and methodically. He dropped one and then paused before the next as he had been trained. A rushed shot that missed would only cost time. Consistency and control produced speed.

As he gained confidence, his pace quickened. One after another, he moved so fast he lost count of the rounds in his magazine. He fired until he pulled the trigger as rapidly as he could, and it didn't feel fast enough.

So he flipped the fire mode selector to automatic and unleashed the remainder of his ammunition. The firing range had trouble keeping up with him. It couldn't populate the targets quickly enough.

His rifle clicked empty, and without missing a beat in his war song, he dropped it on the table and pulled his sidearm from its holster, the grip in the web of his right hand, trigger finger and thumbs pointing downrange. The mechanism of his hand worked on its own, just like it had years ago, just like in his dream. London. The boy. Blood running into the tunnels below.

It felt good to fire round after round. All those bullets carried his rage and disappointment in catharsis.

With the targets continuing to populate and march slowly toward him, Stellan thought about the boy, the innocence lost. The boy's death granted Stellan life in a manner most would never understand. In a way, he had walked the Earth as an undead ghoul, fighting for the wrong beliefs, which he had wholeheartedly accepted. The boy's death showed him how far he'd fallen, and it gave him back his life, even if it was only wreckage.

He hated the Council for leaving him with that. In their campaign for the perfect world, they stepped on anyone who stood in the way, and he'd been the tread on their boots. More maddening to him was the fact that, now that he had awakened, he could not shake them. They would never know what he knew, that humanity could not be made better through inhumane acts. They were driven by an idea, and an idea could never be diverted by individual human compassion. It only left scars on their collectively marred face, people to mourn the past, present, and future; people to resent what they'd become; and people to stand against it.

It had taken him a while to understand he had been part of the cause of the war, not the solution.

When he ran out of ammunition, he could taste the burning metal of his rifle barrel. He could smell the combustion as the rounds hit the air at such velocities they created explosions. And he wanted more.

"I know what you did," a voice said. Startled, Stellan spun around and found Agent Adelynn Skinner leaning against the doorframe.

Stellan didn't respond. He was surprised but careful. He knew very little about this woman, but in a way, he knew her well enough. She worked with her eyes always searching for something she could use, a way to gain leverage. While Stellan and the other Unity Corps soldiers bludgeoned targets from where everyone could see, agents sidled up from invisible places, took what the Council needed, and vanished without a trace. He was vulnerable here, and she wasn't a monster he could just shoot.

"Most people would have just let Edward go. Not you. You're a hero, aren't you? A big, selfless savior. Jesus Christ. That's it, you're like Jesus fucking Christ," Adelynn said with a playful smile. "I don't understand. It just doesn't add up for me. On one hand, you have a guy who's worthless and hell bent on killing himself and doing a pretty good job at that, and on the other hand, you have a guy who's got a loving wife he willingly abandons for the slim chance of saving this one man. One man dies, or two men die? It seems like such an obvious choice to cut your losses, yet you try for the third option, the one most wouldn't even consider. Why is that?"

"I don't know," Stellan said. "Maybe too many good people have died for no reason."

"Indeed," Adelynn said. "What would be the reason if you had died for him?"

"I didn't."

"No, you didn't. You're a survivor, and that's part of why I like you. When your chips are down and your cards stacked against you, you'll do what you have to do to live." She extended a slender, accusatory finger at Stellan. "You're one of those people who's searching for a purpose, aren't you?"

Stellan simply stared at her because the truth was he didn't know what his purpose was anymore. Was it atonement? Did he feel compelled to save Edward to make amends with fate by saving as many as he had taken? He didn't believe there was a cosmic balance, so he considered it odd as well. Truthfully, he didn't know why he had risked his life. He just did. A mechanism inside of him had been in control, and he'd done it out of reflex.

"Well, I can give you one," Adelynn said. She sauntered toward him and ran a finger over his stubbly cheek. She grasped his shoulder and leaned into his chest.

"Indeed," she whispered, and Stellan pushed her to the floor.

She looked up and smiled through a waterfall of golden hair. "I like this side of you," she said with a playful laugh, brushing her hair back.

"What do you want?"

"That's a very good question," she said, standing. "I realized we've been on this ship for weeks, and I know nothing about it or its people."

That's a lie, Stellan thought. He was sure she knew everything about him and everyone else.

"I was hoping you might be able to show me around."

"A tour," Stellan said. "Now?"

"Yes."

"Do I have a choice?"

"Not really," Adelynn said, maintaining that smile like nothing mattered because she was unreachable. "First, though, do you mind?" She motioned toward the firing range, and Stellan stepped aside with bewildered eyes.

"A gentleman, too!" she said.

Adelynn stepped up to the bench with the five targets marching toward her. She drew her weapon with no pause or hesitation, only taking a split second to find her target. Her sidearm was black and sleek with a uniform quality to its chassis that did not reveal its parts. It was not a model with which Stellan was familiar. The built-in suppressor limited the muzzle flash, and though it was smaller than Stellan's, it did not lack stopping power. Stellan appreciated that the rail system must have featured state-of-the-art amplifiers. The weapon must also have had sliding stabilizer systems that countered the hefty kick because Skinner's elbows only bent slightly from the recoil even though the blasts thumped in his chest.

He hated admitting that watching her fire her weapon was beautiful in a way only another killer could appreciate.

She quickly dispatched the five targets, and when the system replaced them, she sent rounds through those, too. She took a third set with her final rounds, and when they were spent, she removed the empty magazine, replaced it with another from her belt, and then returned her sidearm to its home on her hip.

"Okay if I refill this one on the way out?" she asked, waving her empty magazine, and walked away without waiting for an answer.

As they left the firing range, the display at the end of the lane blinked 100 percent. Stellan didn't think Agent Adelynn Skinner had even bothered to look.

Four

Outside the security deck, the halls were still quiet enough that, when Stellan encountered other crewmembers, he could hear their whispers. Stellan and Adelynn were entwined as opposites. While it wasn't out of the ordinary to mention both in the same breath, talk was one thing; seeing them together started people talking. Stellan ignored it because it was beyond his control.

"The layout of the *Atlas* is pretty simple," he said. "This corridor runs the length of the ship parallel to the tram line, which runs straight up the middle, from engineering at the rear to the residence decks at the fore. Some say it's the backbone of the ship. From each tram station, corridors lead perpendicularly into the various decks."

"Sort of like a rib cage," she said.

"Yes." Impatience threatened to overcome him, but he was not impolite. Stellan knew she was merely humoring him, watching him dance like a marionette as she probably laughed under her breath, smiling and sneaking snickers when his gaze turned elsewhere.

"It must be simple, but how do you orient yourself?" she asked. "How do you know which direction is the front and which is the back?"

"You don't. It's a feeling. Sort of like sea legs. Walking toward the back just feels easier. And, if you wore a link," he tapped his wrist, "it would tell you where you were at all times." It also would tell *him* where she was at all times.

"I can manage."

They came to the main thoroughfare of the ship, a clearing in their path where eight corridors intersected. Brilliantly lit, the ceiling of the circular room arched into a dome. With all the halls pouring into the one intersection, the crowd was thick and challenging to navigate even though it wasn't yet time for the shifts to change. Stellan felt a brief reprieve from the judgment of his crewmates, as it was just too busy for anyone to notice anyone else. All you could see was the crowd, a sea of people.

"I'm sure you're familiar with this area," Stellan said. "We call it 'Gamble's Run.'"

"What's the significance of the name?"

"I don't really know. It's as old as the ship as far as I can tell. There are a few stories. The one I like best is a guy owed some gambling debts and was chased through here. Now, remember, we're on a ship in space. Nowhere to go, right? Apparently, it was during one of the shift changes, and he lost his pursuers here, taking off down one corridor while they chased down another."

"Why do you like that one?"

"Because it reminds me not to get overconfident. The guy got away, and they couldn't find him before they docked at Earth. He disappeared. It's easy to get complacent here and think the hull is the border no one can cross, that if someone gets away from you, it's okay because you're bound to run into him sooner or later. Fact is, I've been here ten years, and I think there are still parts of the ship I've never seen. Plenty of places to hide."

"Can't you track people by their links?"

"Yes," Stellan said. "If they wear them, and if they're on. When people are on the run, though, they tend to get rid of them."

"So someone could disappear here."

"Yes."

"That's good to know."

"Why is that?"

Adelynn didn't answer. She impressed Stellan because, even though he didn't trust her, she projected genuine interest in what he had to say. He could see it in the way she turned her head toward him, tilted slightly sideways as if considering his words. Her eyes focused on him and not the crowd, something he was incapable of doing even when he was interested in what someone was saying. Being mindful of his environment was ingrained in his behavior too deeply to tune out the crew. He watched them even as he tried to direct his attention to Adelynn, and he wondered if she willingly lowered her guard to them to feign interest in him or if she was just so good she could maintain focus on everyone and make him think he had her full attention. With so many people crashing into each other, he didn't think it was likely. Still, he wondered, and he begged to know the answer because she most certainly was sizing him up. His mind struggled to keep track of it all, to run continually through possible scenarios for danger. He felt jealous that she made it seem so easy.

"Down that way is the medical deck," Stellan said.

"Maybe we ought to check in on Daelen," Adelynn suggested with an eerie, almost threatening smile. It angered him, but of all things, she wouldn't touch Daelen. Not while he was still alive.

"Down that hall is the main group of lifts that go to the command deck or down to the cargo bays."

He continued on, ignoring her proposal.

"We're walking toward the rear, aren't we?"

"Yes."

"I think I feel it. What you mean. It's almost like I could lean forward, and something would carry me."

They passed another pair of crewmembers, a man and woman, who didn't notice the agent and the chief of security walking together at first. When they saw Stellan and Adelynn, however, an unmistakable look of disgust crossed the woman's face.

"That doesn't bother you?" Adelynn asked.

"No."

"Why not?"

"Because it's not me they whisper about. Does it bother you?"

"No," Adelynn said solemnly, like she regretted the thought but accepted it all the same. "I know what I am."

She looked at him, and Stellan thought she was searching for approval. He considered that the reason for the tour was so she could spend some time with him and, perhaps, gain his trust, something he would never give to her. It wasn't a matter of emotion or logic. It was just something he'd never be capable of doing. If she knew anything about him, she should have known her attempt would never pay off, though he thought it unlikely that she'd misjudged his tenacity. So, like everything she did, Stellan tried to assess the subtext of her actions, what she was trying to accomplish with her uncharacteristic pleasantries.

"So do I," Stellan said.

Five

Ensign Cooper Evans couldn't sleep. It had been hours, lying in his bed, since his sleep cycle began, and the images poured through his mind in a continuous stream. He replayed the security footage that the Council agent reviewed on the bridge. He recalled the look on her face as she watched Daelen break down. She was pleased.

And Cooper was afraid.

He was afraid of her, the secretive agent who dressed in all black like a shadow, as he would be afraid of any agent. Cooper was just a boy, and he knew it. He was old enough and smart enough to fly on the *Atlas*, but he'd led a privileged life. He knew people saw things that changed and strengthened them, and he had not seen anything like that. He feared it. It was a natural aversion to anything that might taint his innocence, a paranoia that had grown into a fear of reality.

What he saw on the agent's face was painful to him. She feared nothing, and he feared everything. That strength was oddly alluring, as was the way her uniform hugged her hips and breasts and the way she swayed when she walked, but he knew straight down to his bones just how untouchable she was.

For her, maybe she had gone so far beyond fear, knowing nothing could touch her, that she found pleasure in the fear of others. It wouldn't have surprised him. Of the stories he'd heard, these agents had the freedom to do what they wanted. They carried the will of the Council, and they were given free reign over the people of New Earth, so they could do the dirty work the Council could not be associated with. They were above the law in such a way that the Council looked the other way when a necessary evil needed to be done. That was why her presence on the *Atlas* put so many on edge.

What necessary evil needed to be done, and why couldn't the Council be connected to it?

The fear was not the only reason he couldn't sleep. Fear was something he'd lived with. Since childhood, he slept with it every night as his only companion in the darkness, carrying with him thoughts that gangly tentacles could reach out from under his bed.

He was awake because he needed to tell someone. He needed to tell Stellan what he'd seen, and he imagined the Council agent had counted on him staying silent because he was timid. She wielded fear like a silent sword that she swung playfully in the air, taunting those she passed with a reminder that they were beneath her.

In the darkness of his cabin, Cooper gazed at his door to the hallway and hoped Stellan would walk through it, but even then, what if the agent was watching him? What if she would know he told Stellan that the agent had appeared to enjoy seeing his wife in pain, that it made him wonder if she might kill Stellan just to watch Daelen collapse? If she were so ready to deal death and pain, retribution would be a nice side dish for her, and no one would be able to touch her. She could push Cooper out an airlock, and not only would it be hours before anyone noticed, she could walk into the Captain's quarters and declare it herself, laughing, and the Captain could do nothing.

It was out of his control. Better to stay quiet and hope for the best. He shut his eyes as hard as he could and prayed she couldn't read thoughts.

"Just go to sleep, stupid," he said.

Exhausted from fighting with himself, he eventually slipped into unconsciousness, and his last dwindling thought as his mind's grasp on reality slipped was everything was all right, a feeling of falling into his mother's arms as her lips hushed his whimpers.

Of course, that was just a dream.

Six

Arlo should have been sleeping. Soon, the *Atlas* would reach the *Shiva*, and every person on the ship would depend on him to guide the carrier in and ensure a successful lock with the excavator. It was something he'd done hundreds of times, thousands if you counted simulations, but experience had not made it any easier or less risky. Neither did it ease his apprehension, but of course, that wasn't something to which Arlo would have ever admitted.

He found himself surrounded by beds but not the kind in which people made homes. They weren't beds built for comfort or to share with a spouse or significant other. These beds were more functional and meant for the sick, injured, and recovering. Somewhere around here were the beds for the dead. The medical deck on the *Atlas* even had a morgue.

Walking the hall between private rooms, his fingers tingled with an excited nervousness that he had to squeeze out. The hallway narrowed and elongated, and the space between doors expanded. They became exit ramps on a highway, each one a marker to his destination, each one a chance to turn around. He tried not to look at them because he wanted to be there, but fear tried to pull him away.

A door opened at the end of the hall, and Rick Fairchild stepped through, walking toward Arlo with his eyes cast toward the floor. When Arlo's boots came into view, Rick looked up, startled.

"Jesus," Rick said. "Son, you look like shit. Aren't you off cycle?"

"Yeah. I'm fine. How's my dad?"

"He's still out. You know, you don't have to be here. Good people are taking care of him. He's going to be okay."

"I know," Arlo said. Rick took hold of Arlo's shoulder and looked him hard in the eyes.

"You should go get some rest."

Arlo couldn't sleep. Pierce's words rattled in his brain like a rock in a can, and the reality of what had happened was just beginning to sink in. The deepest wounds took the longest to feel.

"Thanks," Arlo said. "But I need to see him. I just need to be here. I can't let him be alone. I realize it's more for me at this point."

Rick nodded, squinting, trying to read how Arlo really felt, and then he walked away, rubbing his eyes and yawning so wide his jaw locked.

Arlo could empathize with the pressure Rick was under, but the difference was Arlo's job essentially came down to a single event at the end of each run. Rick held the *Atlas* together every day, and if he let up, over time, the whole thing could fall apart. And over time, the *Atlas* had become harder to hold together.

Arlo continued to the door. He craned his head to look through the porthole window. The room inside was dark with a large silver bullet in the center: his father's hyperbaric chamber. Wendy stood silent, watching over Edward, and Arlo appreciated the company for his father but was embarrassed to confront her in such a sensitive place. Across the room, Doug Fowler slouched in a chair that looked to be made for children in comparison to his large size.

He opened the door, and Wendy hurriedly wiped tears from her eyes. Arlo entered the room and respectfully closed the door. He crossed the darkness, removing his cap and fumbling with it nervously, and it wasn't until he entered the spotlighting in the center of the room, which overlooked his father's chamber, that he spoke.

"Hey," he said.

"Hey," she returned, glaring at Doug. Though it took a moment, the big man got the hint. He stood and walked out of the room, absently leaving the door wide open.

"Captain wanted someone to keep an eye on things," Wendy said. "It's for your Dad's safety."

"As much as anyone else's," Arlo said, missing Wendy cringe.

"How are you holding up?" she asked.

"I'm okay."

"Of course you are," Wendy said with sarcasm, which Arlo spoke as a second language.

"Why does everyone want me to pour my heart out?" he said. "People grieve. It happens."

"We're a family. We try to look out for each other. Everyone's just concerned and maybe a little freaked out because we didn't know how you'd react."

"I'm like everyone else," Arlo said.

"Do you want to talk about it?"

"Not really."

Arlo couldn't take his eyes off his father's chamber. He could feel Wendy searching him; he could feel her disdain. He could feel himself pushing her away.

"Listen, if you do need to talk," she said, "I can be a pretty good listener. Ignore anything Stellan says to the contrary. My listening abilities are somewhat selective."

"I appreciate it," Arlo said with a smile. "Really, though, I'm fine."

"Okay. I'll leave you two alone." She walked toward the door with a few sniffles, again wiping her face.

"Thanks," Arlo said. "It's good to know my dad has such good friends."

"We try to look out for each other," Wendy repeated. "I'm sorry we didn't see it coming."

"It's not your fault. It's nobody's fault."

She nodded solemnly and left the room, taking with her the last distraction he had from his father.

Arlo thought it was odd how the most powerful conclusions were the ones to which you arrived on your own, as if no one could tell you or show you the way. You had to find it yourself, and you might as well have been fumbling in the dark. Finding it struck a match, and you could finally see. You could finally read the writing on the wall, and somehow, it was in your language.

He realized guilt weighed heavily on good people when their loved ones came to harm. It was just a natural reaction. In some sense, he bore the responsibility for what happened to his father, but he realized he wasn't alone in that. His misery didn't want company, but it didn't hurt to have it.

At that thought, Arlo wondered if his father would want him to be there. Arlo imagined, if his father were conscious, he would send his son away, and Arlo knew his father would because Arlo would. They both wanted to be alone in their sorrow.

People like them pushed love and compassion away when they needed it most, and the tragedy was it was pretty common. It was scary to open up. Most people just wanted to cover their vulnerabilities, and it took exceptional friends and family to hold on and stay.

He put his hand on his father's chamber, bending to look through the observation window with both unease and excitement. When they took Edward away from the cargo bay on the maglev gurney, Arlo had seen his father, but he was encapsulated by the quickness with which they moved.

Because of how fast they worked, he knew his father was still alive, and that had been enough. He'd caught a glimpse of his father's swollen blue skin, but only a glimpse. That glimpse planted a seed in his mind, and his imagination had filled out a picture of what his father had become. Although he tried not to form expectations, he couldn't help it, and he knew it would only lead to disappointment.

When he found the nerve to look through the window at his father's face, he found himself relieved that it wasn't as bad as he'd thought. He saw the evidence of the decompression, the swelling of the tissue. He saw the lines of the ruptured veins, but he otherwise looked clean. With the swelling already reducing and the color returning to normal, Edward actually looked okay. Though it was clear that he probably would have some scars, Arlo didn't think his dad looked like a disfigured monster as he had feared.

It would be like it never happened. Oddly, Arlo didn't like the idea that his father's mistakes could be erased. He didn't want them to move on like nothing had happened. Maybe Arlo was giving meaning to a meaningless accident, but he felt like he'd learned something. Pierce had told Arlo to learn from his father's mistakes. Well, Arlo wanted his dad to learn from them, too.

"Are you happy?" Arlo said. "I suppose not, since we stopped you. When you come out of this, are you going to understand that you're not alone, that people are here for you and will listen, that it's okay to open up to us? No, I suppose not."

He stood silent for a few moments, listening to the machinery work, the sounds of restoration and healing. Everything was about trying to make things like they were before.

"You hurt me, Dad. When you hurt yourself, you hurt me. The Captain says I should forgive you for that. Thing is, I don't know that I can. But I'm going to try. It's not my fault that you did what you did. I feel responsible anyway. I hope you don't blame me. I hope you don't blame anyone but yourself when you wake up. For your own sake. It's never too late to make amends, and I think, the longer you wait, the harder it becomes. If it becomes too hard, maybe that's what drives people to bitterness. Don't let that happen, Dad. Just be thankful. Just be thankful Stellan saved you."

When Arlo fell into silence, the tears finally came. Speaking to his father provided the catharsis to ascend from the shock, and he found the depths of his pain. All at once, he began to understand his own emotional trauma and wondered how many others had known it better than he. He wondered who could see it on his face.

A hand pressed his shoulder. He turned and found Pierce's stern face, which was hard to decipher.

"How long have you been there?" Arlo asked.

"Not long," Pierce said. He moved beside Arlo and gazed into the chamber. They stood side by side for a moment, listening to the sounds of Edward's heartbeat in high-pitched, digital tones.

"There's one thing, still, you should probably understand," Pierce said. "Stellan did what he did because he couldn't have done nothing."

"What do you mean?"

"The man grieves for himself. For years, he's been trying to make up for something there's no making up for. He dug a hole in himself, and now, every good thing he does is a rung on the ladder out of that hole. He didn't save your dad for him or you. He did it for himself. So you may feel like you owe him something, but you don't."

Arlo considered whether the reason Stellan had saved his father changed the selflessness with which he did it. He thought about his own reasons for being by his father's side. Edward would probably never know his son was there, yet he came anyway.

"He saved my dad," Arlo said. "He did the right thing. It doesn't matter why he did it."

Arlo turned back to face his father's chamber.

"Aren't you supposed to be off cycle?" he asked.

"I don't think anyone's sleeping tonight," Pierce said. They stood in respectful silence together for another moment.

"Come on," Pierce said, turning. "We'll be in Apophis soon, and there's a lot of work to do. If we're not going to sleep, we might as well do something useful."

Arlo lingered a moment longer and then followed his Captain away from his father's unconscious body, returning to the duty that beckoned, a descent onto the back of a world ender.

CHAPTER 5
THE DESTROYER OF WORLDS

One

The *Atlas* drifted on a backdrop of swirling stars, obscuring whole galaxies with its hulking hull. Its heart, the light drive, had fallen silent, but its thrusters still burned a brilliant blue. Lazing in the endless expanse, the gravity cranes booming deep in its belly, demanding to be fed, the sleeping giant was patient.

But for all its immensity, the carrier approached a far greater entity.

The excavator *Shiva of the Trinity* ensnared Apophis 259 with all the grace of a predatory spider. Its long limbs stretched wide, tiptoeing above the surface of the planet, drilling and pulling earth up the tethers into the *Shiva's* waiting arms.

Pools of red marred Apophis 259's otherwise brown surface, as if blood spilled when the *Shiva* cracked its crust. The planet spun on its axis languidly as if fatigued from the *Shiva's* vampire embrace, slowly dying as it was torn apart mountain by boulder by rock.

A debris field from the excavation obscured the *Atlas'* view, but between the chunks of earth turned asteroids and beyond the planet, Apophis, the dying red giant itself, gazed like a galactic eye.

"God, that thing's close," Navigator Evans said. "The *Atlas* is rated for this level of solar radiation, right, Captain?"

"EM field's holding so far," Arlo said. "We're pushing it, though."

Pierce didn't answer and simply stared straight ahead, focusing on the task at hand. Their EM field would hold. It had to.

"Probe is coming back with telemetric data on the planet's composition," Evans said. His eyes traced down the list of elements on the report. Then he stopped. "Captain, there's water on two five nine."

Pierce grimaced. "If there was any life there, it's gone now."

Arlo, now manually piloting the *Atlas* with precision hand controls on the armrests of his chair, navigated through the chunks of charred earth that had blown out of the planet's gravitational pull when the *Shiva* sank its long fangs into the celestial body's veins.

"Nice and easy, Arlo," Pierce said. "The *Atlas* has thick skin, but some of these pieces look unusually large."

The display on the wall of the bridge served as a front-facing window. An automated proximity detection system drew thin yellow lines to the pieces of earth that posed danger. Arlo's tongue absently brushed his mustache.

"Two five nine must have a brittle crust," Evans said. "Telemetry shows a high concentration of granite."

Or the Shiva *blasted straight into the layer of unidentified material,* Pierce thought.

"I appreciate the concern, fellas," Arlo said. "But this is what I do, and the doing is good."

On screen, one of the yellow lines pointing to a particularly large chunk of earth flashed red, and a high-pitched beeping accompanied the visual warning. Arlo pulled both controls hard right, and the *Atlas* banked so sharply the artificial gravity system had trouble keeping up. Pierce grabbed the rail in front of his platform to steady his balance. The ship rolled as if crashing against a cosmic wave.

The proximity warning turned back to a yellow caution line, and Arlo leveled out the carrier, easing it by the debris while the crew watched with bated breath.

"I think the universe just slapped your ego," Evans said. Arlo acknowledged him by releasing a deep, nervous breath through puckered lips.

A comm channel window expanded from Arlo's terminal, displaying the sound waves of an incoming voice transmission along with a picture of the woman to which the voice belonged. She looked strong and distinguished. Deep wrinkles cut around her pale eyes and mouth, and her

116

silver hair was pulled back into a tight, braided ponytail, striking down like an icicle from the base of her skull.

"Carrier *Atlas*, this is the NESMA excavator *Shiva of the Trinity*," Commander Emra Ashland said over the comm, the voice transmission wave recognition software shaking into form with her thick and hard southern twang. "We have you on scope, and you're clear to dock. Hope you're hungry because there's plenty to go around."

"Roger that, *Shiva*," Arlo responded. "We're already getting an appetizer up here."

"Copy, *Atlas*. The planet's crust was unexpectedly brittle. Apologies," Ashland said. "Bring it in nice and steady. See you soon." Her voice sounded warm and welcoming, like she was glad to see them. Only Pierce thought that was odd. "*Shiva* out," Ashland said. The voice transmission wave flattened, and the comm window shrank back into Arlo's workstation, closing the channel.

"Called it," Evans said.

"They could've sent a sweeper out to pick all this crap up," Arlo said. "You know, tidy up the place since they were expecting company."

"We're early," Pierce said.

"Right," Arlo said. "So it's my fault."

"No, you're right," Pierce said. "I'll bring it up with the commander. Maybe we could cut them some slack though, since from the looks of things, they've been busy."

The *Atlas* ducked under a large asteroid, giving them the first unobstructed view of the Apophis planet. Captain Pierce leaned forward against the rail on his command platform. The surface of the planet bled. Huge craters from the *Shiva*'s gouging had scarred Apophis 259's face, and the dust and debris over the horizon loomed like a storm. The entire planet was encased in a halo of pieces that used to belong to it. Pierce felt like he could fall through the screen into those gaping holes right down into the planet's core. He'd seen the *Shiva* on many excavations. He'd seen it practically devour planets whole. This time felt different. The craters were alluring, almost hypnotizing. They drew him in, and if he hadn't forgotten to breathe, he might have fallen into them entirely, as if his mind were at the edge of a cliff.

"Take us in," Pierce said, and a small pang of fear pinched his gut. It was irrational, but wasn't all fear irrational? Rationality was how the mind defeated fear, but to Pierce, that planet seemed alive. From it, he feared, the *Shiva of the Trinity* pulled its malice along with its life force.

Two

The *Atlas'* belly hovered delicately over the docking platform. Unsecured anchors reached out from the *Shiva* like seaweed at the bottom of a shallow, waving frangibly.

"Every time like the first time," Arlo whispered to himself. "Every time like the first time." Evans looked at him with a furrowed brow, confused. At the back of the bridge, the door opened, and Stellan entered quietly. He let not even the soles of his boots interrupt Arlo's concentration.

On Arlo's workstation, a simple graphic of two circles showed him the alignment of the two ships. A large, unmoving blue circle overlaid a smaller yellow circle, which bounced around inside the larger circle as Arlo moved his controls finely. The small circle grew as the *Atlas* neared, and when its color and size matched, they would have a lock.

Now, Arlo thought about nothing but landing his ship. Later, as he did every time, he would reflect upon how steady his muscles had been. As if they'd been a system of mechanical pulleys and levers, he commanded the slightest movement, precise like a machine.

"Just breathe," Pierce said.

A silence crept over the command deck, though no tension or anxiety accompanied it. They watched in anticipation of a successful lock, as Arlo had achieved many times before without fault. They trusted him. If they didn't, he wouldn't have been their pilot.

The silence was for respect. It took Arlo a few runs to convince himself that he wasn't performing when he docked the ship. He was just doing his part, and by being silent, everyone else was doing theirs. Thinking of it as a team effort in those terms helped with the apprehension.

"Mind your pitch," Pierce said.

"I've got it," Arlo said. Another high-frequency warning shrieked from Arlo's terminal, and the *Atlas* trembled. Stellan took hold of the railings on either side of him and waited for a voice to announce an impact, but that call never came.

"I've got it," Evans said. He pulled a window from the side of his terminal to the center and expanded it with his hands.

"The planet's gravitational pull is stronger here than we anticipated," Evans said. "As a result, our calculations were wrong."

"Our calculations?" Arlo questioned.

"My calculations," Evans confessed.

The warning ceased, and the two circles on Arlo's terminal almost blended. The *Atlas* wobbled as Arlo found the threshold of the *Shiva's* magnetic anchors' pull. Quickly compensating, he eased the ship toward the cradle.

In a moment of anticipation, they held their breath. The quiet was so deathly not even the *Atlas'* holographic user interface system dared chirp. And then it came, a thunderous applause that shook the ship as if a giant rapped upon its hull.

A moment of uncertainty passed. No one moved. No one breathed.

"We're down," Arlo declared, folding his hands. "Thrusters cooling. Seals engaged. No variations detected. Ninety-nine percent alignment. Hard lock achieved, Captain."

Cheers and clapping erupted in the bridge and on the command corridor.

"Good," Pierce said. "Arlo, you have the conn. Stellan, you're with me."

"Why do you do that?" Evans asked Arlo.

"Do what?"

"That thing you repeat every time we dock."

"I've got a five percent cushion on the seal. If I miss the lock by six percent, it could mean both ships and thousands of lives, ours included, turned inside out by the vacuum of space, so I think it's prudent that I remind myself to never get complacent, don't you?"

Evans froze and gaped as his Captain left the bridge, his gaze almost asking for help. Pierce and Stellan walked past the smiling department heads who were flushed with joy.

It never got old. The sensation just before a dock, that moment of reflection where faith waned. It was like they doubted a thing like gravity, something so constant that they could drop a ball one thousand times and expect it to fall one thousand times. But in that moment before they let go, they weren't sure. Every time was like the first time in that, the moments after achieving a hard lock, they would all become giddy and embarrassed at how silly they'd been to doubt.

Pierce and Stellan didn't speak. They understood the words they had to say were not for others' ears. They walked comfortably and confidently, side-by-side, their footfalls in unison without even realizing it. To the department heads outside the bridge, they sounded like soldiers. Those parts of them had not changed, for better or worse.

The lift entrance at the rear of the command deck opened wide, like a mouth, and swallowed them whole, dragging them down into the belly of the *Atlas*.

Three

There was something about the way Stellan could almost feel Pierce's presence. He knew the man so well that he could gauge Pierce's attitude, and he could sometimes read Pierce's mind. It wasn't something time and familiarity had instilled in him. They'd both gotten so close to death that something had rubbed onto them. They'd sipped from the thin ether between this world and the next, and it had changed them.

It had seemed to Stellan at times like a hive mind. A decade ago, when the bullets flew, other men might have seen chaos. But Stellan saw what Pierce saw, and Pierce saw what Stellan saw. Pierce would see a flash out of the corner of his eye, and Stellan would return fire. An enemy would sneak up behind Stellan with his knife drawn, and before Pierce could utter a sound, Stellan would spin with his own blade in hand, as if using Pierce's sight, slashing their enemy's throat.

They never spoke of it, but it was there once. Stellan wondered if it remained, and he felt, even then, almost a decade after London burned, traces of their connection lingered.

"Arlo have trouble navigating the debris field?" Stellan asked. Between floors in the lift, light entered through a screen panel in the wall and splashed across their faces, passing in a constant rhythm reminiscent of the sleeping light drive.

"The *Shiva* was a little overzealous," Pierce said. "It blew half the planet into orbit."

"Brittle crust?"

"That's what it looked like," Pierce said with a deadpan glare.

"Appearances count for something, I guess."

"Just enough to tell what something isn't."

"What's wrong?"

"I don't know," Pierce said. "This place. There's something about it. Part of me wants to kick us back the way we came."

"The other part?"

"It just keeps moving."

The splashes of light between floors slowed, and the lift settled. The doors parted with a mechanical whir upon a circular room lined with ENV suits like guardian statues. In the center of the room, a small crew stood around a ring that looked like a large well. Rick Fairchild had pulled both legs into his ENV suit, but the torso hung down at his waist like a flap of gray, dead skin.

"Someone give me a hand," he said, a cigarette bouncing on his lip. Wendy, fully dressed in her ENV suit, ran toward Rick. Her headpiece bobbed and flapped. Her legs and arms rubbed her oversized suit like sloshing through a pool of water.

"I got ya, boss!" she called.

She pulled up on Rick's suit, stretching it over his midsection and shoulders. She circled behind him and tugged on his collar, locating the seam up the back where it sealed.

"I never get used to how quick it gets hot in these dang things," Rick said. "Hurry up and get my helmet on so I can get the temperature regulator going."

"You could stand to sweat a bit, old man," Wendy said.

"You wouldn't want me to keel over, would ya?"

Wendy laughed, feigning doubt.

"Anyway, why is it you're always the first one suited up?"

"Because," she grunted and tugged, "it's a bit easier for me to fit." She pulled the suit in place and patted Rick's stomach.

"That's it!" Rick cried. "Come here!" He lunged for her, and she slipped through his arms.

"Oh come on!" Wendy yelled. "You walked right into that one!" She screamed with delight and giggled.

Pierce and Stellan watched a fifty-seven-year-old man chase a twenty-year-old girl who didn't look a day over fourteen around the well-shaped airlock hatch.

Pierce thought about old friends, and he knew these ones would never let him down. Stellan, least of all.

He looked to the man he'd come to know as a brother then and clapped him on the shoulder. As Rick tackled Wendy and rolled around on the dirty metal deck with her in a bear hug, smiling and laughing, in suits that were worth more than their yearly salaries, he knew he could count on them all. Wherever these bad feelings came from, they would face them together. It felt good to be confident in his friends.

"Captain," Adelynn Skinner said, stepping from the shadows. Rick and Wendy's laughter ceased when they heard her voice. They had no idea she'd been there. "I'd like to accompany the boarding party if you don't mind."

"No," Pierce said. "I don't mind."

One of the other men who stood quietly around the well-shaped airlock in his ENV suit was Thomas Foster, and he would look none of them in the eye.

Four

The boarding party slipped one by one down through the airlock corridor, a temporary tube in place like an intestine that allowed them to pass between ships. They couldn't help but feel like digesting food.

Fingertips and boot heels brushed the skin of the tunnel, and it trembled. They each descended carefully and nimbly in a slow gracefulness only afforded by weightlessness, pushing off from the circular metal ring frame.

"Do you think they baked?" Wendy said.

"Is this another fat joke?" Rick said.

Wendy laughed. "No, I'm just hungry."

"Do you all like your ENV suits?" Pierce asked.

"Sure," Wendy said. "Why?"

"Peace of mind," he said. "I'd just like to know you'll enjoy your coffin should we tear this thin polymer membrane that's the only thing between us and a burial in the black."

"Buzzkill," Wendy sang.

They landed in a room very similar to the one they left on the *Atlas*; only, the world had turned upside down. The well-shaped airlock port spit them out from the ceiling, and as they hit the deck, their boots engaged their magnetic locking systems to keep them grounded. Each foot fell heavily as they wandered the chamber like robots.

They had arrived in another world. The entire sheen of their environment changed. The very air was sharper, crisper in comparison to the *Atlas*. Stellan thought he might look down at the floor and see his own eyes reflected as if on the broad side of a blade. The walls, floors, and ceiling had a silvery blue, almost mercurial quality to them that screamed of vibrancy and youth, even though the *Shiva*, much like the *Atlas*, was an old fleet asset.

Seeing the *Shiva* made them realize the *Atlas'* metal had a brown tint to it like cancer eating aged bones.

Even still, they missed their home already.

The airlock hatch above them closed with a sound like a sheathing sword. Stellan wondered if it had ever closed on anyone. It would split a man in half without a stutter, hitch, or slip.

"Just like dropping out of the *Atlas'* asshole, isn't it?" Rick said. No one responded because everyone thought it, as they did every time.

The feeling of passing through to another world was undeniable, but Stellan thought the *Shiva* felt different this time. The excavator was a floating city in space, housing thousands of crew, built to tear planets apart piece by piece. A celestial body in itself, it usually felt more like solid ground. This time, it felt more fragile. He didn't know what it meant, but he felt like something could slip or give way here. It wasn't safe.

He looked at Pierce, who did not move but stood relaxed, his arms raised at his sides in the zero gravity. His aging eyes, which had seen many conflicts unfold and no doubt could see them coming, were closed. Stellan wondered if Pierce had already begun to ignore the premonitions of danger he'd felt on the *Atlas*. He didn't think so.

The room rumbled, and compression hit their bodies like springs. Gravity returned, and pressure and air followed. The HUDs on the insides of their visors told them with blue text that pressure, oxygen levels, and temperature were rising.

"It's much quieter than the *Atlas*," Adelynn said absently and to no one, merely an audible observation.

"I like the hissing and humming," Rick said. "That's how I know it's working." His back turned to her, he didn't see her flash her green eye at him as if he'd insulted her. Her blue eye followed along benignly, an elegant companion.

Before them, a door loomed like a giant closed eyelid. As critical environment levels reached norms, the eyelid stirred from its deep sleep. Its heavy metal gears and joints squealed and yawned. The *Shiva* beckoned.

Beyond the splitting doors, an array of motionless faces greeted the *Atlas*' boarding party. They recognized Commander Emra Ashland standing resolute at the head of the *Shiva's* welcoming party, her fingers interlocked in front of her. Her mouth, beginning to show age, like a piece of driftwood, sun-cracked at its corners.

"A lot of new faces," Wendy said.

"Mmm hmm," Rick responded.

Stellan counted those he knew, and he only recognized the Commander and maybe one other. It had been six months since they'd been to this excavator. During that time, the *Atlas* had serviced another excavator breaking down another planet. They'd seen a planet of metals and silicates reduced to a cluster of worthless asteroids like a handful of peanuts in a serving dish. He supposed if they could destroy a whole planet in that time, Ashland could replace members of her crew. He recalled that their chief of security had been close to retirement, and deck hands transferred out of excavator service frequently, exhausted from the long tours in the deep black. Though, he didn't think it likely that the six men who lined up behind Ashland would all be replacements for men they'd seen periodically for years. Still, new faces they were.

The *Atlas*' boarding party marched forward and crossed into the *Shiva*, their footsteps much quieter with the magnetic systems turned off as rubber sole met steel. They removed their headpieces with a hiss of escaping air. Wendy tightened her ponytail. Adelynn's hair fell on its own, and she left it.

Stellan looked up to see the ceiling. The *Atlas* was finishing docking procedures and slowly lowering into place. Soon, the facility's ceiling would open, and the *Atlas'* entire belly would fill the hole. Its rib cage of bay doors would open wide, and the gravity cranes would suck up the entire payload. Then the bay doors would close, and they'd go home.

The measure of the room they entered was magnificent. There was no end in sight. In fact, it went on for miles, only equipment, loaders, packaged material, and personnel to obstruct their view.

The groups stood toe-to-toe, and Pierce and Ashland saluted each other.

"Captain," Ashland said.

"Commander," Pierce said. "It's good to see you."

They shook hands, and Ashland smiled a genuine smile. The color in her cheeks flourished, and Stellan thought even her weary eyes brightened. The wrinkles in her face loosened, and he thought she looked relieved.

"Mr. Fairchild, I'd like you to meet our new senior deck hand, Horton Albright," Ashland said. Horton was young, his cheeks and jawline still boyish and round. His hands looked soft. "Please work with him to initialize loading procedures."

"Ma'am," Rick said with a nod. He shook Horton's hand, and they walked together into the great expansive loading bay, disappearing among the crowds of rushing crew. Wendy and Tom followed, her face upturned, his downcast.

"Keep an eye on them," Pierce told Stellan, but he understood the Captain meant for him to keep an eye on Skinner. "Keep them out of trouble."

Pierce and Ashland walked side-by-side, and Stellan could feel the pull between them, like the magnetic bed that tensed up the entire station when the tram whispered out of the tunnel. Pierce's hand moved to the small of her back, and she didn't react, not to push him away in alarm or even to fire him a glance of warning. Everyone knew there was something between them, but Stellan wasn't sure they were just going to her quarters to enjoy each other's company as usual.

He knew Pierce, and he knew Pierce wasn't happy with the mess the *Shiva* had left in orbit. Pierce would probably say something that would ensure there would be no love this run.

It was all in the way she moved. There was a stiffness, like she was afraid of something. Her knees jerked slightly, as if she would jump at a start. Curiosity tugged at his gut. Curiosity was an instinct he used, a tool like a hearing aid that helped him be more observant, so he could sense trouble before it came.

Trouble would be all they would share, and he was sure Pierce would tell him all about it when they returned to the *Atlas*. That thought satisfied his curiosity for the time being.

Adelynn stood with her arms crossed and her weight shifted onto one leg, her hip jutting and her posture crooked. Uninterested in the apparent inappropriate relationship, she paid no attention to Pierce and Ashland. Instead, she watched the deckhands cross the bay toward a shuttle. She observed the loaders in mechanized suits grab packed crates and haul them away. She examined the doors to the refineries open with rolling clouds of smoke and fumes.

She stood, unmoving, for a long time, silent, just watching. She never said a word.

Five

Pierce followed Ashland into her cabin, and something told him that she needed his help. It wasn't any one thing that spoke to him. A conglomeration of queues created an overall sense that something wasn't right, and now, little details made him question if this was the *Shiva* he remembered.

Ashland had braided her ponytail hastily. She nervously rubbed her palms together like they were dirty. Her neglected conference table displayed an error message. A sock hung from an open drawer like a tongue. All of these things were out of the ordinary for Emra, the woman Pierce had come to know as a creature of order and habit.

"So," she said, "did you bring it?" She walked around her desk, running fingers over the glass top and steel frame. Her leather chair sighed as she sat, and she peered at him with kind, round eyes. When they were together, those eyes changed. In front of her crew, they were narrow and strong.

With him, they opened up and became softer. She was happy, and Pierce thought things could only be so bad if she was happy. Of all the things that seemed awry, at least her eyes hadn't changed.

"Maybe," Pierce said playfully from a small chair in front of her desk. "You tell me what's going on first."

"Gordon Pierce," Ashland said with a scoff and a headshake. "Always business before pleasure."

"Business with you is my pleasure, Emra."

Her smile faded. "Not this time, I don't think. Why do you think something's going on?"

"Let's start with the new asteroid field in the Apophis system." Pierce didn't want to ruin their time together. It had been too long, but he owed it to his men to raise their dissatisfaction with their commander. In service, complaints climbed the ladder until they reached the right person. It wouldn't have been right for him to fail them.

"I told you. The crust is brittle."

Pierce waved a dismissive hand. "Whether the Council told you to dig deep or not, I don't care, but you didn't sweep. It could have cost us the *Atlas*." He didn't need physical evidence to be certain of her orders. He just needed to see her get defensive, and then he knew she wasn't being truthful, that she was hiding something. He wasn't about to accuse her of lying, though. Not only was she his commanding officer, and not only did he want to make the most of their time together, but she was a woman. He had learned years ago women didn't respond well to accusations. They required a more delicate approach.

"Don't be so dramatic."

"Emra, it could have been me."

As if she hadn't considered Pierce would be the last one off the *Atlas* if it needed to be abandoned, surprise stunned her face.

She opened a drawer in her desk from which she pulled a small black brick, and she held it out in her palm. It was smooth and solid with a polish that gave it a lustrous shine like obsidian, but the light reflecting from it was not quite right. Pierce's eyes couldn't quite focus on the brick, and gazing deeper, pressing his concentration, he arrived at the idea that the brick was refracting or distorting light somehow. It was absorbing the light and turning it into darkness.

When Ashland set the brick down on the glass desktop, Pierce expected a solid clang, but it barely made a sound.

"We're having trouble breaking down its chemical makeup," she said. "It's very light and brittle. That's about all we know about it."

Ashland's gaze upon the brick lingered a little too long and a little too deep. Her face appeared reverent, and her head tilted to the side, listening to something Pierce couldn't hear. Her pupils dilated, and Pierce thought, for only a moment, she was being drawn or falling into it. She was letting her mind go to it.

"What do you think it is?" Pierce asked cautiously, uncertain he wanted to break her trance. His words woke her, and she blinked, putting on a smile again.

"Just a rock."

"It looks igneous. Could it be organic?"

He could feel her eyes wanting to return to it, and on some level, maybe it was in his mind, he thought he felt a vague pull, too.

"How many years have you been making runs out here?" she asked.

"I think it'll be a decade soon."

"People talk about the madness," she said. "Do you believe it?"

"The talk?"

"That we lose ourselves. That we get spread thin." She wiped one palm against the other, and Pierce became unsure it was only a nervous gesture.

"I don't know," Pierce said.

"Have you ever seen anyone just lose it?"

"Yes," Pierce said, immediately thinking of Edward, but he decided not to bring Edward up. After all, they wouldn't really know anything until he woke. It was enough to ease Pierce's conscience. Besides, neglecting to mention certain details was not the same as lying, which he knew she'd been comfortable with.

"Daniel Landenberg," Pierce said. "A few years back. Stellan brought him to me, and I was skeptical then. So I told him to go back to work. He shot another one of my men with a crane. It blew off one of his legs."

"I remember that," Ashland said, her voice trailing into recollection. "You turned him over to Wellcare, right?"

"Had to. Had no other choice at that point."

Wellcare was a government-run administration that, as the Council claimed, took in the diseased, sick, and mentally unstable for treatment and rehabilitation. Publicly, their intent was to return societal drains back to civilization once they could be productive members of society. No one Pierce ever talked to knew anyone who'd ever come out of one of those places. Some thought it was a type of genetic cleansing with a friendly face.

"Skeptical then?"

"Still, I suppose. I don't believe anything on stories alone. I don't disbelieve either, though."

"So you think it could be real?" Ashland said, sounding hopeful.

"It could be, yes. It also could be that some people just can't handle the isolation and that madness is an excuse for weakness."

Unexpectedly, Pierce's words didn't please Ashland, who bowed her head and slouched her shoulders, withdrawing.

"What about you?" he asked.

"I never saw anything that made me believe in it," she said, "until we came out here. My crew has been acting strangely all over my ship. We've had more breakouts of violence in the last couple of days than we have in the last couple of years. Fights, beatings, harassment, rapes, and today, my senior engineer, Mr. Fairchild's counterpart, airlocked himself."

Pierce sat unmoving, his face unflinching as a stone. On the outside, he offered Ashland no sympathetic or exclamatory response. Inside, however, electric current lit up his nerves and locked his muscles. Ashland thought it was the old resolute Pierce she knew, but he simply was stunned and speechless.

"Anything on the *Atlas*?" she probed, searching for some company in her confusion. For a moment, Pierce couldn't answer. The message broke down somewhere between his brain and his mouth.

"No," he said, reaching forward and touching her hand with a comforting smile. "I'm sure it's just coincidence, Emra. People see two things together and assume they're related. It's human nature. It's probably how all the stories of the black madness got started. One guy has a legitimate breakdown out on the rim, and suddenly, it could happen to anyone."

"You think so?"

He smiled. "I do."

Ashland closed her eyes, and she wiped away a tear. Puzzled, he wondered why she would want him to convince her that the black madness was real, that it was the reason for the strange behavior on her ship.

He stood and walked around the desk, her round, soft eyes following him. She had never looked so vulnerable, and tears welled under her seafoam irises, red blood vessels streaking across her corneas like lighting. He found her weakness beautiful.

He bent down behind her, crossing his right arm over her chest and his left arm over her abdomen, resting his chin on her shoulder. He kissed her on the neck, and then she craned to interlock her lips with his.

They were silent for a while. Neither pursued any further physical contact. It was just nice to be together, to remove themselves from their duties and responsibilities and just feel another person whom they loved, feeling that love reciprocated like a cycle of emotional healing.

"What should I do?" she asked.

"A superior officer asking me for guidance," he joked. She elbowed him playfully in his gut. "I've always found inspiration more effective than the fist. Don't force them in line. Give them a reason to fall in on their own."

"Hard to believe you were a military man."

"It wasn't at all what everyone thought it was. And anyway, you can lead dogs, but you can't lead men. You have to give them a reason to follow."

"I'd feel a lot better if you stayed for a few days," Emra said. "Tell your men to take their time."

"You know I can't."

"I could make it an order," she said, and they laughed together again. Pierce knew she wasn't serious because she wouldn't abuse her power for her benefit any more than he would. He knew for certain so many things then.

"I'll have some of our security officers detailed to the *Shiva* if you like," Pierce said. "We'll be back in a month, and you'll see then that everything will be all right."

"What if it isn't?"

"We'll figure something out," Pierce said. "I promise." He kissed her softly again. It was the purest kiss either of them ever experienced. There was no physical arousal. Only their minds and emotions touched for a brief, perfect moment, and it was sweet and comforting. It was enough.

"Close your eyes," he said. She complied.

Pierce reached into a cargo pocket in his pants and pulled out a small paperback novel, its pages yellowed with age and its back cover torn off long ago. It was a story about a young boy who left his love to go off and fight a war, but when he returned, he found she had died. It was titled, *The Long Way Home*.

"You remembered!" She clapped and grasped at the book. Greedily, she flipped through the pages, feeling the warmth and crisp paper edges across her thumbs.

"Of course."

"I'll have it back to you on your next run out."

Pierce dismissed the thought with the wave of a hand. "It's a gift."

Six

The refineries on the *Shiva* churned earth with an indifferent malice. The machines moved steadily, their arms dipping and rotating in perfect radial arcs, skimming the fat away from the chunks of rock and ore, and Stellan marveled at how effortless it was. The blades cut; the lasers fired. They did what they were designed to do with a precision and accuracy that was without the taint of intent. The machines didn't mean to do anything. They simply worked. However, Stellan had no doubt that what they did, the continuous eradication of earth, was evil.

The temperature in the loading bay built up from the burning of the waste earth, and the acrid smell of smoldering metal licked the back of his throat. Tears rose in his eyes as he helped buckle a small load of material into a crate for transport.

"What's the matter?" Wendy said. "Your dog die?" She punched him playfully on the shoulder.

"Girl, one of these times, you're going to crack that joke on someone after their dog really did die," Rick said.

"That's why I go with the dog. It's not as serious as a grandmother, and it's just as funny."

"If you say so."

"How do you stand this air?" Stellan asked, struggling with the final latch on the crate. "It can't be healthy."

"We're supposed to wear respirators," Rick said, moving to assist him. "Safety first and all that. But half the time, they don't do a lick of good. They're so old they wouldn't filter a cigarette. Anyway, we aren't getting any of the actual off-gassing. This is just the odor. Those guys next door in the refinery, though, they're getting a face full off this stuff, believe you me." The two men pulled in unison, and the final latch closed on the side of the crate. Rick bade it farewell with an affectionate pat.

"You get used to it," Rick said, "but I've never gotten used to how much earth we waste to get the good stuff."

"What do you mean?" Stellan asked.

"Rick's just being sentimental," Wendy said with a dismissive eye roll.

"One-thousandth of one percent," Rick said. "This twenty-ton crate of whatever the hell this stuff is, it's from two million tons of earth. That means 99.999 percent of what the *Shiva* picks up is destroyed. It doesn't so much excavate as devour."

"And melodramatic," Wendy said. Rick shot her a sharp glance, and she smiled. "I mean it in the best possible way." Innocence was easy for her to pull off; everyone had to play their strengths.

Captain Pierce and Commander Ashland neared, and Stellan noticed when he heard their laughter. Ashland was holding a black brick in her hand, and was clutching a book to her breast. Even though she looked like she hadn't slept in days, a rosy color billowed in her cheeks as she smiled like she couldn't help it.

How could anything be wrong if the commander of the New Earth mining fleet was giddy as a child?

Pierce hadn't told Stellan of their relationship, of how she made him feel. Pierce didn't speak about his feelings. Stellan only knew because of their tone when they were together, that musical language in every person's voice. Pierce spoke softer to her than he spoke to anyone else, and it went beyond respect. The gentleness in his voice touched her as if he would die before he saw harm befall her.

Stellan wondered, then, why Pierce didn't seem more concerned.

"Chief," Pierce said, his voice hard as a rock, "how many men can you spare?"

"That depends on how long I'd need to be without them."

"Commander Ashland has requested a bit more manpower. It would be until the next run."

Stellan felt somewhat relieved that Pierce was concerned enough to order a detail of security personnel, but Stellan needed his men. He needed their eyes and ears on the *Atlas*, and he needed their presence. As a believer in symbols, Stellan thought simply stationing his men in the right places helped their people not only stay in line, but also feel better about their surroundings. The reassurance helped people live and work. It helped establish a sense of normalcy.

"I can work up a list of names and have it to you before we leave."

"Do it," Pierce said.

"Thank you, Chief Lund," Ashland said. "I suppose you men have some work to do, so I'll leave you to it."

"Yes, Commander." Pierce saluted through a smile. Their gaze lingered on each other as she turned and made her way out of the loading bay.

Before Ashland got far, a man screamed, accompanied by a loud crash of heavy metal. The metallic smell grew so strong they could taste it, and they thought they'd never be rid of the taste of iron, like blood, in their mouths.

Seven

The walls of the *Shiva's* loading bay encircled them like an arena of pain, the focal point of all of the excavator's dark desires, which man had given it. It was where the ship brought its prey, thoroughly ravished and finally killed. It was where beautiful things moved on, and they were the carriers of the dead, like Kharon, Hades' ferryman.

Stellan wondered how damned they were, if they'd been dead men helping the underworld all along and if he was finally beginning to see the monsters within. Maybe insanity was simply seeing the world clearly. Maybe the black madness was waking from a dream.

A hatch door opened from the refinery, expelling a fine black cloud like dragon's breath. A man clutched the valve handle on the door, stumbling into the greater hall of the loading bay, a plume of black smoke veiling his face.

Stellan swore he could see the man's eyes, though, closed one moment, lazily opening the next, black streaks running outward from his irises like fractures on an egg shell or jagged fingers of obsidian, hiding just beneath the man's corneas.

He fell to his knees, and Stellan's world began to shake. Almost involuntarily, he was running toward the collapsed man.

The shroud of smoke around the man's face lifted, and Stellan caught him as he fell backward, his head flopping over Stellan's arm like a rag. With his eyes and mouth agape in horror, his pupils rolled, but there was no trace of the black cracks Stellan thought he'd seen.

"Medic!" Stellan screamed.

Rick stuttered to a stop at their side, limping on knees that burned with age and arthritic ache.

"Oh God!" he said. "Tom!"

Tom's feet began to knock the deck like a tap dancer with no rhythm.

"He's seizing!" Stellan said. Rick grabbed a small, cylindrical flashlight from Tom's belt and handed to Stellan.

"Use it as a bit, so he doesn't bite his goddamn tongue off!"

The refinery churned on. The arms dipped and rolled. The machine continued to turn. A crowd gathered.

The hatch door swung out again, crashing against the wall. Two more men stumbled from the room, falling on either side of Stellan, Tom, and Rick. Both were crew of the *Shiva*.

"Take one!" Stellan said. Rick rolled the man over who had fallen on his stomach and braced his head between his knees. He pulled his own flashlight from his tool belt and tried to work it between the man's clenching teeth. Rick worked the man's jaw from the chin, and just when he thought he had it, his fingers slipped, and the man's teeth clamped onto the side of Rick's hand. When he was able to pull his hand free, the man's teeth snapped together, breaking an incisor in half.

Rick didn't pause because he was used to working in tight spaces with plenty of sharp edges to catch some skin on. It didn't faze him.

Pierce emerged from the crowd and didn't need to be told to help the other seizing man. The three of them kneeled in place, bracing the heads of the deck hands and could only watch their feet stutter and wait it out.

Across the loading bay, Commander Ashland looked down at the black brick in her hand and let it roll off her fingertips and onto the deck, like dropping a piece of trash. She watched it lay still for a moment, and then she turned and walked out of the bay, leaving her men to kick and shake on the deck of the loading bay while the *Shiva's* gears continued to churn the Apophis planet to dust.

Eight

Shortly after Commander Ashland left, the three men stopped seizing. Their shaking eased, their boot heels ceasing to knock and instead drawing narrow ellipses on the deck floor, dashing lines left and right, back and forth. Jerking motions settled into lazy, erratic stretching. And finally, simple tremors and the occasional twitch, flipping their wrists like puppeteers, moving their marionettes in choreographed dance routines.

When they were still, Pierce gently rested his man's head on the deck floor. One of the *Shiva's* crew took up for him, and Pierce walked across the loading bay to where Commander Ashland had left so silently, without a hint of the smile he so loved. He thought it was odd, but he excused her, knowing she could have done nothing to help them.

He kneeled and examined the black brick closer. For a moment, he thought its surface shimmered. The lighting in the loading bay was not evenly distributed. The brick lay in shadow.

When Pierce reached for it, he felt a pull so subtle he thought he was again imagining things. It was strong enough, though, to convince him it had happened.

He picked it up, and it felt cold in his hands. With its smooth surface and deep black color, he thought it was nothingness. Like space, it was a vacuum but in solid form, something to lock inside the absence of heat, pressure, air, love. When gazing into it, loneliness surged so powerfully it that it sucked away his entire world, and, like gazing at the Apophis planet, it left only a primal malice that he thought might drive him mad.

Stellan approached Pierce silently, respectfully. He saw the brick. More importantly, he saw how Pierce looked at the brick and was concerned. Whatever it was, it had his attention.

CARRIER

"We should take Tom back to the *Atlas*," Stellan said. "It stinks here. Besides, there's nobody better than Daelen."

Pierce nodded. He heard Stellan's concern in his voice, but he didn't care. A part of him was convinced something was really wrong. The rest of him knew it was too late to turn back. They had entered a jungle unwittingly. If they panicked and raced back the way they came, it would only get them killed faster, as predators had no doubt boxed them in. They had to learn what they were up against. They had to remain calm.

Pierce dropped the black brick in his cargo pants pocket.

"What is it anyway?" Stellan asked.

"A gift." Pierce tried to make his smile comforting, but Stellan saw through it.

Three medics rushed in with maglev gurneys, and when they reached the three men who remained unconscious, Rick stood up and backed away. The medics each took a patient and waved their links. They checked the results of their scans, nodding as if they had any idea what they were looking at, and then commenced loading their patients onto their gurneys.

"We'll take ours with us," Pierce said. The one who worked on Tom nodded in agreement.

Rick wandered over to Pierce and Stellan, deep in thought. His hand stung, so he shook the pain away and examined the gash on the inside of his palm, amazed to find teeth marks like a curved, dashed, red line across his skin. Two streams of blood ran down his forearm, and he wiped them away with a dirty rag from his back pocket.

"What happened?" Stellan asked.

"When I slipped my flashlight in between his teeth, he got a nibble."

"You should have Daelen look at that, too," Stellan said.

"I'll be fine," Rick said. "Should we finish the pickup?"

"Might as well," Pierce said. "We're here. Tell everyone to be more careful. And wear your goddamn respirators."

Rick nodded and walked off to continue the operation, shaking drops of blood from his hand onto the deck.

"That's rather casual, don't you think?" Stellan said. "We might as well continue because we're here?"

"Damage has been done," Pierce said. "It can't get any worse as long as everyone uses their head and watches their ass. Otherwise, if we go back empty handed, it'll be mine. I don't think it's too much to ask at this point."

136

Pierce walked in the direction in which Commander Ashland had left. Only steps away, he reached down to feel his cargo pocket to ensure its contents were still there.

Nine

The *Shiva's* medical personnel stabilized Tom and transferred control of his maglev gurney to Stellan's link, and he navigated the device back to the *Atlas*. He moved slowly and carefully, fearing he would do more harm than good if he rushed.

The air between Stellan and Tom had never been so still and quiet. It felt good to help Tom without his protests.

By the time Stellan got Tom to the medical deck on the *Atlas*, Daelen had been informed of Tom's condition, though the details she'd received over the ship's intranet had been vague. A seizure was serious, and any number of things could cause one. Not all of them were cause for concern.

Stellan floated Tom through the door, and Daelen shot up from her office chair and rushed to them.

"What happened?" she cried.

Stellan told her about the collapse and the seizure. He told her the scream startled him and lingered with him the most. He did not tell her about the blackness in Tom's eyes.

She pried open Tom's eyelids with her fingers and shined a light in them to check for pupillary response. She turned his head from side to side to check his oculocephalic reflex. Stellan peered over her shoulder for those black cracks in Tom's eyes and was relieved to see none. Daelen waved her hand over Tom's body, and several windows leaped from her link, displaying preliminary diagnostics.

"Is he in a coma?" Stellan asked.

"No. He's just unconscious. He has to be unconscious without responding to stimuli for six hours before he's technically comatose, and I have to do some other tests to figure out the cause. Right now, it's just important we keep him stabilized and hope he wakes up on his own."

She leaned over Tom until her face was inches from his. "Tom? Can you hear me?"

He didn't respond, and Daelen stood up with a furrowed brow, deep in thought. Stellan didn't like when Daelen didn't have the answers. She always did; it was a constant, something he could depend on.

"Margo?" Daelen called.

"Yes, Dr. Lund?" Margo emerged from a workstation where she no doubt had been performing endless perfunctory tests.

"Take Tom to a private room, please."

"Should I prep for intubation?"

"No," Daelen said. "Not right now, but we should monitor his breathing. Keep an eye on him, and note his respiration. Take some blood. Put it at the top of the order."

Margo took control of the maglev gurney with her link and navigated it toward the back of the medical deck.

"Tell me what happened," Daelen said to Stellan. "Everything."

"I already told you what I know. He came out of the door, collapsed, and then had a seizure."

"What about before the door?"

"I wasn't there."

"If you had to guess?"

"Daelen," he said, "I wasn't there!"

She could understand his frustration. Stellan's job was to prevent accidents from happening. He saw Tom's condition as a failure just as, if he died, she would see his death as her failure.

She reached out to him, and he recoiled.

"I'm sorry," he said.

"It's okay. What's wrong?"

"What do you mean?"

"I can tell by your look that there's more to this."

"I have a look?"

"You do."

"I don't know," he said. "Something's wrong. I can feel it. I've felt it this whole run. Worse, I feel like my brain knows it, too, and is teasing me. I'm trying to stay in control, but the more I do, the more I feel like it slips away."

"It's okay, love."

She reached out to him again, and he let her cup her hand around the back of his neck. He brought his forehead down to meet hers, and they stood there together for a moment, basking in the silence.

"All right," Daelen said, breaking their contact. She wandered as she spoke, absently speaking with her hands, dictating to herself out loud. "You bring me an unconscious man, and I can't figure out why he won't wake up. He hasn't been struck. There's no evidence of brain trauma. And you say the two other men in the room with him also came out seizing and are unconscious, so it's logical to deduce that whatever happened to Tom happened to them as well. What could put them all out like that and not leave any obvious traces?"

"A gas?"

"Maybe," Daelen said. "We won't know for sure until we get his blood results. Something in that refinery did this."

"You'll take good care of him. You'll bring him out of it."

"It's not Tom I'm worried about, love," Daelen said. "It's everyone else."

Ten

Stellan returned to the *Shiva* to help with the remainder of the loading process, leaving Daelen to put together the pieces of the puzzle of Tom's unconsciousness. All she could think about, however, was that she still hadn't told Stellan about their unborn child.

She worked in Tom's room, performing menial tasks. She just wanted to keep her hands busy so her mind wouldn't run too fast for her to keep up.

No matter how hard she tried, she just couldn't tell him. There never seemed to be a good time. Every moment on this run had been spoiled by something. She just kept telling herself the time would come, and the circumstances would be right.

Her eyes kept dashing to the door. She hoped he would come back. All this time she'd delayed telling him about the child they would have, she'd thought about how easy it was for her to deliver such news to others

139

and how different it had been now that she was in that position. For a while, she convinced herself she held the news from him because she hadn't decided whether she would keep the child. No, that was too easy. As she came to terms with her pregnancy, she grew to love the thought of motherhood more than she thought possible. With that love grew a fear for how Stellan would react when she told him. She'd played it out in her mind many times, and each time, she'd seen a sadness or regret in his eyes, a reaction she wasn't sure she could take.

She thought maybe she would wait until they returned to New Earth, for a quiet time where she might be able to prepare him, for a time when he would not be so preoccupied and she might be able to convince him that this life was good news.

Yes, he had enough on his mind without having to worry about her and their unborn child.

The truth she wouldn't admit to herself was that she was afraid he would bemoan the changes their life would endure, afraid that he would resent them, both her and their child, for having to return to the surface of the planet for which he had so much disdain.

She was so deep in thought for so long that she didn't hear Tom awaken and slowly rise from the table. She didn't hear his low moans or laborious breathing. And she didn't hear him shuffle nearer, struggling to maintain a balance on uncertain legs.

He grabbed her shoulder, and she cried out in surprise, turning toward the pale face and gray lips of Thomas Foster.

He collapsed to the deck floor with a groggy bellow.

"Jesus!" Daelen said with a hand over her mouth. "Tom, you shouldn't be up."

"I called your name. You didn't hear me. What the hell happened?"

"In a moment," Daelen said. "Let's get you back to the bed." She grabbed his arm and pulled him up. He wasn't much help. He was like dead weight, and as she pulled fruitlessly, Margo came running into the room with a mixed look of fear and wonder.

"Give me a hand," Daelen said.

Margo hurried to their aid. She slung one of Tom's arms behind her neck, and together, they were able to get Tom on his feet and over to his bed.

"You could have hurt yourself," Daelen said.

"Maybe you should pay more attention to your patients," Tom said. "Anyway, what the hell happened?"

"What's the last thing you remember?"

"We were loading up the refined rock. One of the others said something I don't remember. Then he pointed behind us. When I looked, I saw something."

"What?" Margo asked.

"Like a shadow," Tom said. "I remember the shape of a person, then just blackness, like there was a void there. I thought about chasing after whoever was there, but then there was this ringing. And then nothing."

"You passed out?"

"No," Tom said. "There was *nothing*, like I was floating out in the black. It actually felt kinda nice. Relaxing. Then I was here."

Daelen and Margo shared an uneasy look.

"We're going to run some tests, and I'd like you to stay here the night," Daelen said.

"I actually feel much better now," Tom said. "I think I just stood up too fast."

"Don't move," she said, ignoring his protests. She waved her link over Tom's body, head to toe. Several windows leaped from the face of her link, capturing diagnostics on Tom's body.

"I'm fine. I'm okay."

"Vitals are good. CT scan is good. When we get your blood results, we'll know more," Daelen said.

"Dr. Lund," Margo said, "I already processed them. Everything is normal."

"See?" Tom said. "I told you. Now let me go."

Tom stood, pushed Daelen and Margo aside, and walked toward the door. "Thanks for the hospitality."

He turned the corner out of the room, and Daelen and Margo were silent until they heard the door out of the medical deck open and close and knew Tom was gone.

"Ungrateful jerk," Margo said. "Why didn't you stop him? Should we call Stellan?"

"I'll let Stellan know. We'll just have to keep an eye on him. I've known Tom long enough to know he's going to do whatever the hell he wants to do or hurt himself trying, and there's no reasoning with him. He's insane, and he's slipping further into it. It'll take something big to wake him up, if he doesn't die first."

Margo turned her attention to cleaning the private room and prepping it for any other incoming patients who may need it. Daelen simply stared at the door for a while, quietly, as if she expected something to walk through it.

CHAPTER 6
BULLETS AND SECOND CHANCES

One

The *Atlas* felt heavier. Certainly, it carried pieces of a world in its belly, having fed from the excavator *Shiva of the Trinity*, taking on millions of metric tons of earth. What belonged to the *Shiva* now belonged to the *Atlas*. The pull on the crew's spirits, however, felt heavier than all the cargo in the *Atlas'* holds, and there was no giving it back.

For most of the crew, the *Atlas* had simply become a vessel for their weary bodies, beginning their long journey to New Earth, a planet that had become less like home and more like just another world. Their life was in the journey, and they felt it in their backs, aching like brittle bones. Nonetheless, they looked forward to the rest between worlds.

For Captain Pierce, the *Atlas* carried a dread akin to premonition. It put him asunder, into a sense of separation from the rest of the crew, a kind of loss or disconnect he hadn't felt in years, when he could somehow know trouble was just over the horizon or around a corner.

He thought of that ability as more of a curse than a blessing. It was never enough intuitive insight that he might be able to prepare. It was just enough to know something was coming, and he could do nothing about it but wait.

Stellan, however, the only other man Pierce ever knew to share this ability, never learned to accept that he couldn't save everyone. He wouldn't admit to himself that simply knowing a storm was coming didn't mean you had access to shelter. Sometimes, they just had to hope lightning never struck. If it did, well, dark times meant difficult decisions.

As they stood beside each other on the bridge, Pierce thought Stellan almost looked happy, as if he knew something Pierce didn't. Perhaps it was ignorance. He wanted to ask what Stellan was thinking. He wanted to know what Stellan could possibly be optimistic about. Pierce settled for the knowledge that, before their troubles were over, Stellan would accept reality. It wasn't something Pierce wanted, but they all had to return their feet to the ground, one way or another.

And so, the *Atlas* cast off from the *Shiva*, its long, tendril-like magnetic anchors hesitating to let go. Like old friends, the ships wanted to stay together just another moment, to share one last embrace.

Arlo pulled up on the controls, and Pierce focused on the comm channel on the wall in front of them, Commander Emra Ashland's face beside gentle waves of her voice. In another life, he would have liked to have found her earlier and under different circumstances. He would have liked to have served under her if it meant more time together, but that would never be possible. If Council politics didn't pull them apart, he knew he'd do something to screw it up.

No, what they had was as good as it would get, and it would have to be enough. The alternative was discharge from the service that provided the opportunity to live on their own terms. They lived free apart or as slaves together. Their choice was simple.

"Farewell, *Atlas*," Ashland said. "Be careful. We'll see you again soon."

Without knowing why, Pierce settled on a word he wasn't sure he'd ever said. He'd always chosen other words without such finality.

"Goodbye, Emra."

Two

The *Atlas* ferried past the floating debris field, two five nine now in its wake, the red giant Apophis itself beaming upon it with indifference, casting a long shadow upon the *Shiva*.

As they distanced themselves from the planet, Pierce and Stellan expected that uneasiness would weaken. It didn't, and they knew why. They carried their dread with them now, so close that it felt they would never again escape it, that it would drive them mad before they even reached New Earth.

"Light drive spinning up, Captain," Arlo said, and that familiar hum rested in their ears once again, like an old friend who talks and talks, never listens, and is impossible to tune out. Still, it meant they were on the move and would soon be gone from this place, and like any fool, Stellan thought, if only briefly, distance would solve their problems. Maybe it was hope.

"Never thought I'd miss it," Stellan said.

"I love it," Arlo said. "Like a bumblebee in your ears sometimes, but nothing says cruisin' like the hum of a good light drive." Arlo looked back over his shoulder at Pierce. "How fast you want to go?"

"Floor it."

"Yes, sir," Arlo said excitedly. He pushed a holographic slider up as far as it would go.

"Has the *Atlas* ever gone that fast?" Evans asked timidly.

"Not that I'm aware of," Arlo said with wild eyes.

"Never been a need to," Pierce said.

"Is there a need now?" Evans asked. Arlo stopped, realizing he hadn't thought to ask why they would risk one hundred percent on the light drive. He simply had heard permission to ejaculate and was happy to do so.

They turned toward their Captain and found Pierce's back to them.

"Where are you going?" Pierce asked Stellan, who was walking out of the bridge.

"To do my job," Stellan said, "the best I can." And Pierce understood Stellan securing the ship was their best chance at making it back to Earth. Speed didn't matter so much as keeping the wolves at bay long enough to get to safety, and there was still an elusive Council agent around, assuming they hadn't left her on the *Shiva*.

Arlo and Evans turned back to their workstations, and as the hum revved up, faster this time, since they'd kept it warm while docked at the *Shiva*, they began the countdown.

Arlo counted down from ten, and the door to the bridge closed behind Stellan when Arlo counted seven. He heard Arlo's voice boom throughout the ship, counting three as the door to the lift opened for him.

"One," Arlo said, and Stellan turned around to face the lift's closing doors.

145

The *Atlas* tore a hole in the black with a streak of light, like the flash of a storm and then an eyewink of a god in the heavens, as the carrier disappeared among the stars.

Three

Jude Washington had always wanted a simple life. He would never have described himself as ambitious. He just wanted to enjoy the time he had. It was why he officially was a deckhand but unofficially tended bar on the *Atlas*. He was drawn to the art of mixing spirits. It brought people happiness and laughter, peace and relaxation, and aboard the *Atlas*, most of his concerns were taken care of for him as long as he kept taking care of his customers.

It was a good life. It was a simple life.

However, no life is difficulty-free, so the occasional signs of dependency showed themselves, and those times were when his life was not so simple. Who was he to tell other adults what was best for them? If they wanted him to keep serving, shouldn't he shut up and keep serving? It wasn't with a sense of obligation, of knowing regret followed excess, that he cut them off. It was because, at some point, he was just piling problems on top of problems even as they flowed out of his customers' mouths like rivers, and if he felt obligated to do anything, it was simply to listen.

Thomas Foster had been the worst. He was drawn to the bottle like a moth to flame. When he started drinking, it would cheer him up, but as he drank and more of his drivel flowed off his tongue, he would reach a point where he would just burn.

So Jude thought it odd when Tom sat in his usual stool, slamming drinks as quickly as Jude could serve them, without uttering a word, staring through Jude, through the wall of liquor behind him, into nothingness. Tom had become a machine, simply playing out his old routine without emotion, without the passion he once had, smacking his lips as he brought each drink closer.

Jude turned to serve someone else and heard glass shatter on the deck. He turned back to Tom and found he had pushed his glass off the bar top. It lay in pieces on the floor.

"You know, Tom," Jude said hesitantly when he saw no reaction or acknowledgement in Tom's eyes, "you're going to have to pay for that." Tom's continued silence disturbed Jude, and he found himself hoping the normal, harmless Tom would return. If he said anything, even if it was judgmental and ignorant, as it typically was, it would have been better than this strange silence.

Jude reached under the bar and pulled out a broom and dustpan and went to work cleaning up the glass shards.

Tom sighed like he'd been holding his breath and snapped out of his trance.

"Oh, I'm sorry, Jude," he said pleasantly, which shocked Jude to a halt. "I'm such a klutz. Let me clean that up." He took the broom and dustpan from Jude and efficiently, almost mechanically, swept the glass off the floor. When he'd collected it all, he offered the dustpan back to Jude with a smile.

Jude wanted to think everything was all right, but that smile was all wrong. Tom smirked. He grinned. He sneered. He never smiled. It amazed Jude how he couldn't tell the difference in qualities of these facial expressions until he saw the wrong one.

"Thanks," he said. "But you still gotta pay for it."

"Okay," Tom said. "No problem. I know when I've made a mistake." His voice returned to that hollow, empty tone, like he was reciting a script with absolutely no feeling.

Jude returned to his post and served Tom another drink, this time a beer in a pint glass.

"Maybe take it easy for a bit," Jude said. "Relax." Tom returned to gazing into nothing.

Jude turned around again to take care of another customer, and another crash reported from the deck. Jude looked back to Tom, his face still blank, the beer emptied, and the glass on the floor.

Jude grabbed the dustpan and broom again. This time, Tom didn't offer to help, and when Jude bent to sweep the broken glass, he saw the bulge behind Tom's waistband. Studying it closer, he discerned the butt of a pistol.

"I'll do that, Jude," Tom leered down at him. "I'll take it real easy."

Jude found himself in the middle of a complicated situation, and he didn't want it. There was an easy way out, though. He sent a message to

Stellan via link-to-link connection, and the responsibility lifted from his shoulders.

Four

Instead of his son keeping him company, Edward Stone had a medical intern and a tall, lumbering security officer by the name of Douglas Fowler, not that Edward minded. He still lay unconscious, a deep sleep that had become a coma.

Margo stared, entranced by the metal casing of Edward's hyperbaric chamber. For her, being in the room with it dropped anchors in her heart. She felt anxious for the time when Edward would awaken and everyone would try to make sense of it all. But Margo never claimed to understand the things people did. She was a scientist, and science was only truth and fact, things you couldn't deny, things you had to accept.

"Can you believe this fuck head?" Doug Fowler said. "Loses his cool, and then he just decides to take a long walk out a door that literally leads to nothing." Doug pounded on the incubator's casing. "You almost got my friend killed, numb nuts!"

"He can't hear you," Margo said rattling a rack of blood-filled test tubes with an unsteady hand. Being alone with Doug made her nervous. He was hostile, he was as clumsy as he was dumb, and he was likely to kill you unintentionally by tripping and falling on you. And she felt uneasy because of the way he looked at her. His eyes sometimes lingered a little too long. She often longed for men to stare at her that way, but she certainly didn't like an ogre such as Doug Fowler looking at her. Not one bit.

"Anyway, space technically isn't nothing," Margo said. "It isn't a perfect vacuum. It contains low densities of particles, magnetic fields, radiation, neutrinos. There's also dark energy and dark matter."

Doug shifted his weight, and Margo flinched as if expecting him to knock something over.

"Listen, squint, you think I don't know that?" Doug said.

"I wouldn't have told you if I did." Margo prayed Doug couldn't hear the rattling of her tubes. She set them on a table nearby. "Why did you call me 'squint'?"

148

"I don't know. Would you rather I call you 'shitheap'?"

"I would rather you call me Margo."

"Polo!" Doug yelled with excitement. Margo's eyes narrowed into a squint. Doug's smile faded.

"Relax," he said. "It's just a joke. You know, 'Marco-Polo'? You need to loosen up and get a sense of humor, or you'll end up like jack-off wagon in here. I've been waiting all night for an opportunity to say that."

"I have a sense of humor," Margo said.

"Really? Make me laugh. Tell me a joke."

"Okay," Margo said and thought for a moment. "Why do chemists call helium, curium, and barium 'the medical elements'?"

"Why?"

"Because if you can't helium or curium, you barium," Margo said and laughed smugly. Doug humored her with a smile, but she knew he didn't get it. Though, she felt more at ease with the giant she was realizing was gentle. The man's piston-like arms were intimidating, but she no longer feared he would use them, unintentionally or otherwise.

"So you said he can't hear me. Is that because this thing's soundproof?" Doug asked.

"No, it's because he's in a coma."

"So if you had somebody you loved in a coma or whatever, you don't believe they could hear you tell them you love them?"

"Belief has nothing to do with fact."

"Yeah, but even knowing what you know, you don't have faith."

"What do you mean?"

"You know, like you want them to hear you so bad that you believe it's possible."

She thought about it for a moment. She couldn't imagine a situation dire enough where she could find herself being so simplistic.

"That's moronic," she said.

"Well, I believe."

Oddly, Margo found the thought endearing, somehow romantic. While she didn't quite understand it, she could appreciate the capacity for human belief to sway one's perception.

"I believe, and I want this guy to know he's a fuck head." Doug pounded on the chamber again. "You hear that, shit stain!? You're a fuck head!"

Though Edward's mind had not returned to him, inside the chamber, his fingers twitched and curled.

Five

Occasionally, the *Atlas* crew had to work long cycles. Someone on the alternate shift wouldn't report for duty or would get ill and, because of the close quarters living, would be confined to their residence. To fill their absence, crew sometimes had to split the difference of the twelve-hour shift. Someone would stay late six hours; somebody else would come in six hours early.

Long cycles didn't bother Doug Fowler. After all, it wasn't like he had much else to do. He'd worked long cycles a few times before, but it had never been like this time. Sometimes, it wasn't so bad. He got to move around and talk to people. This time, however, he was stuck staring at an unconscious fuck bag in a metal tube who couldn't possibly go anywhere, and he was bored. It had to be punishment for something.

The long hours darkened the room like dusk, and Doug became tired. The medical deck had closed and would only reopen for emergencies, which, since most of the crew's work was finished and they could relax, was unlikely.

Fortunately for him, it was quiet, except for the hum of the medical equipment. His chair had stopped being comfortable around hour four, and at about the eighth hour, he wanted to go to sleep. Something happened around the time he should have gone off cycle. He suddenly became wired. It made him angry because, while the squint was able to leave and go play with her chemistry set or read a book or whatever the hell she did when she wasn't annoying him, he had to stay and make sure nothing happened to the shitheap.

They'd all probably thank him if he just put the guy out of his misery, but it wasn't his call.

Doug became more restless by the minute. He could probably just leave and no one would be the wiser, but he actually wanted the asshole to get better. He wanted to see Edward return to full health. And when Edward was back on his feet, Doug fully intended to lay him out on his ass.

For a while, Doug mindlessly flipped through his link files and applications, desperately seeking something to do, and then he thought, why couldn't he get some sleep? The jackoff was out. It wasn't right that Doug, who worked so hard and sacrificed so much and never lost his shit, couldn't get some shuteye, too.

He set an alarm on his link, leaned back in his chair, and closed his eyes. It always helped him to fantasize about women when he tried to sleep. When he tried to conjure one up, the first image that came to him was the squint. It wasn't the first time he'd fantasized of a real woman, but it felt odd for some reason. Maybe it was disrespectful. Normally, he wouldn't have cared, but she'd been nice to him, and while he knew he wasn't the smartest guy in the room, she'd been patient with him without being condescending.

He let the fantasy continue. He liked her small stature. It touched something paternal in him, like she could use protection. He liked her lab coat. It made her different from all the other women, but he had her take it off to be able to see her slim body better. He imagined the curve of her hips into a tight waist. He imagined her taking down her ponytail, and her dark hair spreading over her shoulders. He imagined her thin-framed glasses around her round eyes, but he didn't make her take those off. He liked them right where they were.

As he continued down and found no trouble imagining her touch herself, Doug heard a knock, pulling him out of the fantasy.

His eyes shot open, and he looked around the room.

Moments passed, and he heard nothing else. He decided it was probably his mind playing tricks on him. It had always been a spiteful fuck. It probably was just jealous he was trying to turn it off. Or maybe it didn't like that he was redistributing blood to other parts of his body.

Doug settled back into his chair, and when he again was certain he was alone, he closed his eyes and brought Margo back.

Then he heard another knock. A short moment later, he heard several knocks, enough to know they came from Edward's tube.

Doug stood and walked cautiously over to the chamber. He wondered if the machine was glitching or if someone was playing a prank on him because it couldn't possibly be the fuck bag. He was stone cold out. The doc had said so.

The lumbering security officer approached the chamber cautiously because it was completely foreign to him, and on some level, he was afraid. As he neared, the knocking sounds became more frequent and stronger, as if his mere presence aggravated it.

He inched closer until he could peek into the observation window, and a hand pressed against it. Then a fist beat it. Then, two fists. The hands parted, and he saw a swollen face, dark from bruising, screaming a silent scream. While the face's expression was hard to decipher, he thought it looked like fear.

"Hey," Doug called. "Hey! Help!" No one came. As far as he knew, the medical deck was empty.

The fists continued to pound, and Doug could only pound back with his heavy hands, his way of telling the horrible face to calm down and that help was here.

"Uh, what do I do?" Doug panicked. He looked down at the controls and realized the chamber was electronically sealed. He thought if he cut the power, the chamber would open, so he moved to the back of the chamber and yanked on all the cables he could find. Sparks flew. The tube's interior light went dark. The pounding ceased.

With the cables lying on the floor, Doug moved back around to the observation window, peering closer until his face was inches from the glass. He could only see darkness in the tube, heard only the quiet of powerless machinery.

Then the chamber door flung open and gave Doug the sleep he'd wished for.

Six

Daelen dozed at her workstation, struggling to maintain balance in that space between sleep and consciousness. Her head bobbed like crashing waves, and though she wanted to stay awake, she could feel the tide pulling.

She'd agonized over Tom's test results, poring over them as she'd made Margo do with the blood samples, knowing it would lead to mistakes and the lesson she hoped Margo would learn soon.

Every way Daelen looked at Tom's test results, everything looked right. Still, something about him wasn't. According to the book, he was healthy, but she sensed a change in him, an inconsistency, like someone had moved something in a room ever so slightly, just enough to make her notice.

Her link chirped and expanded a window, waking her from that in-between place. It was an automated message regarding Edward. In her concern for Tom, she'd forgotten all about her black madness case.

She expanded the message from her link, and it told her Edward's heart rate had spiked. She thought it odd, though it wasn't anything to be too concerned about. She decided she should check on him. At a dead end with Tom, she welcomed the distraction.

Setting her glasses down, she rubbed her eyes, trying to regain her ability to focus on anything except the back of her eyelids. Her link chirped again. Another message informed her Edward's chamber had lost power.

"Bollocks," she said with a yawn. Though it was incredibly odd, she was not concerned because, even without power, the chamber would function properly for hours, as long as it remained sealed.

She checked her link for the time and saw Margo was on her sleep cycle. She had gone home hours ago. Daelen should have as well. In fact, she'd intended to when she last left Doug with Edward, emphasizing that he not touch anything before she bade him good night. But Tom's case had drawn her back to her workstation. She supposed it was good that she stayed. She would not have liked to have to come back to the medical deck from her cabin for an equipment failure.

With a deep sigh approaching annoyance, Daelen rose from her desk and made her way toward the back of medical into the private rooms. Nearing the door to Edward's room, she glanced through the window and saw the top of the chamber hatch standing straight into the air.

"What the hell?"

She opened the door and stood at the entrance in an odd state of shock caused by the psychological paradox of seeing something so contrary to expectation. The chamber was open, Edward was missing, and Doug lay on the floor, bleeding from a wound on his head. Her first instinct was to rush to the security officer's aid, and when she lunged forward, a hand swept out from her blind spot in the room and snatched her by the throat.

Unlike Stellan, she had not been trained to check her corners.

The fingers dug into her larynx. Fear, surprise, and the lingering disbelief overpowered her perception so much that she didn't immediately realize she couldn't breathe. She reached for the hand around her neck and tried to pry the fingers away, but they would not yield.

"What did you do to me!?" a voice of agony screamed.

The hand pushed her back on her heels, and she fell to the floor, stumbling and shuffling, trying to get away even as the back of her head bounced off the cold, metal deck. A flash of pain washed out her vision in brilliant white, and when it returned, she saw the face to which the digging fingers belonged. He mounted her and wrapped both hands around her throat.

Her vision darkened quickly, and she supposed her brain was already starving for oxygen, but she saw the swollen and purple face of Edward Stone, the man she'd taken into her care. She wanted to tell him that she was only trying to help him, but only gasps and moans exited her mouth. She clutched at his gown. She beat his arms. Her feet thrashed under his weight and strength. She knew it was the hypoxemia.

After all the struggling, she found herself beginning to let go. Her arms weakened, and she stopped trying to force his hands away from her. Her body became limp under Edward's power, and her vision dulled further. The pressure and pain in her face from the force of Edward's grasp caused blood vessels to burst in her eyes, and it felt like they might pop out of her skull, even though she knew it wasn't likely.

He was killing her, and she knew it. She understood every second in medical and biological detail, and she thought about Stellan, how she wouldn't want him to grieve. They would find the life that had begun to form inside her, and he would take that hard. She knew that, once in his life, he lived close to death. In another way, she did, too. For both of them, the idea of death was harder to accept and live with when it concerned someone they loved. For all of his hardness, he was a sensitive man who appreciated life even though he once took it. It was something she'd always loved about him.

Then Edward's grip loosened, and he began to weep. When she could once again breathe and her vision returned out of the darkness, she saw him above her body, looking down in terror. He left her and slid across the floor, propping himself against a cabinet, nervously biting his fingers.

The fresh air burned Daelen's lungs, and she coughed so hard she worried they would expel from her mouth.

"What have I done?" Edward said, and she reached out to him and pointed to the chamber.

"We have to get you back in there," she said hoarsely. "You've been through a lot of trauma, and the pain you feel isn't going to go away. That chamber is helping you heal."

He stared at her in horror, eyes wide. She imagined his pain was so severe that, whether he had his mind or not, he couldn't concentrate on anything, and what she felt was nothing compared to what he must have been feeling. She struggled to rise much sooner than she knew she should, her weak knees begging to buckle, and as she approached him, his fearful look intensified.

"I'm not going to hurt you, love," Daelen said.

With tears streaming down his cheeks, Edward's voice was just above a whisper. "But I hurt you."

"I'll be all right, yeah," she said, rubbing her neck, already darkening into a bruise.

Then he pointed to her abdomen, and Daelen looked down to see the blood soaking her inner thighs.

She never felt so afraid. Fear stole her breath from her lungs, and she was once again suffocating. It wasn't long before the dizziness overtook her and she fell into a spinning world and then into the black void of unconsciousness.

Seven

The din of the bar crashed relentlessly against Stellan's ears, but it was a sweet sound. The laughter and the upward inflection of the voices meant the crew was happy. Most of their work was done, and for the next couple of weeks, they hoped to relax and enjoy life.

And why shouldn't they? They earned it with their backbreaking work on the *Shiva*.

More than ever, Stellan hoped for a peaceful resolution with Tom. He hoped Jude was wrong, that he hadn't seen what he claimed he'd seen. After all, Jude was a bartender. Stellan wouldn't doubt the man's ability to discover a bottle of liquor in a waistband, and with Tom, that was a distinct possibility.

As doubtful as he was, Stellan had to treat the prospect of Tom with a weapon seriously. If anything, the man's drunken unpredictability made him dangerous, and a weapon could lead to catastrophe. Although, Stellan didn't expect he'd have to do any more this time than he'd done the other times when he simply dragged Tom to a holding cell to sober up.

None of the patrons noticed Stellan standing by the door. Most congregated into small groups around tables and drinking games, intertwined like thread interwoven to create a fabric so tightly compact they wouldn't be concerned with anything happening outside of their group. Some moved between groups but were intensely focused on the others who were losing the drinking games or telling jokes or stories about bad decisions that weren't funny at the time. Even the shrieks of laughter that followed them passed Stellan by.

It was good. They would provide him cover.

In situations like these, Stellan's concern was not the inevitable confrontation and altercation. That would go the way it would go, and all he could do was read it and do his best. His concern was collateral damage. With so many people in such a tight space, he worried, especially with two weapons in play. Even a shot fired straight at the ceiling could ricochet and hit someone.

Safety of innocent bystanders was his primary objective, so he hoped to be able to take Tom down quickly if he, indeed, posed a threat.

Stellan found Tom occupying his usual stool at the bar. Tom sat still, not rocking and cawing with his usual derogatory words and raucous laughter. Enough empty glasses lined the bar top to challenge even Tom's tolerance. Something wasn't right, and Stellan wondered how bad things could be if he worried when someone wasn't falling into an oblivion of alcohol.

At the base of Tom's back, Stellan saw the bulge. He knew immediately that it was a weapon. From the size of the handle, he guessed it was a snub-nosed, semi-automatic pistol. Though not a large weapon, and easy to conceal, it could be deadly.

Jude saw Stellan approach, which was unfortunate. Tipped off by Jude's glance, Tom deftly reached into his waistband and pulled out the hidden handgun, placing it on the bar top like raising a bet in a card game.

Stellan discreetly moved his hand to his sidearm and unbuttoned the leather strap that held it in place.

The voices in the bar settled one by one, sensing the confrontation. They saw Stellan standing mere paces from a man with a gun, and they saw him freeze in his tracks, as if the man were a bomb that might go off. No one spoke. No one moved.

"Where'd you get the weapon, Tom?" Stellan asked.

"You know, something's been really eating at me these last few years," Tom said, a subtle drone in his voice like a buzzing insect. "Why'd you let him go back to work?"

"Who?"

"You know. The prick who took my leg."

"You know what would have happened."

"It happened anyway."

"I couldn't give up on him. Like I can't give up on you."

"That's your problem," Tom said. "You gotta let people go. Cut your losses. You love everything to death. Everything you touch turns to shit."

"What if it were you?" Stellan asked. "Would you want me to give up? Because I can tell you, right now, the only thing that stands between you and discharge is me."

Tom chuckled and answered Stellan by flipping his weapon's safety off. He wiped his mouth and then casually stood, turned, and raised his weapon at Stellan. His face appeared emotionless, blank, but behind that, a blackness swam in his eyes, something more than nothing.

"Put it down," Stellan said, one hand rising with his palm out in a calming gesture, the other hand digging deeper into his sidearm holster, his fingers easing around the handle of his weapon.

"If it were me," Tom said, "I'd rather you pull the trigger, but you don't have the stomach for it."

"What did you say?"

Time slowed. Everything around Tom blurred. All sound washed away except for the click and high-pitched whir of the rail-firing mechanism in Tom's gun and then the blast.

Stellan thought about the boy in London. He wondered if his answer last time had been the right one. Maybe he should have let the boy shoot him, the Council's man. Whether by his death or by his wounding, perhaps inaction may have made a difference.

But he wasn't fighting for the Council then any more than he was now. Conflicts are never as clear as drawing a line between two sides. Then, he fired for himself and for the friends who may have suffered if he hadn't. He fired now for the same reason.

His hand moved, and as he drew, he ducked his left shoulder, dodging Tom's shot, which rippled his clothing like a passing breath. No time to aim, Stellan let his hand guide his weapon, and his pistol answered with its cracking death call.

The bullet struck true in Tom's chest, boring through his sternum, severing his spine, and burying deep into the mahogany bar behind him. The spray of red mist from the exit wound covered Jude's face and several other people at the bar, their eyes agape in shock and disbelief, catching the red rain.

Tom fell to his knees and then to the floor, where he lay in a heap, a light wisp of smoke pouring from his exit wound.

A woman shrieked, but most of the crowd remained silent and still. Jude stood in shock behind the bar, his eyes shifting toward Stellan, projecting something like fear. Some rose from their seats, and they all looked to him, amazed at the spectacle that was his monster, a cunningly quick messenger of death.

Stellan feared that they all saw him now as a killer, no longer as a protector, no longer something of comfort and reassurance, but cold death. It was the identity he'd struggled to hide from them for as long as he secured the *Atlas*. He was afraid it was his truth, the answer to the riddle of who he was before he was chief of security on the *Atlas*, the answer to the question of who he really was.

Stellan holstered his sidearm and walked to Tom's body. He pressed Tom's carotid artery to search for a pulse and found none. He was gone, and as good as Daelen was, she couldn't bring men back from the dead.

Then he remembered Tom's shot had missed, so in a sudden panic, he turned and searched the crowd.

He found his closest friend who was like his adopted sister. Of all the people on the *Atlas*, of all the places she could have been, Wendy had stood behind him.

She looked down in disbelief to her stomach, her hands trying to catch the blood spilling from the dark rose blooming on her jumpsuit. She gasped, her young, pretty face contorting into a ball of pain, and then she fell.

Another shriek and a rustling of people who wanted to help but didn't know how, a murmur of voices expressing shock, doubting the reality of what they were seeing, praying to their gods.

Stellan rushed to her side, tears welling in his eyes. Words could not express his sudden grief.

He could have taken that bullet, but he hadn't. Was it fear that had caused him to dip his shoulder? He didn't know, but he knew this was his failure, too.

He touched Wendy's face and reached under to feel her back. She cried out as he rolled her. No exit wound.

She tried to speak; only shallow, arrested breaths escaped her mouth. She looked at him with such reverence, and he knew she depended on him. Even on the floor with her blood spilling from her belly, she still looked to Stellan as her protector and guardian. It wasn't the urgency of her condition that spoke to him then. It was fear of letting her down.

So he took her into his arms, cradling the back of her neck, and ran as fast as he could toward the door and onward to the medical deck, leaving the crowd at the bar as silent as the dead.

Eight

The medical deck buzzed with tension, a burning at the back of Doug Fowler's brain. He woke slowly, sluggishly, and the pounding on the floor, the shuffling, he needed it to stop. It was like an old-fashioned train he'd seen in the movies, the ones that still used wheels and burned fossil fuel. When they rolled into the stations, they'd always knocked so irregularly on the tracks, like spooked horses stomping their feet, threatening to stampede.

The squint was there, and she was nervous. She wore a big T-shirt that reached down to her knees, and her hair was in shambles, like she'd just rolled out of bed. Her mouth produced sounds, but Doug couldn't make out her words. Then he saw the open chamber and the doc sitting against the wall, the blood beneath her and, in the corner, a man who was little more than a meat bag, sobbing. What a shitheap.

Doug's adrenaline ran through his veins like electrified water, shocking and soothing him at the same time. He stood, the pounding in his head continuing, though it was bearable. He wiped his forehead and found he was bleeding, too.

"Can you stand, Dr. Lund? I need to get you on this table so you can lie down," Margo said.

Doug saw the perplexed look on her face. She had no idea how she was going to lift Daelen off the floor and onto a table.

"I got her," he said, and the big man shoved Edward's chamber off its platform with a loud crash that startled Edward into a high-pitched squeal. He picked Daelen up, supporting her with one arm behind her neck and the other behind her knees. He was gentle, but as he lifted, she moaned in pain.

"What the hell happened?" Doug asked. Daelen and Margo knew she was having a miscarriage. Doug was afraid for her because he'd never seen so much blood, and he knew it was his fault. He could have stopped whatever had happened had he not passed out. Had he passed out? He didn't know what happened to him, but he knew it had to be his fault.

"I'm losing my baby," Daelen said, and between the bursts of pain in her abdomen, her heart sank; verbalizing it had made it real. It made her understand she was the one on the table, and that this crisis was not just a challenge for her to overcome. Her life was changing that very moment. If she lost her child, it would be her tragedy, no one else's. She had not expected she could feel such loss. She'd seen other mothers suffer miscarriages, and she knew their pain.

But feeling was different than knowing.

Surprised at the revelation that Daelen was pregnant, Doug saw the bruises appearing around her neck and pieced it all together.

"You fuck!" Doug yelled, and he lunged at Edward, the sobbing, dripping pile of mess in the corner. Edward launched into unintelligible screams and shrieks of gibberish between his whimpers.

"No!" Daelen said. "It's not his fault."

Another bolt of pain colored her face.

"What do I do, Dr. Lund?" Margo asked, her confusion and distress apparent in her wide eyes.

Stellan burst through the door, and everything stopped. They saw him carrying Wendy, blood dripping down the front of his uniform and down her dangling arm, her head lolling back. When Stellan saw Daelen lying on the examination table with blood darkening her pants, he understood. His balance faltered, and everyone looked at him, completely baffled, their minds a bullet train derailed between stations.

"She's been shot," Stellan said, and it shattered the ice that had frozen time.

Margo looked at Daelen for instruction, and all she found was a woman laid out in agony, unable to give her the direction she sought.

Doug scooped the instruments and what he considered junk off a nearby counter. The crash this time was like shattering glass, and indeed, some of it was.

"Put her over here," he said.

"Yes, that will do," Margo said.

Stellan swiftly carried Wendy to the counter and laid her down. As her body stretched out, the pain surged in her abdomen, and she screamed. That only fueled the searing pain, so she bit down on her own arm. Blood flowed around her lips.

Margo waved her link over Wendy's midsection and inspected her wound. The bullet had entered low and to the side of her belly button, passing through her small intestine without damaging any of her other organs. Fortunately, it had also missed her celiac artery. There was no exit wound, and she found the bullet on her link.

"I see it," Margo said. "She's losing a lot of blood. I need to get her to surgery now, or she's going to bleed out."

Wendy and Daelen moaned in unison.

"Stellan, I can't treat them both," Margo said, her eyes asking if he understood, pleading with him to understand so she wouldn't have say it. He would have to choose Wendy or his child.

He understood, and the feeling went beyond helplessness. Of all the things he ever hoped to give the world in return for the lives he had taken, he realized now a child was the purest thing he could offer. Perhaps the only thing. Though the thought of fatherhood paralyzed him with fear, the potential that person could represent made him feel empowered, as if the future could be brighter. He supposed this was what it truly meant to be afraid, what it meant to feel loss. In one moment, all the hopes and dreams he never knew he had were fulfilled. And he could do nothing to stop them from shattering.

"What about Daelen?" he asked.

"She'll live."

Daelen opened eyes she couldn't bear to wipe dry, the grief and pain intermingling in a way she couldn't understand, fix, or fight. She and Stellan held onto each other's gazes then, a moment they could feel burning into their memories, a time they would decide later if they would reflect upon with grief or with joy because, in that moment, they saw in each other that they both wanted a child. Losing this child would be tragic; from its loss, they would learn the meaning of love, legacy, and creation.

"How I can help her?"

"Keep her comfortable," Margo said, and nothing ever made Stellan feel so helpless. "There are some painkillers in that cabinet. We'll evaluate for a D and C later." For every life he'd taken, he'd known someone was behind it, grieving and feeling helpless. This knowledge brought on his guilt.

But feeling was different than knowing.

"Help me," Margo said to Doug, and he picked up Wendy and followed Margo to another room where they delivered her into the arms of God, which, on the *Atlas*, was a machine that would remove the bullet, repair her broken body, and grant her life once more.

Nine

When Margo had Wendy stabilized, Doug came for Edward, his face a snarl. Doug, so loyal to Stellan, so eager to please his Chief. It appeared to Stellan that Doug was going to bring his boot down on Edward's whimpering head, and Stellan decided he wouldn't stop the big man. However, Doug grabbed Edward and restrained him.

"What do you want me to do with him?" Doug said.

Stellan wanted to tell Doug to do whatever he wanted. For the first time ever, he was sorry to have saved a life.

"Lock him up where he can't hurt anyone else," Stellan said, knowing Daelen wouldn't be able to treat him anymore. He would have to heal the old-fashioned way.

"I didn't mean to hurt you," Edward repeated. "I'm so sorry!"

Her cramps fading, Daelen nodded her approval with the intention that, once she was back on her feet, she would do for him what she could in his cell on the security deck. Pierce had been right. Pierce was always right.

Doug lumbered off, dragging Edward behind him.

Daelen slept. Though the drugs helped with the pain, she was exhausted from the grief that was still too near; her body knew it. When she awoke, she would face the horror of realizing all her medical training and resources amounted to nothing if she couldn't even save her own child. That pain would never subside. It would be a grief she would carry with her the rest of her life, and in the quiet times, when the world receded like a tide, she would remember, and in those times, she would find strength. It would reinforce her will to do better and be better.

Stellan stood over her, watching her breathe. They were alone. They were almost never alone anymore. They slept together every night, but since the *Shiva*, regimen mired those times, both of them too exhausted to do anything other than slip into unconsciousness.

Even after what she'd been through, she was beautiful. Her dark, tangled hair lay in a pile, natural, wild like the summer breeze had styled it with nimble fingers. Her soft face, while fragile and innocent, exuded strength. All evidence of her grief, all the worry wrinkles and tears, were erased from her fair skin.

Then she stirred. She took a deep breath, and her brow tightened. A quiet whimper escaped her mouth, and she blinked in the soft lighting.

She looked to Stellan, and before he could say anything, she said, "I'm so sorry."

"For what?"

"Not telling you. You shouldn't have had to find out this way. Maybe if I'd told you..."

Stellan had never been good with words in times of tragedy, so he remained silent. To let her know he forgave her, he caressed her cheek. Her hand shot up and grasped his, pressing it against her face. Fresh tears sprang from her eyes.

"Everything is going to be all right. Now, you need to rest," Stellan said. "Doctor's orders." He meant Margo, and he smiled at the role reversal. She managed a smile, too, weak though it was.

"I know that."

"Sure you do."

"How's Wendy?" Daelen asked.

"Fine," Stellan said. "Surgery went well. Your protégé already has her in recovery."

Daelen sighed with relief. At least it wasn't for nothing. Their sacrifice.

"You know, I've never been so scared in my life," Stellan said. "I've looked down the barrel of guns. I've looked into the eyes of men determined to end my life. But when I came through that door and found you, I didn't know what was happening. I just knew my world was falling apart, the pieces slipping through my fingers."

He bent and kissed her softly.

A fearful look crossed her face. "Stay with me," she said. "Promise you won't leave."

"I'm not going anywhere."

"After everything we've lost, I can't lose you, too."

"I'm not going anywhere," he repeated, a look of concern crossing his own face as he wondered if she knew about Tom and the shooting yet.

"Rest." He hushed her. "Everything will be all right."

Daelen slipped back into sleep, and a moment after he was sure she was out, Stellan's link chirped. A small window leaped into the air, a voice message from Pierce. His voice sounded grievous and grim. It didn't ask anything. It simply ordered Stellan to report to the Captain's cabin.

Ten

When Stellan stepped into Pierce's cabin, he had the distinct feeling of entering a church, going to make a confession. He smelled the musty odor of aged oak, and the lights had been turned down low, elongating shadows as if by candlelight.

Stellan crossed the threshold into Pierce's office and found the Captain behind his desk as usual, still and silent, staring at Stellan with a hard look that lacked passion of any kind, offering no insight for whether he felt anger or love, disappointment or pity. His chiseled cheekbones jutted like a rock face. His jaw muscles tensed and released. His thumb rubbed the worn spot on the lip of his desk.

The hard, unyielding chair before Pierce offered no relief from the discord in silence. It supported Stellan only in a physical sense. A moment passed where Pierce only gazed at Stellan, as if considering a move in a game of chess. Finally, he relaxed and leaned forward, hands folded and elbows on his desktop.

"I'm sorry we had to meet under these circumstances," Pierce said. "How are you holding up?"

"Fine."

"Good. And Daelen?"

"She's going to be all right."

"Wendy?"

"She'll be fine, too."

"Good, good," Pierce said. "I want you to know this is just a formality. Anytime something like this happens on a Council ship we have to do an assessment. We have to try to salvage what's left."

"I know," Stellan said. "I understand." He didn't like the way Pierce said, "we," when it didn't include him.

"Good," Pierce said. "And I'm here for you as your friend. I chose you for this job because I knew I could trust you, so I know you'd tell me if there was something wrong, if something had compromised your decision-making."

Pierce gazed at Stellan with those stone eyes, neither judgmental nor sympathetic, impossible to read, awaiting a response.

"I would."

"Yes, you would," Pierce agreed with certainty. He opened a document from his link and spread it out over his desk, swiping through pages and passively scanning them.

"From the report one of your officers filed, it looks like it was a clean kill. Tom wouldn't comply. Your life and the lives of your crew were threatened. You defended yourself and them admirably against an eminent threat," Pierce said.

He paused, closed the report, and then leaned forward with a warm smile that felt somewhat mechanical and deliberate.

"You know, I'd give you some downtime if you needed it, but so much has been going on lately that hasn't been right."

"I know."

"I need you at the top of your game."

"I am."

"Are you?" Pierce asked. "You did everything right according to your report, but you've failed to ask questions. The right questions. Remember, I told you the first rule of being a soldier was to stop asking questions, and the first rule of leading was asking the right ones?"

"I remember."

"Really?" Pierce asked. "Then why is it that you haven't really looked into where Tom got his weapon?"

Stellan had asked Tom directly, and when he'd gotten no response, he'd left it at that. At some point, maybe he thought it didn't matter where Tom got the weapon. With everything that happened after, maybe he simply forgot, or maybe it was the fact that seeing someone point a gun at him wasn't so odd. Granted, it had been a long time, but the mind had a way of recognizing circumstances. It was how he knew what to do. It was instinct.

"He must've brought it on board with him," Stellan said.

"Likely," Pierce said with a nod. "The simplest explanations are probably true. Still, so much has not been simple about this run. I have to consider the alternatives, and so should you."

Stellan thought back to the fire in the water plant, the feeling that it had been meant as a diversion. At the time, Tom had been in holding; Floyd slept. Security was completely accessible.

"Skinner," Stellan said.

"Have you seen her?" Pierce asked with a furrowed brow that resembled worry.

"Not since the *Shiva.*"

"Do you think she's still on board?"

"I know she is," Stellan said. "You don't think she caused the accident?"

"Edward," Pierce said. "How did he get out of his chamber? How did a man recovering from explosive decomp overpower Doug Fowler?"

"How could she be responsible for all of that? And why?"

"I don't know," Pierce said. "It's unlikely, but you know how they work. Never see it coming until they hit you sideways. If you find her, maybe you'll get the chance to ask her."

"We done playing nice?" Stellan said eagerly.

"I said I wasn't about to see lives end out here. Now, Tom's gone. By your hand, but it was forced. Edward. Wendy. Daelen. It's time we find Ms. Skinner and have an open discussion. That's what I need you to do now. Find her, and bring her here."

Stellan stood, feeling empowered with understanding. Using his imagination to fill in the blanks, it all became so clear, like wiping the fog away from a window.

"One more thing," Pierce said. "You lied to me."

"What?" Stellan asked, turning uncertainly. He wracked his mind trying to think of when he had lied to Pierce and couldn't come up with anything.

"You're not okay."

"Yes I am."

"No, you're not. Sit."

Stellan sat back in the uncomforting chair, the air between them more open. He again felt they were on the same team, but that confession feeling lingered. Pierce wanted Stellan to tell him something, and Stellan didn't know quite what he wanted to hear.

"You put more of the weight of the world on your shoulders than anyone I've ever known," Pierce said. "You have to learn to let things go. It can weigh you down. It can cloud your judgment."

Of all the things that had happened, one thing stood out, and it wasn't vengeance or guilt.

"I didn't know," Stellan said. "She didn't tell me."

Pierce took a deep breath. "I'm sure she had her reasons. Maybe she was waiting for the right time."

"Thing is, it had never crossed my mind that I wanted to be a father before I walked into that room and knew the opportunity was gone. It's like the guys used to say. Some men get a taste for killing and can't let it go. I feel like I'd been looking for something all my life and just got a taste of it. For a moment, it was real, and now it's gone. Now I can't imagine wanting anything else."

"Well, then," Pierce said, "that's one good thing to take from it, isn't it?"

"I should have known something was wrong," Stellan said. "It was like she kept wanting to tell me something I wasn't going to like, and then she would hold it back. I've just been so absorbed with everything this run with Skinner and Edward and these dreams I—"

"Dreams?"

"Yes," Stellan said warily. "Two different ones. In the first, it's London. Everything happens just the way it did. It's like my brain is trying to remind me of something, trying to reinforce something I'd forgotten."

"You would be lucky if that were the case."

"No," Stellan said. "We have to hold onto it. It's made us who we are. In a way, the other one's connected. I'm on the *Atlas*, and it's deserted. A tram pulls up at a station, and I find a crowd. They've turned into monsters, and they turn on me."

"How are they connected?"

"The boy. He's in that one, too. He turns them," Stellan said. "What does that mean?"

"We all owe a debt to the dead," Pierce said, his eyes glazing over. "One way or another." He fell into silence for a moment and then returned as if out of a trance. "It probably means nothing. Guilt, that's all. It comes back sometimes for me, too. The faces fade and blur 'til they aren't recognizable, and then there's just the idea."

"I remember exactly what he looked like."

"I doubt that," Pierce said with a patronizing laugh. "You've just constructed an image in your mind."

After a moment, Pierce opened a drawer in his desk and reached in.

"When the ash settled on London, when the fighting stopped, I went back to see to the boy. Made sure he was taken care of. We were gentle. Respectful."

Pierce's voice trailed into a whisper, his eyes vacant with recollection. He tumbled something small and shiny in his hands, and then he clenched it within his fist.

"There was so much water. A main must have burst and softened the earth. I found the slug buried into the wall and pulled it out. Had it melted down and recast. It could be fired again. I've kept it all these years to remind myself that, sometimes, even the worst of us get second chances. It's important that we do right with the chance we're given because, like that bullet, we have the potential to make the same mistakes. Then again, maybe we can yet do some good."

Pierce offered the bullet to Stellan, pinching it between his forefinger and thumb. The metal gleamed at the tip, like the beacon of a lighthouse showing the way home.

He dropped it into Stellan's palm.

"What am I supposed to do with this?" Stellan asked.

"Bury it."

Eleven

The first thing Rick Fairchild thought of as he lay under a gravity crane loader in a cargo bay of the *Atlas* was not how warm and wet the floor felt on his back. He did not wonder why a black fluid drained from the exposed guts of the crane or even how the manifold had been removed. He did not feel the sting of the cuts on his forearm or the swelling of the bite on his hand. It didn't cross his mind that the human mouth was a breeding ground for bacteria.

The only thing Rick could think of was that his memory was blank. He couldn't remember how he'd gotten there.

It didn't feel to him that he'd simply forgotten, the way the mind sometimes passively declines to process and store certain memories of places you've been and actions you've committed a thousand times before, a kind of autopilot. It wasn't the fog of weariness for lack of sleep or the haze of a drug- or alcohol-induced blackout. It wasn't a momentary lapse. In fact, the last thing he could definitively recall was the warm shower that poured over his greasy body and the towel he used to dry himself off.

He looked to his link. That was hours ago.

"What the...?" he whispered, his bushy eyebrows narrowing.

In his hand, he held a bolt torque, a hand tool that used powerful magnets to turn bolts. He looked up into the guts of the machine and found a power module missing, a small part that looked insignificant to the untrained eye. Anyone else might discard it as a spare part, but Rick knew it was like the machine's kidney or liver. It scrubbed and regulated power for the crane, and without it, the crane would overpower itself, imploding from an enormous amount of unchecked gravity.

On the floor beside him, Rick found the module, hoses and wires frayed on short ends. It had been ripped out by hand after the bolts from its mount had been removed.

Rick tried to tell himself he was there to fix the machine. He tried to deny that he would ever harm one of these cranes, his babies.

As he struggled to accept what would be so apparent to anyone else, he grabbed the power module and shoved it up into the crane's guts in a futile attempt to put it back in place. Even before he accepted the truth, pieced together the final moments of his missing memory, his mind worked its way through how to fix the crane. It would need new couplings on the power module ports, and new lines and wiring would need to be drawn throughout the entire crane, which would mean taking it apart and piecing it back together.

The crane was dead. Rick knew it and dropped the power module onto the deck beside him.

For some reason he couldn't grasp, Rick laughed, quietly at first, then erupting into an uncontrollable fit, and he knew it was wrong.

Twelve

</// New Earth Space Mining Administration (NESMA)\\>
</// Council Civilian Fleet Identification Number: A9343-7270-G2552
</// Model: Carrier; Class: Titan AAA; Designation: Atlas \\>

</br>
</// Incident Report \\>

</br>
>> Sent: Senior Engineer Arup Manish, Department of Engineering, Fifth Level, Power Plant
<< Received: Department Director Andre Lawrence, Command Deck
</// Subject: Assault \\>

<// Body: Two engineers involved in physical altercation. Junior Engineer Elias Robichaud approached Engineer Martin Hollander. Verbal conflict led to physical violence wherein both men were injured. Robichaud suffered minor lacerations and bruises. Hollander suffered a bite on his forearm. Robichaud seemed traumatized by experience and was unresponsive to questioning. Robichaud restrained. Hollander sent to medical for evaluation. Please advise of punitive measures if any required. \\>

</br>
<< Awaiting protocol response... >>

<// New Earth Space Mining Administration (NESMA)\\>
<// Council Civilian Fleet Identification Number: A9343-7270-G2552
<// Model: Carrier; Class: Titan AAA; Designation: Atlas \\>

</br>
<// Incident Report \\>

</br>
>> Sent: Charles Waterman, Cook, Mess Deck
<< Received: Assistant Department Director Melvin Stoltz, Command Deck
<// Subject: Attempted rape \\>
<// Body: Susanna Barton and Jude Washington were involved in a physical altercation, which led to an attempted rape. Washington and Barton were alone in a storeroom. I overheard shouting and, upon investigation, found Washington pinning Barton to the floor, her shirt raised to expose her breasts, blood flowing from her mouth from an apparent strike. Washington was attempting to take her pants off when I intervened. Barton is off to medical. Washington is restrained and unresponsive. \\>

</br>
<< Awaiting protocol response... >>

<// New Earth Space Mining Administration (NESMA)\\>
<// Council Civilian Fleet Identification Number: A9343-7270-G2552
<// Model: Carrier; Class: Titan AAA; Designation: Atlas \\>

</br>
<// Incident Report \\>

</br>
>> Sent: Maggie Prewitt, Junior Engineer, Cargo Bay 28
<< Received: Department Director Spencer Cutler, Command Deck
<// Subject: Attempted homicide \\>
<// Body: Engineer Robt Mathers approached fellow engineer Dexter Whedon with a pipe and struck him in the leg. Screaming obscenities, Mathers raised the pipe for a deathblow when Deckhand Lonny Sawyer tackled and restrained Mathers. Whedon is on his way to medical with a probable broken leg. Mathers is tied up and not speaking to anybody. \\>

</br>
<< Awaiting protocol response... >>

<// New Earth Space Mining Administration (NESMA)\\>
<// Council Civilian Fleet Identification Number: A9343-7270-G2552
<// Model: Carrier; Class: Titan AAA; Designation: Atlas \\>

</br>
<// Incident Report \\>

</br>
>> Sent: Marcel Wooding, Deckhand, Engine Room
<< Received: Assistant Department Director Augustine Faust, Command Deck
<// Subject: Dead body found \\>
<// Body: Found dead body behind reactor coupling, seemed to have been dragged there. I don't know who he is or what he was doing down

here. All I can tell is he is a man. His insides are on the outside and there's blood everywhere. HELP!

</br>
<< Awaiting protocol response... >>

<< Awaiting protocol response... >>

</br>
<< Awaiting protocol response... >>

</br>
<< Awaiting protocol response... >>

CHAPTER 7
THE PANDORA PROTOCOL

One

Preoccupied by thoughts of Daelen and a burning desire to hunt down Adelynn Skinner for what he was sure she'd done, Stellan almost didn't notice the way his crewmates looked at him as he hurried down the corridor to medical. They looked uncertain, like they didn't even recognize him, and he didn't like it one bit. They seemed ungrateful for the sacrifices he'd made for them, and it made him angry.

But it wasn't thanklessness. He was disturbing them. Stellan didn't see his own wide eyes reflecting the blue glow of his link's expanded holographic interface. He didn't hear his erratic voice or his labored breathing. He didn't see his rigid posture or his hurried gait. They perceived his stress like an electric field emanating from his body, and it unnerved them.

All at once, the *Atlas'* crew had gotten out of hand. As the reports flooded the ship's intranet, he became increasingly irritated with his obligation to his duty. He should have been with Daelen. He'd promised her he wouldn't leave.

Then again, wasn't all duty about personal sacrifice?

Management and delegation had never been among Stellan's strong suits. He was more of a hands-on kind of man. As the requests for protocol procedures followed the predesignated paths over the link system and landed in front of him, he had to find ways to delegate duties to his weakened security staff, which he wished he had back in full force. He would have welcomed back even the most inept of his men because it was becoming a game of sheer numbers. He just didn't have enough bodies

174

for a security presence everywhere he needed it, and he worried something would inevitably slip through.

"Doug, you're going to run roundup," Stellan said into his link. "I want you to take a couple of others with you and put Jude, Robichaud, and Mathers in holding. Keep them isolated. I'll question them when I get back."

"Okay, Chief," Doug said.

"Floyd, I want you to head down to the engine room to secure that dead body. Nobody goes in there. Understand?"

"Oh, I don't do well with blood," Floyd said. A cackle rang through the channel from Doug's end.

"We're a little shorthanded, old man, so I'm going to need to pull you away from that desk for a little while," Stellan said. "I'm sure that body's not going anywhere. Just make sure no one enters the room. I'll be there as soon as I can with a medical team."

Stellan thought about how weak the crew he'd left himself with were, but he'd never thought he'd need to plan for this much trouble. It would have been fine if there were one larger disruption in one location, but the violence was breaking out all over the ship, spreading them thin and making it hard to coordinate. His entire security staff mostly comprised men and women who had no other adaptable skill but wanted to live and work on a carrier. It wasn't hard to teach people how to stand around, keep an eye out for trouble, and call him if they saw anything. Stellan was always the backup, but now he needed them to be where he couldn't. He needed them to support him in a way they never had and in a way he had never thought would be necessary. They were overwhelmed.

The only solace he could find was in the realization that, whatever was going on, it was bound to let up. And he knew that because, if it didn't, they were finished.

"And both of you," Stellan said, "don't touch anything."

Two

Daelen was preoccupied as well. For some reason, while she still grieved for the loss of her child, Tom's mystery continued to plague her. She knew there was a reason for his madness, that it was different than what Edward had experienced. While everyone wrote it off as just another case of the black madness, Daelen remained unconvinced.

With the escalating reports of violence sending patients to the medical deck, Daelen had to be on her feet far sooner than she should have been. She couldn't expect Margo to handle it all. Keeping busy kept her mind from wandering into dark places where nothing made sense, but she still wanted to just sit and ponder Tom's case.

If she knew anything, it was that Tom hadn't had the black madness. With him gone, stowed away in her morgue, it may not have mattered anymore. Still, some instinct pushed her in that direction.

She stood before Susanna Barton, one of the *Atlas'* bartenders. Susanna sobbed in a way Daelen had seen in patients before, and it came from a kind of pain Daelen had experienced herself very recently. While Susanna had several bruises and cuts, she felt a deeper, emotional trauma. It was a loss of power and control. Jude Washington had attempted to rape her. Unfortunately, no counselor was available on the *Atlas*, so Daelen would have to listen. After her own feeling of loss of power and control, it was the last thing she wanted to do.

Susanna sat on the exam table in a private room, clutching her own body like she was cold. Even though they kept the medical deck a comfortable 22°C, someone had given her a gray blanket, probably taken from a fire station in the kitchen where she was found. Her makeup drew lines down her face, and it smeared from where she wiped blood away from her nose and mouth. A faint streak of red remained jutting up to her cheek bone, and Daelen marveled at how blood could stain even skin, a reminder that would only wash away with an abrasive cleaning tool. The last thing that pretty girl needed was to look at herself in a mirror.

"Hi, Susanna," Daelen said. "My name is Dr. Lund. May I examine you?"

"You're Stellan's wife, right?"

"That's right."

"I heard about your loss. I'm very sorry."

Daelen tried to ignore the sympathy because she wasn't ready for it. It threatened to crumble the emotional foundation she was rebuilding.

"Thank you," she muttered, snapping on a pair of latex gloves.

"That's probably for the best," Susanna said. "I feel toxic right now." Another tear rolled down her cheek, and she gasped between sobs.

"They're for your protection as much as mine."

"I'm not really worried about catching a cold."

Daelen nodded while searching for materials in a cabinet. She set disinfectant, swabs, bandages, and a cold pack on the table beside Susanna. She snapped the chemical casing inside the cold pack, and it instantly cooled.

"For the eye," Daelen said, handing the cold pack to Susanna, who placed it over the bruise forming around her left eye. Daelen went to work cleaning up Susanna's wounds, starting with the long, tearing scratches on her arms, which looked to be done by an animal.

"So, dear, do you want to talk about what happened?" Daelen asked.

"I'd rather forget about it."

"I understand."

"I won't be able to, will I?"

Daelen shook her head with as much sympathy as she could. Susanna winced, and Daelen wasn't sure if the bad news or the application of the disinfectant caused her pain.

"It was like it wasn't him at all, like it was somebody else in his body," Susanna said. "The look in his eyes. It was like he didn't even recognize me."

"Sometimes even good men do bad things."

"Jude's not that good of a man," Susanna scoffed. "He's the same as all the others. They all look the same. It's in their eyes."

"What do you mean?"

Susanna's face glazed over, staring beyond Daelen, as if her brain was sending messages her body wasn't receiving.

"Sorry," she said, breaking that trance and shaking her head. "Nothing. It's stupid. It's just that he asked me out a long time ago, and he was pretty persistent. He even grew a flower in a pot for me while we were on one of the longer runs. He *grew* one. I saw the UV lamp he had and everything. Who does that?"

"No one," Daelen said. "No one does that."

"Right!?" Susanna said, missing that Daelen meant what he'd done was exceptionally thoughtful.

"It just seemed like he was so attached and just wouldn't let it go until I told him plainly that it wasn't going to happen," Susanna said. "Even then, I could feel his eyes, watching me. What a creep! It was hard sometimes, working with him. I guess now I don't have to worry about that, do I? I mean, they're not going to let him back, will they?"

"Not likely."

"Good. To be honest, I don't feel bad at all for what I did to him."

"Pressing charges?"

"No," Susanna said. "When he was on top of me, the only thing I could do was bite his arm. Even though I couldn't stand the thought of his blood in my mouth, I bit down as hard as I could and didn't let go until I thought his pulling away would tear out my teeth. It'll leave a scar, I'm sure." Susanna smiled, pleased with herself. Daelen smiled back because it was clear Susanna was looking for an indication that she'd done right by the sisterhood of women. For what she went through, Daelen didn't mind giving her that much.

However, despite Susanna's claims about Jude, which clearly were the skewed perception of a young, beautiful girl, it didn't seem right. Daelen knew Jude, and none of this made sense. Tom didn't make sense. The masses walking into medical who currently were waiting in the front room didn't make sense. Something was going on, and unlike everyone else, she couldn't dismiss it all as fluke or coincidence or something that would go away on its own.

Daelen wrapped bandages around Susanna's arms and finished treating her, making notes on her link, which then retreated into a file stored on the *Atlas'* servers.

"Keep the bandages fresh and clean. Change them regularly. Come back if you have any problems."

"Do you think I could just rest here awhile?" Susanna said. "You might not get it, but I feel embarrassed. I don't know that I could face anyone else right now, especially since, well, you know how people on this ship talk."

Daelen understood. She was sure gossip had become a raging firestorm across the *Atlas.* Even Susanna Barton, a relative stranger, had heard about such a private matter as Daelen losing her baby. She wouldn't be surprised if someone had made T-shirts and stickers in Susanna's honor, and of course, despite the good intentions, Daelen understood how unbearable that kind of thing would be. Everyone would try to be there for her, and she would just want them all to leave her alone.

"Stay as long as you need," Daelen said.

She walked out into the hall, and it was as if everything, right down to the very bones of the *Atlas*, had changed. She surmised it was what people called an epiphany.

Three

Nothing betrays a man like his own body, and although wise men know they are at the mercy of biology, the illusion of control leads young men to believe they can brush off ailments at will, as if they can walk through the fires of mortality and come out the other side without feeling the lick of flame.

But at a point in every man's life, he acknowledges vulnerability and powerlessness. Life is like falling through an abyss, and wisdom comes with learning there is a bottom. It's only a matter of time.

Rick Fairchild understood all of this. However, he also understood living was fighting, and he didn't merely roll over and accept that he would one day perish. Cuts and bruises didn't concern him. If he could move it, it wasn't worth seeing a doctor for, a stubbornness he shared with the rest of his rough and rugged kind. But something in his body was broken, and he could feel it. No bone sent bolts of pain searing up his spine. No nerve burned to indicate torn flesh. Yet, he could sense something inside of him, growing and twisting.

Something was wrong, and he intended to fight it.

When he walked into medical, he found the intern, Margo, examining a young man. Others waited patiently, sitting on exam tables. He didn't come to medical often, and when he did, it wasn't for treatment. But the number of people waiting there had to be out of the ordinary. Daelen and Margo couldn't possibly treat that many people every day. They filled the room with the musty smell of human sweat and sour breath. Most of them were quiet and didn't speak, but their occasional shuffles, scratches, and coughs created the sound of a crowd, growing more restless by the moment.

179

Margo engaged the people in her exam room as doctors, the good ones, do. He imagined Daelen had taught her well and that she had already learned much from her mentor. He thought Daelen must have been proud of her apprentice.

Their eyes met, and she motioned to him to have a seat on one of the other exam tables. He was disappointed that he couldn't find Daelen. He'd hoped he could speak with her, not because he didn't trust the intern, but because Daelen was his friend, and he felt embarrassed for seeking medical attention.

"Keep it clean and dry, and change your bandage once a day," Margo said to her patient, a young man with a gash above his eye. "If you want, you can come back, and I'll change it for you." Rick didn't recognize the young man. He'd never been good with faces and names. Rick knew machines.

The young man hopped off the exam table, and Margo escorted him to the door. When she turned back toward Rick, she offered a half-enthusiastic smile, the kind of smile he could tell she felt obligated to make.

"Rough day?" Rick asked.

"Busy," Margo said.

"A bug going around?"

"No," Margo said. "Lacerations, bruises. People fighting. I'm afraid we might run out of disinfectant and cold packs. It seems to be calming down now, though. What's the trouble with you?"

"I believe they were here before me," Rick said, motioning to the others.

"I've already seen them. I'm running triage out here, and Daelen comes and brings the ones who require her attention to the back."

"There are more people here?"

"Some are waiting for Stellan. He needs to talk to them about the incidents they were involved in."

"Oh," Rick said, feeling a little awkward about having to talk to someone so soon after arriving. He didn't know why he felt this way, but he had expected to have some time to acclimate to the environment, which wasn't as unfamiliar to him as he expected. There were plenty of tools, which intrigued him on a mechanical level. He wondered what purpose they each served, if there was something as ubiquitous as a wrench or hammer, something that had been a mainstay for hundreds of years because the design was so perfect and appropriate for its use that innovation had hit a ceiling. Some things were just so perfect they never changed because they never needed to.

"Well," Rick said. "I was hoping to talk to Daelen. No offense."

"None taken," Margo said. "As I said, however, I'm performing triage examinations, so if you want to see her today, I have to insist you tell me your symptoms."

"You all are that overwhelmed?"

"Yes and no," Margo said. "She needs to take things easy, so I have to do the best I can on my end."

"Is she all right?"

Margo nodded. "She needs time, but she will be. That's all I am at liberty to say."

"Understood." Unlike Susanna, Rick hadn't heard about Daelen's miscarriage because, unlike Susanna, Rick didn't engage in gossip. If he had heard about it, he would have come much sooner, and he wouldn't have come for himself.

"If it would make you more comfortable, I can record your symptoms and have Daelen contact you when she's able," Margo said.

"No, no," Rick said. "That's all right. After seeing what Edward went through, I don't want to wait another minute."

The mention of Edward caught Margo off guard. His name was like a seed in her head, growing guilt. Talking about him reminded her that what had happened had been real, and she could not escape it because she felt like it was her fault.

"Why do you bring him up?" Daelen said from the door to her office. Rick and Margo turned to her in surprise. She looked good, as strong as ever, like nothing had happened. Although, her spirit remained crushed, and what they were seeing was pure willpower to keep going.

"Because," Rick said, eyes darting around the room at the faces that were watching him.

"Why don't you come on back?" Daelen said. She led him to an empty private room and motioned for him to hop up on the exam table. Daelen sat in a chair beside him, folding her hands in her lap. Margo accompanied them and stood in the corner to observe. Along with the privacy, the room looked and smelled cleaner, untainted by the cloud of so many bodies. Rick could breathe easier.

"Is this better?" Daelen asked.

"Yes," Rick said. "Thank you."

"So why do you bring Edward up?"

"Because," Rick said, still hesitant. "I think I have what he had."

"That isn't likely," Daelen said. "From what we know about the black madness, if it exists, and we don't even know it exists outside of known psychological illnesses, which can develop regardless of environment, it isn't communicable. You can't catch it like a cold."

"What if you could?" Rick asked.

It was a scary prospect because she knew if such a thing could be transmitted when they had no understanding of it, the *Atlas* would be doomed. There would be no stopping it. In the pure isolation of the black, the only thing that would stop it would be the *Atlas'* hull, and it would eat away at them until there was nothing left.

"What symptoms are you experiencing?" she asked, opening a notepad application on her link. The holographic window danced and reflected off the lenses of her glasses.

"I've been getting the chills and the shakes, like the flu," Rick said. "I've been feeling run down but having trouble sleeping. Fever dreams. Memory loss."

"Memory loss?"

"Yeah, I just was somewhere and didn't know how I got there. That's never happened before. I'm not a worrier, understand, but I can't help ignore that something's wrong."

Daelen typed furious notes, and her eyes pulled away from what she was typing long enough to see something so obvious she stopped and almost smacked herself for missing it before.

"What happened to your hand?" Daelen asked with a concerned wrinkle on her forehead.

"Oh, that," Rick said, massaging his bad hand with the fingers of his good hand. "I know it's a terrible bandage job, but duct tape really does fix anything. Take my word for it. I happen to be an authority on the matter. You know we once duct taped a crane arm so well it was usable? Of course, halfway through the pickup, the tape gave, and the broken arm shot right out the bay and speared a chunk of refined earth mid-flight. The safety director would have had a fit, but you should have seen the son of a bitch, like the *Atlas* launching a javelin. And this other time—"

"Rick," Daelen said. "The hand."

"Oh, right. Back on the *Shiva* when there was that accident, I tried to get a flashlight between one of the men's teeth. You know, to keep him from biting off his own tongue. I slipped, and he nipped me a little." Rick grinned. "It's not so bad." Daelen humored him with a smile of her own and looked at Margo uneasily. The accident was when Tom started to act strangely, and since the accident, they'd seen increasing frequency of injuries from crew conflicts.

"Let's run some tests," Daelen said. "I can give you something for the fever and something that will help you sleep. Do you mind if we keep you for observation?"

"No," Rick said. "My job on this run is mostly done anyway. There are some things I need to take care of but nothing that can't wait." He actually felt relieved to have someone keeping an eye on him. It meant he wouldn't go tearing up any more equipment that he'd have to figure out a way to explain later.

"Margo, can you compile all the names of the patients you saw today? I might want them in here for another look."

"Sure thing," Margo said, eager to please, and left the room, happy to have a mission in which she could deliver.

Daelen reached into a cabinet and retrieved a syringe to take a blood sample and another to administer a sedative and fever reducer. She placed them on the counter and then loaded one with a vial for Rick's blood. She loaded the other syringe with a cartridge of the drug she would administer.

"I'm sure you'll be gentle," Rick said, "but I hate needles."

"Don't be a baby." Daelen wiped his inner elbow with a disinfecting swab and took a blood sample. He winced, but when he realized it didn't hurt as much as he expected it would, he watched with wonder as his blood spurted into the vial. With the other syringe, she injected the sedative into his shoulder. It self-administered the drug, whirring into Rick's flesh and then retracting.

"I know the accommodations are lacking," she said, packing up her tools and carrying his blood to the door, "but try to get some rest."

Rick lay down on the exam table, already feeling the effects of the drug and the comfort that he was heading off an illness before it had gotten too bad. Daelen knew how to make him better, and everything would be all right. He would just close his eyes for a little while and let her take care of everything. After all, it was what she did. She made people better. She fixed people. She saved them.

Daelen forced a smile because she felt obligated, though it appeared as genuine as any smile Rick had seen before. The difference between a medical professional and an intern was their ability to fake it for the sake of their patients. As she left the room, she closed the door with a swipe of her link over the holographic control.

She tried to be quiet as she tapped the controls, cursing digital and mechanical technology that did not compute subtlety and stealth. The locking mechanism slid into the doorframe with a pop, but she found some relief in the knowledge that Rick had probably drifted far enough into his subconscious already that he hadn't heard a thing.

Four

While Daelen was with Rick, Stellan arrived at the medical deck to question the victims of the attacks. However, there was something he had to do first, something more important to him. He hadn't seen Wendy since the shooting.

The room in which she rested was dark, calm, peaceful. He liked that she had such a place away from the growing chaos. Stellan could make out her body lying in the dim, cool blue light that emanated from some medical equipment and bounced off a mirror on the opposite wall. The light cast a sheen on her upper arm and the curve of her cheek, and he couldn't tell if she was breathing. For a moment, Stellan feared she had died quietly in her sleep, and it wasn't the vanity of his sacrifice that dropped anchors in his heart. It was simply the thought of failure.

"Hey," she whispered. Her voice sounded foreign to him. Normally it jumped with energy. Still, hearing her speak filled him with joy. He knew the pain of a wound to the abdomen and thought it was a miracle she was even conscious.

"Hey," Stellan said. "How you feeling?" He pulled a chair up beside her bed, careful to not let its legs drag on the floor.

"All things considered, not bad," she said. "Your wife has the best drugs. I'm firing my dealer."

Stellan laughed. She managed a smile.

"I heard about what happened," Wendy said. "How are you guys holding up?"

"Haven't had much time to deal with it."

"You'll never have enough time if you don't make time."

"Wise words," Stellan said. "Some philosopher say that?"

She considered it for a moment and then shook her head. "Rick."

Stellan could tell she wanted to say something and was mustering up the courage.

"I know you had to choose," she said. "Why me?"

Stellan didn't know how to respond because he wasn't sure himself. Was it that she had a better chance of survival? Or he couldn't bear for her to suffer? No, he figured it was that the other situation was too complicated. On some level, it just made sense, and he was sure Daelen felt the same way. They sacrificed themselves for their crew.

"Because I love you, kid. I couldn't let you go."

She fell into silent reflection, and Stellan knew all about survivor's guilt.

"I'll do right," she said. "I'll earn it."

"No," Stellan said with a wave of his hand. "None of that. You have nothing to make up for. Thinking that way is unhealthy. Trust me."

"At least let me apologize for yelling at you," Wendy said. "When you missed the game. That stuff doesn't matter anymore. Family comes first. You were right to look after Daelen."

"You think you're not family to me? I should have been there."

"You're there when it matters."

"Not always."

The darkness and calm air made the passing moments of silence between them easier to bear. It felt nice to just be in that room because, although Wendy had been shot, she had lived. Stellan hadn't let her down entirely, and he found comfort in that thought.

"Stel?" Wendy said.

"Mmm?"

"I was curious about something before but was afraid to ask. Now, I feel like I need to know."

"What is it?"

185

"That scar on your shoulder. While you were still out after saving Edward, I visited you. Daelen pulled your shirt up to check something, and I saw it. What happened?"

His scars were evidence of another life in another time, a life he no longer thought relevant because that person no longer existed. Wendy didn't know about the person Stellan had been, and he didn't think she needed to know. History had a funny way of changing perception of the present, and he liked the way she looked at him then. He didn't want it to change. He didn't want her to see him another way. If she knew about the things he'd done, he was afraid she might think he was a monster.

"Experience," he said, but he could tell just by the look on her face, the way she glanced down toward her own belly, that she knew it was a gunshot wound. It was a connection she suspected they shared, and she wanted to share it, to feel company in it. Stellan couldn't give that to her, though. She didn't know how deep his wounds went. She didn't know that it would be too much for her.

He understood when she wasn't satisfied with his answer. He hadn't meant it to satisfy her curiosity, but he hoped it would be enough.

"I have another question," she said. "Do you fear God?"

It caught Stellan off guard. They'd never spoken of religion or faith before, so Stellan's first instinct, as odd as it may have been, was that she was joking. Topics of conversation with depth weren't really Wendy's style, and when Stellan saw on her face that she was serious, he was surprised to find it didn't feel awkward.

"What do you mean?"

"When I was young, this old man used to come around my dad's shop. He'd just sit inside the store and ask people who came in if they were God-fearing people. I never understood it, but it always stuck with me.

"When I looked down and saw all that blood, my first thought was someone had spilled something on me. I didn't feel any pain, even when I realized a bullet had gone through me, and I thought, this is what dying feels like. My body knows it's done, so there's no point in bothering me with pain. Until you were looking down on me. I didn't feel pain until I felt hope that I might live. But even then, I couldn't stop thinking about how afraid I was, and I wondered what it meant to fear God. My mind jumped back to that old man and my curiosity."

"It's funny how, when you're convinced it's over, your mind brings back things you didn't even know were still there," Stellan said, and he thought he'd given himself away. Wendy looked at him with a mix of contempt and curiosity, and with a nod of his head, Stellan apologized for the interruption and asked her to continue.

"What does it mean to fear something that's supposed to love you?" she asked. "The devil I understand. You do bad things; you get punished. Fearing God doesn't make sense because he's supposed to reward you for being a good person. You're supposed to love and fear him? He loves you, but then you get shot? I wonder if it's maybe not him you're supposed to fear but facing him. Judgment. Scrutiny for all your sins. It's yourself you're supposed to fear. Your own worst enemy."

"You getting holy on me, kid?" Stellan asked.

"Maybe."

"You didn't answer my question."

"You didn't answer mine."

Wendy's gaze persisted. She wanted an answer. She wouldn't let him leave without giving one. He wasn't sure which question she wanted an answer to, but he thought they essentially were the same. The scar was a mark of a lesson he'd learned, and that lesson was about as close to the existence of God as he ever got. So he gave the only answer he could, and it was honest.

"God scares the hell out of me."

Five

When Stellan exited Wendy's room, he found Daelen across the hall, gazing at what he didn't know was Rick's door. He knew something was troubling her. His presence startled her from her thoughts.

Meeting each other felt like meeting for the first time again. They were each in their own place emotionally, and neither of them could tell what the other was thinking or feeling. Neither could be sure of what they were thinking or feeling themselves. In some ways, they were estranged, separated by the loss of their unborn child with no time to grieve and heal.

"What are you doing up?" Stellan asked. "You should be resting."

"Can't. Loads to do. Listen, we need to talk."

"Now? Do you have any idea what's going on out there?"

"Precisely."

She walked toward the end of the hall, and even though he was confused, Stellan had no choice but to follow.

When they entered her office and she closed the door, her face was cold and hard. She looked like she was trying to not appear frightened, but she couldn't help it.

Stellan couldn't have known, though, that seeing him had taken Daelen's breath away. He didn't understand the measure of his effect on her. She remembered that feeling when she first saw him all those years ago in the subway tunnels beneath her burning home city. She found a broken man for whom she felt a unique attraction to heal. She understood him then, as he kneeled on the tile floor, a blank stare across his face, water trickling between his legs from a burst pipe, draining down the stairs and flooding the tunnels below.

He'd been a believer, a killer, as much as she hated to admit it, and he was realizing that path led only to destruction. The world couldn't be forged in fire, and there was a kind of beauty in his breakdown, like the royal city, a transformation into something diminished yet better. As painful as it was, razing a forest meant fertile soil. She could help him rebuild. They could start again together, and the *Atlas* had been a great place for that. A new beginning. A reset button. A second chance.

This time, though, she had some rebuilding of her own to do.

The problem was he reminded her of her failures. She feared that feeling might never go away, that every time she looked at him, she'd remember how she couldn't find the strength to tell him about their child and how, if she'd been a better doctor, she might have had nothing to regret.

She understood it was how Stellan felt in those tunnels, acknowledging the full weight of responsibility. Everything he'd done since had been to lift himself from that dark place, to right the cosmic balance of all his deeds.

And even though she thought she understood Stellan better than she ever had, she had never felt so far away from him.

"Are you okay?" he asked.

She wanted to tell him how deep her grief went. She wanted to break down, to fall into his arms and let the sadness flow out of her like extracting poison. But it wasn't a time for weakness.

"Have you ever heard of the Pandora Protocol?" she asked.

"I'm sorry. What?"

"It's the protocol of protocols." She opened a document on her workstation. "In the event that we encounter a biological hazard, there's the chance an alien bacteria or virus could infect the human anatomy."

She could tell she'd blindsided him and that his mind was struggling to catch up.

"In the last twenty-four hours, we've seen more injuries from violence than in the last twenty-four years. All since we left the *Shiva*. All since Tom."

"Let me get this straight," Stellan said. "You think we picked up something that's causing our people to go mad? And now you want put the ship on lockdown based on a theory?"

"Quarantine," she said. "I'm saying what if there's a reason my infirmary is now a triage center? What if there's a reason you're running all over the ship? I've seen this kind of thing before. Have you seen any of these people? I just examined Susanna Barton, who was almost raped by Jude Washington, and she couldn't focus. It was like her brain kept stalling. And then there's Rick. Rick's in the room I just left. He says, ever since the accident, when the man he was helping bit him, he's experienced memory gaps."

Stellan took a deep breath and released it through puckered lips. He rubbed his head, ruffling his blond hair. "It isn't just the black madness? Like with Edward?"

"Maybe. But what if it isn't?"

"I can't believe Jude would—"

"I know."

"And Rick. God," he said. "Assuming you're right, what do we do about it? How do we proceed?"

"The first step is getting Gordon on board. Then he has to issue the command."

"I'll talk to him," Stellan said, still in disbelief.

A moment passed where Daelen expected Stellan to leave, but he refused. They stared at each other, and he detected fear in her eyes.

"Is that all?" he asked.

"Yes."

He pressed forward, and she backed away as if frightened.

"We have to talk about us," Stellan said.

"I know. I just…"

"What?"

"I'm not sure I'm ready. Work's the only thing keeping me going. Besides, it just doesn't seem like a good time. Too much is going on."

Stellan tried to make sense of what she was saying, and he remembered what Wendy had said about time. "Is that why you didn't tell me? It was never a good time?"

"That's not fair."

"You're right," Stellan said. "I'm sorry. I don't mean to be insensitive, and I certainly don't want to upset you. It's just confusing, you know?"

"Yes," she said and then hesitated. "I suppose I didn't tell you because I wasn't sure I was going to keep it."

Even though she spoke softly, Daelen's voice echoed in Stellan's mind. "What? How can you say that? How can you even think that?"

"No children in space," she said with a small voice. "You know this. We have a child, we have to go back to the way things were before."

"It was our child. *Ours.* The decision was ours, not yours to make alone."

She wished she could make him understand her fear, how if they had a child, she couldn't bear to see it grow up without a father, how it took all she had to endure the thought of living without him.

And then it happened without either of them knowing it or intending it. Like the first cracks in a damn, the grief began to overtake her. That barrier of numbness she'd constructed for herself out of pure willpower vanished, and full power of emotional collapse fell on top of her.

"You make it when you jump out airlocks," she sobbed. "You make it every time you put your job before me."

"Don't you put that on me. What happened was tragic, and I only did my job the best I could."

"That's what I'm saying, love," Daelen said, caressing his cheek. "Something's got to give. What's going to happen if you have to choose between your duty and me? What's going to happen if you have to choose between your duty and a family?"

He paced to direct some of his anger anywhere but at her. "I didn't do this."

"No, it wasn't you. I can heal bullet wounds and exposure, but I can't keep my own unborn child safe." And with the realization that all her training and knowledge amounted to nothing if she couldn't save the ones she loved, she understood his fear. She understood he did what he did because, if he couldn't save lives, he had nothing else, nothing but a pit of self-loathing to fall into, something she couldn't save him from.

Stellan embraced her, and she pressed her face into his chest, the warmth of her tears soaking through his shirt. His anger evaporated. Without knowing it, they were taking the first steps toward recovery. They were healing.

He whispered into her ear, running his fingers through her hair. "We're going to fix this. And we're going to fix us. There was nothing either of us could have done."

He suddenly remembered his conversation with Pierce about Skinner. He remembered their suspicion and how agents worked. The confluence of events was their weapon. They manipulated environments to make things work their way so it would appear natural, and he wondered how many people comforted loved ones with the same words he'd just used when, all the while, a Council agent had been to blame. He wondered how many people she'd killed that way, how many spirits she'd broken.

When Daelen was still and quiet, Stellan again kissed her, embraced her, and told her he loved her.

"You should go," she said.

"No. If you're right about this, I'm not leaving you."

"You have to."

"No way. I'm done. Pierce can fix it himself."

"Love," Daelen said, "think of where we are. If this gets out of hand, you're our best hope. You're my best hope. And you can't help anyone from here."

She was right. His best chance of saving her was leaving. Reluctantly, he stood, gently laying her hands in her lap, and walked toward the door.

"It's the bites," she whispered.

"What?" Stellan turned back to his weak, defeated wife and knew he had done that to her. But it had to happen. To rebuild, they had to finish clearing what was broken. They had to raze the forest.

191

"It came from soil, so it's probably a pathogen, meaning it's transferrable by body fluid contact. It's in the blood, but it's also in the saliva and other fluids. I don't know everything. Everything we know about pathogens might not even apply. I know Rick was bitten. Others are coming in with bite wounds. For some reason, people are being compelled to bite. It's probably a function of the infection. Even on Earth, we have behavior-altering infections."

Stellan grimaced.

"It's in the blood. It's in the bites," she repeated.

He left her then, still distracted from the one duty he wanted to fulfill. For the entirety of his time away from New Earth, he'd fought to preserve and protect their way of life, but he needed someone to blame for everything that had happened, someone to direct his anger toward.

Even though he knew a preoccupied mind made mistakes, he also knew, as soon as he found Council Agent Adelynn Skinner, he would kill her.

Six

Pierce's cabin was quiet except for the creaking of his wooden chair's back legs, the front legs rising off the ground in protest. He rocked slowly, biting his bottom lip. He rubbed his stubble and stared into nothing, his attention turned inward. The rise and fall of his chest was barely visible, like a man feigning death. The black brick loomed on the desktop as if it sucked all his life into it, a singularity of human emotion and thought.

The stillness crept over Stellan like icy fingers. He felt a tightening in his shoulders because he wasn't quite sure where to begin trying to make Captain Pierce believe the unbelievable, and all he could think about was the chair's wood splitting with each crack and pop, like snapping twigs. Each sounded like it would be the last before the legs finally gave out under the strain of time, its long career of supporting people brought to a close beneath the weight of a man's nervous habit.

Instead of breaking the chair, however, Pierce broke the silence.

"You know, I miss the way things used to be. Some might call me a romantic, but I miss the clarity of it all. I miss the certainty. I miss the not knowing what I know now. I miss the belief."

"Belief in what?" Stellan asked.

"Something better. A better world, but you know as well as I do that this is as good as it's going to get. They say it's all downhill when you realize your wheels are just turning. They say you don't know what you had 'til it's gone. So true."

Stellan knew what Pierce was talking about as only he could because Stellan sometimes felt the same. Pierce longed for the feeling of the path of righteousness they both thought they were on before the revolution, which they'd helped the Council win. Pierce used to say that, sometimes, a little killing was necessary. Purging the bad seeds was good for the rest. Stellan didn't believe that anymore. He thought perhaps Pierce still believed it but had lost the taste for it all the same. Still, wishing to return to those times was the same as wishing for a lie. They might as well have wished for death.

For the first time in as long as Stellan could remember, he felt like he didn't know Gordon Pierce. He didn't know what the Captain was thinking. That connection they'd shared that served them so well on the battlefield was severed.

Pierce leaned forward, and the pounding of the chair's front legs on the deck startled Stellan.

"So what's the big secret that you had to call me into my own cabin for?" Pierce asked.

"Daelen has a theory that there's a biological hazard on the ship, that we picked up something that's infecting people somehow."

"I know."

"How?"

"It's my ship." Pierce's eyebrows rose.

It didn't surprise Stellan that Pierce's reaction was not what he anticipated. He knew Pierce was guarding his thoughts and feelings. He didn't know why, however, and not knowing Pierce's motives bothered Stellan more than not being able to predict Pierce's movements. It felt like Pierce was hiding something from him.

"She thinks we should enact the Pandora Protocol," Stellan said. "Jettison the load. Quarantine the crew. Isolate the infected."

"We can't jettison the load," Pierce said, his eyes drawn to the black brick, laying like a miniature coffin on his desktop. "We have a mission. We can't just abandon it." Pierce's gaze on the brick bordered on longing.

"What was that crap you said before about being the first one to cut and run if lives were at risk? And what if the stuff we have in our cargo bays is what's causing the problem?"

"We don't know that there is a problem. You said it yourself. It's just a theory."

"What about all the people in medical? And I'm running out of holding cells."

"I see your point," Pierce said, looking away from the brick and appearing more thoughtful. "And we have lost lives, but we can't do anything about them now. I understand Daelen's concern and agree with her assessment. It's better we be safe, but we don't jettison the load."

"It's protocol. No one would blame you. You don't owe the Council anything," Stellan said, and Pierce's gaze fixed on Stellan like a weapon. It was a look Stellan had never been on the other end of. It was the look Pierce gave his adversaries.

"When the fuck have I ever given a shit about protocol? This is about principle. We owe it to ourselves to try and make good on our mission no matter how FUBAR the situation may get, and retreat is my call to make, not yours."

"Gordon," Stellan said, "these people aren't soldiers."

The uncomfortable silence returned. Pierce leaned back in his chair again. The legs groaned in agony.

"The load stays," Pierce said. "Follow containment procedure. Find a way to determine who's sick. Isolate anyone you suspect. I'm going to turn us around."

"Turn us around?"

"The *Shiva*," Pierce said. "If Daelen's right, they're going to need our help. The men we lent them aren't going to cut it." Stellan detected a hint of worry in Pierce's voice, a slight tremble in his throat, at the mention of Commander Ashland's ship.

With the decision made, Stellan stood and walked to the Captain's hatch door.

"We do this right, or no one goes home," Pierce said.

"That's what I've been trying to tell you," Stellan said. "The *Atlas is* our home."

Seven

Pierce walked the length of the command deck as he had countless times before. This time, though, his boots were heavy like they contained leaden weight. He went with reluctance, with no desire to do what he would have to do, but he would do what was necessary. He hoped Daelen was wrong, but if she was right, he would see them all through it. Well, he would see as many of them through it as he could.

The department heads continued to sort through requests for protocol responses and had taken to directing security personnel themselves. As Pierce strode by, one of them tried to ask him for help, but he simply carried on toward his place on the bridge. Everyone would have a place soon. The protocol was clear. Everyone would have a job to do, and success would be contingent on their individual performances.

When Pierce passed the department heads and entered the white light of the bridge, they stared at him. His apparent indifference set them off kilter, like a glitch in a system. Their queries returned no response, no directive, breaking up their rhythm. They did not know what to do.

Pierce knew that, and it was okay. Soon, they would understand. Soon, they would have no question what they would have to do. The protocol would tell them everything they would need to know, and by God, they better be strong enough to carry out their orders. Leadership was not for the weak-willed. Only hard men could lead in hard times.

Their mouths gaped. Their screens flooded with unanswered requests. Pierce reached his platform and leaned upon the railing, his shoulder blades pressing the back of his uniform like hidden wings. For the first time in as long as he could remember, he found himself unable to say the words he knew he had to say. He knew which words he would say. He had already chosen them carefully, but a barrier in his throat or in his mind would not let them pass. Never before had he struggled so intensely to do the right thing. He understood then that ordering men to commit necessary evils was harder to bear than committing them because, when you are the hand, the burden of intent is not yours. It is leadership that bears guilt. It is the mind that remembers.

"What's up, Captain?" Arlo said.

"Turn us around."

"Sir?"

"Take us back to the *Shiva*."

"You leave something behind?"

Pierce thought about Commander Ashland, and he tried to convince himself he wasn't taking the *Atlas* back to help her. He was taking the *Atlas* back to help the crew and, in the worst-case scenario, keep their blight from reaching New Earth, but only in his darkest nightmares had he thought that far ahead.

"Ensign Evans, on your terminal, you will find a document," Pierce said.

Evans moved a window aside on his workstation and found the document of which Pierce spoke. "The Pandora Protocol?" He swiped through it casually and then slowed when he began to understand what it was.

"Yes," Pierce said. "On my mark, I want you to send it to all department heads and officers."

"Sir," Arlo said, carefully. "Do you know what this is?"

"It's necessary," Pierce said. "It's necessary." As if repeating himself might reassure them, as if it might reassure himself, Pierce found the truth was not comforting.

"Execute," Pierce said, and with a single word, he killed the spirit of the *Atlas*. By enacting the Pandora Protocol, he brought the oppression of the New Earth Council across the cosmos.

The tragedy was that it was necessary to keep living, and that was the only thing on Pierce's mind. Soon, he was sure, survival would be the only thing anyone could think about, like a black dawn settling on a horizon where once there was light, an eclipse in his mind.

CHAPTER 8
TURNING WHEELS AND NECESSARY EVILS

One

You'd never know from the odor that the water treatment facility processed so much toxic waste. It smelled like the cleanest, purest part of the ship. The scent of the water rising from the tanks as steam, beading on the walls as condensation, reminded Stellan of the lakes and rivers near the last place he called home on New Earth. He recalled the warm summer days lazing in the shade of the trees, when the world still seemed so big, when he yearned to find his place in it.

The black water in the water plant was hidden away, though Stellan knew, even if he couldn't see or smell it, the stuff that could kill him wasn't far.

Standing on the catwalk between tanks of clean water and gazing at the reflections from the exposed pools dance on the ceiling like ghost stars, Stellan breathed deeply, the air itself cleansing him. It smelled like dew or rain on a spring day when the trees were coming into full bloom. When he closed his eyes, he could almost feel the wind, smell the soil, and see the branches and leaves waving at him, greeting him, applauding him, inviting him.

The hum from the light drive rippled in his head like the water below. It was quiet, except for the gentle lapping against the tank walls, and the urge struck him to turn his link off, dive in, and wash away all his anxiety.

The charred area in the walkway from the burning ENV suit had been expertly repaired. The men in this facility loved their ship, and if Stellan didn't know there had been a fire there, he probably wouldn't have been able to tell. They had paid so much attention to detail to weld the new portions so evenly across the supports and the grating that the seams appeared natural, as if they'd been there all along.

Stellan hoped he could repair the crew with such workmanship. He hoped he could persevere so that their losses would be minimal and they could move on as though nothing had changed. People were far too complicated for that, though. Unlike steel, people were soft, and what would happen over the next few hours would mold them and perhaps take the rest of their lives to smooth out. He hoped they would see their forced quarantine as precautionary and protective instead of oppressive. He didn't want to be that person again.

"Back again, Chief?" Carter Raines said, emerging from the dancing shadows. "I hope there's no more trouble."

The water treatment personnel cared for the water, and in turn, they wanted to be left alone. They'd opened up to Stellan over the years and allowed him to invade from time to time as a reclusive religion that would invite someone who was beginning to see the beauty in their peace.

"Everything's fine, Carter," Stellan said. "But I'm going to need you to shut it down."

"What? The water?"

"Yes."

"Why in the world would you want to do that?"

Stellan saw in Carter's face and heard in his voice that his friendliness was evaporating. Carter's round edges became sharp as he raised his guard, his muscles tensing into alertness, but Stellan didn't think he would fight.

"And then I'm going to need you and your people down in bay seventeen," Stellan said.

With a sigh, Stellan motioned with a finger to two of his men who'd been waiting near the entrance. Andrew Reynolds and Desmond Brannigan swept in and grabbed Carter under his arms. They were good men. They would be gentle, respectful.

"You can't do this, man!" Carter cried. "This place is our home. We live here!"

Carter's face broke in a way Stellan had seen many times before with many others whom he told would have to leave their homes. It was the loss of control and freedom. It was heartbreak from lost trust. Just like on New Earth, it was easy to support your government when it was protecting you, when it was establishing the perimeter around your home, but it was hard for citizens to be patriotic when soldiers knocked on their door and told them they would have to move or they'd be abandoned. They'd have to comply, or they'd be shot. Men like Stellan would go as far as they needed to go if they thought it was necessary. If they believed it.

"Tell us what's going on at least!"

Stellan felt the urge to justify to himself that he was just the messenger. It was how he lived with it before. He'd pulled men and women away from loved ones, but it wasn't his call. He'd fired bullets at children, but he was just the hand, the mechanism.

The problem was there might have been something worse than him out there, and if he left them on their own, they would be unprotected. It was for their own good. It was necessary.

Stellan walked to the far end of the room where the main valve control was accessible through a small door secured by an electronic lock. He had access. He had access to everything. So he waved his link, and the door slid open, revealing a one-meter-wide pipe with an old-fashioned red valve wheel.

"Everything will be all right," Stellan said. "You just have to trust me."

The wheel turned with surprising ease.

Two

Pierce paced along the platform on the bridge, head bowed in thought, chasing down something internally. His crew watched him with electric anticipation. When they decided he would maintain a state of deep reflection indefinitely, some of them turning back to their workstations, he walked to his platform and spoke.

"Arlo," he said. "Comms to all stations."

"Have something you need to get off your chest?" Arlo said. "Because you know you can always talk to me. I'm a good listener." His fingers danced on his holographic interface.

"I need to address the crew." A window expanded before them, displaying the sound wave, a flat line of silence.

"Ready when you are," Arlo said.

Pierce drew in a deep breath. "Attention all hands," he said in a grave tone. "This is the Captain."

Everyone throughout the ship stopped what they were doing to listen. The flowing traffic in the hallways stood still. The tram arrived at a station; no one boarded. The patrons in the bar set down their drinks. The off-cycle crew in their quarters rose from their beds. Pierce's words boomed. Everyone heard him like the voice of God directly in their minds.

"This run has been anything but ordinary. Together, we've dodged the unexpected at every pass. We dove deep into the black, and some of us have paid a price. Coincidence presents itself as a curiosity, and we struggle to connect the dots. The connections may exist. They may not. However, for the betterment of us all, we have to take certain precautionary measures. It's important that we cooperate with each other now and that we all attempt to reserve judgment. We have to lean on each other. We have to help each other. We have to remain united, or we may not come out the other side the same, if we come out the other side at all. We prepare for the worst but hope for the best."

Pierce stood silent for a moment. Arlo and Evans turned toward him, knowing he had more to say. The department heads in the hall craned their heads for a better view. They suspected Pierce was simply allowing his words time to resonate before he stopped speaking in generalities and got to specifics.

"I've ordered the security team to carry out a protocol that puts the ship under quarantine. The crew will be isolated into multiple zones throughout all decks. If you are currently in your residence, remain there until our ensured safety has been re-established. If you are not on the residence decks, you are to report to your nearest quarantine zone, which is being sent to your link now. Do not leave the deck you currently are on unless ordered to. If you are not feeling well or if you know someone who is not feeling well, report it to the nearest security officer.

"At this time, I cannot reveal the specifics behind the reason for this act. However, I ask for your cooperation. Work with our security team, and we will get through this. I will keep you all apprised as we gain new information."

By addressing the crew, Pierce created a sense of calm and order. He answered just enough of their questions to satisfy them for a time. He established enough confidence that the crew knew something was being done. But that calm and order was fleeting at best, and they all knew it. They'd lived freely so long that they forgot about the definition and finality of a strict set of guidelines. They'd forgotten what it felt like to have certain freedoms revoked in the name of civilization. They'd forgotten the oppressive spirit of the planet they'd escaped.

"This is the Captain," he said. "That is all."

Three

The *Atlas'* corridors swelled. Stellan knew it was impossible, but looking down the long hallway leading to the dining deck, over the bobbing heads of the crew who were shuffling toward the designated quarantine zone, he could have sworn the walls pushed outward.

With fear and panic making the air musty, friends and acquaintances found each other and moved quietly together, embracing tightly. All the while, Stellan and his men, now armed to reinforce the message that cooperation would be appreciated, watched over the crowds at pre-established checkpoints. Their weapons added an ultimatum even though no one explicitly stated it. Those symbols reminded the crew what life on New Earth was like before they came to the freedom of the *Atlas*.

Doug stood beside Stellan at their checkpoint outside the cafeteria and bar, a single hatch door leading to a room that was used to being filled to capacity. Now, they were pushing that limit a little further.

"I don't understand," Doug said. "No one will look us in the eye."

Stellan didn't respond. Doug would either get it, or he wouldn't. If someone had tried to explain it to Stellan when he was in the Unity Corps, he wouldn't have gotten it either. So he simply focused on helping people through the doorway.

The sweet elderly woman who worked for housekeeping and changed Stellan's sheets approached. Her name was Bernadette, and Stellan gently took her hand.

"Watch your step, Bernie," he said. She accepted his help but showed no appreciation.

"Spoiled brats. All of 'em," Doug said when Bernadette was out of earshot, the cacophony of sobs masking his words.

"You really have no idea what we're doing, do you?"

"We're helping them," Doug said. "They should be thanking us. We're risking our lives here just to give them a chance."

Stellan shook his head and went back to watching the crowd.

"What?" Doug asked.

"Killing and dying are easy," Stellan said. "Living is the hardest thing a man can do."

Doug's eyes glazed over as if considering a complex math problem. "What does that mean?"

"It took me a long time to figure out that killing and dying are pretty defined terms," Stellan said. "Everyone's got a different take on what it means to live. These people came out here to get away from all of this. It's why I never armed you guys until now. It's why I never needed to. We let them live the way they wanted and asked for little in return."

Doug furrowed his brow, trying to understand. Stellan knew he never would.

"Please!" someone cried. "Don't do this!"

"What are we, cattle?" another yelled.

"Just tell us what's going on!"

Stellan expected Doug's caustic tongue to make matters worse. He didn't give Doug the chance.

"Everything's going to be all right," he said. "Help us help you, and we'll all get through this."

"The last of them are through checkpoint B," one of Stellan's men said over a comm channel.

A moment later, Stellan saw a break in the line of people as the tail end lurched around a corner. Their low heads bobbed and weaved toward the dining deck.

When they all were inside, Stellan turned to see them finally looking at him with quiet, pleading eyes. The crew of the *Atlas* were on the ship because they had no fight left. So exhausted from suppressing their anger, they resolved to the space. Of course, the anger remained. There was plenty of that left.

"Keep each other safe," Stellan said. "We'll come back for you soon."

As he closed the door, the quiet erupted into unintelligible protests and spitting hate. The hatch sealed, and Stellan waved his link over the holographic interface, changing the green light of access to the red light of finality.

Four

One-by-one, the quarantine zone supervisors checked in to verify that everyone had been secured. Every zone had finished with the exception of cargo bay seventeen, the only bay the *Atlas* hadn't utilized because of too many nonfunctioning cranes. It would house hundreds of crew for the time the protocol was in effect, and they were close to being finished, too.

In the stillness and quiet, Stellan had the distinct feeling the *Atlas* was dying. The halls were a wasteland of cold, lifeless metal, the illuminated halls picked clean like bones. Even the light drive's hum was weak and distant.

Stellan checked a schematic of the *Atlas* on his link, marking each active link on the ship with a red dot. On the blue background of the holographic image, the concentration of the links in the quarantine zones looked like clouds of blood in water. He checked his own location, a speck in the starboard main thoroughfare, surrounded by blue for hundreds of meters in every direction. In a place where he was usually no more than a dividing wall away from another human being, the understanding of the physical separation combined with the quiet felt all too isolating.

The schematic returned to his link, and Stellan continued down the corridor. Turning a corner, he expected to see more blank, white hallway. Instead, he found Agent Adelynn Skinner, leaning against a wall with her arms crossed, as if materializing from the nothingness was no big deal.

"Well, hello there," she said cheerily.

The Pandora Protocol had almost made him forget how he knew without a doubt that she was responsible for everything, and he charged her with a war cry he hadn't heard himself make in ages. In an instant, he was on her, pinning her against the wall with his forearm across her neck, with all the conviction of instinct, of knowing her guilt without needing

203

proof. He wouldn't consider until later how she didn't even try to defend herself.

"You did this!" he screamed in her face, feeling satisfaction from the spit that flew from his lips. "Admit it! You did all of this! Why!?"

She grasped his arm and struggled only to allow herself to breathe and speak.

"Why would I do such a thing?" she said. "Your prejudice is clouding your judgment. My mission is to ensure safe delivery of the precious cargo, not maroon us in space. If you let up, I'll explain."

"You're lying!" Stellan pushed his arm into her throat with each syllable. The strain flushed her face with crimson, approaching purple. "What is your mission?"

"I may be a liar. I'll give you that. But about this, I'm telling the truth. Our missions are the same."

"No." Stellan backed off a little so she wouldn't asphyxiate. "My interest is in saving lives. You care only about the material. Why?"

"The Council ordered me to—"

"Not good enough. What's the *reason* they ordered you to bring it back?" He eased back into her, and she struggled against his forearm.

"They want to study it. As I said."

Stellan had an epiphany, his attention drawing away. "They know what it does. They think they can use it to control people."

"Stellan, please. We have a common interest in getting home, and that's what matters. I'm here to help."

"Like you helped Tom get a weapon?"

Her eyes narrowed. "When we got back to Earth, I was going to have his leg replaced, and I was going to get him alcoholism counseling. I have no idea where he got the gun. Maybe he brought it on board with him. Have you noticed, for a security department, you're pretty lax on security? I mean, you didn't even ask for *my* weapon."

She led him downward with her eyes. Her sidearm sat casually in her hand, the barrel pointing at his abdomen. He'd allowed her free hand to retrieve her weapon. Rage had made him sloppy.

As she pressed her weapon into his rib cage, Stellan begrudgingly released her and backed away, expecting her to finish the job she'd sent Tom to do. She rubbed her neck and breathed deeply, coughing. Her face returned to its natural color.

"If I'd wanted you dead, I could have killed you anytime I pleased. You know this. Believe it or not, I'm here to help because, for the time being, we have a common interest in survival." She holstered her weapon. "You know, you sure have an interesting way of greeting people."

"What do you want?"

"The Pandora Protocol was never designed to work with so little support. Putting so many people into so few zones is only going to exacerbate the problem. You have to stop the Captain."

"It's already done," Stellan said. "All the quarantine zones except for the cargo bay have checked in."

Troubled by this news, she retreated into thought, pinching her bottom lip and staring into nothing.

"The whole ship's locked down," Stellan said, "which you should know, although it doesn't seem to be hindering your ability to move around."

She emerged from her thoughts with a mischievous smile. "This is going to escalate. The captain is holding onto the illusion that he has control, but it's already beyond his grasp. As he loses it, he's going to squeeze harder, and it's going to flow between his fingers like water," she clenched her fist and put it on display. "He's very stubborn, and people are going to die."

"I doubt that concerns you."

"No," she said. "It doesn't, but if we don't fix our problems, we'll never get back to Earth. He won't let us."

She'd thought further ahead than he had. Stellan's problem had always been seeing past failure and into contingency. He'd not doubted that, if Daelen was right about the infection, they would be able to wrestle it under control, and he'd not yet seen how fast it could spread. He'd not considered just how contagious the plague that they carried was. In the worst case, he knew what Skinner said was true. Pierce wouldn't let anyone leave.

"What do you suggest?"

"This quarantine was premature, but it has to work. Some have to remain uninfected. There have to be survivors. Returning home is contingent on convincing Pierce there's a reason to bring people home. You have to figure out a way to test for who's infected. Then isolate the ones who are from the ones who aren't."

"And the infected?"

She raised her eyebrows as if the answer was obvious, as if they weren't worth her time to discuss, and then she started to back away.

"Where do you think you're going?" Stellan said, raising his weapon. She showed her hands but continued backing away.

"Save who you can. There's something I need to take care of."

"What's that?"

"Call it insurance. A failsafe."

Stellan felt her slipping through his fingers. He wouldn't shoot her because he had more questions now than he did before, and if he killed her, they might never be answered. Even worse, if he killed her and it turned out that she was telling the truth, he might even have felt guilty. He wanted to pull the trigger, but something told him that, if he did, he'd regret it.

"How do I know I can trust you?" he asked.

"I never wanted harm to come to anyone. I'm not evil. Though I will do what I think is necessary. This mission is perhaps the most important one I've ever taken. It's why I chose this ship and why I chose you. I knew from the first time we met that you were my best chance at success. As I said, you're a survivor."

"You're not convincing me."

"Nothing in life is certain," she said. "You play the odds and stack the cards in your favor when you can. You're going to have to decide for yourself whether it's worth the risk."

Adelynn retreated into the shadows, and Stellan let her go.

Five

Now operating automatically, the tram whirred into the station, and Stellan looked to the front cab, waiting for the operator to stick his head out the window to make sure everyone boarded safely. He alone walked through the parting doors, and no one made sure his heels cleared the gap before the doors closed again.

He rode the tram across the ship, and it stunned him how spacious the car felt with no other passengers. He'd made a similar trip during what should have been his sleep cycle before docking at the *Shiva*, and he'd been thankful for the silence and solitude and absence of bodies. Now, he would have taken even bloodstains. Any signs of humanity would have been better than the total absence of life. Knowing the horror was real would have been better than waiting for it and fearing it. At least then he could do something.

Exiting the tram, his footsteps echoed in the halls. With no one to disturb it, dust already hung in the air and settled on the flat surfaces of the empty station manager's booth and terminal. Overhead lamps flickered on and warmed as he approached. Other lights were dark, detecting no occupancy. Each door he passed through required authorization with his link, and on the other side, he found more nothing. Everywhere were the signs of desolation.

He walked into the security deck and found the signs of negligence even there. It was more of a feeling, like the whole world had moved on and left him alone with the emptiness and the darkness beyond the *Atlas'* hull. All his men were stationed around the ship at quarantine zones, watching the entrances and reinforcing the locked doors with their weapons, as if the message hadn't been delivered with relentless clarity.

Stellan walked past the empty desks, which his men would use for terminal access in filing reports. Most people didn't realize the administrative duties that came with the security post. Even the most mundane events required reporting. They were required to keep journals and note everything they observed. Stellan didn't look forward to having to document the quarantine, and he was sure much would be left out simply from inability to recall. Maybe part of them would be unwilling to remember.

He entered his office and thought his workstation had never looked so lonely. He couldn't remember the last time he'd sat there to file a report, and he wished for those times when the monotony of documentation was a task on a to-do list rather than a suspended formality. Nevertheless, he hoped to have the time later, down the road when things returned to normal.

Flipping through windows on his terminal, he was almost unaware of what he was doing. He wondered if he even wanted to know whether Skinner told the truth. No one liked the feeling of waning belief, and if they weren't on the right path, he feared it might already have been too late.

He found the surveillance files on the *Atlas'* server and navigated back to the date and time of the fire incident in the water facility. When he found it, he gazed at the file for a moment, feeling something like fear.

He almost didn't open it because some part of him argued it would be a waste of time. He already knew he'd find Adelynn Skinner, and then he'd admonish himself once again for letting her go. She'd been so cool when she lied to him. He envied her for that ability.

Yet, she'd been waiting for him. Stellan had no illusion that she allowed him to find her.

He opened the file and watched the screen. The perfect clarity of the digital transmission did the water's dancing reflections justice. He thought about the calm and serenity of that place, the organic effect of the water, its purity.

Realizing he hadn't sat down since beginning quarantine, he zoned out. Exhaustion pulled on his mind, so he shook his head and rubbed his eyes. When he regained his focus on the screen, he saw a dark figure, rays of light dancing on baggy pants, a downcast head, and hunched shoulders. Excited fingers struck a match, and the flame illuminated the face of Edward Stone, dancing in his wondrously mad eyes. He held the match out with a pinch and then dropped it into the accelerant. The ENV suit burst into flames, whiting out the sensitive sensor in the camera.

When the camera adjusted, it showed Edward casually turn, place his hands in his pockets, and walk away, his lips puckered into a whistle Stellan could not hear on the video feed.

Stellan closed the file in disbelief. He had been so sure Skinner had started that fire to distract him. She'd done that to get at Tom, so she could give him the gun, which he'd used to try to kill Stellan.

As Pierce had said, people see coincidence and try to derive meaning. All of his preconceived notions about her came crashing down. He'd been wrong.

With renewed anger, Stellan remembered Edward was in a holding cell, so he stood and walked to the door that led to the holding room. He waved his link over the holographic lock and stepped inside. He found Doug watching over Jude Washington, Elias Robichaud, and Robt Mathers, problems Stellan had forgotten about seemingly ages ago. Stellan and Doug regarded each other with a nod in the dim room.

On the end of the row of cells, Edward wept in a corner, the pain of his injuries consuming his sanity one thought at a time. Stellan didn't care, mostly because Adelynn had been right that Edward wasn't worth it, but seeing the other prisoners made Stellan remember what was important.

He hoped he would have time later, when things returned to normal, to sort things out with Edward. For now, these three men had his attention. They stood in the center of their cells, staring out murderously. In their gaze, Stellan found emptiness, like a blackness that covered malice. He saw it in their unflinching, stone stares. They all looked at him the same way, as if they had all the time in the world to kill him. They eyed him unafraid, pupils swallowing irises.

Seeing them, Stellan knew there had been no mistake, and Daelen was right. Something was consuming his crew. All remaining doubt evaporated, and he had no idea what they were going to do.

"How long have they been statues?" Stellan asked.

"I picked 'em up like that," Doug said. "You push 'em, and they move. Otherwise, they just stand there, like they're tuning into something or trying to find a connection. Somethin' ain't right upstairs." Doug tapped his temple and then banged on the cell bars. The only prisoner who moved was Edward, who shrieked but never left the comfort of his fetal position on his cot.

"I think Jude tried to bite me," Doug said.

"Did he?"

"No."

Stellan's heart sank to see Jude in such a condition. The other two were not so familiar to him. At first, he couldn't quite place their faces, but as he looked at them staring back, images of the gunfight with Tom played in his mind. He remembered his hand acting on its own and his eyes never leaving his target. He remembered the sounds of the cracking guns, and he remembered the blood. There was so much of it. It sprayed everywhere, covering the bar and several faces behind Tom.

And as if someone placed the images in front of him, those faces became clear.

"My God," Stellan said.

"What?"

"Where's Floyd?"

"Still guarding that door, like you told him to."

"We might need his administrative skills after all."

Stellan realized, when he shot Tom, the back spray had covered others. And he remembered them one at a time. Jude was there, but so were Robichaud and Mathers. Daelen said the infection was probably a pathogen, which meant Tom's blood would have carried the contagion. They would need to find out who those people had contact with by tracking their links during the past few hours since Tom died. Even though Stellan had no idea how this infection worked or how communicable it was beyond Daelen's theories, he had to try. If Skinner was right and the quarantine would inevitably fail, it was his best option.

Looking into the murderous gazes of the men in his holding cells, Stellan realized he wasn't waiting for the horror. It was already there, and he felt powerless, knowing it had snuck up on them, using their own fear and skepticism of the black madness as camouflage.

Space hadn't warped these men's minds. Stellan couldn't even be sure they still were men. However, there was one thing he knew with certainty. These men were no longer his friends.

Six

All his life, Floyd Coulson's mind had wandered. When he was young, his doctors had prescribed him medication to help him maintain his focus through school, and until he'd finished, moved out of his parents' home, and officially became a man, he took them. Then he stopped because he liked letting his mind run free. It allowed him to tap into his creativity. Unfortunately, he found he lacked the drive to make use of it, but he didn't care. He was happier. He was the person he was meant to be.

So as he stood guard of the door to the room on the reactor deck in which the body had been found, his mind wandered from the boredom. He thought about writing a book. And he thought about sleep. He thought about it more these days. It was the ultimate way to let his mind go. To dream was sweet and warm, like his mother's potato and dumpling stew.

She'd used the old-fashioned rolling pin to flatten the dough. He remembered the sound it made as it crossed the countertop in their country kitchen. It was a soft rumbling, and it sounded wet when the air bubbles snapped and popped under the rolling pin. Over and over, she'd beat the dough, and he remembered he loved the surprise the best. You'd never know if you'd get a soft potato or a chewy dumpling until your teeth clamped down.

Floyd realized he'd closed his eyes and had almost fallen asleep standing up. The onset of another dream moved into his mind like a passing cloud. The sound of that rolling pin was in his ears.

He slapped himself in the face, and after the ringing vanished from his ear, the wet rolling sound remained. It took a moment for him to realize the sound was coming from behind him, beyond the closed hatch door, in the room where the reactor coupling was. In the room with the disemboweled dead body.

Floyd pressed his ear against the door. It was cold, but he could hear the sliding sound better. It was low, on the deck, and then he picked up on two syncopated taps on the deck before each wet sliding sound. A rubbing accompanied the sound, as well, like dragging boots on the floor.

At this thought, he jumped away. There were only two boots in that room as far as he knew, and Stellan had assured him they weren't going anywhere.

Floyd reached for the door latch. He had to know what the sound was, and even as his mind wandered and the sound grew louder, he knew. But it was impossible. Even his wandering, open mind would not accept it. Because it wasn't possible.

The sound grew louder, and he moved closer. He never felt so foolish in his life. Still, he inched along, dragging his paralyzed body.

A window leaped from his link, and Stellan's face greeted him in holographic glow.

"Floyd, how's it going down there?"

"Fine," Floyd said with a relieved sigh. "Just fine." The sliding sound ceased.

"I'm going to need you back up here. We've almost got quarantine established, but there's something else I need your help on."

"Okay. What about the stiff?"

"It's not going anywhere, and soon, there won't be anyone left out of quarantine to disturb it," Stellan said. "Just get up here." Stellan's face shrank into Floyd's link.

Uncertain, yet still curious, he reached for the door and stopped with his hand outstretched.

"You're being silly," he said aloud. He wasn't sure, however, if it was the fear or the simple knowledge that, if he opened the door, there would be blood, but his hand fell upon the manual locking lever. He pulled it down, and something within the bulkhead wall boomed like a giant gavel.

Wiping his brow, he started back toward the tram, which would take him to the security deck. A few steps later, the sliding sound returned, and Floyd stopped and listened. He ran for the first time in years when he heard the pounding at the base of the door.

Seven

There's a space between sleep and consciousness where dreams overlap reality. Some call it "protoconsciousness," the waking brain beginning to process the real world again. Hypnotists claim it is where they take their subjects to exercise the power of suggestion.

When Wendy awoke on the medical deck, her abdomen still burning from the gunshot wound and the surgery, she thought she was in that place, still sensing her dreams but otherwise conscious and aware, her imagination painting pictures over the real world, her mind creating sounds her ears didn't hear.

She thought she heard a scream, and in the low, ambient glow of the nearby medical terminal, she couldn't tell where it came from. The light in the hallway outside her room filtered through the frosted glass that surrounded the door on the far wall, but it wasn't enough to discern the origin of the voice. Surely, the fogginess of the sound meant it was outside of her room, or it was just in her mind.

Wendy tried to sit up but was only able to make it halfway with her elbows supporting her like shaky pillars.

"Hello?" she called. "Is somebody hurt?"

For a moment, she heard no response. The dead air hung audible like static, and she had enough time to doubt herself again and nearly drift back to sleep before another scream pierced her ears, creating an unmistakable sense of urgency that shot through her body like electricity. The lingering cloud of sleep melted away enough to know for sure that the voice was not in her mind.

The remainder of her consciousness sprang into awareness. Her eyes darted around the room, searching. She found the strength to sit fully upright. She listened.

A pair of feet padded rapidly outside her door. Through the frosted glass on the far wall, she saw a dark shape hurry past. And then she heard a gasp and the squeal of shoes as they slid across the deck. She presumed the series of knocks she heard were the sounds of joints on the human body slamming against the deck. She heard scuffling as that body struggled to rise.

The voices silenced, and she sensed a moment of terror but not her own. Wendy was afraid, but through the silence, she felt a strong, vicarious fear. The person who ran past her room panicked.

Wendy leaned forward toward the door, reaching out from across the room, feebly attempting to engage the electronic lock. She didn't care who that person was or what they were afraid of. She simply knew she didn't want it. She wanted to hide from it and let it pass her by, and locking the door was the only way she could ensure that happened.

But she couldn't move. Fear froze her muscles, and the burning in her stomach became a stabbing that was too great to bear. She collapsed back to her bed in defeat and clutched to the hope that, if she were quiet enough, she might remain unnoticed.

The shape was back on its feet again and was hurrying toward her room. Wendy could tell it was female by the tone of its gasps. Behind the shape followed a faint dragging sound, like a metal rod sliding across the floor. It came at regular intervals. Slowly, at first, and then it picked up speed and was accompanied by the unmistakable pound of a footfall.

Wendy tried to run to her door, but even though her adrenaline lit her veins like fire, giving her the shakes in her limbs and flutters in her stomach, the pain overpowered her again. She could not move when the dark shape crossed once more in front of her room and stopped at the door. The access hologram flashed from red to green and announced the *Atlas'* signature chirp. Daelen entered the room and quickly swiped her link and input a code to close and lock the door.

She backed away, clutching her own heaving chest, not even glancing at Wendy.

"Daelen?" Wendy whispered. "What's going on?"

Another shape appeared in front of the frosted glass. It lumbered and lurched, the slow and regular pound and drag growing louder. It released a deep sound somewhere between a moan and a growl, and Wendy did not think it sounded human.

The shape stopped at the door.

Wendy expected it to pound in frustration. She expected an angry cry. Instead, she heard a sliding sound as the shape ran its hands over the metal door, searching for a way to open it.

They knew that, unless it possessed incredible strength, it would not be able to get through. The door was not a bulkhead or hatch. It would not withstand depressurization. However, it was still a metal plate running into a metal frame. They found relief in that.

Their regaining sense of security waned as the shape's hands moved outward around the door, scratching the frosted glass, its nails leaving red streaks.

Glass was not as strong.

It lowered its arms to its sides and stood silently outside the door for such a time that Wendy and Daelen wondered if it had disappeared. The streaks of blood collected and ran. A moment passed, and they heard its feet shuffle and begin its pound and drag once again. It crept away, and neither of them moved until they heard a far-off scream outside medical, audible through the ship's vents and pipes.

Daelen refused to take her eyes off the locked door as if it might open and let the thing in if she turned.

"What was that?" Wendy whispered

Either because of the shock or because she didn't know how to answer, Daelen didn't make a sound.

Eight

On the bridge, no one would shut up.

Pierce stood at his platform leaning upon his railing, his fingers rubbing his forehead, desperately digging for relief. Voices all around him called out status reports. The department heads shouted information to each other, a stamp of urgency accompanying everything. Problems needed solutions, and Pierce grew tired of answering obvious queries. He needed his crew to take off its training wheels. He needed them to use their common sense. He needed them to give him time to think.

"Sir," Evans said. "Cargo bay quarantine is already requesting provisions. Food and water."

"They're going to have to wait," Pierce said. Something was building within him like seismic activity before a volcanic eruption.

"What should I tell them, sir?"

"Dammit, Cooper! I don't care what you tell them! Just shut them up!"

The cacophony of voices silenced. All the personnel on the command deck stopped what they were doing and looked at him. Instead of feeling relieved, he felt shame. He'd forgotten his own first lesson of dealing with crises. He'd lost his cool.

And he realized he'd been selfish. Like every truth he would never speak of, he realized he wanted them to figure things out on their own so he could have the time to worry about Emra. Anxiousness was like grief in that something inside him wanted it to surface. And as they drew nearer to her, it became more powerful. Work helped to push it down, but eventually, it would have to come up.

"I'm sorry, Mr. Evans," Pierce said, standing upright and straightening his overcoat. "That was uncalled for."

Evans silently accepted the apology with a nod. To do any more would have been disrespectful. After all, Pierce was his captain. He didn't need to apologize to anyone for anything. He did what he wanted and felt was necessary, and Evans trusted his judgment. Although, Evans respected Pierce's humility. It was important for leaders to be right, but it was more important that they knew when they were wrong.

"Sir, quarantine procedures are almost complete," Evans said. "What do we do now?"

"Now?" Pierce said. "Now, we wait."

Nine

Several hundred crew, including Carter Raines and the rest of the water plant crew, were unlucky enough to be assigned to cargo bay quarantine, where so many cranes had been inoperable for the pickup that the bay had been rendered useless. The Pandora Protocol found a use for that space. Anyone who couldn't be quarantined elsewhere was stored there. Trams dropped them off at the nearest platform, and it took more than an hour to feed them all through the tight corridors, down the ramps, and into the belly of the *Atlas*.

Security Officer Desmond Brannigan thought they seemed relieved to enter such an open area after the tightness of the *Atlas*' hallways. It must have felt nice to be able to spread out and put some space between each other, get some elbow room as it were. Any good cheer disappeared, however, when they noticed the young security officer at the hatch door, barring their exit with his rifle, waiting for the last of the crew to make it through so he could lock them in. His grip on his weapon was awkward, but the mere sight of it was enough.

Carter didn't mind the rifle, and the shock of being forced to be near so many people at once had long since passed. He was beyond it and into something else, something primal. He could feel it surging through his veins, throbbing in his head.

It had started when Stellan had told him they would have to leave their solitude. When the news reached his ears, his breathing picked up until he thought his lungs might burst. Since then, he hadn't been able to catch his breath or slow his heart, but it wasn't debilitating. He actually felt empowered.

Everything angered him. The way other people looked angered him. The sounds they made, the way they moved. He wanted them to shut up. He wanted to shut them up.

Oddly, he could sense that same hostility in some of the others. He could tell by the way they looked; their brows pressed together like molded clay, and their faces flushed red as if their blood boiled. He felt a kinship to those people. They understood his mounting rage; they were united.

Out of a murmuring, aimless crowd, Tram Operator Nathan Philips approached Carter. His eyes indicated he was looking for someone to latch onto, someone to console him in his confusion. Carter did not want to be that person.

"Crazy, eh?" Nathan said, his voice ramming spikes into Carter's ears.

"Yeah," Carter grunted.

"A few people party a little too hard. Security freaks. A few bad apples ruin it for everyone."

Carter thought Nathan was ruining whatever serenity he had left.

"You're one of them hermits, right? You live and work in the water plant?"

Carter nodded.

"I always wanted to see the inside of that place," Nathan said. "Still, I never envied you guys up there, shut away from everything. That is, until recently with all the crazy shit that has been going on. I guess we end up in the same place anyway. If you aren't one of them, you're one of us."

Carter resented Nathan lumping them together like that. They weren't alike. They were nothing alike, and Nathan had no right to think they were. But he understood the sentiment that authority would never go away. They didn't want anarchy. They wanted peace, to be left alone, and even so deep in the black, it seemed they would never escape their oppressors.

Nathan continued to speak, and Carter pretended to listen. Although, he would have rather found a quiet corner to sit by himself. He understood that, in times like these, other people wanted the comfort of company, someone to talk and listen to. That wasn't him, and the fear and shock had built in him so much that he didn't feel like putting up with that anymore.

And Nathan just kept talking. The words he chose to use picked away at Carter's skull. Then it was the very sound of his voice, like driving nails into his brain. It built within him, and the more he held it back, the more it built until he knew he would explode.

By the time he let it out, the anger had moved beyond words. It exploded into action. Carter threw fists at Nathan. He threw feet, elbows, knees. Then, when Nathan was on the ground, Carter jumped on top of him and used his fingernails. Nothing registered in Carter's mind, not the blood, not the pain in his own hands, only the satisfaction and pleasure of shutting Nathan up. The man's cries for Carter to stop only made him hit, scratch, and tear harder. And finally, in an act he could not understand, as if something else drove him to do it, Carter bent and sank his teeth into Nathan's neck, tearing away a mouthful of flesh.

The taste of Nathan's blood registered in Carter's mind. He knew what it was, and he liked it. It felt right to destroy this man. It felt like he'd always wanted to do it, like all his life, this rage had built up, and he was finally setting it free. He let out all the hate for the New Earth Council. He

217

released his disdain for his ex-wife who left him and took their child. He set forth his contempt and revulsion of his father, who had abused him and his sister.

When Nathan was still, Carter couldn't stop. A woman's scream attracted his attention, and he jumped onto her, tearing at her clothes and into her flesh. A man tried to pull Carter off, and he bit the man's arm so hard the bone broke.

In moments, Carter's rage downed three people. He was on another when a deafening gunshot stopped the crowd, and he felt a white-hot burning in his chest. Darkness followed as he crumpled and lay still on the cold deck of the cargo bay.

"See?" said Security Officer Andrew Reynolds to Desmond Brannigan. "Easy peasy." The excitement in Andrew's voice disturbed Desmond. Neither of them was exactly comfortable with their weapons, but Andrew had just ended a man's life. And he had enjoyed it.

Feeling saved, some of the crew moved to aid the injured. Nathan Philips was bleeding out on the floor, and a woman removed and pressed her overcoat against his neck, sobbing as she stared into his wide eyes.

Andrew twirled the gun playfully in his hand. He felt powerful. Killing a madman and saving everyone gave him a rush, but one of the injured saw him waving the gun and shrieked. He put out his hand to reassure them it was okay, that he had the situation under control. One of the injured stood with a fiery rage in his eyes like Carter's. His attendants, who only moments ago showed great concern for his wellbeing, backed away. The man tackled Andrew, latching onto his back like a monkey.

The madness spread almost as quickly as the panic, which overtook the crowd, and several hundred of them raced toward the hatch door Desmond guarded. A window expanded from Desmond's link.

"This is the Captain," Pierce said over the comms. "Close that hatch, son."

Desmond couldn't. He knew the finality of it. He knew that, when he closed the hatch, it wouldn't open again until the quarantine was lifted, if ever.

"Andy!" Desmond screamed. "Come on!" Andrew spun with the man mounted on his back, biting into his shoulder. Several others swarmed around him, and then Andrew disappeared into a flood of flailing bodies.

Desmond pulled his rifle to his shoulder, his uncertain hands shaking, and the approaching crowd slowed.

"Don't you do it, Desmond!" Stellan broke in over the comms. "I'm almost there."

"Stellan, get off this line," Pierce said. "Close that door, or we could lose the whole ship!"

"Andrew! Come on! Get out of there!"

Behind the flood of people circling Andrew, blood sprayed into the air as more of the madmen tore into others. Andrew didn't know where all these mad people were coming from. Then he saw Carter back on his feet, blood still flowing from the gaping wound in his neck, using the last ounce of his lifeforce to tear into a woman who was fleeing for her life.

The madness was spreading. The people falling to it succumbed to its control.

In the confusion, no one knew what was happening, and one man figured risking that Desmond wouldn't pull the trigger was better than waiting for certain attack. He ran toward the door. Another followed. Two more joined in, and then they all came rushing toward Desmond, who knew they would not stop.

He debated opening fire and even began to squeeze the trigger only to find he could not do it. He could not take a life. However, when faced with the choice between leaving his friend and succumbing to the crowd of frantic people rushing him, he closed and locked the door, telling himself it was to save the rest of the ship from this breach. It was different than pulling a trigger. It was so others may have a chance.

Through the bulkhead, he felt the wave of bodies collide with the door. He wondered if the hatch would hold.

Pierce's consolations and commendations came through the comm system but did not reach Desmond's ears. He could only watch as people pleaded with him through the porthole window.

A moment later, Stellan appeared. "Out of the way!"

Desmond stepped aside. "I had to! Chief, I'm sorry! I had to!"

Stellan tried to open the door with his link, and the holographic lock would not disengage. He tried to pull it open, and it would not budge. It was the first time on the *Atlas* that he could not access something.

Through the porthole window, he saw the horrified eyes of fellow crew, pleading for their lives, and behind them, arterial sprays launched into the air like geysers. He could see the wave of madness approach them from behind, but it clearly had not reached them. He knew the look of the madness as it stared back at him through holding cells, and these people did not have that murderous gaze. He saw only hope and fear, a desire to simply be given a chance.

"Pierce!" Stellan called. "Open the door!"

"We can't risk it. I'm sorry."

"They're getting torn up! I can help them!"

"You wouldn't know who to save and who to put down."

On the bridge, Pierce thought about acceptable losses. In a time of war, he and his men often joked about being expendable. Ironically, it wouldn't have been funny if it weren't true. The laughter made it easier to cope, to bolster their spirits as if they could demoralize death like the enemy. But when it came down to it, they were resources to leadership, and every man had a price tag. Men could be bought, but they also could be sold if the mission was worth it.

Numbers. When they were soldiers, that's all they were.

Pierce began to understand the coldness of the calculation. Faced with the reality of the situation, he thought about the purpose of the Pandora Protocol. With such a sledgehammer approach to quarantine, they hadn't admitted to themselves they were mingling uninfected people with infected people, and they would have to lose some to save the rest.

When you led, it was about the numbers.

But he couldn't let people in cargo bay seventeen suffer. He couldn't let his men watch the crew get slaughtered by madmen that killed and no doubt spread the madness to them all. Daelen had said it spread through body fluid contact and even could be transmitted through bites. The mad did a lot of that in their thrashing, relentless assaults.

"Ready the fire-stop system," Pierce said.

"Sir?" Evans said.

"No!" Stellan cried. "Open the door!"

"We have to consider them all a loss now," Pierce said. "They've all been exposed."

"No!"

Evans hesitated. He reached out to his holographic interface and froze. Pierce walked down the ramp to Evans' station, steadying the boy's hand with his own.

"It's okay, son," Pierce said. "It has to be done."

Pierce called up the window on Evans' terminal and entered the command himself.

If a soul be damned, he thought, *let it be mine.* He concentrated on Evans' eyes, and he wanted this boy to have a chance. He wanted them all to have a chance, and it was tragic that some had to pay for that.

Pierce forced himself to watch as the fire-stop system sucked the air out of cargo bay seventeen. In moments, they fell down weakly. They moved slowly, gasping, flopping, twitching, one by one becoming still and quiet.

Ten

As Stellan charged toward the command deck, his anger temporarily cleared, and he experienced a moment of perfect clarity. The hallways folded in on themselves, and Doug's labored attempts to appeal to Stellan's sense of reason silenced. In the darkness of Stellan's mind, there were only three residents: Stellan, his instinct, and the innocent boy.

For the first time in as long as he could remember, these three sides of his persona aligned. There was no conflicting guilt, as he'd done everything he could. His compassion, the mechanism that made him a killer, and the boy that split these two sides and continued to haunt him all agreed that what Pierce ordered had been murder. They had other options, and they should have turned to them. They should have tried to save everyone they could.

The clarity faded, though, with the thought of Daelen. Unlike every conflict he'd been involved with, he had an investment. Daelen. Her life was in danger, and Stellan realized it wasn't about seeing the individual or seeing the crowd. Lives, indeed, had worth, and Daelen was worth everything to him. If things got any worse, he'd have to adjust his thinking. He'd have to do what it took to protect her.

The lives of the crew in cargo bay seventeen had been out of his hands. He couldn't bear the thought that Daelen's life could be out of his hands.

Pierce had to answer for his crime, and perhaps Stellan could regain some control. His one consolation was that Daelen was safe in medical, away from all of this madness. Knowing that was the only way he could focus on saving the *Atlas*.

"Wait up, Chief!" Doug huffed. He'd followed Stellan to the cargo bay in hopes he could help. Now, he followed in hopes he could talk sense into Stellan.

"Pierce had to do it," Doug said. "They were getting torn up in there. It was mercy."

"For the ones we'd lost," Stellan said. "Hundreds of others? He killed them."

At the central lift, there was an awkward current between them as Stellan wasn't sure whether Doug followed in support or to rush to Pierce's aid. The doors to the lift opened, and they boarded.

"You shouldn't be doing this now," Doug said.

"Are you going to stop me?"

Doug knew he couldn't if he tried. "No."

"So what are you going to do, Doug?"

"You aren't thinking straight."

Stellan laughed at the thought of Doug being a beacon of rationality.

"I'm serious, Stel. With everything that's happened, you haven't had time to grieve or anything. Are you sure you want to do this?"

Stellan's eyes narrowed. "Do what?"

"Go against the captain. Mutiny. Don't worry about what I'm going to do. Worry about what you're going to do. I just want to keep the peace. Keep us all on the same team. This only leads one way."

"There's no such thing as peace," Stellan said.

The lift stopped, and the doors parted onto the command deck. The frantic tapping of the department heads on their glass keyboards stopped, and they craned their heads in dismay.

"And we haven't all been on the same team for a while now."

Stellan marched down the command corridor toward the bridge, where Pierce stood like a monolith at his platform. The sight of him made the fire in Stellan's stomach rage. It burned in the back of his throat.

Doug lumbered behind him. He could feel the eyes of the department heads lingering.

Pierce stood his ground as Stellan marched closer. Pierce's solid stone face gave nothing away, and Stellan's eyes burned. Some kind of energy sparked between them as the on-looking crew willed them to stay away from each other. Pierce's face changed when he realized Stellan was not stopping. It became a surprised, dumbfounded look that shattered when Stellan's fist connected with the bony line of his jaw.

Doug tried his best to restrain Stellan. In seconds, Arlo was on his feet and there to break it up. None of that mattered because Pierce showed no will to fight even as Stellan tried to break from Doug's hold and hit him again.

"I know you're angry," Pierce said, wiping his mouth and rubbing his jaw. "We did what we had to do."

"No!" Stellan screamed. "It didn't have to go like that!"

"I made the call!" Pierce said. "Would you rather I let you in there to join them in quarantine?"

"They weren't soldiers! They didn't sign up for this! They were innocent people who deserved a chance!"

"Everyone deserves a chance," Pierce said. "Can you give it to them?"

"How do you know I'm not sick? How do you know *you're* not sick?"

"If we are, we all are, and we're all dead anyway," Pierce said. "Someone had to make the call. And goddammit, I'd do it again if I had to! Anything to save as many as I can."

"We owed it to them to try! We owed it to ourselves to try!" Stellan said, finally shaking Doug's arms off. Doug reached for him again, but Stellan showed no desire to continue his attack. The time for throwing fists had passed.

"What if you'd failed? What if you'd gone in there and the quarantine failed and it got out? You would have given your life for nothing. As much as you seem to want to do that, what then? What about the rest who deserve a chance? What about Daelen?" Pierce asked.

"Don't you dare!" Stellan said, again reaching for Pierce. Arlo and Doug struggled to hold him back.

"I know you won't let this go, Stellan, and that's fine," Pierce said. "In time, you'll see it clearly. I know that, too. For now, do your duty, and go with Officer Fowler into holding. You've been through a lot. Cool off. We'll get you if we need you."

Stellan shook Doug and Arlo off. "This won't work. No one's going to make it. We're all going to die."

223

"Get him out of here!" Pierce said, and Stellan went willingly.

Eleven

The *Atlas* shuddered, and the light drive's drone wound down into a silence that left an absence in their bodies like a destructive addiction that was no longer sated. They noticed it instantly, and while their minds cleared, a part of them wanted it back.

For the time, the light drive had fulfilled its duty and would rest. The run junkies, the *Atlas*' crew who lived in that space between worlds, would have to wait. They had returned to the *Shiva*.

Pierce leaned on his railing, set on his platform above the crew, weary and haggard like a tired watchman. Though he had no cue from the sun, no regular cycle of daylight, his body knew the hour was late and that it was overdue for a sleep cycle. It had been a long time since he last slept after leaving the *Shiva*, and even then, he had not slept well, wracked with worry over the accident, the planet and its precious cargo, and Emra.

Most of all, he worried about her, his last bastion before total obscurity. He looked forward to the few days he was able to spend with her each month because she didn't look at him like everyone else looked at him. She admired and respected him, but she felt those emotions as an equal. She was the only person he could connect with. She was the only person in the universe he could allow himself to be vulnerable with.

Even through all that had transpired on the *Atlas*, the deaths of his crew and the pursuing madness, his mind dwelled on her. For a moment, he wondered if the exhaustion had affected his judgment. He wondered if the desire to bury his face in her warm chest made him selfishly endanger the lives of his crew. He wondered if the way he justified his decisions to himself, that the sum was greater than the parts, that some would need to be sacrificed to save the rest, was all so he could see her again and to just ensure she was okay.

Perhaps that was true, but the fact remained that he was saving more lives by allowing some to perish. Letting go, as it was, never troubled Pierce when he thought of it in this light, focusing on the good. Yet, it concerned him that, if he pulled his scope out far enough, even letting them all die was preferable to allowing the epidemic that plagued his ship to reach New Earth. Of that much, regardless of his emotions, he knew he'd done right, and his conscience was clear.

"Sir," Navigator Evans said. "The *Atlas* is showing substantially more debris than before. I'm not sure we can squeeze through."

"Arlo?" Pierce said. His pilot bit his lip and gazed nervously at the proximity readout interface before him.

"All stop," Pierce said. "On screen."

The *Atlas* placed an image of what lay in front of them, and it made Pierce stand at attention, fully awakened in every meaning of the word. Exhaustion no longer buzzed in his mind. All he felt was loss and heartache.

The *Shiva of the Trinity* lay burning on the face of the Apophis planet, its arms wrapped around the celestial body's surface in a lover's embrace. Pierce's command for all stop suddenly held more meaning, as no one on the bridge moved or spoke.

Time dilated in a way Pierce had never experienced before as he struggled to comprehend the meaning of what he saw. It takes the tenacious mind time to recover when it sees something that is contrary to what it believes absolutely. For a moment, the expectation or prediction of what it might see overlaps what it actually sees, and the resulting paradox leads to physical pain as the brain dumps a cocktail of emotions into the body.

"No," Pierce said, his eyes refusing to blink for fear that closing might be a kind of finality, that in that split second of darkness, his brain would process and accept what he saw.

Someone on the bridge gasped. Another cried. Most stayed silent. The destroyer of worlds had taken its last life: its own.

As he began to admit the reality of what he saw, Pierce could look upon it no more, and he had to see something, anything other than the screen.

"Sir," Evans said. "I'm picking up a beacon in the debris field." Pierce's stomach fluttered with the hope that it was a lifeboat, a chance that she could still be alive.

"The prefix in the signature reads as a comms buoy," Evans said. No life forms. Comms buoys were used to relay or leave messages. This one would tell the *Shiva's* final tale. It would be its crew's collective epitaph.

"Let's hear it," Pierce whispered. Evans instructed the *Atlas* to play the message.

225

In place of the image of the *Shiva's* wreckage, a video of Commander Ashland's face appeared. She looked harder than the last time they'd seen her, and her blue eyes peered at them ghostly, almost transparent. Behind her hung pictures on the wall that Pierce recognized: her grandchildren running in a field of tall grass, another picture of them with their parents: Ines, Emra's daughter, and Ethan, Ines' husband. Pierce was the only one who knew what they meant to her, and he was the only one who knew they were the reason Commander Ashland had committed herself to the space mining program so entirely on an excavator, isolating herself in oblivion. They had all died in an accident years ago, and like so many on the *Atlas* would have understood, she had used service to NESMA as a way to create a junction in her timeline, to effectively start a new life.

The pictures placed her at her desk in her cabin when she recorded the message.

She spoke: "This is Commander Emra Ashland of the NESMA excavator *Shiva of the Trinity*. We have failed. This message is a warning. Beware this place.

"Several weeks ago, we arrived at Apophis 259 and, as instructed, immediately began digging for the layer beneath the crust, which was an unidentified material. We refined, processed, and packaged it per established procedure, and by all accounts, this crew performed exceptionally. Something went wrong. I don't know where it started. My crew began to act strangely. We thought it was the black madness. We thought being so deep in the black and spending so much time in FTL was playing tricks with our minds. The death of my senior engineer was sobering. Others died of bizarre circumstances, and violence broke out all over the ship. We barely had enough unaffected people to hold it together.

"That's when the *Atlas* showed up to make its pickup. During transfer, there was an incident, and two of my men were exposed to direct contact with the material, in direct violation of containment code article 252.59. Against my better judgment, I allowed a third man, from the *Atlas*, to be brought back to be treated aboard his home ship. I know now how grave a mistake that was.

"When my men awoke hours later, they seemed fine. Healthy. But they descended quickly into madness. We tried to restrain them, but they attacked several other crew before we could subdue them. One was killed in the struggle.

"The crew they attacked also began to display signs of madness, and several hours later, the man that was killed emerged from the morgue, attacking everyone in sight. We barely managed to control that situation. We wouldn't be so lucky again.

"The ones he attacked, if they didn't die immediately, died within hours. A fever accompanied their dementia, and eventually, death. They, too, rose from the dead. I've personally observed instances of this, and as a result, we've lost control of this ship. Even the extra security forces we borrowed from the *Atlas* only staved off the inevitable.

"This plague or curse, whatever it is, we couldn't stop it, and it can't be allowed off this ship. It can't be given the chance to get back to New Earth. So I'm going to take the *Shiva* into what remains of the Apophis planet, killing all aboard. If you find this message and find my ship still in orbit of the Apophis planet, you'll know I have failed, and I beg you to put this crew out of its misery. If I succeed, that hopefully won't be necessary. To be sure, burn this place.

"There is one loose end that is beyond my reach. The carrier *Atlas* was almost filled to capacity with this material. That it is the cause of our blight, I have no doubt.

"Gordon, if you are the one to find this, I am sorry. All I have left is hope that you won't have to do what I must do, but I have to order you to destroy your ship, its contents, and all the crew if you cannot ensure the safety of New Earth. Nothing is more important. This thing kills humanity, the good with the bad, everything that makes us what we are.

"My only regret is the time we shared was limited. I know you will do what is necessary."

Outside the vantage point of the video message recorder, pounding, gunfire, and distant screams distracted Ashland. She regarded the sounds with indifference. If her concern escalated, she didn't show it.

She fixed her eyes deliberately in the center of the screen.

"I love you, Gordon," Emra said. She then reached down into a drawer in her desk and removed a handgun. Placing it on the table, she stood, reached behind the camera, and the message ended. The image on the screen cut to black, and then the *Atlas* display faded into the burning wreckage of the *Shiva*.

Ashland had succeeded, and now it was Pierce's turn to do his duty. He wasn't ready to execute that order yet, however. Returning to the *Shiva* was isolation in itself, and they had bought some time.

Pierce walked toward the lift at the back of the bridge. "Get that shit off my ship."

"Sir?" Evans said timidly. "If we open one, we open all."

"They're gone now, and there's nothing we can do for them," Pierce said. "We're not giving up on everyone else. Not yet."

As Pierce walked toward the lift, he knew more than anyone the urgency of their situation. He knew he must be strong, and he knew all of their lives depended on his leadership, but he needed to do something before executing his final options. Before he could be strong, he needed to feel vulnerable again, even if it would be for the last time.

He remembered, in his desk drawer, beneath some pictures of his daughter at a young age, some medals, and a certificate of honorable discharge from the Unity Corps, his sidearm, which was very much like the one issued to Emra, lay in an oak box. He had no doubt anymore that he would need it.

Twelve

Pilot Arlo Stone and Navigator Cooper Evans watched the surveillance feed from cargo bay seventeen on the holographic wall of the bridge. The bodies lying on the floor said nothing, but in a way, the dead spoke to them. And they listened. Out of respect, neither of them wanted to disturb the silence.

It wasn't long, though, before the bodies began to move.

Carter was the first to reanimate, and Arlo and Evans couldn't believe it. Even when Carter stood on the very floor he painted red, they didn't believe it.

"Holy shit!" Arlo said. "Are you seeing this? Am *I* seeing this!?"

Carter slowly rose and then looked around like he wasn't aware of his surroundings.

"How is he still alive?" Evans asked.

"He can't be," Arlo said. "He's got a fucking hole in his chest the size of my fist, and there's no oxygen in the entire bay." Arlo looked at Evans. "There's no oxygen in that bay, right?"

Evans moved some application windows around on his terminal. "Right."

Carter swayed side to side in a lonely dance. His jaw opened and closed absently, mouthing the words to some song they couldn't hear, and they wondered if there was something in that place where Carter existed, a world between theirs and the next.

"Is this what someone stuck in purgatory looks like?" Evans asked.

"I don't think so," Arlo said with a grimace. "That's not Carter. He's long gone."

"If that's not Carter, who is he?"

"I don't even think it's human."

The idea that the thing they were seeing was no longer a man had not crossed Evans' mind. When he looked closer, into the thing's eyes, he wondered if the body was simply a vehicle. The man they knew was gone. He had no doubt about that, but there was something behind those eyes, an emptiness, like the blackness of space.

In the vacant stare of the man that was Carter Raines, something remained behind the wheel. Something drove the limbs that were once under the power of a reasonable, logical man, but as Evans watched Carter and considered the things he'd seen this thing do, he knew it lacked reason and logic.

More than anything, however, Carter now lacked the restraint of conscience and awareness, of empathy and sympathy. The void in those parts of his being released his body to commit the acts they'd seen on the surveillance feed. Evans didn't think a human being would ever be able to do what Carter had done relentlessly, and he realized what made a being human was what had been purged from Carter's mind. He now was just a being, and Evans resented it for even appearing human.

"Commander Ashland said people went mad before they became like this. She said the bites changed them. What do you think it wants?" Evans asked.

"It's trying to survive, I think," Arlo said. "People get bit and then become like him. I think it's trying to spread."

"I keep thinking," Evans said, "what if this is it? What if we're sick and don't even know it, and what if this is all in our minds?"

"You're not sick."

"How do you *know*?"

They couldn't take their eyes off the screen. The fact that Carter moved but didn't move, an aimless wandering of body parts, hypnotized them, and then movement elsewhere caught their attention. The flick of a wrist. The twitch of a foot. The curl of a finger.

"Did you see that?" Evans pointed at the screen.

"I don't know," Arlo said.

Then, they could not mistake the movement of an arm reaching out from under a pile of bodies and digging its fingernails into the deck floor. A leg bent and worked its knee to the floor for support. Some of the dead, the ones attacked by the madness, began to rise. Some slithered out from under other bodies. Others trembled clumsily like children learning to walk, unsure of their appendages. A few stumbled. Once they were fully upright, they each looked around like amnesiacs, having no memory of where they were. And then they joined Carter in his unpredictable swaying. All the while, Carter didn't even notice.

"They're alive!" Evans shouted.

"No," Arlo said. "They're not. They're like Carter."

"How do you know!? I mean, how can you be sure?"

"He isn't tearing them apart."

Evans' hope vanished when he realized Arlo was right. Even though he knew it in his heart, Evans refused to believe it until he looked into their eyes and saw what he had seen in Carter's eyes. The nothingness prevailed, their humanity extinguished.

"Promise me something, Arlo," Evans said. He moved some files around on his workstation and then swiped his hand across the interface and confirmed that the *Atlas* had begun to depressurize the cargo bays one by one. The artificial gravity system deactivated, and the dead who had risen floated in the cargo bay along with the dead who would not return. They kicked and swung their arms, feebly struggling to regain their footing. That much, Evans thought, survived in them. The inclination to maintain balance was innate in the human vehicle they now drove.

"What's that, Coop?"

"If that happens to me," Evans said, "I don't want to hurt anyone. Promise me you'll put a bullet in my brain."

Evans pressed the command on his terminal to open the cargo bay doors and jettison the load. Arlo's terminal prompted him to confirm. He removed his cap and rubbed the top of his balding head, the finality of it almost too much to bear.

"I don't think you'll have to worry about that," Arlo said. "One way or the other, the captain's going to have that under control."

Arlo pressed the command to confirm, and they watched in silence as the *Atlas'* cargo bays opened wide, the ship unzipping a coat and exposing itself to the vacuum of space. The floor of the cargo deck, the very underbelly of the ship, slid away, and their cargo drifted down and out as the ship pulled away from that which was not attached to it. Amid the scattering payload, the dead drifted into space. Some of the crates carrying the Apophis material knocked together and smashed some of those intermingling bodies.

Arlo and Evans gaped in disbelief as the reanimated dead continued to kick and swing their arms without concern, still unaware of what was happening to them as the deep freeze of space halted their limbs and the knocking payload shattered their frozen bodies, like the hands of an invisible alien giant crushing the monsters it had created.

Thirteen

It hurt.

In Pierce's quarters, everything hurt. In his head, he hurt. He hurt in his heart and in his stomach. Deep down, in what he knew was his soul, he hurt.

The pain was what convinced him he was not evil.

Pierce sat at his desk, rolling a glass of whiskey across his forehead. His terminal played back the message Emra left in the beacon, and the meaning of it left him in despair. It wasn't the sight of the *Shiva* burning on the surface of the planet. The source of his sadness was the realization that everything she'd done would create her legacy, and that was all that existed of her now. He'd lost many men in combat and knew many of them well. He'd made peace with even his own inevitable death. But he couldn't handle the thought of Emra existing only in memory. She existed now merely as a piece of public record, and he wondered if maybe the senselessness of it was what made it difficult. The most beloved person to him had died for nothing. At least, when he believed in the righteousness of killing to make a better world, he thought his men died for a cause.

Pierce began to weep for the first time in as long as he could remember. He allowed himself to shed tears because he knew it might be the last opportunity he had.

The tears provided some respite, physical confirmation of his guilt, and he thought that, if he felt guilt, real physical pain, for the lives he'd sacrificed in hopes that others might live, he could not be evil. Could he?

After all, what was the nature of evil? How did it occur naturally? As in all things, the illusion humans constructed was that mankind created it. Mankind wanted to believe in a perfect world without it, where warmth came from fire that would not consume, where the lion would be beautiful without feeding. However, the king of the jungle was a predator. Evil was necessary for balance.

He considered the nature of sacrifice. Was it nobler to give your life or your soul so that others may have a chance?

When his tears cleared, it occurred to him that Emra had said something that rang his old soldier's bell. It couldn't be allowed to reach New Earth. Nothing was more important. Her death and the deaths of her crew were for a cause, and it was to protect innocence.

Suddenly, her death made sense. He began to accept it not because he had to, but because he'd understood it in terms to which he could relate.

Her death had been necessary for the greater good.

There was no such thing as a perfect resolution. Only perfect resolve to make things as right as possible, to do what was necessary to see through good and evil, right and wrong, and to remove the chains of morality, to accept that someone had to be the bad guy because sometimes it took a bad guy to move forward or prevent an even greater disaster.

Sometimes, people just had to die, and it wasn't about simplicity. It was about efficiency. When the ends were worth it, the means were irrelevant.

The door to Pierce's quarters scuffed, and Pierce stood up purely on instinct and reflex, flicking off his sidearm's safety and chambering a round.

Agent Adelynn Skinner peered around the corner from the foyer into his office. He couldn't help but appear shocked. As she'd expected, while the crisis on the *Atlas* elevated, he'd forgotten all about her.

"Where have you been?" he asked.

"Around," she said, stepping carefully through the doorway into the room. She flashed her green eye at him, a warning, and proceeded to move toward him. Pierce felt frozen.

"I know," she said. "About your loss. I know how deep it cuts, deeper than Commander Ashland. You've taken a wound you'll never recover from, and I know how that feels."

"You do," Pierce said. "You're too damn young for it. We're all too damn young."

She smiled and sauntered around his desk. She touched his shoulder and leaned close to his ear.

"You did the right thing," she said in her best consoling voice, which would have sounded alien to anyone else. "You did what had to be done."

Pierce trembled. Not because she told him anything revolting. He trembled because she was right.

"I always knew you were disappointed," Adelynn said. "With all your strict lessons, you really only taught me one thing. No one likes change, and everyone will hate the one who changes everything. That hate will blind them to the fact that the changes are for the better. One day, they will see."

She leaned in closer and then wrapped her arms around his broad shoulders. He did not return the embrace.

"I was never disappointed, Addie," Pierce said. "Life is confusing, and if anything, I was proud of your strength to choose a path. Being a parent means accepting the child you have raised, not the person you hoped he or she would become."

Pierce felt her smile as she rested her head on his shoulder.

"We can't ever stop hoping," Pierce said. "That's why I hope you can forgive me."

"For what?"

He wrapped his arm around her waist, and the tightness of his grip alarmed her.

"At first, I deluded myself into believing you wouldn't lie, not to me. Now I know I lacked the clarity to see what I had to do, not for good or evil, but with the hopes that someday, it would be right."

She raised her eyes to meet his.

"I know now why you're here," he said, "and I can't let you do it."

Pierce placed the barrel of his sidearm to Adelynn's abdomen, and she did not fight back.

Her body muffled the gunshot, and he heard the spray from the exit wound splash against the wall. Her knees weakened, and her body trembled. Slowly, she fell to the floor, and he let her go.

Pierce didn't look back as he left his cabin. If he had, it would have been the end of him. He wouldn't have been able to handle it. Instead, he focused on what was necessary. Even as he closed the door and she spoke, he was too focused on moving forward to hear it.

"It's already done," she said.

Fourteen

Pierce descended in the lift. He didn't think about the past. He didn't have time for reflection. Harder times lay ahead, but he knew they'd get through them. They just had to keep moving their feet and pushing forward. They couldn't let anything get in their way.

The lights flickered, and the lift stuttered and stopped. The holographic control panel changed to solid blue.

"What the hell?" Pierce said. A moment later, the control panel returned to its familiar command display. Pierce pressed the button for the command deck, and the lift continued its descent.

When the doors parted, Pierce jumped forward out of the lift. The sounds of his footfalls had no effect on the department heads, who frantically worked at their stations, some of them crying out in frustration.

He passed them and walked straight to his command platform. "What the hell just happened?"

"Network's down," Arlo said.

"What!?" Pierce said. "How in the hell did that happen?"

"No idea. It's supposed to have redundancies out the blowhole, but it's crashed."

"Do we have maneuverability?"

"Yes," Evans said. "All the systems work independently, but they no longer have the ability to communicate with each other. Integration is lost without the network. File access is gone. Comms are down, too."

"Yeah, yeah," Arlo said. "Thrusters are responding. IR's good. EM shield's holding. Proximity systems are still online. All that is just gravy. Tell him the bad news."

Pierce's increasingly worried eyes darted between his control team.

"In the event of a network failure or disconnection, for safety reasons, any affected equipment returns to its default state," Evans said.

"English, Cooper," Pierce demanded.

"Quarantine has been lifted throughout the entire ship," Arlo said. "We can't reinforce it from here."

Throughout the *Atlas*, hatch wheels turned and released a flood of bodies.

Fifteen

When you fail the man whom you respect absolutely but to whom you've never adequately conveyed that respect, what do you say? If you're Douglas Fowler, a large dam of a man whom many avoided out of fear and, therefore, ignored, how could you put a positive spin on arresting the only good man you've ever known, the only man with relentless good intentions, the only man who ever gave you a chance?

Doug couldn't. There was no way to bring light to such a dark situation. Even if he had the words, they would be inadequate. He felt hopeless because he was not a freethinking man. He did as he was told. He followed orders.

Stellan told him it was all right, that he understood all too well the chain of command, and Doug felt it was okay.

Still, he wished he didn't have to do it, and then it occurred to him that he didn't. He had a choice. He looked at the cuffs around Stellan's wrists and wondered about the chances of a mutiny with him because, if it were unsuccessful, he might regret it. Furthermore, it could just be a waste of time. It could cost lives, if not the entire ship.

And, as if Stellan could read Doug's mind, he said that it was not a good idea. The crew was more important, and putting him away would make things easier. He told Doug that he was counting on him, and Doug swelled with a pride he'd never known.

That was when the madmen set on him. He heard them, echoing through the corridors, their position difficult to discern and pinpoint. The moans and growls rose from the belly of the *Atlas*. Shadows danced on the walls in the irregular light, which hadn't been the same since that blackout moments ago.

Finally, he saw them, and the choice was made for him. Their pace slowed when they found him. He could tell they were evaluating him, trying to work things out in their minds. It bothered him that he wouldn't be able to claim the nobility of standing up for what he believed was right. He wouldn't be able to share in that glory and respect he'd earned through sacrifice. Doug released Stellan not because Doug was as good of a man as he. He released him now because he needed him to have his weapon in his hand. Doug needed Stellan to save his life.

What was really messed up about it was, on some level, Doug resented him for it.

CHAPTER 9
THE HUNT, THE KILL, AND THE EXECUTION

One

Stellan grew up in the Appalachian Mountains of the Mid-Atlantic, District of America, part of the former United States of America, a country that global unity had dismantled. Although, some said the spirit of that once-great nation had long since died, one of the last inevitable cornerstones to fall and give way to the New Earth Council.

When Stellan was a boy, there were still stretches of land in those mountains where people lived away from civilization by their own rules, independents that the Council allowed to exist. The New Earth Registration Act changed all of that, and some said it birthed the revolution.

For a time, Stellan knew nothing of politics or corruption. All he knew of the New Earth Council was that, while it could reach out and take them if it wanted, it seemed satisfied to let them be. He experienced pure, unbridled freedom. Maybe that was why he later sought out life on the *Atlas*.

Freedom didn't come without a price, though. Life was simpler in those hills, but in some ways, it was more complicated. While other children learned about base ten mathematics, how to work around Einstein's laws of relativity, and the subtleties of sociopolitical interaction, Stellan's family hunted for its own food.

He would never forget killing his first deer, how eager he was to contribute, to make his father proud, but sentimentality did not burn it into his memory. Horror did.

At the age of thirteen, Stellan had more experience with firearms than most people ever had in their lives. He had never fired at a living target, though. His father only let him shoot at painted bales of hay and stacks of wood. Learning to put the bullet where it needed to go was the most important part of shooting, he had told the boy. It was a responsibility. Stellan wouldn't be allowed to fire at a living animal until he could accurately place his shots, which was hard for a boy who struggled to hold the weight of his father's old-fashioned, bolt-action hunting rifles.

The morning he became a killer, the autumn sunshine poured through the treetops and spotlighted the grassy forest floor with golden rays, burning away the mist. The leaves had turned, but most still clung to the branches. They would fall soon, leaving little cover for hunters.

Stellan had grown up accompanying his father on hunts. He learned to appreciate the anticipation of the kill. The waiting had seemed uncomfortably indefinite, but as his mind matured, he began to understand that they weren't simply waiting for an opportunity to present itself. They had to be ready, and they had to recognize it when it was there. A large part of hunting was maintaining focus for long periods of time. Remaining still but in a state of readiness was hard, and it was something snipers trained years to master: the power of will and patience and having enough energy to focus it on the target at the right time.

It took Stellan a long time to master his attention span, and on the morning of his first kill, he had not yet mastered it. So, his father spotted the doe one hundred meters away before Stellan did.

Stellan's father placed an index finger over his lips and then pointed into the distance. Even though Stellan's eyes were young, they were not as well-trained as his father's, and he could not decipher the fawn fur through the turning foliage.

Stellan shook his head to indicate he could not see the deer. His father lifted his rifle and motioned for the boy to look down his scope. Stellan did as he was instructed.

He peered down the high-powered scope, scanning the edge of the tree line before the clearing. His crosshairs passed over a whipping tail, and Stellan followed the curvature of the animal's flank until she seemed to stare right back at him, as if she knew he was there.

"Let your weapon fall until it finds its target," Stellan's father whispered.

Stellan let the barrel of his rifle descend until it settled on the doe's chest. She looked in their direction, ears twitching. The wind blew through the trees like a sigh.

"Breathe," Stellan's father said.

Stellan breathed deep and then released the air through puckered lips. His heart slowed, and his body became still. His hands never felt so steady.

"Take your time," his father said. "You have all the time in the world. Imagine you're holding the bullet in your hand, and when you're ready, just let it go."

He listened for a lull in the wind to ensure minimal bullet trajectory variance. He smelled his father's chewing tobacco, the cordite on their hands, the conditioner on his weapon. Under his father's watchful gaze, Stellan thumbed the safety and curled his finger around the trigger. He heard the creak of their tree stand and the distant caw of a crow.

Peering down the scope, his whole world became the deer and the trigger. He squeezed gently and was surprised when the rifle stock recoiled against his shoulder. The gunshot rolled over the hills like the voice of God, speaking a language he was only just beginning to understand. That crow he'd heard took flight.

The space between the bullet leaving his weapon and entering his target felt like powerlessness. He battled doubt for just an instant.

The wind picked up through the trees again but, this time, stronger, more of an applause.

The doe fell to the ground in a fine red mist, and Stellan looked to his father with excitement. He'd never felt so proud of himself. The bullet had landed its mark, and he knew most men would not have been able to make that shot.

His father's gaze had lingered on the doe through a pair of binoculars. He did not smile. He lowered the binoculars and let them hang from his neck, looking at Stellan grimly.

"Good shot," he said.

They shouldered their rifles and climbed down from their tree stand. His father said nothing as they walked toward the doe. He made no effort to conceal their movement, snapping twigs underfoot, and Stellan didn't understand why. The gunshot would have spooked any other deer off, but he felt powerful enough that, if they saw another, he would shoot it, too. He wanted that chance.

When they emerged from the forest into the clearing, Stellan understood. He hadn't killed her. The bullet had penetrated her shoulder blade and was on track for her heart. It should have been a clean kill, but it ricocheted off of a bone and shot up through her spine. She had writhed while Stellan and his father walked from their tree stand.

She tried to drag her paralyzed hind legs, her front hooves proving ineffectual at grasping the damp soil. She trembled quietly. Sometimes deer cried out before they died. She did not.

Stellan raised his rifle again to finish it, but his father gently pushed the barrel downward.

"No. We will mount this one. Now watch and understand why discipline and accuracy are important. When you fire your weapon, you have to mean it. You have to kill with mercy."

She died in minutes. It felt like hours. The memory lasted a lifetime.

Two

Stellan watched the infected madmen bring Doug to the deck, tear into his flesh, bite his arms and legs, rip his uniform to shreds, and dance in his blood as if in celebration. He knew then that this thing, whatever it was that turned men and women into senseless animals, would make him choose between his wife and his duty because he couldn't save them all.

Doug had been right next to Stellan one moment, and the next, a flood of bodies overwhelmed him like a crashing wave. Stellan could only gawk in disbelief at the shrill screams of delight coming from the mouths of the madmen between bites.

His sidearm felt light. Almost all of the thirteen rounds in the magazine were gone, emptied into the crowd, yet they still came. Out of dark corridors, they came. From every side passageway, they came. He could feel more on the other side of the walls, beating with their fists, trying to find a way to the feast. There were so many, so fast that they must have been drawn by the gunshots. Bullets were of no use against their unrelenting numbers.

As circumstance pushed Stellan, the ease of choosing to turn and run for his life surprised him. The immediate guilt did not surprise him. It felt natural, instinctive, but he felt he was leaving a piece of himself behind, the piece that would accept no loss. He had to face that they weren't losing the *Atlas* anymore. It was already lost, and they had to salvage what they could.

He began with his own life and ran. He didn't swear to redouble his efforts as he'd done with Wendy bleeding in his arms. He just ran. He ran for Daelen and would help anyone who needed it along the way, but with his duty to the *Atlas* sworn off, he no longer felt pulled in many directions. He felt a distinct pull straight as an arrow.

The ship didn't matter anymore. Daelen was everything.

Before he could get to her, he'd have to stop along the way. If they were to survive, they would need weapons.

Stellan knew he had always fought for himself. Even as he fought for others, he fought to save his own soul. He didn't know if there was a God, but he knew, at the end of his time, he would judge himself, and that was enough weight to carry.

For now, he would fight for himself and the survival of his loved ones because he could do no more.

As he ran, he hoped he wouldn't encounter any more of the madmen because he had drawn a line in his mind and knew he had already crossed it. They were on the other side where he couldn't reach, where he couldn't help them except to do as his father taught him. He would kill with accuracy. He would kill with mercy.

Three

Captain Pierce didn't know if it was when he accepted his promotion to lead third platoon in the Unity Corps or if it was the reason he was promoted, but his allegiance to his duty was absolute. He would die before he lost the *Atlas*, and as far as he was concerned, he no longer had loved ones.

He told himself it was what was expected of every enlisted man. That was why he understood he had no chance of surviving if the *Atlas* didn't make it, if he didn't save it regardless of who he sacrificed.

He was no longer enlisted in the military. However, when Stellan had told him he no longer owed the Council anything and Pierce had responded that they owed it to themselves, he meant it. The principles of his actions defined him.

As he watched his department heads trickle off the command deck, looking to him with both fear and shame, it was not with dwindling hope. With the network down, they could no longer do any good here, and it was just as well that they go and find their loved ones and try to keep them safe. Perhaps, in the field, they would be of some use.

Still, he felt obligated to point out the obvious.

"If you leave the command deck, you will not be allowed back," Pierce announced. "I cannot guarantee your safety."

Some of the department heads hesitated and looked back, but he knew they had no intention of returning before the end, whatever that end may be. It was only a lingering sense of obligation to duty, one last payment of respect to him before titles and rank became irrelevant.

Arlo left his workstation and joined Pierce in that lonely corridor.

"You're just going to let them go?" Arlo asked in both hope and disbelief.

"They'll be a liability for what I have in mind. I need soldiers."

"What about when we get the ship back under control? We'll need them."

Pierce looked at Arlo grimly. "We're going to have to get our hands dirty if we're going to take the *Atlas* back. Is there some place you would rather be, Arlo?"

"Well, I might like to check on my dad."

Pierce looked back at Evans and found his waning resolve. His navigator would be of no use to him, but they would need someone to stay on the command deck. For someone like Evans who was so wracked with fear, such a command would be a blessing.

"When you flew for the Corps, they taught you to handle a weapon, right?" Pierce asked Arlo.

"Sidearms, hand-to-hand, and the assorted small arms and MGs outfitted on every helo and gunship."

"Good enough," Pierce said. "Evans, drop the anchor. You're staying here. When we leave, lock down the command deck. Only person you let back in is me. Understand?"

Evans nodded and didn't bother to ask what he should do otherwise because he knew the standing order was to do nothing. He knew the *Atlas* wasn't going anywhere.

"Arlo," Pierce said. "Come with me."

"Terrific. Today's a perfect day for a walk in the park."

Pierce walked toward the lift, and Arlo followed. Though Pierce felt guilty for taking his pilot off the bridge for what may be the last time, he didn't have time for guilt anymore. He'd let the last of his vulnerability out and knew this would be their last shot. For it to have any chance at success, he would have to be relentless. He owed both the dead and the living that much.

Four

After running for what felt like miles, Stellan stopped to listen. He expected to hear the footfalls of his pursuers, but there were none. All he could hear were the sounds of his own labored breathing, the pounding of his heart, and the emptiness, like the *Atlas* had died straight down to its bones.

Then those bones rattled with a shrill scream. It reverberated through the corridors so that he could not determine its origin. The return to silence disturbed him more than the voice itself. No one called for help. No one opened doors in concern or even curiosity. No one rushed to offer assistance.

The voice belonged to a woman, and Stellan realized he should be the one going to investigate and give aid. It was his responsibility, and he felt the tug in his gut, pulling him in a direction, any direction, so that he might help that woman, so that he might make amends for his past life. Like an addiction, it was hard to let go.

He told himself it was too late. He told himself he could not help her but that he could still help others and that the situation had gone so far out of his control that triage and prioritizing the needs of the *Atlas'* crew had become necessary.

The truth was he was afraid, not for himself, however. He feared that woman's voice belonged to Daelen. It was illogical that she would have been in that part of the ship. She should have been in medical. Daelen would have wanted to help, and that was where she would be able to do the most good. She knew that, and Stellan knew she would act on it. Still, he doubted, and his love for her compelled him to investigate to be sure. If he left her, she would most certainly perish. If he went to her aid now, he might still have been able to help.

He didn't know what to do.

The conflict was peculiar. Stellan had experience with concern for others in high-risk situations. In battle, he and his squad mates had agreed they were all more than brothers. They said, when you were willing to die for someone, the knot that held that bond was greater than any that blood could tie. More than genetics bonded them. They needed to lean on each other. Otherwise, their chances of survival dwindled.

Co-dependence made them stronger as a whole.

He had seen his battle brothers die in combat. He would never forget the faces of those who fell, some of them condemning him, pleading with him, asking why he had let them down.

But none of the loss and guilt he'd felt then compared to the thought of losing Daelen now. He had to know she was all right. He had to continue toward medical. It was mathematics. Each moment that passed that he was not with her, ensuring she was alive and well, diminished their chances.

The portside fairway was just ahead of him and around a corner. The corridor stretched nearly the entire length of the ship, and it was a gamble to use. With the *Atlas'* friendly population waning, it was likely any of the madmen would be able to see him if they were anywhere in the stretch of that corridor. But it was the quickest way to the medical deck, and he had to risk it.

Speed meant greater risk to him, and that meant less of a chance harm would come to Daelen. It was a trade he was happy to make.

Stellan turned the corner to the fairway and realized their problems went far beyond the concerns of the living.

Five

Stellan wondered about the meaning of the word "victim." He wondered if it was a matter of perspective. In all the madness that ran amok on the *Atlas*, he couldn't determine anymore whose loss was greater, the living who fought for their lives, the madmen who had lost their minds, or the dead who had no words.

Stellan was not a religious man, but surely, there must be something after death, even if it was simply peace, a prevailing nothingness.

Death did not scare him. It was a part of life he had to come to terms with years ago. In fact, the only way they could come to terms with it was to believe they already were dead. This belief was not to discourage them or so they would be reckless or more courageous. It simply allowed them to cope, so they could function and do their duty.

The thought of not being able to rest, however, scared him, though it was not with fear or disgust that he looked down upon the man in front of him now. It was with pity because it was clear that death was no longer the final grant of peace. This man was not allowed to rest. He had come back in the most horrible way Stellan could imagine.

Judging from his torn jump suit, the man had been an engineer. The blood had dried black like a splash of gravity crane oil. He had been a young, attractive man with broad, muscular shoulders and clean-cut dark hair, like a movie star whose name escaped Stellan at the moment.

Stellan felt guilty not knowing this man's name. The *Atlas* was like a small town. He knew almost everyone, but he could not come up with a name. The man deserved the dignity of an identity.

Stellan saw the man he had been, but he had become something else entirely. He realized the infection that took their minds took their bodies as well, and after death, when everything of their identity was gone, it assumed full control, driving them like a vehicle.

One of his legs had been eaten away, leaving only a femur extending from his waist, white and dry like it had been licked clean. His abdomen was exposed with intestines coiling behind him like tendrils. Even as he tried to drag himself toward Stellan with his lone hand, the other arm ending in a stringy stump at the elbow, his mouth gaped and chomped with dusty rasps, lips chewed away revealing perfectly straight and white teeth that even then could have served as a model for a dentist's work.

Stellan marveled at the torso-wide streak of blood that extended down the fairway about one hundred meters, reminding him of the distance to the clearing and the doe that deserved mercy.

No one deserved this.

Stellan looked grimly to his sidearm, which he held with white knuckles.

Stellan's only skill had ever been killing. Growing up in the mountains, he had been a product of his environment, learning how to hunt at an early age. He wished he had been an artist or a scientist, someone who had the ability to contribute to society. The source of his self-loathing had only been that he was a bringer of death.

He remembered his first kill, the doe. He remembered how she tried to drag her paralyzed hind legs and how ineffectual her front hooves were at grasping earth. He imagined her agony and how frightened she must have been as her killer watched her bleed to death. He wondered if and when she had realized what was happening.

Regardless, death came. The time she spent in pain was definite. That was not true for the man who lay in front of him now. Stellan did not know whether he felt any pain, but something wasn't allowing his body to die. He was undead, in a kind of stasis, a checkpoint between this world and the next.

Perhaps Stellan could use his skill just this once to free someone of the torture of being trapped in their own body. Perhaps he could send this man on to where he belonged.

The man grasped Stellan's boot, feeble fingers trying to scratch through the leather, perhaps clawing to escape, begging for release.

He aimed his weapon at the man's head; he looked up into Stellan's eyes. So ghostly white, Stellan thought there unmistakably was a person in there, locked in a prison of enduring life.

Sometimes, death was better.

The dead man continued to grasp Stellan's boot, rocking like a boat, rolling onto his side to compensate for his stumped arm.

Stellan tried to think of the words to say, some kind of eulogy. He thought he should apologize, express sympathy that something so horrible had happened to this man. He thought he should accept responsibility for failing to protect him. But no words came to restore some of this man's dignity. Stellan tasted only inadequacy and the brine of his own tears.

He squeezed the trigger to do good, and the blast startled him. The bullet entered the top of the dead man's head and exited the back of his neck, then ricocheted off the deck. His reaching arm fell limp. His raspy chomping ceased.

The lack of blood spatter surprised Stellan. He'd never seen a gunshot so dry. The blood that splashed against the floor had the consistency of tomato paste.

Stellan turned away, looking down the other end of the corridor. The others had most certainly heard the gunshot, but he didn't care. This man deserved death, not because he was wicked, but because it was merciful.

Wiping his eyes, he faced the portside fairway. The corridor was so long that the walls appeared to meet at a point impossibly far away. Facing the sheer length of the empty, uninterrupted hallway frightened him. No one hurried toward destinations unknown. No couples gathered along its walls to share a moment of public affection. No groups congregated to block traffic.

Nothing stopped him from seeing the horribly endless possibilities and understanding what this meant for the road ahead.

Six

On his way to medical, the security deck would offer a place of refuge for Stellan to muster his wits and prepare to make the rest of the trip. It also would offer a place for him to gather his strength in the form of weapons and ammunition. Even executioners were tradesmen, and tradesmen needed tools.

He approached the entryway to security slowly and carefully. The door was closed, and the holographic control panel glowed red, which meant it had been purposely locked. He wasn't sure if that was a good sign. He'd left three infected madmen in holding. Perhaps they'd fallen into a coma like the others. And perhaps, when one of his officers checked for a pulse, they'd come back. Perhaps, with madmen on the loose, someone had escaped and locked the door behind them.

With his worst nightmares coming true, anything seemed possible. Stellan could imagine it, so he had to expect it. He'd learned long ago that people didn't make mistakes because they didn't expect the unexpected. They made mistakes because they lacked the imagination to dream the darkest dreams, to truly see how bad things could get.

Stellan crept upon the door, back against the wall, using the various lips and support beams jutting from the bulkhead as cover. The enemy didn't have guns, but stealth tactics remained the same. As monstrous as they were, they still had human sensory limitations. At least, he hadn't seen anything to lead him to believe otherwise. Skepticism might have prevailed and frozen him in place, but he had to keep moving.

He waved his link over the control panel, and it chirped and flashed to green. He pushed on the door, but it wouldn't budge. The manual lock on the other side had been engaged, which was a comforting thought. Someone on the other side was smart enough to use the manual latch, perhaps someone who was old enough to remember a time when these doors only *had* manual locks.

"Floyd," he whispered. "Are you in there? It's Stellan."

A moment of silence passed. Then the lever on the inside fell, and the locking mechanism slid out of the frame. The door cracked open, and a beady blue eye with a wild white eyebrow peered out.

Stellan smiled. He found comfort in the thought that someone under his command still lived. Floyd opened the door with a gasp and sigh of relief.

"Oh, I'm so happy to see you, Chief!" he said. Stellan hurried through the door, and Floyd hugged him. Stellan pushed him away and quickly closed the door.

"I'm sorry. I'm happy to see you, too, but keep your voice down."

"You're right," Floyd said. "I've just been hearing so much that's set me on my heels, and no one's answering any calls."

"I know. The comms system is down. I can't access the ship's intranet either. Have you heard anything about medical? Anything about Daelen?"

"No," Floyd said. "Some of the boys were supposed to finish their sweep to that point, but I never heard from them. The rest of them, well, they just took off a while ago."

Stellan made his way past Floyd's workstation without paying much attention to what he was working on. Much of the security office held little meaning to him now. It was at the center of a duty that could no longer serve the dying *Atlas*. It was remnant of an old, lost world. His only concern was the weapons closet. Symbols no longer meant anything. Only strength and force would be of any use.

"Wait," Floyd said with scared eyes. "Where's Doug?"

Stellan looked back grimly, unsure of how to answer the question. He didn't have to say anything, though. That inability to speak was all Floyd needed to know their friend had fallen.

"Oh no," Floyd said with understanding. "Oh no."

"You better stay here, old man. It's not safe out there." Stellan had little time for empathy and sentimentality. He stored those emotions away because doing so now would increase his chances of allowing himself to feel them later.

He entered his office and confronted the doorway to the weapons closet. The monsters inside, *his* monsters, would rival the madness preying on the crew of the *Atlas*. They beckoned, calling out to him warmly, inviting him as a friend, telling him that, no matter how long or how hard he tried to deny them, he needed them. He would always need them, and they would always be there for him. He would never be rid of them, and in this moment, he was glad for it.

"What are you doing?"

Stellan waved his link over the holographic lock, and the door slid into the wall. The lights flickered on with sunrise affection.

The Kruger MK7C assault rifle was the first thing he reached for. He aimed down the sights and then checked the chamber. It felt as good as he remembered.

"Preparing," Stellan said.

"That mean you got a plan?"

"Not exactly."

He replaced the magazine in his sidearm and then stuffed the pockets of his pants and overcoat with spare clips. He needed to be well-armed, but he had to remain mobile. If there were too many of them, he would have to run.

And then he started to wonder what if the worst happened. What if they got to him? There wasn't much he could do about his arms and legs. He needed them to be free, but the weapons closet had some ballistic vests. They were dusty and intended for riot gear, but they could stop knives and most small-arms caliber rounds. He was sure they would stop teeth and fingernails.

Stellan removed his coat and shirt and put one of the vests on underneath.

"Are they shooting now?"

"No. I'll be the only one shooting," Stellan said. "You didn't see what they did to Doug."

A cry erupted from the holding room. Stellan had forgotten all about the men in lockup.

"They been any trouble?" he asked.

"First peep I've heard in hours." Floyd shrugged.

Stellan shouldered the rifle and walked toward the holding room. Another cry erupted. And then another. Stellan ran to the door and then peered into the porthole window. The lights were dim, but all was as he left it. Edward and the three madmen were in their cells. Edward no longer huddled in the corner and, instead, appeared lucid and alert, eyes focused and brow narrowed in concentration. The three madmen swayed lazily, dancing to some tune Stellan could not hear.

He entered.

"Stellan, I'm so glad to see you," Edward said. "These three, I swear they were dead. One by one, they lay down and didn't move for hours, and then they just got back up. I thought they went to sleep, but they seem different now."

Stellan walked closer to Jude's cell. The young man, once so full of life and energy, now looked fragile and vacant. His head lolled back on his shoulders, his mouth agape. A quiet moan escaped his throat. He looked lost.

Stellan put his hand on the bars. He felt faint but not for any physiological reason. The sudden realization that everyone in his life was gone hit him like a blow to the chest. Everyone but Daelen, and he had to get to her.

A strange scream woke him from his stupor. It sounded like an adolescent boy who had yet to gain full control of his deepened voice. Jude lunged at him, and he jumped back in reflex. Jude's hand grasped at Stellan through the bars. His fingers curled into claws, tearing at the air. His face cast a look of anguish, hate, and, perhaps, hunger.

The thing that killed him and brought him back now wanted to do the same to Stellan.

Facing the pure horror of its simplicity, Stellan resented it. It stared back at him through Jude's eyes. It used his friend's body as a tool to spread itself. And it wouldn't hesitate to take him down. Or his wife.

Stellan drew his weapon.

"What the hell are you doing!?" Floyd said. "That's Jude. These people need our help."

"That's not Jude anymore," Stellan said. "And there's only one way we can help them."

Stellan walked to the end of the row of cells and took aim at the man who used to be Robt Mathers. He pulled the trigger, and after the thunderclap, Robt's body crumpled to the floor. It already felt natural.

"Stop!" Floyd cried.

Stellan moved to the next cell and put down Elias Robichaud's reanimated body with the same coldness, and it began to feel like a process, something methodical.

"No!" Floyd covered his ears and doubled over, vomiting in the corner.

Stellan moved onto Jude, and the resemblance of the grasping, moaning monster to his old friend made Stellan hesitate as if, with Stellan's gun in his face, there was a chance Jude might give up the act and confess it was all a joke. But Jude showed indifference to the deadly end of the weapon. It was less like he did not know what the weapon was and more like he did not even see it. He looked past it, hungrily, murderously, at Stellan.

"This is madness," Floyd spit onto the floor.

"Yes," Stellan said. "It is."

Stellan pulled the trigger once more, and the crack of the gun sounded far away, like even their ears had gotten used to the killing. Jude's body lay in a heap on the floor, and Stellan watched it bleed for a moment, not really thinking about anything. The viscous blood seeped from Jude's skull onto the floor. The spatter on the far wall ran slowly like syrup. On the outside, they looked human. The insides weren't.

He moved to Edward's cell, and instead of holstering his sidearm, he aimed it at the last inmate.

"He's not infected?" Floyd asked, confused. He lunged forward and put his back against the iron bars, ready to stand between them. "He's better now. He's not mad."

251

"Agent Skinner asked me why I saved your life, and at the time, I didn't have an answer," Stellan said to Edward. "You weren't in your right mind, and I couldn't just let you go. Things have changed. Sanity is in short supply right now, and I'm not sure anymore if even I'm still thinking straight. If you ever want to get out of that cell, you're going to have to convince me you were worth it, and you're going to have to do it right now."

Stellan wanted to pull the trigger. With the way things were going, he could claim Edward had been infected, and even if everything turned out all right, no one would question it. With the black madness messing with the dials in his brain, everyone would believe he was mad with the contagion.

"Please," Edward said. "I can't fix the things I did. I know in my heart it wasn't me that did those things, even though I remember my hands doing them. That isn't an excuse. That is to say I will find a way to make it right, and I've never been more certain of anything in my life."

Stellan surveyed Edward's face. It wasn't a matter of trust so much as doubt. Stellan doubted himself. He doubted he had the strength to survive in this new, insane world, to do the things that were necessary. He promised himself he wouldn't let anything stand in the way of that simple objective, survival. However, right now, Edward wasn't threatening anyone, and he might yet make Stellan's potential sacrifice worth it.

He holstered his weapon.

"Things are out of control," Stellan said. "Don't expect me to save you again. When you leave this cell, you leave all the protection I can offer."

"I know," Edward said, and Stellan waved his link over the holographic control. The cell door slid open. Floyd had been holding his breath and exhaled through puckered lips. Then he wiped his mouth.

"If you're finished with that, I have something to show you," Floyd said. Stellan followed him out of the holding room and to his workstation. A moment later, Edward timidly left his cell and joined them, blinking in the bright lights of the central security room.

Stellan and Floyd huddled around his terminal, which projected a blue, 3D model of the *Atlas*. Floyd's fingers danced across the controls, and Stellan leaned back as if watching a show.

"You asked me to track where these links had been and find who they'd been in contact with," Floyd said. "We were lucky in that two of them were, in fact, off cycle. They both went back to their quarters and slept most of the time. Jude, though, he was a busy man. If you include everyone in the bar at the time of the shooting, this happens."

The blue holographic image bloomed red clouds, eventually engulfing every deck of the ship.

"There's no way it could be that bad," Stellan said. "Daelen said it would be transmitted through body fluids. This seems like it's airborne."

"As far as we know, it isn't. Otherwise, we'd be out there looking like the others. But that's not the point," Floyd said. "I've run it a thousand different ways and even calculated a low rate of transmission. Every scenario ends up the same way."

"Everyone goes mad," Stellan said.

"There was no way we ever could have stopped this thing."

Stellan wondered if Skinner had known the madness was unstoppable and if she'd planned for it. He assumed she did. Agents knew and planned for everything. It was how they were able to mold circumstance. Knowing that was why he listened to her at all, why he had given her a chance.

"Well, we're not infected," Stellan said. "That's a start. We just have to keep it that way."

"How do we know who's not mad?"

"For starters, they won't try to murder us."

"Foolproof plan, Chief." Floyd smirked.

"Smart ass," Stellan said. "Pierce was always the one to make the plans."

"You say that like he's dead." With Floyd's smile lingering, the main entryway's control panel flashed from red to green, and the door burst open.

Stellan drew his weapon. Pierce drew his.

"Speak o' the devil," Floyd said.

Seven

Stellan and Pierce aimed their weapons at each other, killer intent flaring in their eyes. Floyd couldn't help but marvel at how far apart they'd fallen. Until now, he'd not doubted that their friendship would endure.

He'd lived these past ten years watching them run the *Atlas* together. He knew about their history. Yet, they had diverged. He didn't know why.

"Lower your weapon," Pierce said.

"Lower yours," Stellan said.

"Shouldn't you be in a cell?"

"Doug's dead," Stellan said. "What are you doing here?"

"Unless I missed something, one of us was relieved of duty, and the other is still the captain of this goddamn ship."

"Gentlemen, please!" Floyd cried. "We all want the same thing here!"

Neither Pierce nor Stellan appeared willing to yield. A not-so-distant cry of anguish rattled through the halls, and everyone looked nervously at the open door. Their time was running out.

"I hate to be a bother," Arlo said from outside the doorway. "I mean, tell me if it's too much to ask. But would you fellows kindly settle this later when one of us isn't dangling like a worm on the end of a hook? If you missed it, I'm talking about me out here, and I'm speaking figuratively to convey my sense of urgency."

Pierce relaxed and holstered his sidearm. "I need your help."

Stellan lowered his weapon as well. "A lot of people out there need help."

"And we're going to give it to them." Pierce crossed the threshold into the room. Arlo hurried behind him and closed the hatch door, flopping against the broad side in an embrace. He kissed it, lips smacking.

"Metal never tasted so good," he said.

The schematic of the *Atlas* on Floyd's workstation drew Pierce's attention. The animation of the red cloud continued to loop, and it drew Pierce's fascination.

"What is this?" he asked.

Floyd explained everything about how the infection started and how his analysis included many variables, always the same result. Everyone would be mad within a matter of hours. The *Atlas'* hull ensured that because, on an island in space, there was nowhere anyone could go. It was only a matter of time.

"What are we going to do, Captain?" Floyd asked.

Pierce considered the graphic in front of him. The red cloud swelled from one of the *Atlas'* foredecks. Multiple clouds formed and then were isolated in quarantine zones across the ship. It spread throughout those zones, thickening and deepening like a boiling rage. The entire residence deck grew to a large, throbbing blister. And then, with the server crash, the clouds erupted and consumed the *Atlas* until no corner was left untouched.

"What do *you* think we should do, Officer Coulson?"

"Abandon ship. The lifeboats, they would give us a chance."

"No," Pierce said. "The lifeboats are meant to save the crew from a damaged ship. In this case, we need to save the *Atlas* from her crew."

"I knew the ship was female!" Arlo cheered. His father, appearing lucid, shushed him with a disapproving glance as, even when a child becomes an adult, only a parent can do.

"The way I see it," Pierce said, "the solution is pretty simple, although it may be hidden for some. Once you see it, there is no denying its necessity. There is an enemy on the *Atlas*. We must eliminate that enemy."

"How do you propose we do that?" Floyd asked.

"Stellan, do you remember Operation Phalanx?"

"Of course. How could I forget?"

"You see, Floyd, we faced something similar to this in a small city in South America some years ago. We were told insurgents were holed up somewhere within city limits, using it as a hub of operations. The problem was that's all we knew, and the Council wanted action. We had no way of telling friendlies from enemies. IFF systems are inaccurately named. They don't identify friends and foes. They only identify registered friendlies wearing their IFF tags and other people. The insurgents knew that, and they got the people to flood the streets. With thousands of innocent civilians surrounding us, their strength was in their anonymity in the crowd. They knew who we were, but we didn't know who they were. In a way, using the people, they outnumbered us. We lost seven men before we even knew they were on us. They used their knives. They were quiet."

Floyd's rapt eyes glistened in the light. "What did you do?"

"We pulled out. We set up grids throughout the city and marched down each street, announcing our presence and then instructing those who supported the Council to surrender to our protection. They had one chance. Anyone who didn't come out would be treated as hostile. Anyone who did come out would be given food and shelter, things they desperately needed at the time because the rebels were bleeding them dry. At least that's what we were told."

"I don't understand. How does that apply here?"

"We go deck by deck and announce our presence at the bulkhead. If friendlies respond, we take them to safety. If hostiles respond, we seal it off."

"And then what?" Floyd asked.

"For Phalanx," Stellan said, gazing into the nothingness of recollection, "we didn't know it at the time, but after we cleared the city and told them there were no more friendlies in the area, the Council ordered aerial bombardment of the entire grid. They leveled it. They said the rebels blew it up and that we were to be commended for the evacuation. They said we saved lives, that we were heroes."

"I hope you pardon any inferred insubordination, Captain, but how is that at all similar to our situation now?" Floyd asked.

"After we clear each deck, we purge it."

"Is that your solution to everything?" Stellan said. "Just airlock it?"

"Space kills."

Arlo sighed. "It certainly does."

"This is madness fighting madness!" Floyd said. "We can't be sure we won't be sacrificing uninfected people, never mind the chance we could actually cure the sick!"

"Some innocents *will* be sacrificed, but it isn't so dissimilar to how you would treat an infected limb. Even today, surgeons remove infected limbs and replace them."

"You can't replace people!"

"No," Pierce said. "No, you can't."

He fell into silence, which Stellan found unbearable. Stellan knew Pierce was thinking about the loved ones he'd lost, some more recently than others. He knew Pierce probably was thinking of all the men he led into battle who never came back. So many of them were good men. It frustrated Stellan that Pierce didn't seem to be fighting for those loved ones who still remained. He was fighting for an ideal in a no-win situation. Pierce wanted to send them into battle but didn't realize they would be fighting themselves. After a moment, Stellan stood and walked to the door.

"Where are you going?" Pierce asked.

"From what I've seen, there's only one way we can help some of these people. There's a lot we don't know. I know I'm not sick, and I know I'm not going anywhere or doing anything without Daelen or until I know she is safe. That's all I've got, and it's all I care about right now. So I'm going to medical. Hopefully, she'll have something more for us there. Come if you want or go off on your campaign. Either way is just as well with me."

With a measure of contempt, Pierce watched Stellan raise the manual locking lever on the hatch door.

"And Pierce," Stellan said. "You're forgetting one thing about Phalanx."

"What's that?"

"It failed. The insurgents were based elsewhere, and the attacks didn't stop. That's why the Council pinned the blame on the rebels."

Eight

A closed door represents possibilities as well as an open one. It offers mystery. There's intrigue and suspense. You want to open it. Before you do, you imagine what's on the other side. A closed door, however, allows the mind to take the thought of what's behind it to a dark place, to fear the unknown.

Stellan tried not to think about what he would find when he opened the door to medical, but when his mind went there without his permission, all he could imagine was blood, the walls dripping with it.

It was too much for him to bear. Part of him needed to know Daelen was safe; the other part could not even begin to prepare for a revelation that she was not. Something in his subconscious resisted it. Without knowing the truth, he couldn't call it denial. It was tenacity in a belief because his mind knew thinking otherwise would cause pain.

If the door held his worst fears, his mind would break.

When he left the relative safety of the security deck, the others followed after loading up on weapons from the supply closet. Pierce made his resentment known, but they all knew they had to go somewhere and do something. Stellan's certain purpose, his definitively forward movement, attracted them.

They approached the bulkhead doorway to the medical deck in single file, Stellan on point with his Kruger MK7C assault rifle fixed in front of the line. He held the rifle tight to his shoulder, scanning for movement ahead, his upper body rigid and twisting to dart between potential targets.

His feet continued to push forward. They always pushed forward. *Steady and easy,* he told himself. *Keep moving.* He had begun to remember how to move when every corner and every room potentially held someone or something that could kill him. It was releasing from his bones, seeping into his muscles, old instincts returning like fossils that had been stored deep within his body.

They heard a distant scream. Or was it nearby? Stellan couldn't tell, so he stopped the line with a raised fist and crouched against the wall of the corridor. The others followed his lead, finding nooks for cover behind struts and support beams. Pierce stood overwatch for Stellan, aiming his rifle in front of the group. Edward and Floyd followed, each with sidearms and no knowledge or wits to use them. Arlo pulled up the rear, spinning around to watch their backs with his own MK7C.

The *Atlas* had fallen mostly quiet, though the occasional scream ricocheted through those corridors like bullets. Sound had a way of traveling in those halls when its only combatant was the silence. Its walls had become a giant amplifier. The demons in the dark had voices that spoke from within their own minds.

"We have to keep moving," Pierce whispered over Stellan's shoulder. "We're almost there."

Stellan glanced back sternly at Pierce. He knew both of those things, and he wondered if Pierce's haste meant he was afraid. The captain's voice trembled, but it could have been exhaustion.

"We can't risk detection, Gordon," Stellan said. "We use our weapons as a last resort. Where there's one, there are many, and one gunshot is enough to draw them all."

The truth was, while Stellan felt it important to be careful, he wondered if he was stalling because he was afraid in a different way. He wasn't afraid for his life. He was afraid for Daelen's life, and that fear threatened to paralyze him. He found a kind of safety in not knowing because uncertainty meant nothing changed, and he wondered if he would turn from the truth if it were in front of him, if it were something he could not accept.

His feet started again on their own. Perhaps his mind knew it was the only way, that his subconsciousness would have to take over to move them into a hopefully secure area. As they drew nearer to the closed door to the medical deck, it became easier to move, as if whatever wanted to freeze him had given in.

Stellan touched the door with one hand, holding his rifle up with the other. He crouched again and listened. His group came to a rest behind him. They tried to quiet their own breathing, tried to conceal any indication that they were living beings.

He didn't hear any shrieks or cries of pain. Outside of his group, he heard only the sounds of silence, nothingness, and death. More than ever, he missed the sounds of laughter and conversation, the sounds of hurried boots on the deck, of concerns that now seemed trivial to him, as they always did in a time of war when lives were at stake and nothing else mattered but keeping the blood flowing through your veins and not out onto the ground.

That silence was what convinced him he needed to let go. It didn't mean he couldn't love and cherish Daelen and wish she were alive and well. It simply meant he had to get used to people dying again, to remember how to cope with war, to expect the worst and to know he was already dead. He just didn't like that it now required him to think of her that way, but he knew he'd have to if he was going to keep moving. To save her, he'd have to believe she was already gone.

Pierce waved his link over the control panel to unlock the door, and he and Stellan burst through, rifles drawn, sweeping the corners, taking the room and everything in it by storm. They moved outward along the perimeter of the room, watching each other, seeing what the other was seeing. It felt like old times.

The group filed into the main medical room, Stellan and Pierce taking positions on either flank, Floyd and Edward shuffling clumsily into the center, fumbling with their pistols. Arlo closed the door behind them, dropping the manual locking lever with a boom.

The main examining room had been ransacked. Various drawers hung open, their contents lying on the floor. A table lay on its side. Cabinet doors along the wall remained open, their contents also spilled onto the floor and countertops.

It wasn't vandalism. Someone had frantically searched for something.

A trail of blood led to a small pool. A roll of gauze lay partially unspooled like a flapped tongue. A box of bandages lay nearby, some individual packages emptied. It looked like someone had field-dressed a wound.

Stellan's heartbeat rose into a thrumming in his chest, neck, and head. It was the precursor to his nightmare. Had she been bitten? It was a lot of blood, and not many would have known how to dress their own wound.

They heard a clattering toward the back, from the surgical room, a sound like pieces of metal falling to the deck. Stellan and Pierce instinctively aimed their weapons in that direction and waited.

Stellan actually felt calmer, more comfortable with a physical threat. If anything came out of that room and down that hall, he and Pierce would unleash a hailstorm of bullets. It was a problem for which he knew they had a solution.

They waited. They breathed. No one spoke, but everyone knew what to do, even Floyd and Edward. It was the beauty of instinct. The desire for self-preservation, to recognize and point a weapon at danger, was innate. It was natural.

Nothing came, and they knew they could not remain on a sealed deck without securing it. They also knew they had come for Daelen, and if she wasn't there, they would have to search elsewhere. She was their key to the ship. Like London all those years ago, she was their mission.

His mind fought him, but Stellan moved. He didn't want to know what was back there because he feared it could bring his uncertainty into horror instead of relief, but he had to know. It became a physical necessity. His heart, stomach, head, every part of his body cried out to know something for sure.

The hallway toward the rear of medical never felt narrower. It seemed to constrict as they moved farther down the passage toward the surgical room and morgue. They passed Daelen's office, and Stellan knew it was futile to look for her there. He looked anyway and resisted the urge to call her name.

He backed out of her office and into the swallowing hallway, and they found more blood on the exterior frosted glass of Wendy's recovery room. Smears that looked like handprints dripped to the floor.

The door was open.

Around it, the streaks of blood swept in wide arcs like someone had tried to make angel wings on the doorframe. Stellan covered Pierce as he leaned in the room, searching with the barrel of his rifle. Pierce signaled that the room was clear.

Another clattering came from the surgical room, and then they heard the cry of a woman. Stellan forgot himself. All his training and combat experience vanished. He acted on pure instinct, lowering his rifle and sprinting toward what he knew was the sound of his wife's voice.

"Stellan!" Pierce said.

He didn't care if one of the mad or dead attacked him from one of the open exam rooms on either side of the hallway. He didn't care if a horde of them lay in wait in the surgical room. He knew he *should* care about these things, but he just didn't. His reality simplified with the sound of Daelen in distress.

"It's not secure!" Pierce and the rest of the group hurried behind their chief of security, glancing quickly into the exam rooms Stellan so heedlessly passed.

For Stellan, knowing anything, even if it were pain and death, would be better than the doubt, the not knowing if Daelen was safe. She was all that mattered to him in the entire universe. He was never so convinced of it, and he knew then that she was beyond that door. She had to be, and if he didn't get there as fast as he could, she would be gone to a place where he could not follow. If his legs didn't push harder, if he didn't move and think faster, it would be too late, and he would have once again let down someone he loved, the person he loved most of all.

And then all his allegiances would mean nothing. He would be nothing.

He did not encounter any madmen in the hall. Beyond the door to the surgical room, he did not find a horde of the dead with their vacant stares and dripping mouths.

He just found one, and looking upon it broke his heart.

Nine

Doors, again, Stellan thought. They never ceased to contain surprises. He stood in the doorway to the surgical room, the sounds of the *Atlas* receding from his ears, the hollow footsteps of his group rushing behind. He was vaguely aware of the sobbing in some corner of the room.

His eyes, however, took in everything, and he couldn't believe them.

On the table in the center of the room, a man struggled in restraints. He kicked and thrashed, his face a snarl. He grasped at the air with clumsy fingers. It wasn't until Stellan looked into this man's eyes and saw that dullness, a ghost-like gray vacancy, that he realized it was no longer a man. Its skin and bones were that of his friend, Rick Fairchild, but under the bright task lighting of the surgical equipment, Stellan saw no recognition in Rick's eyes. It was like an estranged animal, flailing in a room of people it no longer recognized as friends but prey, for it lacked the ability to conceive the idea it could not reach them and that it was at their mercy, which had taken on a whole new meaning.

Margo bent beside the table, picking up a tray of instruments that had fallen to the deck. When she saw Stellan, she stood and froze. Makeup ran down her cheeks from tears that had dried not long ago.

Daelen stood in full surgical gown, wearing gloves and a plastic face shield beside the table on which the thing that was not Rick writhed. Cloth, that's all she wore. It would not protect her from a baby's mouth if one possessed the relentless will to feed as these things did.

When she reached across the table, over Rick's snapping jaws, the whole world rushed back to him on a tidal wave of fear.

"No!" Stellan rushed to her. He wrapped his arms around her waist and pulled her away, legs kicking in the air. Another clattering on the deck accompanied her protests as she dropped a small drill and her face shield fell off.

"Let me go!" Daelen cried. "Let go!"

Stellan thought she fought him because she feared he was one of the infected madmen, but when he put her down at a safe distance from the table, she turned on him. She pounded his arms and chest with half-closed fists. Her face twisted in rage and darkened.

"What are you doing?" Stellan said, seizing her wrists. "It's me."

"You son of a bitch! You could have stopped this! You could have saved them! You should have seen this coming! And now they're all gone! We're all gone! I can't—I can't." Exhausted, she collapsed into his arms, pressing her face to his chest. Her frustrated sobs told Stellan she did not mean what she said. She simply felt responsible and could not bear to place all the blame upon herself.

"I'm sorry," she said when her sobs quieted. "It's my fault, not yours. Rick's gone, and there's nothing I can do."

"It's no one's fault," Stellan said. "We can't save them all."

Stellan felt everyone's eyes on them. Even Rick eyed them, albeit hungrily.

"But there are still some we can help," Stellan said.

Daelen was quiet. She simply wanted to feel Stellan's strong arms around her. Margo finished picking up the spilled equipment and noticed Pierce staring at the man on the table, the man that used to be a senior engineer and friend.

"He was bitten and came to us when he started to see symptoms," Margo said. "After Tom, we knew what would happen, and when we told him, he asked us to use him to study it, to use him as the index case. We monitored the change. We saw how it works."

"What do you mean, after Tom?"

"His body reanimated in the morgue," Margo said. "It worked its way out and killed Susanna Barton. Then it came after us, but we'd all hidden. Eventually, it wandered off."

Pierce said nothing while he struggled to process what Margo told him.

"You keep calling him 'it,'" Floyd said. "These are people."

Margo squinted at him. "*Were* people."

"You were able to study it? Do you have a cure?" Pierce asked.

"No. We saw how it works, but we haven't been able to identify or characterize it yet."

"How does it work?"

Daelen sniffled and brushed her hair back behind her ears, emerging from Stellan's embrace, wiping her eyes with shaking hands.

"It spreads through body fluid contact," she said. "Once in the bloodstream, it attacks the brain and nervous system. Symptoms include muscle and joint aches, fever, dementia, and eventually coma, and death. Tom came back, so we knew the same would happen to Rick. Anyone who dies of this comes back, but we think the time varies. After three hours and fourteen minutes, Rick came back. We were prepared." Daelen motioned toward the restraints around Rick's wrists and ankles. "The infection reanimated his brain stem and nervous system, but his higher order functions are still dormant."

"Dormant?" Pierce asked. "Can they be brought back?"

263

"No," Daelen said. "The brain needs oxygen and nutrients from the body, and when Rick came back, his brain wasn't getting any. The infection doesn't seem to need anything from the body to sustain it, so I don't think it's a virus."

"What is it then?"

"We don't know. I might be able to learn more if we studied whatever it came from. Its source. What it was before it entered the bloodstream. Once in the body, it's an organism. I just don't know what kind of organism or how I could potentially treat it."

"It had to have come from the material we mined from the planet," Pierce said. "Perhaps when Tom and the others inhaled the dust."

"Yeah, the material we jettisoned into space," Arlo said. "Too bad we don't have any more of that lying around."

Pierce ignored him.

"We do," Stellan said. Pierce shot his gaze to Stellan. The rest turned their attention as well.

"Gordon, you have a brick of it in your quarters," Stellan said. "Last I saw, it was just sitting on your desk."

"Good luck getting there," Arlo said. "When we left the lift from the command deck, we heard a big group of them. We got out of there lickety-split, but it sounded like they were coming our way. That's funny. Why do you think they group up like that?"

"People have always congregated," Margo said. "Since early man, tribal mentality has been a natural phenomenon."

"Strength in numbers," Arlo said. "We're getting weaker while they're getting stronger."

"Daelen," Stellan said, "if we get that brick, there's a chance you could cure this thing?"

"I don't know," she said. "Maybe. From what I've already seen, though, those who are like Rick are gone for good. His brain is almost entirely dead, and I can't cure that. Rick is gone."

Rick's animated body thrashed on the table as if it knew they were talking about it.

"The others?" Stellan said.

"Theoretically," she said. "If I can stop the organism before it kills the brain. It's much easier said than done, especially here. I can synthesize vaccines for new strains of the flu, but this is way beyond that."

"We have to try," Stellan said, turning to watch Rick's body attempt to break its bindings, curling its gray lips back in huffs of frustration. It collapsed after a moment, seemingly exhausted even though Stellan wasn't sure it felt fatigue. He didn't know if it felt pain or loss. He didn't know if it could empathize. Stellan looked at Rick's reanimated corpse and realized, as much as it looked like Rick, as much as it looked human, it wasn't. Even so, he locked eyes with it, and in its debilitated state, Stellan thought it was pleading with him. It could not speak, but Stellan saw an unmistakable plea for help. He felt pity.

Then it lashed out, nearly tearing its own arms from their sockets in a backbreaking contortion in which it tried to get its mouth just a little closer to Stellan's throat. Its teeth smacked together on air before it feebly fell back onto the table again.

"His last request before he lost lucidity was that we make sure he could rest when we were finished," Daelen said, looking to the drill on the floor. "I was just about to destroy his brain. Once they've come back, once their nervous system is independent from the rest of the body, it's the only way to stop them."

"The only way to give them peace," Stellan said.

"How do you know?" Pierce asked.

"Susanna," Margo said vacantly. "When she came back, Tom had left her immobilized. Her limbs were paralyzed, and she had been disemboweled. There was almost nothing left, and there was nothing else we could do for her."

"It's a mercy," Floyd said, "isn't it?"

"Yes," Daelen said.

Everyone averted their eyes, but Stellan could tell they were looking at him, even if only in their minds. The world constricted like the hallway again. The man who used to be Rick Fairchild had been a good friend, and all he had wanted in life was to fix machines and be left alone. That's all any of them really wanted, to live free, and for that, they had been struck a blight that led to their ruin.

Even if they survived, Stellan knew they would never be the same. The *Atlas* was done. It may return from the dead, but like the madness that killed the crew and reanimated their bodies, the *Atlas'* spirit, essence, the thing that made it great, would be gone. Most of the survivors would probably opt to return to the relative safety of life on New Earth, accepting the conformity as a necessity they could no longer deny.

Stellan wondered what Rick would do if he were given the choice. If Rick had survived, would he go back?

It was silly to think about because Rick hadn't survived. He was already gone, so Stellan stepped forward, unholstered his sidearm, and fired before he or anyone else could dwell on it any longer.

There was nothing else they could do for him. It was necessary.

Peace was the only thing Rick had ever wanted. He deserved it more than most. Stellan used his gift to grant mercy to another soul.

"Rest easy, my friend," he said. Out of respect, no one looked at Rick's body. They chose to remember him as he was before the alien organism had killed him, a modest and wise man who led without even knowing it.

Stellan heard that sobbing again. In the corner, Wendy's weeping erupted into howling as she sat on a countertop, curled into a ball. She had turned away and couldn't watch Stellan, her best friend, end the life of a man she had considered a second father.

He went to her, and the stunned group watched because they could do nothing else. Stellan embraced her, and when he touched her, she cried out in a pain he recognized as only coming from emotional loss. Some part inside of her had died. She cried so deeply and for such a time that Stellan worried she would never stop, but he would hold her until she did. He would not let her go until he knew she was ready.

After a few moments, a hand pressed his shoulder.

"It's time to go," Pierce said.

Stellan nodded but didn't leave until Wendy fell into silence and sleep, and then he carried her into a recovery room where he hoped she would be safe from the inescapable monster that hunted them throughout every deck on that carrier ship, the horrible thing that penetrated bulkhead walls and hatch doors through which even the black could not pass.

He wanted to hide her from their enduring sadness.

CHAPTER 10
EDWARD'S WORTH

One

When checking ocular motor function, Daelen was supposed to verify that both pupils were equal in size. She was supposed to ensure they reacted by constricting when she shined light into them. Abnormalities could indicate a patient was under the influence of alcohol or drugs. They could indicate eye diseases. They could indicate stroke or brain injury or tumors.

That was what the books told her.

When Daelen looked into Edward's eyes, however, she looked for something else. Maybe she hoped to find someone she could trust, as she could no longer offer much in the way of dependable care. Perhaps desperation drove her to look for the metaphysical, but she couldn't care for a patient if they were to be on the move. They all needed someone they knew they could count on. They all needed to be able to lean on each other. The black madness hadn't just taken Edward's sanity. It took his dependability, and now, he was a liability, creating a strain on the group.

Pierce had asked Daelen to examine Edward, and she wondered what the captain would do if she declared Edward incompetent.

Looking into the black of Edward's eyes, she felt no fear, and it wasn't because Stellan stood watch in the same room. Something had changed within Edward, and she'd recognized it even as he'd held her to the deck with his hands wrapped around her throat. It was clear something inside of him had broken. Like a dam, the waters burst forth, creating a time of turmoil. Eventually they settled, leaving a changed landscape. The important part was the waters were still.

"You say you've been feeling well, yeah?" Daelen asked.

"Better than I have in a long time," Edward said. Edward's eyes drifted down to the bruises that lingered on her neck. "I didn't mean to hurt you. I don't mean to make it sound like I'm making excuses, but that wasn't me. It was somebody else."

She looked to him doubtfully and held her palm over his chest while her link unfolded several windows and took his blood pressure, heart rate, respiration rate, and core body temperature.

"How have your tremors been?" Daelen asked. "Headaches? Blurry vision? Fatigue? Memory lapses?"

"No, no," Edward said. "None of that. Clear as day."

Daelen held up her palms. "Push against my hands."

He reluctantly pressed his palms against hers, and Stellan eyed him carefully. He pushed until she pushed back and understood he was not to push any more even though he felt the strength to do so.

"Good," she said. "Now interlock your fingers with mine and pull." Edward again followed orders and pulled until she resisted.

"Good," she said, releasing his hands. "Now stand up straight and close your eyes." Edward did as he was told, and her hands grasped his shoulders, pushing him sideways, testing his balance.

"Stand on one foot." Edward complied and felt his body's desire to topple but only because of age and his round belly, not due to nervous system defect.

"Put your foot down."

His motor functions were fine, but she felt like she needed confirmation of what she already knew. For the time being, Edward's madness had vanished as suddenly as it had come. It might return. Until they got him back to New Earth and did more tests, they would know nothing with certainty. But by her assessment, he could move on his own.

She looked deep into his eyes then and saw a confidence in him that she had not seen since he first came onto the ship. Since then, he'd been riddled with grief over the loss of his wife, Arlo's mother. Daelen looked deep into the black of his eyes, and instead of the nothingness that had prevailed when his fingers clenched her throat, she found a new man, one still grief stricken, yes, but compassionate nonetheless. The redness from the burst blood vessels had subsided as well, and the swelling of his tissue had all but vanished. Outward appearances told her he was healing well.

"If I could, I would take it back," Edward said. "If I could give my life to make it right, I would."

It wasn't until then that Daelen realized she had not allowed herself enough time to grieve. It wasn't until the tears flooded her eyes and she looked at Edward unashamed and unwilling to let those tears flow that she remembered she still had some healing of her own to do. She wondered about her own liability. If someone leaned on her, would she be able to hold him or her up?

"Thank you," Daelen said because she didn't know what else to say, and maybe she said it because it was something Edward needed to hear. He smiled a small, genuine smile, the kind of happiness that bleeds through grief and sadness during hard times when such emotions are inappropriate.

"Are you finished?" Stellan asked.

Daelen nodded.

"Let's go." Stellan grasped Edward's shoulder with cold, powerful strength. He pulled Edward off the examination table and ushered him into the common room as if he were still a prisoner. Stellan didn't yet understand that, now, they all were, and it was time to let Edward go.

Two

In the common room, Pierce, Arlo, Margo, and Floyd huddled together, whispering conspiratorially. When Stellan and Edward approached, they hushed and looked guilty.

Stellan pushed Edward into their company and continued to the door, stopping only to retrieve his rifle, which lay on the thin padding of an exam table.

"Where do you think you're going?" Pierce asked.

"To your cabin," Stellan said. "To get that brick."

Pierce's eyes narrowed, and Stellan thought he saw a glimmer of panic. "It isn't worth the risk. It's a waste of time. You have to know that."

"Maybe," Stellan said. "But we have to try if it could mean we fix this."

Stellan checked the straps of his belt. His sidearm hung securely to his upper thigh. He slung his rifle over his shoulder and counted the spare magazines in his pockets, then counted the four magazines for his rifle and calculated that he had one hundred and twenty-eight rounds. He also carried four magazines for his sidearm, which meant he had fifty-two rounds, minus the one he used for Rick. It was probably more than enough ammunition. Firing even one round would likely draw the attention of others, and by himself, he could only put so many down. If his dreams had taught him anything, he had learned that much.

"We don't even know if Daelen can cure it," Pierce said.

Daelen came out of the private exam room. She looked to Stellan doubtfully, acknowledging the uncertainty of it. The lack of confidence in herself bothered Stellan because he believed, if anyone could save them, it was her, and he predicated the risk he was about to take on that faith. Stellan walked over to her and gently touched her elbow. He looked long and hard into her eyes.

"Should I do this? If I get that brick, is there a chance?"

Daelen considered it for a moment and then, with a deep breath, nodded. "If I know what it is, there's a chance I could even have something here to treat it."

"That's good enough," Stellan said, and he leaned in and kissed her.

"Stellan," Pierce said with a frustrated huff. "I'm ordering you."

Stellan looked over his shoulder and sneered when he found the dark eye of Pierce's sidearm staring him in the face.

"What makes you think I give a shit about orders anymore?" Stellan said. "Put your weapon down. You may be a murderer, but you won't shoot me. Not when you need me."

"That's right," Pierce said. "We need you."

"Give me thirty minutes."

"Those people out there don't have any more time."

"Exactly," Stellan said. "Those who are infected, the ones we can still save, they're running out of time."

"I'm still the captain of this ship goddammit!"

"What ship!?" Stellan said. "A ship needs people to run it, and if we're all that's left, this isn't a ship. It's a tomb. There are people out there who are sick and dying, but they're not dead yet. They deserve a chance. Save as many as we can. That's what you said, and that's what I'm doing. If we don't owe it to them, we at least owe it to ourselves."

Stellan waited for a response; Pierce had none. As he turned his back on Pierce's weapon and headed toward the door, a part of him feared Pierce would respond with a gunshot.

"So be it," Pierce said, lowering his sidearm. "I hope you find what you're looking for, but I won't let you risk the lives of anyone else. If you go, you're going alone."

It was just as well. He would be better off alone. He could move faster and quieter, and he wouldn't have to worry about anyone else. He knew, with the potential force they faced, it didn't matter how many guns they had. Stealth would have to be his weapon.

"Wait," Edward said. "I'll go."

Stellan stopped and closed his eyes. Though the nobility of the offer touched him, Edward was the last of them he wanted along. Stellan turned with a smile.

"I appreciate that, but I'll be okay. You should stay here where Daelen and the others can look after you."

"I know you don't think I'm well, but I don't want to continue to be a burden," he said. "I feel fine. I feel better than I have in a long time actually. I can help. I know it."

"Dad," Arlo begged.

"No, son," Edward said. "I have to do this, too. I have my reasons."

Stellan looked to Daelen for approval, which she would not offer. She could only return an anxious stare and await his decision.

Against his better judgment, Stellan nodded, and Edward marched forward eagerly despite Pierce's protests.

Edward handled his weapon clumsily, and Stellan watched, fearful that he would drop it.

Three

Stellan couldn't stop watching Edward. Nervous Edward. Despite the progress he'd made, the bruises were still visible, and some of the swelling remained. In places, his skin was a deep purple or light gray. It made him look like one of the dead. At first glance, Stellan nearly turned his gun on him.

Part of him wanted to. They were alone now. He could claim the madmen got him, that there was nothing he could have done.

However, Stellan himself would know what he did. He felt dirty just for having those thoughts.

Yet, if Daelen had died, he didn't know that he would have been so forgiving, but Edward was with him now. They used to call escort missions "babysitting." Both Edward and Stellan would have agreed, however, that it was more of a test to see if Edward was worthy of Stellan's risk when he leaped out of an airlock and brought Edward back from oblivion.

They moved stealthily down the silent halls. They had to be quiet because it was true the madmen and the dead were grouping together. They would not dare discharge their weapons unless they were certain it would not attract more attention than they could handle or if they had no other choice.

Stellan didn't have much to say to Edward anyway. As long as Edward didn't get him killed, he would be fine, and Stellan thought that went without saying.

The way Edward moved irritated Stellan. He held his weapon as if it were a snake, his feet fell heavy and flat, and his breathing was loud and unsteady.

"Quiet," Stellan whispered.

"I'm sorry!"

Edward was trying, but trying only counted in training. In combat, they could only accept doing. Stellan pulled Edward into a dark room where the eyes of the mad or dead might not be able to see. He cleared the room and closed the door.

"You're making too much noise," Stellan said. "If you're going to be with me, you can't be a liability."

Edward hung his head in disappointment. Stellan could see his good intentions. Unfortunately, the madmen wouldn't care about Edward's good intentions. They would chew right through them.

"I'm sorry, Chief. I'm trying."

"Bend your knees," Stellan said.

"What?"

"You're walking heavy," Stellan said. "Bend your knees when we move, and make sure your feet land heel to toe. Keep your body steady like you're gliding."

Edward did as he was told, testing the bounce of his legs.

"Hold your weapon like you mean it."

"I'm sorry. I've never used a gun before."

"It's not a gun. It's never a gun. It's a weapon," Stellan said. "Hold your weapon with both hands. One is its foundation that it rests on. The other is the wall it leans against."

Edward raised his sidearm and pointed it at the wall. Stellan adjusted Edward's body to show him the correct stance and posture. Edward closed one eye to aim down the sights of the pistol and curled his tongue out over his lip.

"Don't do that," Stellan said. "Use both eyes. If you have to close one eye to aim, you're trying to shoot something that's too far away. You need both eyes open, especially here. Use your peripheral vision. Watch your corners."

Edward nodded, perfectly attentive. Stellan thought he was actually learning.

"Keep an eye on me," Stellan said. "I'm on point. When I move, you move, not the other way around. Point your weapon at things I don't point mine at. Cover corners I'm not covering. Watch doorways I'm not watching."

Edward absently held his sidearm up and to the side. Stellan pushed it down gently.

"When you're not pointing your weapon at something you want to kill, point it at the deck."

He grabbed Edward's other hand and pulled it under his other to support the weapon. When Stellan let go, Edward let his sidearm fall too low.

"But not so you'll shoot yourself in the foot," Stellan said. "This is your best friend. Get close to it, but never get complacent. It'll hurt you if you let it."

Stellan took a moment to stare into Edward's eyes, to hopefully allow his crash course in soldiering to sink in. It reminded him of looking into Rick's eyes, not because of any resemblance but because of the differences. Rick's eyes used to burn with a light. Stellan could always tell Rick was trying to figure something out. His brain was always working. The deep, defined lines on his brow were a testament to the years he'd spent inside his own head.

Edward was less of a thinker. Stellan didn't suspect Arlo's father had any mental handicaps, but he certainly was more consigned to a lower class of thought. He had always been quiet and did what he was told, never demonstrating any leadership qualities. Stellan supposed Arlo had spent at least part of his adult life trying to not be like his father. Perhaps it was why his tongue was so sharp and why he feigned such an ego.

Even so, Edward's eyes, while somewhat dull, flashed brighter than Rick's had when he lay restrained on that table. Edward's eyes engaged the world more than the man Stellan found as little more than a torso in the hallway on his way to security. And they were sharper than even Tom's eyes before Stellan had killed him in the bar.

There was something there. Edward was a human being, full of compassion, love, and understanding. Like all humans, he was capable of terrible things, but the point was that he chose not to do those things.

The madmen acted like they had no other choice. Was it free will that differentiated them? Stellan wasn't sure. In that moment, though, he was thankful for Edward. He knew he had done the right thing by saving his life, even if it cost him the life of his child.

Edward's life held value because he still had the potential to do good.

Four

Stellan had hoped Arlo had been wrong about the group of the dead he'd heard near the entryway to the central lift. Unfortunately, he was right.

When they approached the main corridor to the lift, a breathing sound arose like the swell of the light drive. Although, while the light drive's waves crashed evenly and rhythmically, this breathing sound was chaotic and punctuated with popping and clapping noises like vocal cords slamming together with unintentional, short coughs. A putrid odor wafted down the corridor, and as they drew nearer and its strength grew, Stellan identified the stench that he could never describe but, once he'd smelled it, never forget.

At its base, the miasma gagged him like rank earth filled his mouth, the insects crawling down the back of his throat. On the next level, curdled milk and vegetables rotted into gelatin gave it a wetness like an invisible fog. The top note was the sweet smell of vinegar, burning just enough to start the flow of tears.

It was the fetid smell of decomposing flesh.

Stellan stopped Edward with a raised fist, and they hugged the wall between two jutting support joists, partially concealing themselves in shadow. Edward sniffed the air and recoiled, stifling the urge to vomit by pressing his mouth and nose into the crook of his arm.

"What is that?" he whispered. Stellan didn't answer because Edward would figure it out soon enough, and knowing what it was wouldn't make it any easier to bear.

Even with the grand reverb of the empty hallways, they distinguished the sounds of scuffing shoes as the dead moved aimlessly around in the lobby before the lift. They moaned softly like lost children, and they grunted heartily like dogs begging for attention. With their heads cocked and lolling, constricting their airways, their breathing was raspy and dry.

Stellan guessed they didn't need to breathe. From what he'd seen, the dead ones' blood coagulated, and the loss of limbs didn't bother them in the slightest. It might slow them down, but losing blood concerned them as much as the drool that dripped onto their shirts. It didn't appear that their bodies had much use for any of their old support organs anymore.

Daelen had said, while the higher-order brain functions ceased, the brain stem remained active. He knew the brain stem controlled things like breathing and heartbeat. Maybe those parts of the body continued to function because some semblance of who they were remained. Maybe they simply were bored and liked to play with their windpipes to entertain themselves, some weird form of necro-masturbation, a living organism playing with a dead body like a toy.

In any case, it was relevant to him because he knew, even though they breathed, they wouldn't flinch if he shot them in the chest.

Stellan led Edward to where their hallway intersected with the main corridor that would bring them to the lift. He crept slowly toward the corner, crouching low, running his palms along the wall for balance. His fingertips curled around the edge, and he looked back at Edward with authority, a look that told Edward to stay put.

Stellan leaned out of cover and peered at the group of the dead crowding the lift lobby. His training rushing back to him, he took a mental picture so as to expose himself as shortly as possible. Then he returned to where he would be unseen.

"What'd you see?" Edward whispered.

"Nothing good," Stellan said. "We can't go this way."

"How many?"

Stellan reviewed the picture in his mind. "Twenty. Maybe more."

"We can take them," Edward said, holding his weapon as Stellan had shown him. Stellan smiled at Edward's enthusiasm.

"You forget about the 'maybe more' part," he said. "Others may be nearby, and they will come at the sounds of our gunfire."

Edward retreated into thought. "It's odd. I understand them grouping up. That makes sense. But why here?"

"Maybe they remember," Stellan said. "Maybe they're waiting on the lift. A lot of people use this lift to get around the ship. Maybe they're playing out a routine. Maybe something of what they used to be is still there."

They heard the *Atlas'* signature chirp, and Stellan peeked around the corner again. One of the dead was pressing the call button. Even as the lift doors opened, he pressed the button, his mind stalled on that one action as the bright light held his attention.

"So what are we going to do?" Edward asked.

"We can double back and hit a service ramp up a level and catch the lift there."

"What if there are more of them?"

"We'll figure something out."

They were preparing to move when they detected a faint ringing sound like a bumblebee with tiny bells attached to its wings. It was far off, but after a moment, Stellan identified it as metal dragging against metal. It bounced around in those corridors as if emanating from the very walls.

Pinpointing its origin was impossible, but Stellan guessed it was coming from the congregation of dead by the lift. If it wasn't, knowing how they would react to the sound was valuable information. As in any recon mission, he had to look for signs that his position had been compromised, and it wasn't always as obvious as the enemy opening fire. Even something drawing attention in his area could be disastrous, so he had to make sure the dead weren't moving toward them to investigate.

Stellan carefully peeked around the corner once again and saw them aimlessly wandering as they were. He watched each individually. None of them made the sound.

Then the dead picked up on it, too. One by one, they began to lazily crane their heads and search in every direction. The ringing continued to grow, and they all fixed their attention down the same corridor with their absent, puzzled faces, stupidly wondering about everything and having answers for nothing. He supposed the infection could kill everything else human in them, but for better or worse, the human propensity for curiosity would endure. After all, curiosity had them in this predicament to begin with.

A man emerged from one of the side corridors. Behind him, he dragged a pipe, blood soaking its end like motor oil and leaving a spotted trail on the deck. He gazed dreamily at the dead ahead of him and then stopped, eyeing them like familiar strangers.

The dead at the lift moved toward this man with their moans and puzzled faces. Almost in unison, their pace began as a slow stumble, and as they got closer, it became an awkward run, their faces growing hungrier as they neared.

"I told you to leave me alone!" the man with the pipe roared, striking one of the dead in the head, splashing gobs of red paste against the wall.

Behind him, several other men and women emerged. One of the women looked frantic. She was middle-aged, her silvering hair in tangles. She wore an apron covered in blood.

"Have you seen Justin?" she asked sweetly. "He's such a good boy. The Council man took him away to that war. He should be back any day now."

One of the men in this new group grabbed one of the dead by the collar of his partially disintegrated shirt, singed and charred by some fire that might have even continued to rage.

"It's my land! My home! I can fly whatever flag I choose!"

It took a moment for Stellan to understand the conflict. Knowing the madness' desire to feed and spread, he realized this new group was infected, too. Like Tom in the bar, before Stellan put a bullet through his chest and helped this epidemic start by showering the patrons in Tom's blood, this new group was far along. They'd fallen to madness but had not yet died. The dead sought to hurry the process along for them.

"Why are they fighting each other?" Edward asked.

"I think the ones with the weapons are still alive. They're just mad," Stellan said. "The other ones are trying to kill them. Because then the infection has full control."

"Can it be so smart?"

"It's fighting itself."

Before he was taken down, the man with the pipe swung and caught two more of the dead in their heads, probably putting them down for good. But he succumbed to the group, and when he screamed, it was not of a man who accepted his fate or even of a man who was unaware of it. It was of a lucid man who knew, in those final moments, he was going to die and fought against it with everything he had even as his entrails rose above the crowd like ropes.

In the end, for him, as well as all mankind, that will to live was one of the strongest enduring human traits that even an alien infection could not suppress.

Several of the dead tackled the woman looking for the boy named Justin. She didn't understand what was happening to her. She giggled as if they were playing with her. Indeed, in a matter of seconds, one of the dead toyed with one of her limbs, turning it up and sucking on the bloody end.

As the dead killed and accepted the new members into their ranks, Stellan saw an opportunity. Just before the scuffle, one of the dead must have absently pressed the call button for the central lift, and the control panel announced its arrival with a chirp.

It was reckless, but it would take a long time to double back and catch the lift on another level. And he couldn't be sure there wasn't another group of madmen or the dead congregated there or somewhere along the way.

"Come on," Stellan said to Edward. "Run!"

They both swung around the corner, and when Edward saw the dead dancing with entrails high above their heads, he slowed.

"Oh, Jesus!"

"Move!" Stellan grasped Edward's shirt, pulling him so hard they both stumbled.

Stellan's heart beat faster when one of the dead saw them, freezing as it identified new prey. His legs pumped harder than he thought possible, and then two, three, four of the dead turned their heads, fixed their unblinking eyes, and began to rise. Stellan saw something in them after all. An eagerness, a happiness, as if they were children receiving presents.

Ahead of them, the doors to the lift started to close, and Stellan thought it would be the absolute worst way the scenario could have played out. The doors would close, and they would be in the open against twenty-plus dead. They would have no choice but to use their weapons, and it would probably draw more of the madmen and dead. He hoped they would live long enough to figure out that problem.

Edward struck out like lightning and dove for the door, hands splayed out, interrupting the doors just before they closed. With the doors opening, he froze and curled into a ball, fear convincing him the dead were right on top of him. Stellan picked him up and dragged him into the lift.

Stellan felt a brief moment of relief. They had made it, but the doors remained open.

Edward frantically slammed the door close button on the holopanel. Stellan aimed his rifle into the hall. He would not fire unless he had to.

He prioritized his targets. The first to fall would be the man in front of the pack wearing an engineering jumpsuit. His head weaved as he lunged forward, but at this distance, Stellan would hit his mark.

The second to fall would be a woman who was missing half of her face in a tear that mirrored the way her shirt had been torn down the center from the collar, exposing one of her breasts and several bite and scratch marks on her abdomen. She had been a course in a feast before the infection gained control of her dead body and grasped eagerly for them.

The third to fall would be a man in an officer's uniform. Stellan recognized him as one of the department heads from the command deck. He thought his name was Dennis. He forgot Dennis' last name, but he didn't have time to wish them dignity or merciful peace. They turned on him now as predators, and he could not afford to pity them.

The dead reached out. Stellan feared the man who led the pack would trigger the lift door's obstruction sensor again, and if he did, the rest would pour in. Enclosed in a hanging box of steel, Stellan and Edward would have no choice but to open fire. If that first one tripped the sensor, they all would get in, flowing in like water through an open valve.

Stellan's finger began to pull. His instincts took control and knew where the threshold on the trigger was. If he pulled it any farther, his rifle's rail system would engage, charged by an efficient yet powerful amplifier that would accelerate a high-density, tungsten carbide projectile at a supersonic speed with a thunderclap.

His gut screamed for him to pull the rest of the way, that if he shot the first one, there would be a better chance the others would not reach the lift before the door closed. His mind agreed.

So he dropped the first one. In the lift, his rifle's bark was deafening, concussive. His eyes watered. It put Edward on his knees with his hands over his ears.

They were too close. He had to drop the second one. The bullet entered her forehead cleanly, exploding out the back and spraying the dead behind her with globs of red and chunks of gray. She fell peacefully, and the others stepped over her indifferently.

Stellan couldn't take anymore. The sound was too much. If he fired again, he and Edward both would be deaf. Surely, that would be better than dead, but he felt good about the chances that the doors would close before his third target reached them.

Through his tear-filled eyes, Stellan had trouble gauging depth, and as the group reached for them, he wasn't sure there was space between the closing doors and their fingertips.

Stellan clenched his rifle's trigger, ready for a final blast, when the doors closed without obstruction. The dead pounded on the outer doors in frustration.

They were glad for the ringing in their ears then, and for some reason, laughter overtook them, as Stellan understood sometimes happened when you were so close to death's mouth you could feel its breath and then were miraculously pulled away by the hands of God.

The laughter must have come with the realization, albeit perhaps only temporary, that of course there was a God, a great happiness of overwhelming and sudden faith, and in such circumstances, he was showing you what it would be like without him.

And you were supposed to be thankful.

Five

As they ascended the central lift, the ringing in their ears began to recede and allow them to hear the creaking steel and suspension cables that pulled them upward. The remnants of the concussive blasts lingered in the form of sharp pains splitting the hemispheres of their brains.

The laughter and cheer abandoned them, as well. Like a spring of euphoria that had run dry, doubt returned, and they were no longer preoccupied with things like faith in the divine.

But they felt safe, and some parts of them wanted to simply stay in the enclosed lift. In that box, they would be free to live without fear that they'd be torn to pieces. It wouldn't be a long existence. In the end, death would come all the same, but it would be free of fear and pain. And it would be their choice. That much appealed to them.

Stellan stopped the lift between floors.

"What are you doing?" Edward asked.

"Give me a hand." Stellan pointed toward the ceiling. "I'm not going to let these doors open without knowing what's on the other side."

They had passed the command deck, the facilities deck, and the services deck and were just below Pierce's private residence deck. This lift offered exclusive access to Pierce's cabin. It was relatively secure and isolated from the rest of the ship, but Edward thought it was smart to do something a little less reckless after their last encounter with the dead. After seeing one deliberately pressing the call button, it was possible they were using the lifts. One of them could have taken this lift to the top. Several could have followed. It would fit up to twelve people comfortably. That many infected, whether dead or mad, could pose a significant problem for them, especially in a confined space.

Edward interlocked his fingers for Stellan's boot and hoisted him up. Stellan opened the maintenance hatch in the ceiling and climbed onto the lift's roof, his boots booming like distant thunder.

"What do you see?" Edward asked.

Stellan found himself in what must have been one of the darkest parts of the ship. It wasn't often he saw maintenance areas, and he forgot many parts of the *Atlas* didn't need to be lit most of the time. He supposed elevator shafts were included, and he had no idea how to turn on any lights.

"Not a whole lot," Stellan replied.

To make do, he opened some windows on his link. The cool blue glow coated the walls in a sheet of ice. Shadows danced around the shaft walls and on the greasy suspension cables, which he grasped for balance. He stepped carefully because he wasn't sure what he was stepping on.

The door to Pierce's residence level gazed at him like a fine cat's eye. A sliver of light shone through.

Edward heard Stellan pry open the door, and the lift groaned under Stellan's weight as he pushed off and onto Pierce's residence deck.

Edward began to feel nervous. With Stellan gone, there was no way he could get out of the elevator. He couldn't reach the maintenance hatch himself, and he wouldn't dare take the lift to another floor and risk a flood of the dead spilling onto him. Suddenly, the safety and protection of the lift interior felt like a prison. He couldn't imagine a worse way to go.

He wasn't convinced Stellan was coming back. If he were Stellan, he would consider just leaving him there. Pitiful Edward. Awkward, stupid Edward. Maybe he should get cozy after all, he thought. Maybe he should just curl into a ball and wait for death.

"Stellan?" he said.

The worst part about it was Edward wouldn't have blamed him. Edward had cost Stellan so much already, and all he wanted was the chance to pay him back. If it meant being left behind, he supposed he would accept it.

"Chief?"

A couple of thuds struck the lift's roof, and Edward's first thought was not that Stellan had returned. Panicked, Edward first thought it was one of the dead coming to get him. He heard a dry dragging sound as whatever was up there shuffled its feet, no doubt preparing to climb down the hole for him.

So Edward held his pistol at the ready and pointed it at the maintenance hatch. He wasn't going to give up without a fight. No, not lonely Edward.

A pair of boots dangled through the hatch, and then they dropped.

Edward wanted to squeeze the trigger. In his moment of panic, firing seemed like it was the only choice. It was better to be safe than sorry.

The boots landed on the floor, and when Stellan saw the gun leveled at him, he put his hands up.

"Jesus, man!" he said.

Relief and then embarrassment flooded Edward's face. "I'm so sorry. It's just that you left, and I didn't know where you went, and you didn't answer when I called and—"

"Edward," Stellan interrupted. "Would you put your weapon down?"

Edward looked at his pistol dumbfounded, like he had forgotten he was holding it. "Right." He lowered it to his side. "Sorry about that."

"Stop apologizing. Let's just agree to not point our weapons at each other."

"Agreed." Edward nodded. They both took a breath. "What did you find?"

"All clear," Stellan said. "Something strange, though."

Edward looked to Stellan questioningly, but he simply started the lift once more, completing their ascent to the top of the *Atlas*.

Six

They found Pierce's cabin mostly as it should have been. The hall from the lift to the door was quiet and clean, but Stellan had found the hatch door left open, and a stack of books had been knocked over into the middle of the living room. A bottle of Pierce's whisky stood on the table in the corner, missing some of its volume since Stellan had last seen it.

Most concerning, however, was the large pool of blood on the floor in Pierce's office.

"Blood?" Edward said. "I thought you said you found something strange."

"This deck is sealed," Stellan said, grimacing as he crouched to investigate. "Few people can get here. Blood here is strange because there shouldn't be any infected up here."

"Then what was all that in the lift?"

"I said 'shouldn't'."

The conclusion seemed obvious yet illusive. Pierce had shot someone. Whom? And why? From the irregular way the pool had settled and the smears on the floor, Stellan could tell Pierce had left his victim lying on the deck. When Pierce had gone, this person had gotten back up. The question that perhaps plagued him the most, however, was whether this person had died before it got back up.

"What's that on the wall?" Edward asked.

"Blood spatter."

"What would do that?"

"The exit wound from a gunshot."

Edward jumped at the sudden realization that this blood had not come from a bite, scratch, or tear, as if wounding by gunshot had become more unusual than cannibalism. It revolted him, and Stellan could see the onset of nausea. The pigment flushed out of the flesh that was not bruised and swollen. He swooned, and after momentarily fighting it on his feet, he looked for somewhere to sit. He wobbled toward the chair behind Pierce's desk but didn't make it before he leaned in the corner and retched into a potted fern. With the contents of his stomach evacuated, he collapsed into Pierce's creaky wooden chair, wiping his mouth with his sleeve.

"You all right?" Stellan said.

"Fine," Edward said, slouching with his eyes closed. "I just need a minute."

"You got it. While you're back there, maybe you can open some of those drawers. Look for a small black brick."

It wasn't on the desktop where Stellan had last seen it. Pierce must have moved it. He searched the shelves on the far wall, pulling back books to see if he'd hidden it behind one of them. He dug in the trashcan. He looked under the chair. He even checked the fern. They searched Pierce's entire cabin and couldn't find it anywhere. Why would Pierce have hidden it? Perhaps he'd disposed of it. If so, why didn't he tell Stellan before they left medical?

As they stood in Pierce's living room, trying to think creatively about where Pierce could have hidden the brick of alien material, Stellan heard an odd hum. It was higher pitched than the *Atlas'* air circulation system, and he felt certain it hadn't been there a moment ago.

He followed the sound out into the hallway. It became less muffled and tinnier. He heard a squeal and then the groan of the lift's suspension cable.

The lift was moving.

Stellan ran to the doors and dug his fingers between them, struggling to pry them open.

"Give me a hand," he said, and Edward jumped to his aid. Together, they opened the lift's outer doors, and that's when they heard the moans and shuffling. The lift was rising, and it carried with it a cargo of the dead.

"What are we going to do?" Edward said. "Should we hide in the captain's cabin? We could seal the hatch."

"No," Stellan said. "We'd just be trapped, and there's no telling how long they'd wait out here for us."

Stellan hoped the lift would stop on one of the lower floors. He peered down through the maintenance hatch, which was still open, and he could see several heads rolling and bobbing as if they were on the cusp of falling asleep but would not allow themselves to slip into unconsciousness. He couldn't get an accurate count.

He thought about putting their backs to the far wall and trying to take the mob out as it spilled forward. He knew their chances would diminish with the greater numbers in the lift, but he saw no other choice.

He turned to move Edward into a strategic position, prepared to give him a pep talk, and Stellan found himself once again staring down the barrel of Edward's sidearm.

"What—" Stellan said, and the report from Edward's weapon interrupted him.

The bullet whizzed over Stellan's shoulder and through the open lift doors. The pang of metal against metal was almost as loud as the gunshot itself, and the lift immediately cried out in agony. The cable snapped, and the lift fell before its emergency brakes caught it in the shaft, frozen somewhere on a deck below. The moans and growls of the dead inside professed their displeasure.

Stellan looked toward Edward, amazed.

"I figured we couldn't risk trying to take them all," Edward said with an innocent smile. "Then, before I really knew what I was doing, I was squeezing the trigger."

Stellan looked down the shaft, dumfounded, to ensure it wasn't going anywhere.

"That's called instinct," he said, one of the dead peering up at him through the open maintenance hatch with its mouth agape. "Just one problem. They may not be getting in, but we're not getting out."

Edward looked at him quizzically. "What do you mean?"

"You killed the lift. How are we supposed to get down?"

"The fire escape, of course."

"Fire escape?"

"Yes. When they built the ship, code required an alternate route of egress for every deck in the event that something could block escape from a fire."

Edward scanned the hallway, his eyes working under a furrowed brow. "There should be one around here somewhere," he said. "Ah!"

He ran past the hatch door to the dead end, the purpose of which Stellan had always questioned.

"They're hidden and sealed, ensuring they won't compromise other decks in the event of depressurization. If the *Atlas* detected a fire, it would direct the captain here and reveal a control panel and a doorway," Edward said, feeling the wall. "But you can access them manually if you find the right spot."

Edward found a square tile and pushed in on it. It flipped 180 degrees, revealing a touchscreen. He pressed his palm against it, and the wall opened to reveal descending stairs.

"There," Edward said. Stellan gawked at him. "What?"

"You kind of remind me of Rick."

Edward smiled, but before he began his descent down the stairs, Stellan stopped him. The moans of the dead trapped in the shaft behind them rose into the hallway.

"Just one thing before we go any farther," Stellan said. "We agreed no more pointing our weapons at each other."

"I didn't point it at you," Edward said with a smirk. "You were just in the way."

"Fair enough," Stellan said.

The two of them descended into the darkness below. Stellan found some comfort in the knowledge that they were moving into parts of the ship with which at least one of them was familiar.

Seven

Edward seemed to have lost his way.

The fire escape led into a darkened service tunnel. Their links illuminated the walls of metal grating and pipes around them. After a few turns and intersections, Edward spun around and bumped into Stellan. He paused, calculating something in his head. Then he continued on in his original direction.

"Do you know where you're going?" Stellan asked, and Edward promptly shushed him. In the cool glow, Edward placed a finger over his lips and then pointed upward.

Stellan didn't hear anything, and that newfound confidence in Edward waned. He wondered if Edward's mind was regressing, if he was losing his sanity again.

"You have no idea what's in these dark places," Edward whispered.

"And you do?"

"Spend enough time in these tunnels by yourself, and you'll see it. The *Atlas*' history. It's taken a lot of lives, not all of them rocks."

"People are killing each other, and then they're getting back up. You're worried about ghosts?"

"I'm worried one of them could come out of the darkness," Edward said. "If that's not a ghost, what is? Anyway, I can get us out of here. I'm just not entirely sure where we're going to end up."

A shriek bolted through the narrow passageway, and they stopped. Edward cowered. Stellan pulled his rifle to his shoulder. In the darkness, somewhere not too far off, he thought he heard breathing, but he couldn't tell which direction it was coming from. He waited. Nothing came.

"These tunnels would be used for evacuation, right?" Stellan whispered. "Why are they so damned hard to navigate? I can't even tell which way is up." The tight quarters and stuffy air had begun to get to them, forming beads of sweat on their brows.

"They would double as an evacuation route, but they mostly serve as maintenance access. If there was a fire or an emergency, the floor would light up and show the way," Edward said.

"Yeah, well I guess they didn't program the *Atlas* to recognize this kind of emergency," Stellan said.

"The servers are down," Edward reminded him. "I'm sure weird things are happening all over the ship. Everything is probably falling out of sync. Independent systems try to perform their functions, but without the central server, they can't communicate. It's like an orchestra trying to play without a conductor."

The breathing returned. It sounded long and effortless, impossibly deep, as if it were part of the air circulation system. Every few seconds, they heard a short growl unmistakably from a pair of vocal chords. And the breathing occasionally stopped.

"Get up," Stellan said. "We have to keep moving."

"What if it's in front of us?"

"It could also be behind us. We have to keep moving."

They pushed forward cautiously, Edward making use of the stealth tips Stellan had shown him, rolling his feet lightly on the grated floor, heel to toe, heel to toe. The corridors seemed to go on for miles, but in truth, they had gone mere meters. The fear threatened to paralyze them, and it offered their minds the clarity to register every moment in its entirety, stimulating it with the full capacity of their senses.

As they moved, they listened. They realized these maintenance tunnels carried sounds all over the *Atlas*. Screams they knew were distant darted past them like bullets down a rifle barrel. Wherever they went, turning around bends at crossroads, that breathing followed.

Then Stellan picked up on something else. He stopped Edward, and as if the sounds of the ship were keeping tabs on them, the silence returned. Before they continued, Stellan heard it again, an irregular rattling, not far off.

"Was that you?" Stellan asked.

"I didn't move!"

Stellan spun around with his rifle, the glow from his link illuminating the corridor. It battled the darkness with everything it had. Still, he wished it had more power. He wished he could push the darkness back. Down there, in the tiny veins and capillaries of the *Atlas*, the darkness surrounded them. It encroached upon them like cold hands, waiting for their lights to go out so it could take them.

The breathing and rattling came again. Closer now.

"What's there!?" Edward said.

"Maybe nothing," Stellan said.

"If it's something?"

"Then it probably isn't good. How much farther?"

"I don't know," Edward said.

"We have to move faster," Stellan said, pushing Edward forward.

The rattling of their own boots on the grating beneath them masked the sounds of anything they might have heard. Their own movements deafened them. In their haste, they betrayed themselves and lost the only sense they had left.

Stellan imagined one of the dead behind him, gaining on them. He felt a tingle on his back, his body's warning mechanism that something was watching. He wanted to turn and fire into the darkness. Even if he hit nothing, his muzzle flashes would reveal glimpses far down the tight corridor.

"I see light up ahead," Edward said, and the hand Stellan had held on Edward's back to keep him moving slid away as Edward moved faster.

Ahead of them, the passageway came to a dead end, but a sliver of light crept under the wall from the other side.

Their boots pounded the grating hard, and Stellan knew, with the way the sounds carried, every madman and walking corpse who shared whichever deck they were on would know they were there and that they were afraid.

Within a few meters of the dead end, they tripped a sensor, which told the door to let them through. It slid to the side slowly. Edward pressed against it anxiously, sliding his body through as soon as he could fit.

Stellan followed, watching the opening with his rifle. It closed again, and Stellan lowered his weapon. They found light. The corridor they found themselves in revealed all of its corners. They were safe.

"We made it!" Edward declared.

Behind him, the *Atlas* chirped, and the wall split open. The lift they'd dropped from above hung cockeyed and in between their deck and the deck below. A chorus of surprised moans crescendoed. Sickly arms with gaping wounds and ragged clothing lashed out and grabbed Edward's legs like whips, dragging him to the deck. He cried out in panic and dropped the weapon he so awkwardly held. Stellan dove, but there were too many, pulling Edward too fast.

By the time Stellan interlocked fingers with Edward, they were already biting into his legs. Edward's screams mingled with the dead's cries of pleasure and eagerness as ones in the back pushed the ones up front out of the way to get their share of the meal.

Stellan leaped to his feet, still pulling with all his might.

"Don't let them get me!" Edward screamed, and Stellan thought about how he pitied Edward. He was good at his job. He was good with machines and fixing things, but it hadn't registered that he was already gone one way or another.

Until then, Stellan hadn't thought of it either. The dead had won that match before it started.

Stellan stopped struggling then. He stopped trying to pull Edward out of the jaws of the dead and held him as still as he could. He gazed into Edward's eyes and saw the fear from the realization of what was about to happen.

"I'm sorry," Stellan said.

He let Edward go.

The dead pulled him into the lift, focusing all their attention on him, pouring all of their rage and malice onto him, and extracting their bloody delight.

Edward's screams meant he was still alive, and it meant Stellan could grant him mercy.

He edged as close as he needed, took aim with his rifle, and silenced the man he'd saved in vain. No matter whom he saved, death always won in the end. The will to survive and to save others was nothing but vanity. Never mind that he would not have made it this far without Edward, as fruitless as their endeavor had been.

When Edward was gone, the dead lost interest in him. They looked at Stellan with predatory eyes and moved toward him slowly, stalking him. He counted at least fifteen. He thought briefly that he stood a chance of filling the hole with bodies to keep them from pursuing him.

He dropped five of them before they began to climb out of the lift.

That was when Stellan turned his back on them and ran, and it seemed, wherever he went, the dead followed.

CHAPTER 11
THE DEAD COLLECT DEBTS

One

For most of the time Stellan was gone, Pierce thought about two things. His mind dwelled on them, digging like fingers into damp soil.

First, he thought about how nothing ever seemed to go as planned. He'd cover all the angles, think everything through, but he always missed something and would have to improvise. Actually, he enjoyed the challenge; however, just for once, with so much at stake, he wished things would be simple. He wished the solution would be obvious and that he could just walk out that door and make it happen.

Pierce looked to the sidearm he held affectionately, wishing the solution to their problems were as simple and pure as firing a bullet.

Second, he thought about how he would have killed someone for a glass of whiskey. He wanted to feel the fumes dance in his nostrils and prick his lips. He wanted it to make him feel warm again. The loss of control had made him feel cold, and if he couldn't have the heat of a foolproof plan, the excitement of the acquisition of power, he wanted the warmth of whiskey in his belly. He wanted to breathe fire.

"Where are they?" Arlo said, cracking his knuckles and pacing around the room. "They should have been back by now." The young man had grown increasingly restless after his father left, and little of Arlo's apprehension materialized on his face. Arlo wasn't joking around anymore, and that was a bad sign. At this point, Pierce knew nothing he could say would calm Arlo down. All Pierce could do was wait and hope the pilot didn't erupt. It was a side of Arlo he'd always known was there, though he'd never seen

291

it beyond shadows and silhouettes. He had no way of telling what would happen.

"Captain, maybe we should go after them, you know?" Arlo said. "After all, you wanted to go hours ago."

"We wait," Pierce said. He couldn't remember the last time he felt so inexplicably calm. Even through the frustration of lingering failure, he found a solid foundation. It was true he'd wanted to leave hours ago, and in fact, he'd been furious. But something inside of him knew there was nothing he could do and simply defaulted to a relaxed state. Until Stellan got back, they could do nothing, and he never doubted his friend would return.

"I hate to be the realist here," Floyd said, his arms crossing over his belly, "because I know none of you want to hear it. Hell, I don't want to say it. But what if they're not coming back?"

"Don't say that!" Wendy cried from the corner.

"They're coming back," Margo said definitively.

"They're just hung up somewhere is all," Arlo said.

"Enough!" Pierce said, quieting the rising panic. They were all ready to explode.

"All I'm saying is we can't stay here forever," Floyd said.

Their denial proved that, in truth, they all doubted. Their words persisted and reinforced their resistance to the idea that Stellan and Edward had perished. Pierce had considered his friend would not return, but he honestly couldn't believe it. He sensed something similar in Daelen, as well.

As plain as her face was, it held a blank puzzle. She simply gazed at the door with indifference, not a hint of worry, concern, or anxiety, as if she knew without a doubt that it would open.

In her, he found the strength to believe, even if it was unrealistic, even if it was a delusion. In her, he found hope, and he was thankful. Pierce knew Daelen was a wonderful woman, but he knew then why Stellan had married her. She made everything all right.

She broke her gaze from the door and looked at Pierce. For some reason, whether it was an automatic response or a deliberate attempt at reassurance, he smiled and immediately regretted it. His smile was out of place. Her face remained unchanged, and then she returned her attention to the door.

"We wait," Pierce said.

Two

The heart leaps at the most inexplicable things. The mind cannot comprehend what only the heart knows. It does not speak logic or reason. It cannot lie like the mind lies. It speaks only truths, and the power of will is nothing compared to the strength of even the weakest hearts.

As Daelen watched the door to medical, she thought she'd convinced herself Stellan would return. She thought she had no doubt he would be okay. But when the holopanel flashed from red to green and the hatch wheel spun, she didn't know what to think. She wanted it to be him, but it could have been anyone.

The room had been static. Nothing changed, and until she saw activity, progress on the path to learn his fate, her certainty had been unshaken. From the safety of the medical deck, she perceived no threats, though she knew they were out there.

Pierce drew his sidearm and swept around beside the door so he could catch whoever it was in their blind spot. He crept to the door with his back against the wall, ready to let his weapon fall like a hammer.

The hinges groaned, and when Stellan spilled into the room gasping, Daelen's body began to tremble, having held back the shaking until she knew something definite. Something in her body relaxed, and she hadn't known until then that it had been tense.

Until she knew Stellan was alive, she hadn't allowed herself to think otherwise. Like stepping into traffic and feeling the wind brush her face as vehicles raced by, she didn't know how close she'd been to breaking down until she knew she wouldn't have to. She didn't know how close to death he'd been until she knew he lived.

He fell to the deck, and she rushed to him, instinctively scanning his body for wounds. Pierce craned his head out the door left and right. With screams and growls chasing Stellan through the corridors, Pierce slammed and secured the hatch.

Arlo couldn't take his eyes off the door, his face wide open in disbelief. A shadow fell over the room. Edward had been with Stellan. Why hadn't he returned? Thousands of explanations ran through their minds, all of them attempts to deny the obvious, all of them causing painful, paradoxical schisms in their consciousness.

Pierce was the first to accept it. He knew Stellan wouldn't return without Edward unless the worst had happened, so he approached Arlo with a deep sigh, knowing the pilot would have great difficulty with it.

Realizing he'd made it to the safety of medical, Stellan's attention turned to Daelen. He embraced and kissed her passionately, looking deeply into her eyes so he could know she was safe. He wanted to hold her longer, but there would be time for them.

"Where's my dad?" Arlo asked, trembling. "Open the door! He was right behind you! He had to be right behind you!" The tears of a breakdown, of a world of belief crashing to the ground, spilled from his eyes.

The heart speaks only the truth, and Arlo couldn't bear to listen to it. He dashed for the door, but Pierce took his shoulders and steadied him.

"It's all right, Arlo," Pierce said. "It's going to be all right."

"No!" Arlo said, throwing Pierce's hands off. "Where's my dad!?" He paced back and forth like a lion in a cage.

"I'm sorry," Stellan said, and Arlo shuddered, threatening to swoon. Pierce held him steady.

"He trusted you!" Arlo cried. "He trusted you!"

Stellan knew they all had trusted him, and he had let them all down again. He looked around the room from face to face; none of them could look at him. Whether it was fear or shame or sadness, things had changed.

Nothing could have been truer. He'd seen what had become of the *Atlas*. He knew what the madmen and dead were capable of, their utter lack of remorse and restraint and respect for humanity. These people had no idea, and he felt some resentment that they would dare judge him.

"I tried. God, I tried," Stellan said. "They just, they came out of nowhere." To this, Arlo did not respond. He only sobbed in Pierce's arms and would not even react to Floyd's warm, compassionate touch on his shoulder. Even Wendy found the power to stand, using a table for support. She gazed through her own tears and gasped into her trembling hand.

Daelen comforted Stellan, as she understood the feeling of failure. She understood the feeling of powerlessness, that even with all the medical equipment and training she had at her disposal, they couldn't save everyone. That's what Stellan had told her, and now she believed it.

It didn't lessen the pain, but at least she could live with herself.

Arlo's cries eventually quieted. For a while, no one had the heart to move. They wanted to, but all the energy was drained from them.

When Stellan felt the fire of Pierce's gaze burning on his skin, he knew judgment fueled those flames.

Three

Pierce closed the door to Arlo's lingering sobs. The others would comfort him for now. Daelen's office offered privacy for the conversation Pierce needed to have with Stellan, who wasn't exactly in the best frame of mind for a debriefing, but Pierce didn't have time to wait for his chief of security to gather himself. No one had time for that.

"What the hell happened out there!?" Pierce demanded.

"They came out of nowhere," Stellan said, collapsing into Daelen's office chair. "There was nothing I could do."

Pierce moved in so close to Stellan's face that the heat from his raging nostrils licked Stellan's cheek like dragon's breath.

"I couldn't give a damn about Edward!" Through the large window that looked out upon the main common room, Pierce and Stellan saw Daelen looking disdainfully at them as she cradled Arlo's head. Pierce touched the holopanel by the door, and the glass frosted like the private rooms in the back.

"You left us for a fool's errand," Pierce continued, "and you came back empty handed."

"This about you saying you told me so?"

"No. This is about your inability to focus on what's important and it leading to failure." Pierce shoved a finger into Stellan's face, and Stellan slapped it away.

"I thought we wanted to save the *Atlas*!"

"That's right," Pierce said.

"So what am I missing?"

295

Pierce scoffed and turned away, shaking his head. When he looked back, it was with the eyes of a predator.

"You're not trying to save a ship," Pierce said. "You're trying to save souls. You're grasping at redemption."

"It was worth it, Gordon. If there's a chance to cure this thing, we have to try."

"And risk our lives? Edward? Wendy?" Pierce said. "Daelen? No, what you miss is that you think you're only risking your own life? You're playing with all of our lives now. We have to preserve what we have left."

Stellan wanted to jump up from his chair and strangle Pierce. He wanted to shut him up with his hands, and he felt confident he could.

"You're sure the brick wasn't there?" Pierce asked.

"We looked everywhere."

"And the server room?" Pierce said. "You said you were able to get there?"

"Toast," Stellan said. "Looked like there was a fire."

"Sabotage?"

Stellan shook his head. "I don't think so. If someone were trying to destroy the servers, it would have been neater, more focused. It looked like an accident. Old equipment and no one to monitor it. Maybe it was overloaded by all the activity."

Pierce took a step back and let the news sink in. "All right. We tried it your way. Now we're going to do it mine."

"Phalanx?"

"It's our only option."

"Gordon, do you really think it will work? These people, they're not soldiers. They might do for a little while, but they're going to break. We can't rely on them like that."

"Every soldier I've ever known has fallen apart at some point or another, including you. They pick themselves up, figure out they aren't the same person, accept it, and learn to live with it. They don't have a choice. We don't have a choice."

"There has to be another way."

"And that's probably why Edward is dead. That's probably why Doug is dead. You hesitated. You couldn't cut your losses. You couldn't do what was necessary because you were too busy judging yourself. We're not going to do that anymore. You're in no capacity to make decisions. You got them killed, and for what? No brick. No cure. There's no chance that way."

"It can't be done," Stellan said. "Only three people trained to use a weapon, two doctors, one injured engineer, and one retired old man. No way."

"We have to do something," Pierce said. "We can't stay here. We have no food or supplies. We have to move."

"Getting ourselves killed isn't what we should do," Stellan said. "You don't know what it's like out there."

"I'm tired of trying to avoid the unavoidable," Pierce said. "To save the ship, we're going to have to take it back by force. We can't afford compassion or weakness. We have to be ruthless. Like them."

"Then what's the point of surviving?" Stellan asked. "We found the blood in your cabin, too." At the mention of the blood, Stellan had Pierce's undivided attention. "What happened?"

"I thought it would be obvious," Pierce said.

"Enlighten me."

"I did what you couldn't," Pierce said. "I stopped Agent Skinner."

"Christ! Why?"

"She sabotaged us," Pierce said. "I had to put an end to it."

"I don't know what's worse," Stellan said, "the fact that you've changed or that I recognize *this* Pierce."

"Don't you dare judge me like I take life on a whim. Don't you dare assume it means nothing to me," Pierce said. "Someone has to do what's necessary."

"We don't shoot the living anymore," Stellan said.

"I killed her for this ship," Pierce said, as if he was trying to convince himself.

"She isn't dead," Stellan said.

"What?"

"Her body wasn't there," Stellan said.

Pierce's eyes moved from rage and into that ether of contemplation all men look to for guidance.

"Was she mad?" he asked rhetorically. Stellan saw an odd nervousness in the way Pierce paced, the way he scrubbed his stubble, the way his hand landed on his forehead.

"What were you thinking?" Stellan said.

"I should have done it a long time ago," Pierce said. "But I kept believing. I kept deluding myself. She was here to sabotage us. Eventually, I saw that clearly, so I stopped her."

"Gordon, she's here to help us get back to Earth."

"No." Pierce shook his head. "She's responsible for everything. I know it."

Pierce stormed out of the office, pulling the door open so hard it slammed against the wall, trembling on its hinges and disturbing everyone in earshot.

Four

The three former soldiers, two doctors, one injured engineer and one retired old man stood in a circle in the medical deck common room among exam tables that weren't of much use anymore. It was hard to fight the feeling that they would never be needed again. It was hard to believe the *Atlas* would ever be more than a tomb. Yet, they looked to Stellan and Pierce for strength. One man believed they could reclaim the ship; the other believed they could save people, and each man believed hard. The problem was neither understood those weren't the same objectives. At least for a time, they were aligned, but the others wondered what would happen if they weren't.

Instead of a place of healing, the medical deck had become a base of operations for a small strike team that would attempt to secure the *Atlas* deck by deck until they were satisfied they'd saved everyone they could. Then they would open all the airlocks in an emergency purge that would allow the black to penetrate to the *Atlas'* core and suck the infection from its bones.

The final part of the plan would no doubt work. Pressing a button for salvation was the easiest thing they could ever do. The hard part would be attempting to save others. Of course, the more they saved, the greater their numbers would become. Pierce hoped each crewmember they saved would take up arms with them. Just as the infected added to their ranks, so would they, and through a campaign of superior firepower, they could reclaim the ship.

Pierce expected it. It was his vision. Stellan knew each conscript they gained would only be a liability. The soldier had become a rare commodity.

"The plan is simple," Pierce said. "We make our way back to the residence deck. We go cabin by cabin until we've secured the deck. From there, we work forward until we reach the command deck. The objective is to find as many survivors as possible. Once on the command deck, we'll do an emergency purge and open all the airlocks on the *Atlas*."

The natural cadence for these kinds of explanations placed Arlo making a joke here, and Stellan took note that none came. Arlo sat quietly, staring at the deck with his arms crossed and shaking a crossed leg.

"I've no military training like you two," Floyd said.

"Three," Pierce said. "Arlo flew for the Corps."

"Pardon me," Floyd nodded at Arlo who could only manage to look up. He decided he wasn't quite ready for eye contact and returned his attention to the deck. "As I was saying, I'm having trouble understanding something. If we're to go out there and find people who aren't sick, how do we know who's infected and who's not?"

"If they've been bitten or are showing signs of madness, we'll isolate them," Daelen said.

"Surely, we're bound to run into some of them out there. What do we do then?" Floyd asked.

"We'll take each situation as it arises, but you all will be armed," Pierce said, and Floyd's eyes widened at the mention of violence. "Stellan, Arlo, and I will use force if necessary. The rest of you will be our backup if we need it."

Dread set into the group. They recoiled and turned inward, unable to determine if they would be able to answer that call if it came. Stellan noted how Floyd, in particular, suddenly became quiet as if he couldn't stomach any more answers to his questions.

"I don't understand," Wendy said. "Why don't we just go straight to the bridge and do the purge now?"

Stellan never expected her to say such a thing. There no doubt were survivors remaining on the *Atlas* who deserved a chance, and Wendy was proposing they take the easy way out. It was the safe way, but Stellan regarded it as a failure to his mission objective. He didn't hold it against her, though. She was scared. They all were. It was why using them to help secure the ship was a mistake.

With Pierce's interest piqued, he leaned forward, elbows on his knees. "Because there may be others out there who are still alive," Stellan said.

"Why is that our concern?" Wendy said. "We know *we're* alive, and we have a chance. Why risk it?"

"Because we owe them that much."

"Maybe *you* do," she said with some disdain. "*We* don't. Why not just let us stay here?"

"It's secure," Floyd said. "And Ms. Lin is still injured."

Stellan looked to Daelen. She felt his gaze like all lovers know when the other is looking, and she turned to him. Her smile was uneasy and forced.

"We'll have to take our time for Wendy, but I've treated her so that movement shouldn't be a problem," Daelen said.

"I'm not letting you all out of my sight again," Stellan said.

"We have to stick together," Pierce concurred. "We could just head to the bridge now and do the purge, but I'm not ready for that. Not just yet."

The word "yet" stuck with Stellan because he wouldn't be ready for that until his part of the job, the part where they saved as many souls as they could, was done.

Pierce asked for questions; no one spoke. Stellan brought over a bag of guns and ammunition they'd taken from the security deck and placed it in the center of the circle, digging in and doling out the weapons they would best be able to handle without experience or training. He offered a small pistol to Daelen. She shook her head. Her entire life had been about saving people, not slaughtering them.

"It's just a precaution. It would make me feel better knowing you have it," Stellan said.

"No," she said. "I'm not a killer." She spoke without conviction, but the implication struck him as if she were revealing she'd known about one of his secrets all along.

"Think of it as mercy," he suggested, forcing the weapon into her hand.

"Mercy?"

He pulled her close and kissed her forehead. Small strands of her dark hair that had escaped from her ponytail tickled his nose.

"Kill fast," Stellan said. "And mean it with all your heart. Know that it is the right thing, and don't hesitate."

"*Are* we doing the right thing?" Wendy asked no one in particular.

Everyone looked to Stellan, not Pierce, waiting. Stellan looked begrudgingly toward Pierce. He felt like a conduit of authority.

"We have to do something," Stellan said.

Even through Pierce's solid face, Stellan knew he was gloating, celebrating a victory. And Stellan hated him for it. Anger brewed in his stomach like a boiling stew. Stellan knew that, for the most part, Pierce was confident. It was a simple plan.

But Pierce had already forgotten about his earlier revelation that nothing seemed to ever go according to plan.

Five

The moment they left the safety of medical deck, the *Atlas* felt infinitely larger, and in those once well-known spaces, the unknown awaited them. Every meter they crawled elongated until familiar distances seemed foreign. Every sound portrayed the unknown. With every step, they descended farther into an abyss. Any optimism they'd had vanished. Their new mission seemed impossible.

For most of them, the ambience of the corridors had become alien, like tunnels in a tomb. Even the density of the air changed, becoming heavier in their chests.

They moved in single file, hugging the walls. Pierce and Arlo led the line, the barrels of their rifles pointing the way, and Stellan covered the rear. Back there, Stellan felt excluded, but more than that, he felt the loss of control. They were moving blindly through the darkness with no idea what lay before them. All he could do was watch the distance grow between them and the safety of medical deck. It took most of his willpower to not visualize that distance as their diminishing chances, but he knew that's just what it was. Perhaps he was unwilling to admit it to himself, or perhaps the undermining of his authority cut so deep it even severed his self-confidence. But it wasn't just about letting Pierce see with his own eyes

301

the depth of the madness anymore. Maybe Stellan needed to see it again for himself.

Though, he knew the stakes were higher this time; he had more than just one person to look out for and defend. He focused on Daelen, whose survival meant more to him than his own. It meant everything.

"This is crazy," Daelen said. The sidearm in her hand trembled. "Pierce has lost it."

"I think we've all lost something," Stellan said, steadying her hands with his. "We have to do something, and there's a chance we could make it. If we can save even just a few more people, it'll be worth it."

"Do you really think we can?" she said. "Do you think anyone's left?"

Stellan looked down at her sidearm. "After all this time, I can't believe I never showed you how to handle a weapon. I guess there never was a need."

She looked perplexed, her thin lips drawing in, her brow narrowing as she tried to understand his recollection. Her fair skin wrinkled with concern, and when he touched her face, she relaxed.

"We'll find others," he said with a smile. "We'll save everyone we can because that's what we do."

"We do. I'm afraid that isn't what Pierce does anymore."

"No," Stellan said. "It isn't."

Her perplexed expression returned, and Wendy leaned in quizzically, overhearing what he'd said. Hers was more than a look of concerned curiosity. She was afraid, and Stellan saw it in the way her chest heaved, the beads of sweat on her brow, the way her lips and eyes trembled. Outside the confines of the safety of the medical deck, she must have felt naked.

"Don't worry," Stellan said. "We're going to make it. We're all going to be just fine."

Daelen knew it wasn't true. Her husband was a dreamer, but he was so convincing she didn't know if he understood himself that he was lying. She revered him for it, his attempt to brace his loved ones from the terrible truth that they probably all wouldn't make it through the next few hours.

She wondered, then more than ever, if the goodness in him that made him into a kind of bodyguard from realism and truth required he believe the things he said absolutely.

If that were true, would he see the worst coming?

She wondered because, even without seeing the things he'd seen, she knew just how bad things could get, and if he didn't, she didn't know how he could protect them.

Six

They heard the dead somewhere ahead. The moans and shuffles carried down the corridors in a continuum of noise, the natural reverb morphing the sounds into static. Stellan hoped it was only because of the distortion of echoes that they couldn't tell how many of them were there. In reality, he feared there simply were too many to count.

"What do you think?" Pierce whispered to Stellan.

He thought that it didn't matter how many of them were ahead. When he and Edward had risked running by the group earlier, they'd been extremely lucky. Afterward, he decided taking such a risk again wouldn't be worth it.

"See what we're dealing with," Stellan said, "but if they're in our way, we should find another route."

"There isn't any more time for delays." Pierce scowled. "If we can take them, we take them. Understood?"

"I don't think—"

"This isn't a discussion," Pierce said, and Stellan understood what Pierce was really saying. If Pierce thought he could take them, he would, and Stellan would have no choice but to help because the dead would come until it was done.

Stellan nodded begrudgingly, and they instructed the rest of the group with hand gestures to move forward.

Daelen was even more frightened than before. The dead didn't scare her. Pierce did. Daelen's eyes pleaded with Stellan to do something. Short of taking Pierce down silently, Stellan didn't know what he could do. Pierce led them now not because he still commanded the authority of the *Atlas*. With the *Atlas* floating lifeless in the black and the majority of its crew now mindless killers, Pierce no longer had a ship to command. Pierce only led because of his stubbornness. He refused to follow anyone else, and the others followed for fear of what he would do if they didn't.

The group continued on, and as they drew closer to the dead, they picked up the smell. It wasn't just decomposition this time. It was something else they couldn't quite identify, a large accumulation of them amplifying the odor and carrying it down the corridor. It was an earthy, musky scent, like mold, settling on their tongues and palates like dust.

"Christ," Floyd said. "Is that what dead bodies smell like?"

"I've never smelled decomp this bad," Margo said.

"It's in my mouth, my eyes. It's in my ears," Floyd said, wiggling his pinky in his ear canal. "This stench can't infect us, can it?"

"No," Daelen said, and they looked at her uneasily. Still, Pierce and Stellan pushed forward with their rifles leading the way.

Around the next bend, they'd find Gamble's Run. Stellan hoped the dead would not be congregating there, but from what he'd seen of their behavior already, he knew they were. He imagined, one by one, they lurched down the corridors into the intersection and were caught up in the growing crowd, which became too confusing for them to escape. He could sympathize. Even with his full brain capacity, Stellan had a hard time navigating that intersection.

They moved down the corridor and peered around the bend, finding a mass of dead shambling in Gamble's Run, a whirlpool of reanimated bodies. For all intents and purposes, it was an impassable wall.

"We have to go another way," Stellan said.

"We're out of time," Pierce said with wild, amazed eyes. "Just look at them."

His gaze lingered for a moment as he estimated their numbers. Stellan knew Pierce no longer recognized the people the madness now controlled. Once, he knew them all, same as Stellan. Now, to Pierce, they were the enemy, an obstacle to overcome.

"We're going to take them," Pierce said. "Stellan, Arlo, and I will be the front firing line. Ten meters in front of us will be the kill zone for the rest of you. None of you shoot unless one of them enters that zone. Margo, you provide Arlo with magazines when he needs them. Daelen, you have Stellan. Floyd, you have me. Wendy, you're the floater. Fill in where necessary."

"Oh, God!" Wendy cried, cradling her head.

"I don't know about this, Captain," Arlo said.

"Don't worry," Pierce said. "This corridor is narrow, and they will pile up and slow themselves down. It will be over much quicker than you can believe."

"Pierce, this isn't a good idea," Stellan said. "They're attracted to sound. The more we shoot, the more will come."

"Good," Pierce said. "Let them. When we're done here, it will be easier to move."

Stellan and Arlo shared an uncertain, fearful look. The others were worse off, trembling with adrenaline. Daelen shook her head in disbelief.

"Captain," Stellan said. "We can't do this."

"We can," Pierce said. "And we will. Remember, aim for their heads."

Pierce stepped out from around the bend on his own, his body as calm and relaxed as ever. He took aim with his rifle, peering down the precision holographic sight, and then he waited for what seemed like minutes. Finally, one of the dead, formerly an *Atlas* engineer by the look of its tattered jump suit, a dark stain down its side that looked like oil but most certainly wasn't, noticed Pierce and looked at him stupidly, as if to wonder who would be so bold. It cocked its head and turned jerkily toward him. It meandered closer, squinting its eyes in an oddly human way. Finally, when it recognized Pierce was one of the living, its eyes spread wide. Its jaw dropped, and it moaned a deep, baritone wail of not pain or loss or confusion. It was a battle cry. The others slowly turned in that jerky, twitchy motion like robots with rusty hinges.

They were coming.

If Pierce hesitated, it was only that moment where he waited to be discovered, where he invited them down that corridor to just try to take his life. He didn't taunt them. He merely waited for the right moment. When he found it, when he felt it, as Stellan knew engaging in battle was more of a feeling than a conscious decision, he exhaled, and all the world silenced. Pierce squeezed the trigger, and his rifle spoke for him, informing the dead what awaited them if they advanced.

The round entered the mouth of that former engineer, who was still moaning, and it burst out the back of its head like a volcanic eruption. Its rigid limbs relaxed, and it fell loosely to its knees in a sickening, hollow thud that was oddly clear after Pierce's rifle blast backgrounded all other noise. When it finished toppling to the deck, the others came into focus, and the world rushed back to Stellan's ears.

The dead did not hesitate. All the bodies filling Gamble's Run lurched with their twitchy, circular movements, their heads lolling and waving on their shoulders, their eyes wide and starving for light to penetrate their cloudy corneas, their fingers clawing at the very air to pull their victims closer.

They all marched together in step to an inaudible symphony, a ghostly conductor waving his baton at their feet.

Pierce fired again, dropping another with expert precision; it was like the soldier never left him at all, that he had merely hid that version of himself away right where he could always find it and bring it back out if he should ever need it. With another round, another body fell to the deck, tripping others advancing behind him. Stellan and Arlo remained in cover.

"Open fire, goddammit!" Pierce screamed between reports of his rifle, his eyes never leaving his targets. "What are you waiting for!?"

Stellan hesitated, but he was not afraid. Pierce had invited the dead, and they had locked onto him. They would pursue him until something stopped them, be it a high-density, tungsten carbide round from his assault rifle or an impassible obstacle, such as a sealed hatch.

Stellan looked back at his wife and the others, wondering for a moment if they would be better off without Pierce. Perhaps this was the way they could be rid of him. Perhaps abandoning him now meant they could find a safer way. Would sacrificing his oldest friend mean they could save others? Would that justify it? Make it right?

Stellan knew, no matter what conclusion he came to, he wouldn't be able to live with it; he couldn't leave Pierce behind. He couldn't abandon him. He couldn't give up on him. Stellan was incapable of letting his friend succumb to the death he so defiantly invited. Be it ego or pure madness, Stellan would follow Pierce into oblivion because that was what he did.

Stellan jumped out beside Pierce, and Arlo followed, joining in the fight. Stellan crept up to the firing line, heel-to-toe, keeping his shoulders steady and level, firing on the move. The kick of his MK7C's stock felt warm against his shoulder like an old friend playfully tapping him. The holographic sight leveled over the heads of his targets, careful not to cross Pierce or Arlo's firing lines, trusting them to take care of their own.

Floyd, Daelen, Margo, and Wendy fell in behind them, ready with their sidearms, tossing the bag of guns and ammo to the deck for easy access. They cursed in fear, but the frontline of men didn't hear them. The rifles breaking the sound barrier with their projectiles drowned out all noise. In that corridor, they fought the dead with blasts of sound itself.

However, as the bodies filled the corridor, the sounds of gunfire dampened, the dead in the back pushing the bodies up front closer, an unstoppable force crashing into a wave of bullets. Their flesh absorbed the shockwaves of the cracks and blasts. The sound dug deep, rattling the living's teeth and bones.

The gunfire surely rang throughout every deck on the *Atlas*. Somewhere deep within the carrier, anyone still alive would know there were others who were fighting for survival. There was still hope, but it hinged on dropping the dead fast enough to punch a hole they could pass through because there was no end in sight to their numbers. The size of the horde had to number in the hundreds.

The gunmen fired over and over, dropping dead bodies as fast as they could. In such close proximity, Stellan killed two of the dead with one shot, driving a bullet through one's skull and into another. In the midst of a sea of bobbing heads and clutching fingers, those two fell simultaneously limp and crashed to the deck like piles of laundry.

A particularly large specimen with the body shape of an egg wandered into the corridor, and Arlo took him, his round snapping the dead man's head back and up. The body relaxed and fell backward onto its brethren, who tried to push through him. A pair of others succumbed to all that dead weight, and the egg man fell onto them, his enormous gut trembling as they struggled to free themselves.

The dead surged forward like a slow-moving wave, a single volume of bodies. While they couldn't be sure how much time had passed, at some point, it appeared that the survivors were winning. The dead began to fall on top of each other, filling up the corridor and slowing their advance, just as Pierce had predicted. However, they kept coming, and they kept piling until they were forming a barrier. There was no end to their ranks.

"Cease fire!" Pierce ordered.

Arlo and Stellan stopped.

"We have to keep shooting now or fall back," Stellan said. "If we fill the hallway with their bodies, they won't be able to get through."

"We won't be able to get through either," Pierce said.

"I'm more worried about surviving," Stellan said. "We can find another way."

"Let them come," Pierce said with glowing eyes. Some men get a taste for killing and can't let it go.

Just as he wished, the dead continued to spill over the bodies of their fallen comrades, tripping and tumbling down the mound of motionless limbs, and Pierce opened fire on them again. Arlo joined in, his lips curving in either a grimace or a smile, which, Stellan couldn't decipher. He had no choice but to continue their campaign.

In spilling forth, the dead reached the interior kill zone, and Margo was the first of the secondary line to open fire. Floyd fired his handgun with uncertainty. Wendy and Daelen fired their weapons, too. None of them were very effective and burned through the ammunition.

The dead spilled into the corridor faster, and the ammunition dwindled. Stellan was forced to drop his rifle and switch to his sidearm, which was just as well. At this distance, it would be faster anyway.

His HC30 took a few of the dead down before an alarm began to buzz in the back of Stellan's mind. Like an instinctual fear, he knew something was wrong and had to spare the seconds, which were precious, to turn.

One of the dead pinned Daelen to the ground. Between chomps of its jaws, a loose tongue dangled like a snake, dropping saliva onto her cheek. She pushed and punched its chest but was powerless under its weight.

How had they gotten through?

No time. He drove a round through its skull, and its arms and tongue fell limp.

They had attacked from behind, called forth by the survivors' thunderous weapons. Margo and Floyd were pinned as well. Wendy huddled against the wall, safe but frantic. Stellan was able to save Margo, but by the time he got to Floyd, he was already dead, his throat torn out and his limbs still, his attacker lapping the blood from the deck like a dog. Stellan put it down and felt a surge of vengeance but did not have time to dwell on the failure.

While Daelen rolled the lifeless corpse off of her with cries of disgust, screaming pain seared into Stellan's left shoulder. His arm raised in reflex and pushed against a cold, solid mass. Stellan looked to the source of his pain and found two familiar eyes gazing up at him with that cloudy vacancy.

The body that used to belong to Thomas Foster had locked its jaws onto Stellan's shoulder, attempting to tear straight through to the bone.

A wet warmth streamed inside Stellan's sleeve. His overcoat darkened. Blood flowed at the corners of Tom's gray lips.

Placing the barrel of his sidearm under Tom's chin, their eyes met for the last time. Stellan saw no spark of recognition, no spite or glow of victorious vengeance. Yet, he felt the object of all of these human emotions. He felt the hatred and wondered if it was his own.

Stellan pulled the trigger, and the top of Tom's head exploded in a fountain. The teeth that sank into his shoulder retracted as the jaws loosened their grip. Fingers slid down Stellan's arm almost as if reaching out to him. Tom lay in a heap on the deck again, and Stellan put one more round into Tom's brain just to be sure he wouldn't get up this time, feeling like he should have done that a long time ago.

Daelen helped Margo shove the body off of her. They looked to Floyd, weeping even as Arlo and Pierce continued to fire on the front line. The barking of rifles drowned out the women's cries, and as they gazed upon Floyd's lifeless body, Stellan put a round through Floyd's brain as well. They didn't have time for compassion now. They could grieve later. For now, they would have to understand Stellan granted Floyd mercy because his body would no doubt rise again. Stellan's gunshot silenced their cries. Their faces turned to stone.

"We have to move!" Stellan cried. "Fall back!"

As the dead continued to advance from Gamble's Run, Pierce reluctantly nodded and then slapped Arlo on the shoulder, telling him he was retreating. Pierce grimaced at Stellan's shoulder, though he could not afford to pause.

The survivors withdrew from the bottleneck at Gamble's Run. As they raced for their lives, the gunfire continued. Arlo had remained on their kill line, the same mechanical focus in his eyes as when he docked the *Atlas* with the *Shiva* seemingly a lifetime ago.

"Arlo! Let's go!" Stellan called, but Arlo kept firing. With each round, he efficiently dropped one, but two others advanced. When his rifle clicked empty, he dropped it to the deck and switched to his sidearm, and that was when they took him.

One more gunshot cracked the walls of the *Atlas'* corridors as Arlo ended his own life.

Stellan felt the failure of another loss. With everything crumbling around them, he focused on Daelen. He had to get her to safety.

The survivors fell back the way they had come, fighting through more of the dead their fighting had summoned. These were easier to overcome. With their ammunition dwindling, Pierce and Stellan were able to handle them. In the panic, Margo entered a side passageway in an attempt to get anywhere but that corridor of death. After Pierce and Stellan dispatched the dead, she would not respond to calls of her name.

"Margo!" Stellan screamed.

"We have to go!" Pierce said, pulling Stellan's shirt. "Now!"

They filed back into the only secure place they knew. Daelen and Wendy reached the medical deck with Stellan and Pierce trailing closely behind. When Stellan arrived, he found Wendy and Daelen clutching each other in the common room, and he had just enough time to turn and find the barrel of Pierce's sidearm.

"I'm sorry, old friend."

Pierce pulled the trigger, and the force of the blast threw Stellan to the deck. All of the air left his lungs. Through a haze, he watched Pierce slam and lock the hatch door.

Before falling to blackness, instead of feeling the ache of betrayal, Stellan thought about the dead and how his debt to them was surely paid in full.

CHAPTER 12
ACROSS THE THRESHOLD

One

Desperation makes people illogical. It makes them do things they would never otherwise do. It pushes them. It makes them flexible. It makes them adopt beliefs they would normally belittle. It makes them pray to gods they never believed in. It makes them try anything.

Belief doesn't work that way.

When Margo found herself separated from the rest of the remaining crew, she didn't panic. It actually appeared she was safe for the moment. Though the dead screamed by her door, it wasn't long before the scuffs of their shoes and the limbs knocking into walls faded into the distance.

They passed her by.

After a moment of silent celebration, she believed she was okay and retreated farther into the room. Somewhere in her head was the answer. She just had to find it. This problem had a solution.

The storeroom's emergency lighting flickered. Shelves of supplies jutted from the wall. Bottled water, canned and dried food, a first aid kit, even a portable emergency breathing apparatus. It was no ENV suit, but it would suffice in case of a loss of air circulation. She could last in here for weeks. She had all the time in the world. She could finally breathe.

In a rear extension to the storeroom, Margo found a table and some blankets. She made a bed under the table and curled up. She wanted to just sleep through everything. At some point, NESMA would notice the *Atlas* was overdue. It would send a search-and-rescue party. She just had to hold out until then.

Margo would have been embarrassed to know how common her thoughts had become. She couldn't have known that hundreds of people across the *Atlas* thought the same thing as they huddled in dark rooms with barricaded doorways, waiting for help to come. Fear and desperation reduced them all to their most base elements.

Something knocked. From under the table, she could see nothing. Shadows enveloped the room.

She stopped breathing, would have stopped her heartbeat if she could, and heard a whispering, like air continuously passing through a vent.

That's all it is, she thought. *The room sensors detected occupancy, so it turned on the air processors.*

Two boots stumbled out of the darkness, choking her relief. She caught a scream in hand, hoping those boots would pass her by like the others.

The table shook when the thing bumped into it and stopped. Still, Margo thought it could have unwittingly walked into an obstruction and was just turning. She hoped. She believed. She prayed.

It kneeled and peered down at her, a face that carried with it the darkness of the shadows from which it came. Margo shrieked and backed out from under the table, her legs flailing, struggling to gain traction on the blankets. The thing lunged at her, missing its catch, and then slithered after her, whining like a child who'd lost its toy.

She ran for the door but heard more of the dead out there, perhaps stragglers, now pounding on the other side. She could not guess how many but certainly more than the one in the room with her. She would have to face it.

She pressed her back to the door and watched the thing emerge from the table and rise to its towering full height. When it stumbled into the light, Margo saw its face. She screamed.

It dragged a length of its entrails on the floor like a leash with no master. The flesh had been torn from parts of its thick arms. Its security officer uniform had been ripped down the center, and claw marks on its chest had long since stopped bleeding and become simple, gaping holes.

All of this was new. Before it all, she'd known the man who lurched even when he was alive. She'd known him as Doug Fowler.

"Oh my God," she said, catching another scream. "Look what they did to you!"

It moved slowly toward her, part of its small intestine wrapping around its leg and snaking under the table.

"Doug, it's me," she pleaded. "Remember? Don't you remember me? The squint?"

She thought it slowed for a moment and cocked its head. She wanted to believe the recognition was reciprocated and that, not unlike a coma patient, he'd just snap right out of it.

"Doug, can't you hear me? It's Margo."

Her words may as well have never even crossed her lips, and as it crept closer, the realization set into her that she was helpless. She'd thrown all her logic and reason out for the belief that this man, whom she might have once considered friendly, might hear her and stop its advance.

She realized this thing *used* to be a man. It used to be Doug Fowler. Now, it was only a shell, its former master like a lingering whisper in her memory, a memory this thing did not share.

As it fell on top of her, breaking her bones with its incredible weight, she knew how foolish she'd been. She shouldn't have left her friends. Fear had won. Her faith in something real waned, and as she searched for something she now knew was not there, she felt ashamed.

Margo didn't think her friends were any better off. She thought they were all damned; however, that didn't mean she wanted to die. In fact, she wanted every last moment, and when the thing that was once Doug tore her throat out, her dying thought was that she didn't think it was an unreasonable request for just a little more time, just a few more moments without the pain and the incredible solitude of space, just to remember what it was like.

She begged for mercy. She pleaded for pity. She did not know on whose deaf ears her requests fell. This thing that was not Doug would not relent or reason or know humanity, even though it looked human. And she certainly wasn't crying out to God.

As much as she tried, even at her end, she could not believe in an almighty being. Heaven was a nice thought, but Margo knew nothing awaited her after the cold, black silence.

Two

When Stellan emerged from the darkness, he found no air in his lungs, and as hard as he tried, he could not breathe. An immense weight lay on his chest, the hand of God pushing down on him.

Daelen was kneeling over him, tearing open his shirt, the veins in her arms and hands bulging with adrenaline.

She would not let her husband go. After everything she'd lost, his life hanging in the balance restored her confidence. She no longer questioned if she could save him. She simply had to.

She searched for the wound in his chest, beneath his clutching hands as he begged oxygen to flood his lungs. They burned so hot that, even if the air were on fire, he would welcome it.

He convulsed and rolled onto his side, curling into the fetal position. The muscles in his stomach twisted and wrenched as he tried to kick start respiration.

"Baby!" Daelen cried. "Let me see! Let me see!" She tried to roll Stellan onto his back, but she couldn't stop him from curling. He was too strong, and Wendy could only sob. Everyone she'd ever loved and counted on was gone, and now Stellan, her best friend, was writhing on the deck and surely dying.

"I need your help!" Daelen told her.

Wendy timidly complied, and as soon as she placed her hands on Stellan, he coughed. His lungs rattled dryly in their depths, and he gasped, the air feeling like ice water in his throat. After a few deep breaths, Stellan relaxed and rolled over, exposing his chest.

Beneath his shirt, they found the thin ballistic vest. In the middle of his chest, they found a black circle from the bullet impact, the heat from the friction as it left the barrel and traveled through the air at such a high velocity singed and charred the fabric.

Daelen touched his chest and then, in disbelief, searched his back for an exit wound. She scanned him with her link to be sure. The vest had stopped the round.

It didn't make sense. Blood dampened most of his upper chest area. She inspected him further and found the shoulder of his coat had been torn, so she slid it down his arm and found his undershirt drenched in crimson.

Then she saw the two jagged, curved wounds and knew.

"Oh no!" she sobbed hoarsely. "Oh no, no, no."

She looked into his grave eyes and caressed his cheek, almost reticently. The thought that she could somehow fear him made her feel ashamed.

"Margo," Daelen said. "Where's Margo?"

"I don't know," Wendy said. "She got separated from us."

Daelen's mind raced for answers. Everything was a roadblock. All the old routes were inaccessible. She didn't know where to go. She felt lost.

"In that cabinet," Daelen's finger shook, "there's some disinfectant and some gauze. Get them for me, please."

Wendy hurried to the cabinet.

"It's okay," Stellan said.

"Also, there should be some pain relievers."

"Love," Stellan said, "it's okay.

"No!" Daelen cried. "I'm not going to lose you, too!"

She looked into his eyes again and hated what she found. Acceptance is the last stage of grief, and it was in every corner and crease of his face. She could never see herself reaching that stage. She could never visualize a life without him. Stellan had become a constant in her life. He was always there, and he would always be there. What she saw then couldn't have been possible, but it had to be real. Her mind struggled to rationalize it any other way, and she understood that acceptance was a decision. Acceptance was the mind giving in to the exhausting task of attempting to explain its reality in a less painful way.

She thought she may one day reach that point, but she already knew it would be a long time. She also understood knowing that was the first step, so she shook it from her mind.

"I'm not giving up," Daelen said.

"Neither am I," Stellan said. "We have to stop Pierce."

"He's gone," Wendy said. "He could be anywhere."

"I know where he's going," Stellan said, "because he *has* given up."

Three

Stellan sat shirtless on one of the exam tables and allowed Daelen to clean and dress his wound. She took her time, careful to wipe away the blood that was already becoming gummy. She knew what was going to happen, and while she lovingly, yet mechanically, secured the bandage, her mind blazed, searching for a way to fix him.

"How do you feel?" she asked. For a moment, they stared at each other across a threshold of seemingly infinite space.

"Are you asking about my shoulder?" Stellan said. Her gaze persisted. "I feel fine."

Wendy brought another box of bandages and set them on the table beside Stellan. Daelen had already discarded a baseball-sized wad, which she'd used to stop the bleeding. Wendy was careful not to touch it.

"How much time do you think we have?" Daelen said. "Before the purge, I mean."

"Pierce has to make it to the command deck. Assuming he does, then he has to set each deck to do it individually, since the network is down and can't coordinate that on its own. He'll open outer airlocks first and work inward."

"Is there a protocol for that or something?" Wendy asked.

"Not that I know of," Stellan said. "It's just how I'd do it."

"So how much time?" Daelen asked.

Stellan shrugged. "An hour. Maybe less."

He rolled his shoulder to test its mobility and winced. Daelen watched him closely, but he seemed fine, like himself. His face remained as solid and plain as ever, a seriousness accompanied by a politeness that conveyed his good nature. His ghostly blue eyes calmed her like still waters that she could wade in, as if he could hold her there forever and keep her safe.

Forever now had an expiration date. It pained her to think that, even if they were able to stop Pierce and somehow make it to safety, their time together was finite.

Death always won in the end. Time was its accomplice. And now Stellan's life, their life together, was not measured by years but hours. If she could stop time, she would be able to find a solution. In time, she could beat it, but time was relentless.

And none of it would matter if they couldn't stop Pierce from ejecting them into the black. As much as she hated it, to even give Stellan a chance, they had something more pressing to address. Old, resolute Pierce was determined to keep them from ever leaving the ship alive. While the scientist in her agreed with him, the lover in her couldn't accept it. After everything they'd been through, her heart was stronger than her logic and reason. Their will to survive prevailed.

"We should probably move then?" Daelen asked.

"Yeah," Stellan said. "First things first, though. Pierce locked us in here. Wendy, I know your specialty is fixing things, but that also makes you good at breaking them. Think you can get us out?"

Distress lingered in her eyes, as if the very thought of action frightened her.

"Open the hatch?" Wendy said. "Aren't those things out there?"

"They would have followed Pierce away from here," Stellan said.

"Are you sure?"

"Yes."

She hesitated and looked doubtful. "All right. I can try."

"Good," Stellan said, touching her shoulder affectionately, sensing her urge to recoil. He wanted her to feel useful and empowered. If her mind worked on something familiar, maybe she'd feel more in control. Maybe it would calm her.

Wendy walked to the door and popped the control panel off the wall with Rick's switchblade, which he'd given to her before he turned. She gazed at it longingly for a moment and went to work on the wiring.

"So we stop Pierce," Daelen said. "And then what?"

"We'll figure something out," Stellan said.

"What do we have left to fight with?" Daelen asked. "Wendy and I both were out of ammo and tossed our weapons in the escape. And we left the bag at Gamble's Run."

Stellan looked at her grimly. He pulled his sidearm from its holster and released its magazine, showing Daelen that it was empty. They were completely out of ammo.

"Oh," she frowned, but her resignation served as a catalyst for Stellan's mind, and he patted his pants. From his cargo pocket, he pulled the bullet Pierce had given him, the same bullet with which he'd destroyed that boy in London a decade ago.

Stellan held it in an open palm, staring wondrously at the glint along its side. It looked perfect.

"Second chances," he whispered. With a thumb like a hammer, he snapped the bullet into the magazine, and then slapped the magazine into his weapon. Racking the slide, the bullet ascended into the chamber.

He gazed at his sidearm almost lustily, and Daelen watched him with wide, worrying eyes.

With trembling fingers, she took his steady hands, and lowered the weapon to the table. It sounded heavy against the metal tabletop.

"We may yet have one," she said. Her words pulled him from his trance, and he smiled.

"I was thinking about something," Stellan said. "Do you remember our first run?"

"Yes," Daelen said fondly.

"I remember seeing Earth from orbit for the first time. Endless oceans and mammoth mountains became almost insignificant, but I found them beautiful in a way I'd never thought possible. The whole planet looked untouched, and I remember thinking everything was a matter of perspective. As the station came around in orbit and the sun set, I remember feeling like the possibilities were endless. We were leaving a whole world behind but gaining the universe. I remember thinking everyone out here was trying to escape something, some kind of clock or I don't know what, but I felt like we were running toward something. Freedom. The freedom to live how we wanted, without fear of judgment or persecution. I thought I might miss it. Home. The smell of trees, the sound of wind. But I knew I traded all that for you and that, wherever you were, that was my home. This life, it wasn't ideal, but it was enough. And that made it perfect."

"Dammit!" Wendy said, huffing in frustration. For some reason, Stellan and Daelen found it funny.

"I remember the first jump made us so sick we were useless the whole run," Daelen said, and they laughed again. "Even though neither of us could hold a meal down, you were there for me. You took care of me when you could barely stand yourself."

"Not Pierce, though," Stellan said. "His stomach must have a padlock."

Returning their thoughts to Pierce brought back the shadow over their mood, though even in reminiscing about him, they found good memories.

"When we were in the Corps," Stellan said, "he used to go shot for shot with new guys in our squad. Whiskey, of course. He'd say, 'Gentlemen, drinking whiskey is like taming a wild horse. The more willpower you have, the better you can stay on top of it. If you let it, it will kick your ass. But only if you let it.' It was his way of demonstrating mind over body. The stomach wouldn't roll if the mind wouldn't let it. He sent every single one to the toilet before each night was through, and he'd lead the charge in belittling that guy. It may sound silly, but the message was clear. He didn't need to dish out punishment to assert himself. He just had to prove he could take more than us."

"Men are so weird." Daelen shook her head. "But he can certainly keep his drink."

"Yeah," Stellan said. "He wouldn't let anyone else ever see him the next morning, though. See, Pierce was a morning-after guy. He could drink anything, and if it was going to come back up, it'd be the next morning."

"He was a good friend," Daelen said.

"Yes," Stellan said. "He was."

Wendy cursed in frustration again and pounded the panel beside the door. The holocontrol flickered and then change from red to green.

"Tough love," she whispered in disbelief. "Done!"

"Time to go," Stellan said with renewed vigor, and for a moment, the fear vanished, replaced by hope and good cheer. Somewhere along the line, they forgot that, even if they were successful in stopping Pierce, their problems went far beyond him and the dying *Atlas*, but it was sensibility that made them take one step at a time. It was also perhaps sensibility that kept them from losing control and giving up.

Four

Pierce sat at Evans' workstation. Like a spent match, his aged face was pale and wrinkled as if years had passed in mere hours. His mind, as sharp as ever, cut through emotion and doubt. He saw clearly what needed to be done, and he knew he was the only one who could do it.

He glanced back at the body of the young boy lying on the floor. Evans was dead. The guilt weighed almost as heavily as the responsibility to his duty, and again, the remorse he felt proved he was not evil. It hurt, so he must have still been human.

He had to do what was necessary because only he could stomach the guilt. He owned the burden because only he could carry it, the fate of an entire world on his shoulders.

A window expanded from the workstation, and it reflected his face like a mirror. He removed his glasses and placed them gently on his armrest, intending to never pick them up again. Massaging his forehead, Pierce pressed the record command.

"I have failed," he said, his voice low and rough. "We have failed. The only course is to ensure our cargo never reaches New Earth. That cargo is no longer inanimate material. It's people, the crew of this ship. The stakes are too high. It is a scourge.

"The material from Apophis two five nine, it changed us. Initially, we just thought it was the black madness. Being out here, so far away from the planet we were meant to live on, moving faster than we were ever meant to go, we broke the rules, so it seemed fair it would break our minds. We expected it, but we never expected what happened here.

"I would advise whoever remains of my crew to find a weapon, put it to their head, and pull the trigger because this thing feeds on our minds, our thoughts, and uses our bodies to spread that sickness. We must destroy its food, or it threatens any chance we have left as a people to remember what we were and the freedoms that made us great.

"I still hope we can get there. That is why it is not a coward's way out to take our lives. It has become necessary, a necessary evil for the greater good, and I hope, if there is a God, he forgives us. We had the best of intentions.

"I cannot take that path. My burden is too great. I must see the *Atlas* is properly disposed of, and I pray I am strong enough to follow through."

Pierce glanced at a picture of Commander Ashland he'd isolated on his link and took a deep breath.

"This is Captain Gordon Pierce of the Titan class carrier *Atlas*. Beware this place. Burn it. Remember the sacrifice of this crew. Forgive us. Save yourself."

Pierce stopped the recording, and the window retreated back into the workstation with the *Atlas'* chirp of acknowledgement.

"I'll see you soon, Emra."

Moments later, a beacon, much like the one the *Shiva* had left, launched from the hull of the *Atlas*. A red light blinked at the tip of its antenna. Small thrusters pushed it a safe distance away from the *Atlas* and then stabilized it in a fixed location, where it would remain until the red giant Apophis expanded and consumed whatever remained of their mistakes. The warning wouldn't be necessary after that. The cosmic balance would right itself, and the universe would continue as it always had.

Life would go on.

The *Atlas* turned lazily, lurching toward the rocky debris, the Apophis planet, and the remains of the fallen *Shiva*, which still burned trace oxygen and atmosphere like dying embers of a once great bonfire.

Five

Working against the clock with a definite objective, Stellan moved quickly. The question of what waited around each corner and in the dark shadows and unseen places was no longer the sole plague of his mind. Survival was no longer contingent on remaining undetected. They had to stop Pierce before it was too late.

The balance was delicate. They couldn't be careless, but they had to keep moving. While Stellan's own life did not concern him anymore, Daelen and Wendy tempered his pace. He couldn't leave them, and he couldn't lead them to peril.

In that regard, not much had changed.

Outside medical, Stellan, Daelen, and Wendy found quiet corridors and trails of blood leading toward the command deck. Stellan knew the pasty blood couldn't belong to Pierce. Rather, the dead had left them breadcrumbs. He could follow the trail to Pierce because they would follow him until something else caught their attention. The dead had become an asset.

Although, if nothing diverted them, they would inevitably be an obstacle for Stellan and his two followers.

One step at a time.

They mostly found drops and trickles. Occasionally, crimson handprints stained the walls where one of the dead had lost balance and caught itself. They also found the odd, unidentifiable lump of flesh, gray and sitting as a mound in a shallow, sanguine pool.

They found signs of other survivors. Barricades, trashcans, and desks piled in front of doorways, blockades that didn't hold. At security checkpoints, vacant chairs taunted them, relics of another time when it was acceptable to rest. A message on the wall scrawled in blood read, "They're not dead." Stellan, Daelen, and Wendy knew, and the cryptic lack of bodies delivered that message better than words. Everywhere were signs of struggle, blood pools with red boot prints leading away like ghost steps, smashed vending machines and computer equipment, smoke billowing from terminals as plastic circuit boards still smoldered. But there were no bodies, and they knew it was because they'd all gotten up and walked away.

Daelen and Wendy followed Stellan's lead, hugging the walls, darting between shadows. Wendy trembled, her breath shaking in her chest, but Daelen was calm. She was a strong woman. She would be okay.

"The quiet is unnerving," Daelen said. "I know they're out there, but it's even quieter than the height of sleep cycle on the residence deck."

"All we need to know is they're out there," Stellan said.

A distant boom echoed through the ship. The deck shook, and the lights shimmered. It reminded Stellan of the pound of mortar shells above a bunker. They were safe, but it was impossible to ever come to terms with the thought of being bombed.

"What was that!?" Wendy whispered.

Instinct controlled Stellan. Without a thought, he checked their immediate area, ensuring their safety. His sidearm automatically followed his darting eyes. Nothing moved.

"We hit something," Daelen said. "Or something hit us."

"There is a lot of debris floating around out there," Wendy said.

Stellan crouched and pressed his palm to the floor, closing his eyes and opening his ears. The sounds of the ship flooded his mind, and he let them run so deep he could feel them in his chest. The remaining active systems washed over him like waves. He reached out to other decks and found the stillness and quiet. Through the silence, he found the subtle whisper of the thrusters, which, until then, he'd thought was the air circulation system. He opened his eyes, and there it was, the slight pull of inertia.

"We're moving," Stellan said.

"Why would Pierce move the ship if he's going to do a purge?" Daelen asked.

"He wouldn't."

They tried to blend in with the quiet, and Stellan continued to listen. Like a rising buzz in his mind, he thought he could hear the light drive spinning up.

"Hear that?" Stellan said.

"The light drive," Wendy said. "We heading back to Earth?"

Stellan gravely shook his head.

Light drives were one of the most destructive forces man had ever created. They bent space with almost no limitations but their area of effect, meaning they could tear any solid matter apart. When the technology was created, the Council banned its use anywhere in New Earth's solar system so as not to disturb the orbits of its planets. The light drive's pull was as powerful as a black hole.

"How long does it take the light drive to spin up?" Stellan asked

"It depends how cold it is," Wendy said. "The only reason it has to spin up is to maintain an equilibrium of temperature. If the core got out of sync one way or the other, either it would tear us apart or it would get hotter than the surface of the sun."

"I know talking through this stuff calms you down, but give me the short version."

Wendy calculated, her eyes rolling up into her furrowed brow. "As long as it's been down? About twenty minutes. I think."

Another impact shook the *Atlas*, and Stellan wondered if they could make it to the command deck before the debris of the dead planet tore a hole in the hull so deep that they'd be purged as Pierce originally had planned.

Six

As the impacts increased in frequency and intensity, they knew for sure they were heading toward the dead planet, not away from it.

With every step they took, they raced the clock. Even as they tried to push forward faster, fear and the inevitable threat of meeting the dead or madmen slowed their pace.

And then they stopped.

In a long stretch of corridor, Pierce had apparently turned to take down some of the dead that followed him. Bullet holes marred wall and ceiling panel lights, some still flickering. Red smears drew erratic cone shapes from the back blasts of exit wounds. And in all the chaos of the hallway, bodies littered the floor. Most of them lay face down, thick, soupy blood still seeping from their wounds. The corridor had all the appeal of an uncovered mass grave, and they had no choice but to walk through it.

"Don't look at them," Stellan said. Wendy caught a whimper before it turned into a scream. Daelen moaned and turned away. Even Stellan's stomach desired to retch.

They stepped nimbly but quickly, arching their legs over the bodies like bridges over toxic waters, spanning the distance between safe zones. They avoided the pools of blood that gathered, afraid that they could cause them to slip into the death beneath their feet.

It became easier by the time they made it halfway through. The sight, the smell, the very presence of the lingering, tainted corpses became somewhat normal, as if their bodies adjusted to a temperature change or their eyes to darkness.

Ahead, Stellan thought he saw movement, and he raised his sidearm. He wanted to scan ahead, but he couldn't do that to Wendy and Daelen. He had to keep them moving, and even though he wanted to look down to be sure he wasn't stepping on or in anything, he had to keep his eyes trained ahead.

Fingers crunched underfoot, and Daelen and Wendy gasped. Still, they had to keep moving. A few steps later, Stellan caught the edge of a torso and almost fell.

Stellan had to look down. When he did, he found the movement he thought he'd detected. Several of the corpses writhed and wiggled like worms.

Pierce hadn't killed them all. Some of them lay asleep or somehow dormant. Perhaps the force of Pierce's weapon dropped them to the deck but hadn't stopped their malice. It lingered, if somewhat paralyzed.

A surprisingly powerful hand seized his ankle. He tried to pull away, but the fingers would not release.

"Go," Stellan said. "Go!"

Daelen and Wendy jumped around him and ran as fast as they could through the corridor of bodies. The sounds of their hurried footfalls awakened more.

The hand grasping Stellan's ankle pulled.

With his other foot, Stellan rolled over the thing that clutched him. A gaping hole adorned its face under one of its eyes, and its teeth chomped. Its raspy throat gurgled.

Stellan drove his foot down into its neck, stopping the rasp. His boot connected with the jaw and broke its front teeth. Still, it chomped with no regard for his boot.

Stellan twisted and felt the snap of the spine from the base of its skull. The grip on his ankle loosened, yet the mouth continued to chomp feebly.

Ahead, the dead began to stir, waking from a slumber. Soon they could be up and between him and Daelen and Wendy.

He moved deftly, finding no trouble in watching ahead as well as below, and when he reached the last of them, the terror in Daelen and Wendy's faces caused Stellan to turn and look behind him.

The writhing bodies were rising to their feet.

Stellan's sidearm would be no use against them. They had one shot and needed to save it. He offered it to Daelen.

"Take this, and keep moving," Stellan said.

"No!" Daelen said. "We can outrun them!"

"They'll be on us until we get to the lifts, and we don't know what's there. We could be boxed in. You have to go now."

He recognized the look in her eyes. She feared she would never see him again.

"There's no time," Stellan said. "I'm right behind you. Just go."

Wendy pulled Daelen's shoulders with fingers that dug insensitively into her skin. "Come on!"

As they ran, Daelen's gaze lingered over her shoulder, but Wendy didn't look back.

Stellan turned to face the dead, armed only with his fists and the hard rubber soles of his boots.

Seven

Stellan was right. They were boxed in.

Daelen and Wendy found a crowd of the dead huddled around one of the entrances to a working lift, pounding on the metal and squealing their bloody hands down the siding.

Pierce hadn't killed all of his pursuers. He'd only slowed them down and thinned them out. The crowd he left still posed an impossible obstacle. Whether it was five, fifty, or five hundred, Daelen and Wendy found an impenetrable wall of the dead.

"We're going to die," Wendy said, crumpling into a ball on the floor.

"We're not going to die," Daelen said, peering around the corner at the dead. "We'll figure something out."

"What if they got by Stellan, and they're coming after us? We don't have anywhere to go."

"They didn't get by Stellan," Daelen said. "He's right behind us."

"There were so many of them."

"I said he'll come!"

Daelen's voice caught the attention of a few of the dead surrounding the lift door, and they turned around. She ducked back around the corner.

"Shit! Shit!" Wendy said.

"They didn't see us," Daelen whispered. "Just be quiet, and stay calm."

Like any infectious disease, doubt is contagious. Faced with their situation and Wendy's despair, Daelen found it more difficult to believe Stellan would save them, and they had to do something. For the first time, while she felt naked without him, she thought that, if she could survive this, she might be okay without him. For the first time, she faced Stellan's possible death without feeling lost. The loss would be great, but she would not lose herself.

A symphony of moans and growls rose behind them, pressing her harder to do something. With only one bullet, she couldn't possibly take them all down. Again, she needed more time. She needed more time to think.

"Shit!" Wendy said. "They got past him!"

As she despaired and resigned to search for a place to hide, she detected hurried footsteps accompanying their pursuers' moans.

"No," Daelen said. "Wait."

She tried to separate the sounds. In all the disorder, there was a rhythm, a constant voice in the chaos. A steady beat prevailed.

Stellan sprinted around the corner, breathing heavily, his eyes wide and alert.

"Take them all?" Daelen said.

"Not quite," Stellan said looking over his shoulder. "More at the lift?"

"Yes."

"How many?"

"Loads," Daelen said.

Stellan peered around the corner, counted thirteen, and then looked back at the rising voices.

"Give me the weapon," Stellan said, and Daelen complied.

It was worthless in this fight, too, but he would need it for the fight that lay ahead, if they could get there.

"We have to force our way through," he said. "Stay close."

"No!" Wendy said. "I can't! I can't!" She hugged her knees and rocked.

"I know you're scared," Stellan said. "But you have to move. If you trust me, I'll get you through this. I promise."

She wouldn't budge. Terror froze her muscles and joints into a self-clutching position. Stellan looked to Daelen, and she knew she would have to get through to Wendy. Daelen nodded in understanding and bent to speak to Wendy.

Stellan didn't hear what she said because his attention had already turned. He rounded the corner out of cover and approached the crowd of dead at the lift, his breathing coming under arrest one breath at a time. Time slowed, and he felt somehow lighter, as if there was a freedom in this. With the fear of infection gone, he could be ruthless. There was nothing they could do to him anymore. His time was short, but he felt like a god, sending the damned to the underworld.

Even so, he couldn't hope to take them all with his bare hands. He moved for the metal pipe one of the madmen had brought to the fight earlier. It lay at the feet of a dead man who turned, a searing intent to kill in its eyes, and it wandered toward him on unsteady limbs.

Stellan flipped it and crushed its skull under his boot. One down.

He did not hear its final chomp and gasp or its moan. He only heard his slow and steady breathing, a metronomic beat for the kill.

One at a time, the rest of them turned, and in that moment, Stellan realized he no longer recognized them as human. Whether it was their mutilated bodies or the way the blood painted their faces, the tattered, blood-soaked clothing that more or less draped over their bodies was the only thing that tied them to humanity anymore.

He no longer pitied them. He hated them. Without the link of humanity, killing flowed easier, more naturally. He was born and raised to do this. The kill was the reason he lived, and he'd forgotten that.

One of the dead shuffled and kicked the pipe in his direction. It rolled to him, and he grabbed it and swung it up into the head of his closest target.

Moving his hands with mechanical precision, he took them down methodically, removing the closest threats first and shoving others back so he could break spinal cords and crush skulls.

Each target was the same. The look, the movement, it became a regimen. They each looked at him with no regard other than predatory, and they must have recognized a similarity in him because he could have sworn they looked at him differently. They looked at him with a familiarity, as if they knew him, and he thought they were afraid.

Each one paused momentarily, a fault that would lead to each of their ends. One-by-one, he took them down and disabled them like pieces of machinery. He didn't think about it; he just did it. At some point, he felt like he was just watching his body react and hands work.

He remembered what battle felt like, the fluidity, the complete lack of thought. It wasn't a time for thinking. Instinct prevailed.

Before the symphony of his killing spree resolved, three of the dead remained, and they did not hesitate. Stellan knew if he'd been facing humans, noticing their dwindling numbers, they would pause to re-evaluate the situation. There was no such moment with the dead. They lunged for him all the same.

He stood his ground. They drew into a tighter formation, and as they neared him, their speed grew, more eager and hungry for their meal.

Stellan turned to see where Daelen and Wendy were, and they had come around the corner, their eyes agape with fear and surprise.

"Stay close!" Stellan said. Daelen stepped forward, holding Wendy's hand.

"Look out!"

Stellan turned back to the dead in front of him just as they were crashing down like a wave. Instinct instructed him to drop the pipe, go with it, and take them to the ground, and he took the closest one by the neck and twisted it over him as they fell. He felt the familiar snap of bone between his fingers as he drove it head first into the deck.

The others missed, battling each other for the first bite. One of them got ahold of Stellan's boot and pulled. Stellan could feel its fingers clutch and climb his leg like a ladder.

With his boot heel, he found its throat, and pushed it away. It rolled and then staggered, trying to stand on shaky limbs.

The other one was on him again, and with his fingers digging into its throat, Stellan held it at bay, using the time to look for Daelen and Wendy.

So focused on him, they didn't hear the group from behind finally close in. Their arms reached out and swallowed Wendy, lifting her away in a red veil to the sound of her shrill screams.

"No!" Stellan cried, watching her slash frantically with Rick's switchblade and bury it into a skull. She fought, but they took her all the same.

Daelen recoiled, and a couple of the dead from the group turned their attention to her. They approached like intrigued, shy birds. Their heads bobbed and weaved stupidly, and their eyes stared like empty buckets that filled with murderous intent as they drew nearer.

Stellan realized he'd been mistaken. There was one more thing for the dead to take from him, one more debt for them to collect.

Daelen backed away, but for every step she took, they closed two steps. Stellan watched total failure near.

The one on him snapped its jaws, trying to bite his hands, and something boiled inside of him, something so primal he'd not yet been able to tap into it, something that screamed from his chest that this was it. This was the end of everything.

He rolled with the one that pinned him and kicked it away. He shot up to his feet and dashed for Daelen, grabbing her in his arms and pulling her away just as one of the dead lunged for her, snapping its jaws at the air she used to occupy, crashing to the floor in a crumbling tower of flesh and bone. He kicked the other back into the horde from which it had come.

They ran for the lift. He sent Daelen toward it as he tackled one of the dead that had regained its footing.

Daelen called the lift and put her back to the door. Stellan joined her.

The dead approached. This was it.

Cornered and embattled, Stellan cradled Daelen's face and gazed deeply into her eyes.

"Look at me, not them," he said.

She stared back, fear, panic, despair, every emotion that plagued humanity emanating from her face, measuring her helplessness.

Just when they believed it was over, that no one would survive the madness of the *Atlas*, the lift announced salvation with the system's signature chirp, and the doors parted. They spilled into it.

Fearing the grasping fingers of the dead would cut off the doors from closing, they knew they'd put their lives into the hands of the *Atlas*, a dying, mechanical deity. They hoped and prayed the doors would close before the dead could stop them.

Powerless as they'd become, the *Atlas* granted them the one last chance they sought, sealing the doors inches before the fingers of the dead could pry their way in.

Eight

The moment the doors closed, the voices of the dead faded. Even as their limbs crashed into the metal frame, it seemed to Stellan and Daelen they had entered another world. In an instant, they'd been whisked away just before their lives had been taken from them. They were in a safe place, but death still felt incredibly near. The echoes remained, calling their names.

In some ways, Stellan and Daelen *were* between worlds. They didn't know quite what to expect when they got to the command deck, but they knew it wouldn't be the same. Of course, they still had obstacles to overcome, though they were of an entirely different nature now. Getting through one offered them a few moments of respite, and what they each did with that time differed greatly.

Daelen looked to the past. She marveled at how far the *Atlas* had fallen. Everything had changed in the last few hours, and everyone they knew and cared about was gone. Even their closest friend, Captain Gordon Pierce, was, in a way, gone, disappearing into the black along with everyone and everything else.

Daelen's and Stellan's minds met on the thought of Pierce. Stellan looked to their future. The next few minutes would determine their fate, and if they couldn't outmatch Pierce, their changed world would burn. For Stellan, however, it had become much simpler than saving the *Atlas*. If he couldn't stop Pierce, he wouldn't be able to save Daelen, and all his sacrifices, all the crew's sacrifices, would have been in vain. Daelen had become the embodiment of all his success and failure, the last remaining survivor of the *Atlas*. In many ways, she was his last hope just as he was hers.

They gazed at each other from opposite walls of the lift, breathing, living, wondering what the other was thinking. In their silence, the lift's humming and creaking spoke for them. It said they needed to enjoy their time together because every moment they'd had and would have was a gift.

"I love you," Stellan said.

"I know. I love you, too."

Always, their eyes held onto each other, and it was all the embrace they needed before the lift halted and opened its doors onto the command deck. A blinding light screamed through the opening. In all the gloom and death below, they'd forgotten the brilliance of the command deck, which appeared untouched by the madness. They were thankful for that.

They stepped carefully out of the lift, and it felt like stepping back in time to a safer world, a simpler world where the *Atlas* was just a carrier. Their eyes blinked with wonder, struggling to adjust.

It had never felt so empty. Vacant workstations had fallen dim, no longer filling with requests for department heads to process. The staccato tapping of those same workers' fingers on the glass keyboards was silent. No banter flew between Arlo and Navigator Evans. For all the stillness, the bridge at the end of the command deck loomed, its brilliant white light shining like static, and resolute Pierce stood on his platform as always, arms crossed behind his back like nothing had changed, watching Apophis 259 draw nearer.

Though the dead no longer clutched at their heels, their well of time was running dry. They had to move forward, aware Pierce had to know they were there. Still, they crept slowly and carefully. Their minds and bodies had already adapted to that new world below, which now belonged to the mad and the dead. On the command deck, only the damned remained.

"You can't stop this, Stellan," Pierce said. "But you and I both know you're going to try."

Stellan paused, suspicious of Pierce's intent. Pierce playing possum had been an advantage, a tactic Stellan thought he was using to draw them out. Why would he simply discard it like that?

"There's still hope," Stellan said. "We can still save lives."

Pierce bowed and shook his head. Stellan continued to creep down the corridor toward the bridge. Daelen followed, terror trembling on her lips, which she tried to still with her fingertips.

"Even now you can't see it. What's important."

"I think you and I just differ on that," Stellan said.

"This is bigger than us," Pierce said. "It has to stop here. It would destroy Earth if it ever got there. Nothing is more important."

"What's the point if everything that makes us great—hope, freedom, love—is already gone?" Stellan asked. "This madness, whatever it is, can't kill that. Only we can."

"What do you mean?"

"You shot me. After everything we've been through, you aimed a gun at me and pulled the trigger. You gave up. What happened to you? The Gordon Pierce I knew would never give in like that."

Pierce turned slowly, and even though his hands had been empty only a moment ago, when they could see his face, blank and solid as a monolith, he held his sidearm. It surprised Stellan, and he drew his own in reflex.

Across the threshold of the bridge, they aimed their weapons at each other.

"I'll do it again if need be. Only this time, I'll put it where it counts."

Pierce's weapon lingered on Stellan for a moment, and then he fixed it on Daelen. She stepped back in terror.

"Drop your weapon," Pierce said. "You and I both know you have nothing left."

"You dropped quite a few of them yourself on your way here," Stellan said. "How do I know you're not empty?"

"Because I plan ahead."

It was a game, and they had no choice but to play it. As long as Pierce stalled them, he won. If he shot Daelen, he won.

Stellan turned his palms up and slowly knelt, placing his weapon on the deck and kicking it to the side.

Looking down to the workstations before the platform, Stellan saw the body of Navigator Cooper Evans on the floor. He had two bullet wounds, one in his thigh and one in his forehead.

"He wouldn't follow orders," Pierce said. "I warned him, and he still wouldn't. Penalty for mutiny is death."

"Have you lost your mind!?"

"On the contrary," Pierce said with genuine sorrow. "I'm the only sane man left on this ship. In a few minutes, it's not going to matter anyway whether he went by gunshot or fire or decompression. Nothing matters anymore except ending it here and now."

An asteroid shook the *Atlas*, and Pierce didn't even flinch.

"You know," Pierce said, "to your credit, I should have listened to you. I accept responsibility. You were right. This run was fucked from the beginning."

"Indeed," a voice said from the shadows. They all looked, their attention drawn, surprised to find a woman emerge from a blind corner. Her bare feet rolled quietly on the metal deck, and she limped into the light, holding in one hand the black brick of alien material and, in the other, her sidearm, aimed at Pierce. His expression of surprise and recognition widened beautifully. She clutched at her abdomen, any remaining color in her skin seeping from her wound and soaking through bandages that wrapped around her waist.

"While you idiots shot up the place," Council Agent Adelynn Skinner said, "including yours truly, I rationed my ammunition. Who'd like to bet I don't have enough in here for all of you?" She winced at a fresh bolt of pain, and as it passed, her ghost eye exploded with life, as if she'd somehow become more human. Purely out of reflex, Daelen moved to assist, but Adelynn flashed her a look that said they weren't that friendly. In spite of her outward frailty, Stellan recognized the fire, a relentless will to pull the trigger, and he didn't question whether she could because he saw in her face that she absolutely would.

"Now let's play nice," Skinner said. "Whaddya say? One big happy fucking family?"

"You won't," Pierce said.

"Why not? You did me. Code of Hammurabi. An eye for an eye." She smirked. "Call it cosmic fucking justice." Her hand trembled. Daelen knew she wouldn't last much longer.

Skinner held out the brick to Stellan. "Take it."

"No!" Pierce said. Skinner pressed the barrel of her sidearm into Pierce's skull, and he winced, not entirely from the pain, also from the fear.

"You should really get that shoulder looked at," Skinner told Stellan. "Your pretty wife did a nice job on the bandages, but it's going to need more than that. If you don't take this, she'll never be able to cure you."

He looked at it with wonder, and he wanted to take it. He knew Pierce was right, but some part of him hoped for a second chance. That part of him screamed that he wanted to live, that he deserved to take this risk, and he reached out to take it.

"No! Stellan, if you take it, I will kill her! Do you understand me!?"

Stellan's fingertips touched the brick, and a gunshot clapped in the bridge.

He pulled away and looked to Daelen in a panic, finding the barrel of his own sidearm staring in his direction, her hands still shaking, reverberating from the recoil.

Pierce lay on the ground, blood pooling in his lap from a gaping hole in his chest, and Stellan rushed to him, kneeling, paying no heed to the blood because it didn't matter anymore. Everywhere he looked, everything had become red.

"Don't," Pierce said weakly. "You can't."

Skinner tapped Stellan on the shoulder. "Take it. There's still time. Take the lift up to the services main concourse. You can launch a life boat from there." He was frozen. "Stellan, this is my failsafe. You."

"If you come with us, I may be able to stabilize you," Daelen said. "Give you a chance."

"No," Adelynn shook her head. "You and I both know I wouldn't survive the trip. Anyway, that's not important. I wasn't lying when I said my mission was to ensure the delivery of that material. Because of you, I won't fail."

She smiled at Pierce, who wore a look of spite even as his life force drained from his abdomen. "Besides, we've had this coming for a while."

"Stellan, you can't," Pierce whispered. "If you leave, you risk everything!"

Stellan looked at Daelen affectionately. "Maybe. But it's a risk I have to take."

He took the brick from Skinner, and it felt like taking a bribe from the Devil. Daelen and Stellan turned their backs on Pierce and Skinner, and as they walked toward the lift at the rear of the command deck, their hands found each other. Stellan clutched the black brick to his chest as if its mere presence already worked to cure him.

"Stellan!"

Pierce's voice echoed behind them until they entered the lift and the doors closed on the whole mad world.

Nine

When the lift reached the services deck, Stellan and Daelen found it easy to let go and feel the excitement. Forgetting felt good. For the first time in a while, they looked forward.

When the doors parted on the lonely, desolate concourse, a wide and long corridor that resembled a cavern, any good cheer they felt evaporated. They were tired of the fear, tired of the anticipation, tired of the unknown. The emptiness of the once-bustling halls reminded them that, like the *Atlas*, they had nothing left.

"On the bright side," Stellan said, "it's empty."

Daelen nodded with unmistakable regret.

The lifeboats weren't far from the lift, but they still felt exposed when they stepped into the corridor. At that point, the exhaustion felt like a hole in their chests. It reached up and pulled on their eyelids. Every bone in their bodies ached.

The desire to simply lie down was so strong that Stellan wasn't sure he'd be able to defend them if something had been there. The only thing that pushed them forward was the uneasiness of that hallway and the occasional asteroid impact that shook the ship and reminded them their time was running out.

Even without knowing how much time they had left, visualizing a closing door before them, they could only stagger at a walking pace.

They came to doors that lined the corridor on either side. They'd often passed doors like these all over the *Atlas*. The holopanels had always glowed red, and they'd never seen behind them. Now, the panels were green, and even through everything, they felt a twinge of excitement, as if they were venturing into undiscovered country.

Stellan waved his link over the panel, and the door opened, sliding smoothly into the wall frame, revealing darkness beyond. A cold draft swept out of the space. They stood silent and still at the threshold, waiting, as the lights warmed and showed the path beyond.

The doorway contained a narrow hallway that led up a ramp. The red emergency lighting helped them see obstructions, and at their feet, spotlighting shone through metal grills, revealing the path and any tripping hazards.

Even though they couldn't be certain what lay ahead, they felt compelled to move into that alien space because there was nothing left for them on that ship.

Stellan helped Daelen up the ramp, which seemed to go on for miles, turning on landings between floors and zigzagging to the top of the *Atlas*. On each landing, they found more doors, which they assumed led to other decks. On their side, the access panels were red, signaling they had to keep moving up the ramps.

A heavy asteroid rocked the *Atlas*, setting them off balance. They felt the ship drift as if losing traction and slipping. Non-emergency lighting flickered. Internal systems sputtered. The ship veered.

The *Atlas* was dying. It hadn't yet slammed into the Apophis planet, but that it soon would was now unavoidable.

The thought made them hasten up the ramps with renewed vigor, and after a few more flights, they found another row of doors in the narrow passageway. This time, the doors were only on one side and spread farther apart.

Stellan waved his link over the first access panel they came to, and again, the ancient door that had never been opened did as it was commanded without hesitation.

It opened into a circular room. The walls were lined with stasis chambers that reminded Stellan of the hyperbaric chamber Edward had inhabited to heal after his exposure.

Daelen crossed the threshold into the room. Stellan remained in place. She turned with a frightened look.

"I can't," Stellan said.

"Yes, you can." Daelen reached for Stellan's hand, and he did not recoil. "I need you to."

"Pierce is right," Stellan said. "It has to end here." He looked down to the black brick.

"No. I can't lose you. I won't," Daelen said, taking the brick from his hand. "With this, I can fix it. I just need time, and stasis will give us that. We owe it to ourselves. You owe it to yourself to try. We made it this far. We deserve a chance."

Stellan weighed the decision. He knew what he should do, but at the threshold of his fate, he found the will to survive overwhelming. Standing there, looking into the eyes of his beautiful, grief-stricken wife who was pleading for him to join her, he wanted to walk into that room. Still, he hesitated.

"What's a second chance if you don't take it?" Daelen asked.

In the end, it was something Wendy had said that made his feet move. He wasn't ready to face judgment. He wasn't ready to face himself.

As he stepped forward slowly, Daelen pulled him gently, and Stellan fell into her. She caught him in an embrace that sped up her heart and warmed her cheeks. Knowing she would get her chance to help him, the risks they were taking, she never felt more alive.

"There," she said. "Not so hard."

She detected guilt in his smile.

They moved into the room, and a small holographic display expanded over a table in the center, the lifeboat's control interface. Daelen entered the command to jettison the lifeboat and guide it away from the Apophis planet. Without a light drive, the lifeboat would not be able to reach New Earth, but it would give them a chance that a recovery team would find them.

As the boat launched, she recorded a brief message that would go out on a beacon to be transmitted into the depths of space. Hopefully, a Council ship somewhere would find them.

With the message stored, the lifeboat detached from the body of the *Atlas* and burned thrusters through the asteroid field and out to a safe distance. They undressed without saying a word, feeling freer than they'd felt in days, perhaps years. Though the thought of their lost friends weighed on them, the knowledge that they had made it meant their friends hadn't died in vain. Someone had lived. Someone could carry the beacon of hope. They couldn't offer a better tribute to humanity. A man and woman so madly in love they were willing to risk everything.

Stellan looked around at the stasis chambers that surrounded them. He counted twenty-six, thinking about whether he should consider twenty-four failures or two victories.

The holographic display in the center of the room showed the *Atlas*, now being bombarded by debris and falling to pieces. It dove down farther toward the Apophis planet, and a warning accompanied the feed informing them that a light drive event had been detected. They felt the lifeboat's thrusters push harder for minimum safe distance.

The *Atlas* descended into a swirl of earth and metal, and it began to blur and phase out. Slowly, it stretched like a rubber band, pulling the debris over and around it and launching it out the back in fine dust particles. It picked up pieces of the planet that the *Shiva* had not touched and turned them around the ship and into dust as well.

And then, like winking out of existence, the *Atlas* burrowed into the red planet, shooting through it like a cosmic bullet, turning the insides of the planet outward toward the dying red giant star, and crushing the outsides inward into a dense, packed celestial body for an instant and then erupting into a world-ending explosion.

The shockwave rattled the lifeboat so terribly that the lights went out, and in the darkness, only the solid floor on which they stood reassured them they were not dead, floating in the black expanse.

A moment later, the lights returned, and the lifeboat's systems rebooted.

Daelen walked Stellan to a stasis chamber and helped him inside. He lay back, and she smiled.

"I'll see you in my dreams," Stellan said.

"Really?"

"I know it."

She closed the lid for him and then kissed her hand and pressed it against the glass. He reciprocated from inside. She stepped back, adamant that she would watch him until he fell asleep.

As the stasis chamber took hold and pulled him down, something strange accompanied it. His body had never felt stasis, but something was wrong. His heart rate should have slowed, but it quickened and boomed. Even though the lifeboat had no light drive, he swore it rose into a swell in his ears. His instinct was to fight it, but his limbs wouldn't move. A darkness crept over him, and even as he descended into his subconscious, he knew that, when he woke, he would carry it with him for as long as he lived.

ACKNOWLEDGEMENTS

I would like to express my sincere gratitude to some people who played a part in helping me tell this story and get it out into the world. First, to my parents, Paul and Theresa, for their guidance and sacrifices that got me through those harrowing formative years and whose influence shapes me still. To Nicki and Sam, whose courage, strength, and love are enduring inspirations. To my wife, Heather, for her support even on those lonely nights when she surely wondered why she had committed herself to such a recluse. To Bruce Watson, teacher and friend, who instilled in me a deeper appreciation for the art form of storytelling and who read a very early draft of this novel and held nothing back. To my other advance readers who saw the things I couldn't. To Craig DiLouie who offered the advice and guidance to plant this story's seed in the ground. To Felicia Sullivan, who revealed my weaknesses to me with her edits. And to the good people at Permuted Press, especially Michael Wilson and Anthony Ziccardi, who were willing to take a risk.

ABOUT THE AUTHOR

Timothy Johnson is a writer and editor living in Washington, D.C., with his wife and his dog. He has an English degree from Virginia Tech, where he won the Fiction Award for his graduating class. He is a member of the Horror Writers Association. Carrier is his first novel.

Find him at www.timothyjohnsonfiction.com.

14

Peter Clines

Padlocked doors.
Strange light fixtures. Mutant
cockroaches.

There are some odd things about
Nate's new apartment. Every
room in this old brownstone has
a mystery. Mysteries that stretch
back over a hundred years.
Some of them are in plain sight.
Some are behind locked doors.
And all together these mysteries
could mean the end of Nate and
his friends.

Or the end of everything...

PERMUTED
PRESS

THE JOURNAL SERIES
by Deborah D. Moore

After a major crisis rocks the nation, all supply lines are shut down. In the remote Upper Peninsula of Michigan, the small town of Moose Creek and its residents are devastated when they lose power in the middle of a brutal winter, and must struggle alone with one calamity after another.

The Journal series takes the reader head first into the fury that only Mother Nature can dish out.

Michael Clary
THE GUARDIAN | THE REGULATORS | BROKEN

When the dead rise up and take over the city, the Government is forced to close off the borders and abandon the remaining survivors. Fortunately for them, a hero is about to be chosen...a Guardian that will rise up from the ashes to fight against the dead. The series continues with Book Four: *Scratch*.

Emily Goodwin
CONTAGIOUS | DEATHLY CONTAGIOUS

During the Second Great Depression, twenty-four-year-old Orissa Penwell is forced to drop out of college when she is no longer able to pay for classes. Down on her luck, Orissa doesn't think she can sink any lower. She couldn't be more wrong. A virus breaks out across the country, leaving those that are infected crazed, aggressive and very hungry. `

The saga continues in Book Three: *Contagious Chaos* and Book Four: *The Truth is Contagious*.

PERMUTED
PRESS

THE BREADWINNER | Stevie Kopas

The end of the world is not glamorous. In a matter of days the human race was reduced to nothing more than vicious, flesh hungry creatures. There are no heroes here. Only survivors. The trilogy continues with Book Two: *Haven* and Book Three: *All Good Things*.

THE BECOMING | Jessica Meigs

As society rapidly crumbles under the hordes of infected, three people—Ethan Bennett, a Memphis police officer; Cade Alton, his best friend and former IDF sharpshooter; and Brandt Evans, a lieutenant in the US Marines—band together against the oncoming crush of  death and terror sweeping across the world. The story continues with Book Two: *Ground Zero*.

THE INFECTION WAR | Craig DiLouie

As the undead awake, a small group of survivors must accept a dangerous mission into the very heart of infection. This edition features two books: *The Infection* and *The Killing Floor*.

OBJECTS OF WRATH | Sean T. Smith

The border between good and evil has always been bloody... Is humanity doomed? After the bombs rain down, the entire world is an open wound; it is in those bleeding years that William Fox becomes a man. After The Fall, nothing is certain. *Objects of Wrath* is the first book in a saga spanning four generations.

PERMUTED
PRESS

3190105987227